Sophie Sullivan is a Canadian author as well as a cookie-eating, Diet Pepsi-drinking, Disney enthusiast who loves reading and writing romance in almost equal measure. She writes around her day job as a teacher and spends her spare time with her sweet family watching reruns of *Friends*. *Ten Rules for Faking It* is her rom-com debut novel, but she's had plenty of practice writing happily ever after as her alter ego, Jody Holford.

Visit her website: **www.sophiesullivanauthor.com** and find her on Facebook **/SophieSullivanAuthor**, on Twitter **@SophieSWrites**, and on Instagram **@authorsophiesullivan**.

Praise for *Ten Rules for Faking It*:

'Impossible to read without smiling – escapist romantic comedy at its heartwarming best'
Lauren Layne, *New York Times* bestselling author

'A wholesome, slow-burn romance that will warm your heart and offer a glimpse into social anxiety disorder. This is a Hallmark movie in book form'
Helen Hoang, *USA Today* bestselling author of *The Kiss Quotient* and *The Bride Test*

'I adored this book! Sophie Sullivan has written a fast-paced, sweet romance full of heart and truth. Once you start reading, you won't be
Lyssa Kay Adams, author of

'A funny, sweet rom-com from
Everly's social anxiety was insta
for her every inch of the wa
Andie J. Christopher, *USA Today* bestselling au
Not the Girl You Marry

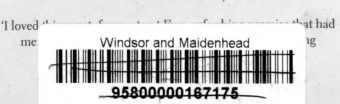

'I loved ... at had
me ... ng

Ten Rules for Faking It

SOPHIE SULLIVAN

Published by arrangement with St Martin's Griffin,
An imprint of St Martin's Publishing Group.

First published in Great Britain in 2020
by HEADLINE ETERNAL
An imprint of HEADLINE PUBLISHING GROUP

1

Cataloguing in Publication Data is available from the British Library

ISBN 978 1 4722 8071 8

Typeset in 10.78/13.725 pt Electra LT Std by Jouve (UK), Milton Keynes

Printed and bound in Great Britain by Clays Ltd, Elcograf S.p.A.

Headline's policy is to use papers that are natural, renewable and recyclable products and made from wood grown in well-managed forests and other controlled sources. The logging and manufacturing processes are expected to conform to the environmental regulations of the country of origin.

HEADLINE PUBLISHING GROUP
An Hachette UK Company
Carmelite House
50 Victoria Embankment
London EC4Y 0DZ

www.headlineeternal.com
www.headline.co.uk
www.hachette.co.uk

To the people on my laminated list

Ten Rules for Faking It

[1]

While there might be varying degrees of magnitude as to how much, Everly Dean firmly believed that birthdays sucked. This one, her thirtieth, more than most. Even more than her seventh when her parents decided the best time to announce their first separation was *at* the party right before they brought out the piñata. At least back then, there'd been a papier-mâché donkey to beat up, followed by an explosion of sugary treats.

She'd attacked that thing with such vehemence, they'd bought her one each year after for her parties until she got smart and hid the one from her twelfth birthday in the back of her closet. When her mom couldn't find it, she'd suggested the kids try spin the bottle. Everly had quit parties right there. That didn't break the cycle, though. At least today wasn't quite as bad as her twenty-first, when she'd spent the night in the ER after getting tonsillitis while still dealing with bronchitis.

Today hovered somewhere between the two; maybe an eight or nine on the suckage scale. What made her think, with her history, showing up at her boyfriend's house with coffee and bagels *before* work was a good idea? When he'd said he was going to bed early last night, she'd believed him. *Ha. He probably did. Just not alone.*

She gripped the steering wheel of her car, knowing she needed to get on with her day, which involved leaving the car.

Baby steps. She got out, leaned against the door. The nearly 10:00 a.m. sunshine warmed some of the chill out of her bones. How did she always end up here? Her muscles tightened.

How? You pick immature men who you have very little in common with, hoping their extroverted qualities cancel out your introverted ones.

"Well said, Dr. Everly." Her words ended on a sigh. Dating wasn't easy. *Understatement of the year.* If she got ready to go out without breaking into hives, she called it a win. Low expectations resulted in less-than-stellar outcomes. She seemed intent on proving that ad nauseam.

As she walked across the parking lot, humiliation heated her skin more than the sun. *Focus on something else. Something good.*

If this was thirty, she needed some guidelines. Rules. Just because today sucked didn't mean she wanted to turn into a bitter old woman, collecting cats or birds or newspaper clippings to ease the ache. *Rule one: No animal hoarding.* Though, maybe one would be fine. Hmm . . . maybe she should get a cat. *Rule two: Find the positive. No, wait, that should be rule one. Rule one: Focus on the good. Rule two: No hoarding—animal or otherwise.*

Once she was inside, lost in work, her mood would shift. Hopefully. *There's a positive.* She loved her job as a radio show producer for a light listening station. Decent hours even if it wasn't the coveted spot, good pay, she didn't work with jerks, which was always a bonus. She and the deejay, Stacey, had become fast friends three years ago after they realized they both adored *Veronica Mars* and hated seafood pizza—the staff had ordered in lunch one day, and they'd both gagged on the smell—instant friendship. Plus, Stacey had more dating disaster stories than Everly, which was comforting even if it was because she dated more often. The fact that they had to work closely together on most of the programming only improved their bestie status.

An ache settled under her rib cage, winding its way over and under each bone, burrowing in for the long haul. She breathed around it, but it didn't fade. The desire to turn around and go home and curl up in bed got stronger the closer she got to the door. *Just breathe. You're fine.* Fingers curled, nails pressed into the softness of her palms, her breathing evened out. Everything would be okay. *That's what you thought this morning. Just get through today.* She'd been saying that to herself for about twenty-three years.

She'd keep her head down, get to her producer booth, seek solitude inside the eight-by-eight isolation square. She'd send fake smiles through the glass and maybe keep the door locked. Plan made, she pulled open the back door of the old building that housed 96.2 SUN. Work and home were her happy places. At least here, she couldn't crawl back into bed and rate her birthdays by level of disaster.

Everly straightened her shoulders and let the door close behind her but paused at the bottom of the ancient, carpeted stairwell.

Thirteen stairs, less than a hundred steps to her booth. She'd avoid idle chitchat—even her friend's—like a Kate Spade blowout sale. Stacey insisted the deals on her favorite bags were worth the crowds, but in Everly's mind, that was her own version of the nine circles of hell. One level below someone massaging her naked body and a couple above moving back in with her parents.

She rubbed her left palm with her right thumb. *Head down, straight to the booth.* She didn't "people" well at the best of times, even with her coworkers. They probably all thought she was a snob. Something weird happened to her ability to form words whenever she got in a room with more than three people—it was like she'd eaten a spoonful of peanut butter. Easier to stay quiet. Especially on a day when her emotions were swirling like a tornado.

"Just go to work already," she told herself, curling her fingers into fists.

Up the steps, through another door, she made it all the way into the booth without looking up or tripping over her feet. Well, the first one, anyway. She had to go through Stacey's deejay booth to get to her spot because the outside door to the production booth had jammed shut about six months ago and no one had fixed it. It wasn't time for their show yet, but the early show host would have left the music playing so they could make the shift change work. Stacey was already in the booth, earphones on, hips moving, staring at the computer.

It seemed like that would make it easier to sneak by, but apparently, having her head down didn't make her invisible. Unfortunately.

"There she is. The birthday girl," Stacey said.

Everly winced. There. Birthday acknowledged. *You didn't go up in flames*. Time for work. "Hey," she muttered, staring down at her purple Converse.

"My eyes are up here, sunshine."

A small laugh escaped. "But your feet are so pretty. Are you wearing orange polish?"

"I am."

Everly walked toward the door that separated their booths and had her hand on the knob.

"Ev?"

Inhaling deeply, locking her lips into a smile, she turned her head. Everly looked straight at her friend, right into her eyes, hoping Stacey knew her well enough to read her mood—to *know* she could not handle any conversation right now. Even without knowing the details, surely Everly's mood transmitted clearly. Was she visibly shaking?

Any other day or maybe one when she hadn't found her now-ex entertaining a very well-endowed—and flexible—woman in his bedroom at 6:00 a.m., she could do this. But if she said anything right now, she'd be a volcano set for eruption.

"You, my lovely, beautiful friend, are thirty," Stacey said, a smile on her pink lips—the woman actually got out of bed early to put on makeup. When Everly argued they were in the booths all morning, why bother when no one saw them, Stacey told her there was never a reason not to look her best. And she *always* did. Everly liked her in spite of this.

Everly offered a weak smile. "Thanks for letting me know."

Undeterred, Stacey added, "It's a big deal."

"Hmm."

"A day worth celebrating."

"Sure." Her hand tightened on the knob.

"And to start that celebration, I'm going to sing 'Happy Birthday' to you," Stacey said, taking a step closer.

Please no. "Pass."

Stacey laughed. Everly turned the knob. *Just a few more steps. Hold it together.*

"You can't escape." Stacey started to sing. Loudly. Loudly enough that the rest of the station might hear and, God forbid, come join in.

Everly let go of the knob and took a step toward the deejay. "Stop," she hissed.

Stacey shook her head and drew out the words, throwing her arms out dramatically, her voice growing louder. "*Happy b—*"

"Stacey Joanne Ryan, stop singing right now!"

Her friend's words died abruptly. Fittingly, like radio silence. She blinked. "Huh?"

Everly hated that her breath shook along with her hands. She hadn't been in love with the jerk or looking to have his babies. She'd thought if she tried to let him in on what was, to most people, a celebratory day, it would bring them closer. *Ha. Any closer, you might have lost an eye.* So much for putting herself out there. Blinking away tears, she did her best to give her friend a quick rundown.

"It. Is. Not. A. Happy. Birthday." She leaned in closer, her chest uncomfortably tight. "None of them are particularly great, but this one is an epic disaster. I found Simon in bed with his personal assistant this morning. You do *not* want to know how she was assisting him. Lucky me, I stood there like an idiot until they finally noticed me. After which, I mumbled something incoherent and ran from the room, dropping bagels and coffee all over the floor. So, while I appreciate your friendship and your enthusiasm and your inexplicable love of acknowledging the date of my birth, I do not want to celebrate or be sung to. No cake. No presents. There's a slight possibility I'll want a stiff drink after work if you're up for that. But if we go out? I don't want to meet anyone. I don't want anyone else buying me drinks. I want to forget what today is, forget what happened, and while I'm at it . . . you know what? You can throw men onto that list. I'm done."

Stacey's eyes widened at the same time her jaw dropped open. But Everly didn't stop when her friend started to speak. That was what happened with a dormant volcano; it was quiet forever, and then it blew, destroying everything in its path.

She pointed at Stacey. "No birthdays. No men. Actually, you know what? I'll amend that. If you happen to find a man who looks like Chris Pine, acts like Chris Hemsworth, smiles like Chris Pratt, and has a body like Chris Evans's, I'll rethink things. But until then? I am officially off the market." She nodded as if she agreed with herself. She felt oddly exhausted after the outburst. "Understood?"

Stacey nodded, her lips trembling, and guilt crashed into Everly with a thud. The other woman's eyes were bright with unshed tears. Everly hadn't meant to be so cruel, but she was having a hell of a morning already and just wanted a few minutes to absorb what had happened. Now she'd done this. To someone who cared. Like the crash that followed a junk-food binge, all her energy and anger evaporated.

"I'm so sorry, Stace. That was completely uncalled for. I—"

"Stop. Stop talking. Right now." She actually put her hand on Everly's mouth.

Everly's gasp was completely muffled, along with her words

when she tried to speak around her friend's palm. Stacey shook her head frantically. "Stop. Stop. I'm so sorry."

Why was she whispering? She tried to look around, but no one else was hovering nearby. Everly pushed at Stacey's hand, but Stacey was surprisingly strong.

"We're on-air, Ev. We're live. Stop. I'm so sorry."

Everly thought she knew what rock bottom felt like. She definitely knew it *looked* like a very tall, stacked blonde perched over her boyfriend. She hadn't known, until this moment, that it was possible to fall further. At the bottom of the drop, the red On Air sign shone like a warning light. Mortification swamped her like high tide pulling her under. Her brain went a little fuzzy. Her skin tingled.

Stacey pulled her hand away, index finger at her lips, and backed away, swiping her hand over the control buttons. As soon as she'd done that, as soon as they weren't live, her friend charged her with a tackle hug. "I am so sorry. What a jackass bastard. I cannot believe that. I will buy you as many drinks as you want. For life. You deserve it."

No. No. She had not just announced to all the listeners that she was off men and the reason why. But she had. She couldn't give a speech to a group of her closest friends, but she'd just shared her love life with thousands of listeners. Her stomach nose-dived even as her skin heated. *No.* Pulling out of Stacey's embrace, she lost the battle against tears. Everly swiped the first few from her cheeks. "I can't believe this. Why the hell were you live?"

Stacey's face crumpled. "I wanted to sing 'Happy Birthday' to you on the air. To make you feel special. I'm so sorry I did this to you."

They stood there staring at each other, and Everly felt like she'd slipped into a different dimension. One that was upside down and backward and full of potholes.

Luke, the morning janitor, popped his head in. "You got dead air, Stace."

Stacey gasped and hurried to the board, pressing buttons.

"Damn it! No. Okay, thanks, Luke. My bad." Her eyes found Everly's, and Everly could tell her friend wanted to say more, to apologize again. It wouldn't change anything.

It just kept getting worse. Everly stepped backward, her hands up, her purse shifting awkwardly on her shoulder so she almost dropped it. "I can't do this. We can't talk about this right now. The day has barely started, and it's already horrible. We need to get to work." She could handle work. Quiet, solitude, and her job.

Hurrying into the production booth, she got herself set up and tried to avoid Stacey's regretful gaze through the plexiglass. This birthday just got bumped up to a solid 9.5. *Rule three: Stay home on birthdays.*

Calls started coming into the station almost immediately. Typically, it was Everly's job to screen the callers, but the phone lines lit up like a Christmas tree and she couldn't keep up. They ignored them for the time being while Stacey tried to laugh off sharing her producer's personal drama. Everly hoped that was the end of it. Just another thing about the day to forget.

Hopes of the wish coming true vanished when the station manager came into the deejay booth. Through the glass, his eyes locked on Everly's, tipping her stomach upside down. Her stomach always went a little weird around him. Nerves, most likely, since she didn't think he liked her all that much. Today probably lowered his opinion.

Walking forward, his lips pressed together in a tight line, he pushed open the door. With his broad shoulders, assessing gaze, and the light scent of his cologne, he filled the space without even trying. Everly swiveled in her chair, her heart jumping around like a kitten who'd gotten his tail caught.

"Mr. Jansen. This is a surprise. Good morning," she said. Yup. Total peanut butter mouth. Sweat beaded along her hairline. He wasn't particularly friendly to her on a good day, and as she'd already established to thousands of listeners, today was not one of those. Everly didn't know what she'd done to rub him the wrong way, but since his arrival at the station less than a year ago, he'd kept his distance. With others, he laughed and joked and seemed like a regular guy in addition to a boss. With her, he took off his cloak of approachability, offering a nod in passing or being as succinct as possible if he had to speak to her about something work related.

"Is it? I'm surprised you think so after the morning you've had," he said, his voice quiet. He wore his light brown hair perfectly trimmed and styled in a way that made it seem purposely tousled. It probably took him way too long to make it just right. *Good God, focus.* Maybe he wanted to say happy birthday. A bubble of nervous laughter fought to escape. The fire blazing in his hard-to-identify-the-exact-shade-of-green eyes suggested otherwise.

"Uh . . . you heard?" *Why would you ask a question you know the answer to? As if you haven't made yourself sound dumb enough. Great follow-up.* If only invisibility shields were real, she could disappear right now. Slip away to somewhere else. Anywhere else.

When he straightened, his perfectly tailored, coal-black suit jacket moved easily with his body, showing not only the quality but his ease. She tried not to look. But clearly her eyes were dumb.

When she glanced up, she saw something that looked a lot like sympathy in his gaze. "Yes, I heard, Ms. Dean. *Everyone* heard. We're being inundated with calls."

If a sinkhole opened up under her rolling chair, she would not have been disappointed. When, after a beat, it didn't, she stared at the wall just beyond him. If she didn't want to talk about her lousy morning with her friend or their loyal listeners, she definitely didn't want to talk to the by-the-book station manager about it. Especially when he usually went out of his way to *not* talk to her.

"You should go."

Her eyes snapped up to his. "What?" *No. No. No.*

"Go home. Take the day. You don't need to be answering the phone and fielding these calls. Consider it a birthday present."

She stiffened. "I don't want presents."

One side of his mouth tipped up. "I heard that, too."

Stacey burst into the room. "It's not her fault. Don't send her home. Please, Chris."

He turned, glanced at Stacey. "I got that. But I can't send the voice of the show home, can I? We'll let the calls go to voicemail, but in the future? Your job description does not include personal shout-outs to your friends. Or singing live."

If a person could burst into flames from embarrassment, Everly would have lit the station on fire. Instead, she stood up, knocking her chair, making it roll across the linoleum. She hated the awkward tension that hung in the room. If she left, she could crawl into bed and wait for the day to be over.

"Stace, it's fine. I'll go home." She looked at her boss. "You're not going to fire me or something, right?"

She couldn't lose her job. It was her *thing.* She sucked at crafting and couldn't stand running. She had no patience for the adult coloring craze, so that was out. She didn't mind jotting her thoughts down in journals, but it wasn't something she'd call a hobby. Work was where she excelled. But nothing was ever written in stone. The station had been undergoing programming and staffing changes for the last couple of years. Chris was one of three new managers they'd had since Everly had accepted her position. The numbers for their show weren't great, but they had a following.

She met his gaze, refusing to back down. Everly couldn't leave wondering what would happen next. She hated not knowing.

Pinching the bridge of his nose, he sighed deeply. "Not to my knowledge, Ms. Dean. Just go home, do something for yourself. Hopefully, the attention from this will fade away by tomorrow and it'll be a normal day."

Ms. Dean. He was so damn professional and standoffish with her. What had she ever done to him?

"I'll apologize to the audience again. Just let her stay," Stacey said.

He looked back at Everly, and she thought she saw his eyes soften for a split second. His voice was anything but soft when he said, "This is for the best. I'll contact you."

Everly nodded and gathered her purse and lunch bag, wishing she'd never gotten out of bed this morning. As she walked down the thirteen stairs, her boss watching from the top landing, she decided this birthday was now a definite ten. At age thirty, she finally reached maximum suckage.

[2]

Technically, she'd accomplished rule three by heading home for her birthday. As she walked up the path to the converted mansion where she rented an apartment, the front door opened. There were four units in the house, two on the top and two on the bottom. With only four homes, the neighbors knew each other's basic statistics, but none of them hung out together or anything.

The woman from unit 4, Shannyn, and daughter, Lexie, held hands. Everly was ready to nod and wave—her standard greeting of choice, but Shannyn's gaze caught hers, and Everly's stomach sank.

Her neighbor's eyes darted right and left, then landed back on Everly. "Sorry about . . . about your day."

Everly smiled too brightly, trying to tell herself it was great that people listened to the show. Meanwhile, her skin started to itch. "Thanks."

She didn't want to say anything more, so she headed for the stairs, let herself through the front entrance, and took the next set of stairs up to the top-right unit.

When she made it inside, she pushed the door closed with her foot and hung her keys on the hook. Leaning against the door, she thumped her head against it and didn't even care that it hurt. She stood, staring at what she could see of her apartment, and realized she didn't want to be in it right now. She also didn't want to go out. Normally, she loved coming home, but not once, not even when she'd broken the ice cream machine *at the ice cream shop* where she worked, had she been sent home.

Her house was clean—not obsessive clean, just comfortable and organized. She liked living alone and had always preferred to. But right now, coming home to an empty place in the middle of the day added to its dismalness.

"Rule three," she said out loud just to fill the silence. "Stay home on birthdays. Come on, Ev. You like following the rules."

She slipped off her Converse and headed for the kitchen. She could use the day to catch up on something. Maybe make a bunch of meals that she could put in the freezer and pull out each evening. That sounded like something someone in their thirties might do.

Opening the fridge, she grabbed a can of diet soda and cracked the top. Pulling a glass from the cupboard, she poured it in, watching the bubbles with more intensity than needed. After all, they'd pop whether she watched or not.

God. Sometimes, she annoyed herself. Being inside of her own brain reminded her of a hamster on a wheel, after he'd been given too much caffeine with a side of uppers. Round and round. One thought after another like a chain-smoker who lit the next cigarette with the one they were putting out. The thoughts collided into one another in passing until she physically felt the exhaustion creep into her head and her body. She took a sip of her soda. Maybe she should do something to turn the day around.

"Ha. How about unseeing Captain Jackass and his sidekick, Flexy Girl?" Being able to do that would be a definite mood changer.

Everly pulled her phone out of her back pocket, entertaining the idea of calling her mom or dad to see if they wanted to grab lunch. She decided against it, not sure if she was up to the whirlwind that was her parents' relationship. Theirs was a back-and-forth that rivaled the Swift–Kardashian drama. Even on her best days, and theirs, Everly's visits with them made her feel like she leaning too far over an edge with nothing to hang on to.

No lunch. Not with her parents, anyway. Her chaos limit was maxed out for the day. Instead, she grabbed a bag of pretzels from the pantry and took them and her soda to the living room and settled on the couch. She was content with her life. Her job. Her home and friends. There was nothing wrong with any of those things, and yet . . . restlessness coursed through her veins. She hated the duality of her feelings. Wanting to *do* something but not go anywhere, wanting to *see* someone but not have to entertain.

Her phone rang, and since it was Stacey, she picked up.

"Hey."

"Hi. I only have a minute. I'm so sorry."

"You've apologized more for this than Simon did for cheating on me. It happened. It's over. I'm not mad at you." She wasn't. She was mad at herself for thinking today would be different from any other birthday and for letting her emotions bubble over at work.

"I'm coming over later. I'm bringing reinforcements."

Everly laughed, knowing that meant chocolate, salty foods, and alcohol of some sort.

"Sounds good. I'm sitting here contemplating life." Which was a lot better than thinking about what had happened this morning. If she replayed it in her head, she'd end up hiding under her blankets. *No hiding. Thirty is too old for that.* Leaning her head back against the cushions, she stared at the popcorn ceiling.

"No time like the present to break out of ruts. Maybe we should do something crazy tonight. Ever try a Brazilian?"

This time, her laugh was more of a squawk. "No, and if you have, we'll put it in the TMI category."

"I didn't know that existed between us," Stacey said.

Everly heard the smile in her voice. "Apparently, it needs to.

I think I've done my crazy for the day. Doing a tell-all on-air is enough for me. Besides, I can't go out."

That was technically true, and technicalities mattered. A lot of things got dismissed in courtrooms because of them.

"Why's that?" Music sounded in the background.

"New rule. Number three. Stay home on birthdays."

"Since when?"

Everly sat up, tilted her head to keep the phone tucked in the crook of her neck, and opened the pretzels. "Since today. I've got a whole list of them."

Three was a list. There weren't more at the moment, so that was the *whole* list. Technically. Details mattered. A grin tugged her lips up. Maybe she should write it down so she could back herself up with documentation.

"I want to see this list," Stacey said, easily ignoring Everly's groan. Why had she said it out loud? To Stacey of all people? She might actually make her go through with completing something *on* the list. Or the list itself. A text sounded in her ear at the same time Stacey added, "I have to go. See you later."

Everly hung up, checked the text.

> **DAD:** I want a last name on this Simon character. Call me when you're done at work. You'll come for dinner tonight. You should be with your family on your birthday.

"Uh, hard no. Sorry, Dad, rule number three—I can't." She stared at the text for another few seconds wondering if he realized she'd often been with her family on her birthday and this had never helped make it better.

She set her phone down and focused on her pretzels. A list wasn't a bad idea.

She bit off one loop of the pretzel. What else could she add? Three things wasn't enough, really, to be considered a list. Five didn't seem like enough either. Ten? Ten seemed doable, and in truth, maybe thirty was the time to actually make a list of rules or goals or some grown-up shit like that. It wasn't like her unguided life was leading her in amazing directions. She didn't have any complaints and liked most of what life had thrown her way, but it wouldn't hurt to be a little more . . . purposeful.

Blowing out an exaggerated, lip-fluttering breath, she swore out loud when pretzel crumbs littered her pants. She looked down at her legs as she swiped off the remnants, then realized now she'd have to sweep.

"Nice job."

She tossed the bag back on the table, getting up to grab her broom from the narrow closet slash cupboard—way too narrow for even Harry Potter but perfect for cleaning supplies. As she swept up the crumbs, she considered items for her list. By the time she sat back down, picked up her soda, all she'd come up with was: Eat healthier. She didn't eat unhealthily, but everyone could stand to eat better, right?

"That's a resolution, not a rule." She'd have to be careful not to mix the two up. Rules provided structure and organization. A way to proceed. That's what she needed. A set of guided principles to help her make decisions. Ones that wouldn't have her walking in on her boyfriend getting busy with a woman who could easily be nicknamed Elastigirl.

"Better yet, guidelines that would demand you make better choices in that department all the way around." Not that she'd purposely chosen a cheater. Could people actually *tell* if someone was predisposed to cheating? Everly wasn't sure, but she could be honest enough with herself to admit the men she chose were unlikely to be her soul mates. It was like she thought she could absorb their qualities—being sociable, funny, spontaneous—by becoming their girlfriend. A sort of dating osmosis.

After drinking down almost half her soda, she worried her bottom lip for a few seconds before pushing up and walking to the antique-looking, multi-drawer cabinet that sat against the wall between the door and her hallway. It looked like a great-great-relative had left it to her. She liked things that looked old but were actually new. Which she was pretty sure should be Pottery Barn's actual tagline.

Inside one of the drawers were notebooks, used and unused. Now and again, when her thoughts crowded too much of her brain, it helped to let some of them spill out onto the page. It wasn't something she did with any regularity, though. *That could change. Your regularly scheduled programing could stand an overhaul.* The first one was red with the word *gratitude* written across it in gold. She moved it aside. That could be for her forties. The next two already had some writing in them, so she dug deeper and laughed when she saw one Stacey had given her a few years ago. Untraditional, like her friend, the small font on the front read: SEIZE THE DAY (AS SOON AS YOU MAKE A PLAN). That fit. Snagging a pen from a different drawer, she went back to the couch and flipped through the pages. Some were plain, others colorful or decorated with the kinds of doodles Everly could never pull off. A few had quotes that made her grin.

The pen needed a few random squiggly circles to get it going. She wrote across the top of the first page: The Rules for Turning Thirty.

Focus on the good.

No hoarding, animal or otherwise.

Stay home on my birthday.

***

She could add to it. *Would* add to it. It didn't have to be today, though.

She'd told Stacey it was a *whole* list. That meant thinking about what she actually wanted for herself, what she wanted for this chapter of her life. Thirty was supposed to mean something. Everly put the pen cap between her teeth. She'd told herself the same thing about twenty. And probably her teens. Every twelve-year-old vowed to really live it up once they finally hit thirteen, right? And then told herself maybe next year. Or the year after.

She went back to 4 and wrote: Try new things. *Like getting a Brazilian?* She shuddered and crossed it out to write: Try something new once a month. That was specific enough. Something she couldn't let herself slip out of on one of those technicalities.

Tapping the pen against the book, she thought of other ideas and dismissed them almost immediately. Wear high heels to work (or anywhere), go to a costume party, go to a concert, do a workshop on broadcast journalism at her alma mater. They'd been asking for two years, but speaking in front of a crowd was second on her levels-of-hell list. These weren't *rules.* She needed to add things that would push her to be . . . more. *Add something for work. Hello, comfort zone.*

"Push the boundaries of your comfort zone," she told herself. She'd been thinking about something for a while now and hadn't had the guts to bring it up to the team or Chris. Her inner cheerleader, which, funnily enough had Stacey's voice, chanted, *Write it. Write it.*

Pitch producing a podcast associated with the station.

***

The idea stemmed from a segment she and Stacey started called "Straight Talk with Stacey." Once a week, the deejay shared something that seemed popular and gave her unadulterated opinion on it. Their numbers for the show overall might have been low, but they got a lot of feedback on that segment. Listeners chimed in on social media. It made for some fun conversations online and around the station.

Producing something outside of the show would level her up in her career, so to speak. Maybe even give her and Stacey a shot at the coveted morning spot. She scanned the list. God, she was boring.

"You don't need excitement." It stressed her out. "You just need to push a little. Stop always choosing the status quo." *Nah.* More than a little push was necessary. She needed a shove off a ledge.

Do something exciting. Something that gives you a rush. Even if you get hives. *Roller coaster? Impromptu trip to Europe? Driving without a license.*

There. Now you're pushing yourself.

The buzzer alerting her to a visitor pulled her out of her self-congratulatory thoughts.

When she asked who it was, her mom's voice came through the tinny speaker. Everly opened her apartment door in time to see her mom bounding up the steps with the energy of someone at least ten years younger. She carried a bag in each hand. Long dark hair bounced with each step, and her eyes sparkled when they met Everly's.

"There's the birthday girl," her mom said, her smile rounding out the apples of her cheeks.

"It didn't work out so well for me the last time someone said that to me today." If her father heard, her mother would know, and vice versa. Even during separations, they stayed in contact. Hence the reunions.

The good news, Everly realized as she stepped aside to let her mother come in, was that even if thirty sucked, all indicators suggested she'd age well. At fifty-four, Jessica Dean had plenty of energy and enthusiasm that showed in her youthful skin and stylish way of dressing. A registered massage therapist, her mom attributed her strong core—Everly's words as Jessica used the term *seductive curves*—to weekly yoga. She was forever trying to get Everly to join.

Locking the door, she followed her mom to the kitchen, amused by the overflowing grocery bags.

"I have food, Mom."

Her mom glanced over her shoulder. "Not mom food."

Unable to suppress her grin, Everly teasingly pointed at her mom. "You're right. Is there a special store where you get food sold only to mothers?"

Setting the bags on the counter, Jessica closed the distance, pulling Everly into a hard hug. "Your father called me at the office to tell me what happened. I'm sorry. I'm just glad we never met him. I'd hate to have gotten attached to one of your boyfriends only to have him treat you like this."

It finally worked in her favor that she opted never to introduce her parents to the guys she dated. Not that there were all that many. *At least you saved Mom from getting attached.* Everly held in the sigh, which made her chest ache.

Her mom leaned back, then cupped Everly's cheeks the way she'd done for as long as Everly could remember. "Any chance you'll let him grovel and make it up?"

That her mother would even ask said a lot about the differences between them. "No."

The corners of her mom's lips tilted down, but she nodded and patted Everly's cheeks before going to the bags and beginning to unload.

Everly tracked the items getting put on the counter: kale—no, thank you; orange juice—sure; salad fixings—fine without the kale; cupcakes—now we're talking. And one, two, three issues of *Cosmo*.

Everly arched her brows. "Really?"

Her mother had a long history of attempting to "educate" Everly about being a sexually fulfilled woman. While she appreciated the sentiment, Everly strongly believed these discussions were best between girlfriends. Sometimes her mother forgot the rules *and* their roles. She'd been sure, once they'd had "the talk" when Everly was twelve, her mother would let it go. They could avoid the conversations much like the STDs she'd warned against.

By sixteen, her mother stuck just-in-case condoms into the pockets of Everly's handbags. Once Everly discovered that, she'd taken to tucking them away in the piñata that, to her knowledge, still sat in the back of her childhood closet.

Mom shrugged as she loaded the fridge. "The articles are top-notch, honey. Let me tell you—"

Everly covered her ears. "Oh God, please don't. Don't tell me anything you learned in *Cosmo*."

Her mother laughed and waved a hand at her. "Stop it. Now, we're going to turn this birthday into a happy one. I know your dad asked you to come over, and I also know you won't. That's okay. You're a grown woman and can make your own choices. But that doesn't mean I'm just going to let you sit here and wallow."

Because she knew she'd be eating more than one of those cupcakes, Everly pulled a banana from the bunch her mom brought to even things off right out of the gate.

"I'm not wallowing. How'd you know I was home?"

Her mom's chin tilted down, and she looked at Everly the way someone would if they were peering over the tops of their glasses. Only she wasn't wearing any, so it seemed strange. But Everly knew the looks; this one was "I'm your mom. I'm supposed to know."

"You went to the station?"

A quick nod, and she finished loading up the fridge.

"I did. Stacey told me you'd been sent home. I'm sorry, honey. You aren't in any trouble, are you?"

Everly broke off a chunk of the banana, ignored the instant stomach swirl even the thought of trouble brought, and said, "Don't see why I would be," before popping the bite in her mouth. She was happy her voice sounded more positive than she felt.

"Good. Because you don't want to start looking for a career at your age. Especially since you should be focused on finding a husband."

Everly rolled her eyes twice because she was sure it would be warranted by the end of the visit, but at the moment, her mom's back was turned.

Possible rule seven: Take the opportunities presented to you.

Ha! See, she could totally come up with a cool list. Pitching projects and seizing moments was exactly what she needed to get thirty off the ground. Even if those moments included behind-the-back eye rolling.

"Not sure if you've heard, but they no longer require you to get married to keep your woman card. You should bring that up next time you're at the Mom Food Store."

Laughing as she grabbed a banana of her own, her mom tilted her head. "Sharing your life with someone makes it more meaningful."

Everly's heartstrings tightened—like someone gave one quick, hard tug. They were both right; she didn't need a husband to make her life better, but sharing her life with someone would make things more special. *That's what Stacey's for; you can share plenty with her tonight.*

"You want a cupcake now or later?" her mom asked, finishing up her banana in record time.

Everly gave her the over-the-fake-eyeglasses look, making her mom laugh. Finishing her healthy food, then grabbing a couple of plates and some forks, they took their treats to the built-in nook in the corner of the kitchen.

"I'm going to give you some motherly advice," her mom said after a few minutes of quiet.

"Mom. I don't need advice. I just need today to be over." She let the soft, delicious chocolate sit on her tongue a moment. She should have started her day like this instead of surprising her ex. *At least you didn't waste much time on him.* It'd been a step forward for her, though, the idea of letting Simon be part of a day she dreaded. *It's over. Stop dwelling.*

"Sweetie." Her mom covered her hand with her own, doing the full head-to-the-side tilt. That, combined with the sad eyes, was her "You don't know what you need" look. Now *that* would be a long list: her mother's many looks.

"Really, I'm good. I dated a loser. This is what happens when you do that." There'd be less chance of traveling the same path once she had her rules.

"Did you stuff his balls down his throat?"

Everly nearly choked on her bite of cake. Her eyes watered. "Uh, no. That would have involved touching them, and I really didn't want to do that."

She frowned. "Did you yell? Tell him what you thought of him?"

Everly shook her head. *That would have meant sticking around for longer.*

Her mom leaned in closer. "Did you call him names? Swear? Slam a door? Wreck something of his?"

She swallowed, wished for some water to magically appear, and shook her head again. "No. No. No. And no. I did drop the coffee and bagels I'd brought us all over the floor and didn't stick around to clean it up."

Widening her eyes in mock horror, her mom pressed a hand to her chest. "Wow. Remind me never to cross you."

She didn't have either of her parents' tempers or flair for the dramatic. In her opinion, the less conflict the better. They loved hard, laughed hard, and fought hard. Everly usually just watched from the sidelines.

With a small smile, Everly slid out of the bench seat and went to grab a couple of bottles of water from the fridge. She passed one to her mom and opened hers to take a long drink.

"I'm good. You don't need to worry."

"Of course we worry. We love you."

Some months it was *we*, some it was *your father and I*. "Well, don't. And I love you, too."

"You know, I know what I'm talking about. You should take me more seriously. I have a client who just got married. She's twenty-three, and when I tell her secrets to a good marriage? She laps it up like I'm the patron saint of weddings or something. I have been married for twenty-five years."

The volcano of emotion that had gone dormant throughout the day started to rumble. This woman didn't have Everly's first-hand knowledge that her parents weren't the gurus of marriage. Normally, she'd bite her tongue, let her mother wax poetic about relationships but she didn't have the energy to hold back. She couldn't fight this, too. Looking down at her cake, she counted to ten in her head. When she looked up, she said, "You keep your office furnished with a pullout sofa for when you're mad at Dad. You dive headfirst into a new hobby every time you're fighting. You break up and make up frequently. No offense, but I don't want that kind of relationship. Or a pile of handmade crafts I'd have to store." These rules were really perfect. No odd hobbies, because rule number two said *no hoarding—animal or otherwise.*

Her mom's eyes didn't flash with hurt or anger. No. Jessica Dean could take a punch and keep going. It was one of the things that made it hard to be mad at her—she made no apologies for being exactly who she was. She also didn't bullshit, so she'd be okay with Everly stating the facts.

Her mom laughed, pressed her index finger to the crumbs on her plate. "You do have a point. *Despite* that, I still know a few things about making a man happy. Besides, it never hurts to have a spare couch. There are many uses for that. Like when your father is being a sweetheart and bringing me lunch."

Everly plugged her ears again but couldn't help the laughter bubbling from her chest. "Stop it. I think I need to worry about me being happy before someone else. But thanks."

Her mom yanked on the crook of one of her elbows, joining in on the laughter. "Anytime, sweetie. I know your dad and I are a little wonky and maybe not the best role models when it comes to love, but everyone is different. You just need to find what works for you."

***

After her mom left, Everly picked up the notebook again, looked through the rules. She wanted ten. A nice, even number. Proof that she was taking this decade seriously so she wouldn't hit forty and think about all the things she wished she'd done differently. *Right. Because you have plans to use that decade for gratitude.*

She had a solid rule seven: Find what makes you truly happy. And hang on to it.

[3]

The headache Chris Jansen woke up with came back with attitude and a Thor-size hammer. He would have dropped his head to his desk if he wasn't working so hard to keep himself together. The look on Everly's face kept flashing in his brain like a neon sign. How one woman could be so gorgeous and unaware of it was beyond him. He wasn't supposed to think of her like that. Chris put considerable time and effort into *not* thinking about Everly Dean, but just seeing her smile opened Pandora's box in his chest. In a small town over an hour outside of LA, he had a simple task: boost station ratings, get the place in shape, move on to bigger and *much* better things. Things he'd actually gone to school for, things he *wanted* to do.

That was the short-term plan when he'd agreed to take the job as 96.2 SUN station manager.

"*Agreed* suggests you had a choice," he muttered.

Maybe that was true if he didn't mind choosing between proving himself to his father or not living up to a long legacy of familial expectations. Chris hadn't paid much attention when his dad purchased the station, along with a number of other businesses under the same umbrella, because he hadn't realized, at the time, it was going to be his final stepping-stone. Nathaniel Jansen loved setting out hoops for people to jump through, and as the youngest of Nathaniel's four kids, Chris had the most to prove. His brothers were already working in their preferred areas of their father's companies. Not that they didn't get shoved through the wringer on a regular basis, but at least they were doing what they loved.

He leaned back in his leather chair, ignoring the groaning creak it always made, and closed his eyes, covering his face with his hands. Nope. Couldn't unsee the sadness in Everly's expression. Or the way her backbone had gone ramrod straight and she'd pulled on that goddamn titanium shield. She was the toughest woman he'd ever met. It was all kinds of attractive, but it also kept her slightly removed. A bit untouchable. *Definitely untouchable.* He had to remind himself of that all too often. Quiet, a little socially awkward from what he could tell, and very talented, she was like invisible lightning. When he was near her, energy burst through his veins, making him abnormally tongue-tied. *You're her boss. Who has one foot out the door.*

Her angry, on-air confession ran through his head again. The listeners would get over that. Most would laugh it off, not that there was one funny thing about it. Remembering the humiliated tinge of her voice carved a hole in his gut. Professionally, the dead air was a slightly bigger problem. It shouldn't be a big deal—glitches happened. But his father kept him under a microscope, waiting for him to screw up, for any chance to tell Chris that he hadn't earned his right to ascend the ranks. He hadn't worked this hard, come this far, to have something minor block him from the prize.

His door slammed open, and Stacey Ryan stood in the opening, hands on her hips, glaring at him like somehow *he* was the enemy.

"This was my fault. I overstepped, but you shouldn't have sent her home. You *know* how good she is at her job. How much it means to her," she started, her gaze burning into his brain stronger than the headache.

He knew, but only because the deejay told him. Whenever he was around Everly, they did an awkward dance of him offering curt sentences and her giving back polite nods.

Chris loosened his tie, wishing the windows in his office actually opened so he could get some fresh air. "I didn't send her home to be a jerk. This is better than having to field calls about her goddamn love life to all the people who are already phoning in. She'd hate that, and *you* know it." He pointed at her and stood up, pacing the pathetically small room.

The thought of Everly *having* a love life unsettled his stomach. It had to be some sort of karmic irony that he met a woman who intrigued him more than any other at a time when keeping his eye on the end goal mattered more than ever.

The phone hadn't stopped ringing since Everly's detailed confession. What the hell kind of idiot would cheat on that woman? He thought of his father and cringed. On *any* woman. But especially someone like Everly. She was five and a half feet of pure awesome, and maybe he didn't tell her that—he had no right—but the guys in this town couldn't be stupid enough not to realize it on their own. She was better off without Simon the asshat. He just hoped she knew that.

"So far, the calls have been in her favor. They want to help her and maybe strip Simon of his boy parts," Stacey said.

Chris winced. The laugh that burst from his chest turned into a sigh. He leaned against the low windowsill. Stacey stayed in the doorway, crossing her arms over her chest. The two women couldn't be more different, but he knew they were good friends. Stacey was about the only person at the station who'd broken through Everly's well-built walls.

"She wouldn't want that either. What were you thinking, going live like that? She constantly shies away from being in the limelight, but you thought it'd be a good idea to put her on the radio?" Everly spoke on-air now and again when she and Stacey went back and forth about something or she told Stacey who was calling in, but those times were few and far between.

Guilt flashed across her features. "*She* wasn't supposed to be on the air." Stacey's shoulders slumped. "She hates birthdays. I wanted to do something fun that might get her excited for the big three-oh. I thought it'd be funny and she'd get dozens of shout-outs from listeners on social media."

Chris sent her a wry grin. "That's already happening."

She nodded, her eyes studying the carpet. "Not exactly the way I'd hoped."

There was probably a protocol to deal with the deejay's lack of professionalism, but Chris wasn't looking to make her feel worse. Though, in the end, he wasn't in charge, and his father was looking for ways to point out his failings. The ratings needed to go up, not down—particularly in this segment.

He didn't want to discuss this anymore. He needed some air, a drink, a hard run . . . something. Pushing off the sill, he walked closer to Stacey. "It'll be okay. We'll field the calls and comments, and it'll go away. Isn't it quitting time for you?"

"Pretty soon. I'm getting some things ready for tomorrow, then I'm going to go and buy Everly five pounds of chocolate, a six-pack of wine coolers, and a really big vib—"

"Don't," Chris groaned, his lips twitching, "finish that sentence."

Stacey grinned unabashedly. The phones continued to ring, and he knew their listening audience—mostly women in the fifty-five-plus age bracket—would love the chance to share their opinions.

"Well, I'm heading out. I have a meeting with a couple of new sponsors." He hesitated, tried to infuse his tone with a casualness he didn't feel. "You think Everly is okay?"

Stacey regarded him for a moment, and Chris had to work hard to keep from giving anything away. Boss and employee. Practically strangers. He was just asking for a friend. Wasn't that what all the cool kids said? *How the hell would you know what they say?* The truth was, he'd never cared much about what others thought of him. But he cared about what Everly thought. And if she was all right.

"Yes." Stacey's expression didn't match the certainty of her tone.

"I didn't mean to make her birthday worse."

"I'm not even sure that's possible," Stacey said in an uncharacteristically quiet voice.

He hadn't even known it was her birthday. *Because she never talks to you!* And he never asked. It was easier to keep a wide berth between them. The attraction he felt—which he was quite certain she did not reciprocate—had been almost instantaneous.

After another uncomfortable minute of Stacey looking at him too closely, she left. Chris tunneled his fingers into his hair. Never mind the dead air, if his father got wind of his . . . whatever he felt toward Everly, it'd be one more excuse to prolong his purgatory. Chris had no intention of staying in San Verde, California. He loved the weather, but this city wasn't on anyone's list of most important places to see. While his father hadn't exactly asked if he'd wanted to come here, the station was the most intriguing subsidiary of the communications corporation his father had bought. Career came first, and he couldn't change that for a shy woman who made his chest feel too tight when he wasn't even sticking around.

Chris fought the urge to pace or, worse, call Everly. He had an hour or so before his first meeting. He couldn't spend it thinking about Everly, so he did what he was used to, what he was good at—he buried himself in work.

***

Despite the fact that San Verde was a smallish town, it had its perks. Though he wished it were on the water, the ocean was only an hour away. The cost of living was a lot better than bigger cities, and there were some excellent restaurants. The one where he'd just had lunch—and signed on new sponsors—had a chocolate-caramel pie that made his mouth water.

He glanced over to the passenger side, still unsure why he'd asked for an extra to go. *Right. You're so unsure you're already heading toward her place.* He'd felt slightly guilty looking up her address but told himself it was her birthday. She deserved something to turn it around. Chris couldn't stand the thought of Everly's entire day being ruined. Was she hurt—or worse, heartbroken—over Simon? *None of your business.* Not only was there a strict no-fraternization policy at the station, it'd be one more strike his father could put next to his name.

Parking across the street from her apartment building he grabbed the dessert and got out of the car. *Maybe you should call her, let her know you're coming. I'm not visiting. Just dropping off some deliciousness and seeing for myself that she's okay.*

He hesitated after only a step. Everly didn't strike him as a "drop in anytime" sort of person. Leaning against his vehicle, he thumbed a text.

Okay if I drop by to talk to you?

A couple of kids were drawing chalk rainbows on the sidewalk. It made him smile and think of Manhattan. It wasn't something he saw there since there were too many people hurrying along the pavement to get any good sidewalk space.

There were lots of things—like crowds—that he didn't miss about living in a big city. Streets like this one, lined with blossoming trees and a sense of calm, made him think about how nice it'd be to come home every night to a place like this. Unfortunately, towns like this didn't come with high-powered firms that specialized in corporate communications.

His text tone signaled.

Okay. Should I be worried?

No.

Tucking his phone in his pocket, he crossed the street, passed the kids playing, and took the couple of steps up to the entryway landing.

Buzzing number 3, he waited.

"Hello?" Everly's voice sounded scratchy through the speaker.

It took him a second to find his voice. "It's Chris."

The pause made his breath hitch until she asked, "Pine?"

His lips twitched. "No."

"Evans?"

"Wrong again." He glanced around to make sure no one was watching this ridiculous exchange.

"Pratt?"

"Let me in, Everly."

"Oh. You do know my first name."

Stopping himself from smacking his head against the side of the house, he sighed, pressed the button again. "Of course I do."

The buzzer sounded, and he pulled the door open. The house was charming with a wide staircase leading to a couple of upper units. His grandmother lived in a heritage home just outside of Hell's Kitchen. Chris hadn't seen her in too long, but he'd always loved going for dinners there. They were simple and delicious. Before he'd passed, his grandfather insisted on gathering as a whole unit at least twice a month.

Grandmother never allowed business discussions at the table, and though she had more money than the San Verde bank, she didn't care much for "things." She believed in family, forgiveness, and hard work. Most of that had rubbed off on Chris and his brothers. The jury was still out on his sister. Chris always felt close to his grandmother. She saw through smoke screens others didn't and knew, unlike the other men, or women, in his family, he craved what she and his grandfather had shared before his passing.

Shaking off his maudlin thoughts, he took the stairs up and veered to the right. Everly's door swung open before he knocked.

"What are you doing here?" She was dressed in a pair of pink sweatpants and a plain white T-shirt, and her long, chestnut-brown hair was pulled up into a ponytail. As usual, her face was free of makeup, but even without it, her skin was flawless. Her blue eyes watched him warily. She had the most expressive gazes. He could tell when she was nervous or excited just from a glance. *Maybe that's a sign you're paying too much attention.* What would it take to make her lower her shield? To open up.

His arms itched to wrap her up in a hug, but he wasn't sure if she'd accept it, if it would be over the line, or if he'd be doing it more for himself. Sticking to safer territory, Chris thrust the brown paper bag toward her.

Her eyes narrowed. She took a small step back. "What's that?"

He smiled, amused by her wariness over something so simple. "Dessert."

Her eyes snapped up, and she scowled at him. As she turned and padded into her apartment, she said, "I don't like birthday cake."

"I heard. That's not what this is." He let himself in and shut the door. He'd never been in her apartment—there'd never been a reason. *Probably isn't one now.*

Glancing around, he saw it was simple and quiet with small splashes of color—teal cushions on the gray couch, a pale pink blanket that looked like she'd been wrapped up in it draped over the back. The television was paused on a show he didn't recognize. Light filtered through the gaps in the closed blinds. It made sense that his apartment here didn't have much character, but in this tiny space, Everly created a stronger atmosphere of comfort, of *home*, than his apartment in New York, which he was temporarily leasing out but had owned for years. There was a hallway to the left and a dividing wall to the right. He assumed one went to the kitchen and the other to the bedroom and bathroom. She headed to the right.

"Good thing I came home so I could greet visitors. Want a drink?"

Around the wall was what he expected—a small, narrow, clean kitchen.

His jaw tensed. Visitors? "Your ex didn't show, did he?"

She looked over her shoulder. "No."

Thank God. He hoped she never had to look at *Simon* again. "I'll take a water, thanks."

She grabbed a bottle from the fridge and passed it to him. He offered her the bag, opened the water, and took a long drink to ease the dryness of his throat. *Excellent. More dead air.* When he set his water down, his eyes landed on the multiple issues of *Cosmopolitan* sitting on her counter. Biting his lip to hold back a smile, he reached for them.

A small noise escaped Everly's mouth. She set the bag on the other counter and took the magazines from him, shoving them into a drawer. He tried to peek before she closed it and was pretty sure he saw more issues. *A closet* Cosmo *junkie. Didn't see that coming.*

Her cheeks were a subtle, but noticeable, shade of pink. He wanted to tease her, make that blush spread over her skin. Everly backed up, and Chris cleared his throat.

He didn't want to make her uncomfortable, ever, so he stuck to safer topics.

"Who came to visit?"

"My mom." She closed her eyes and sighed.

Say something. She shouldn't be embarrassed by wanting to know ten ways to please herself in bed. Damn. Do not think about Cosmo. *Say something. Break the silence. Now. What? I'm sorry you'd dated a loser. You deserve more, and I want to be the man to give it to you. Shit. No. Do not say that.*

Everly opened her eyes. "My mom has it in her head that *Cosmo* is some sort of Bible for all single women. She brings me several issues each time she visits."

Chris chuckled, thinking it was nice to know something about her—something small and personal.

He shoved a hand through his hair. "It's nice she wants

you to be happy." *Way to go not saying* pleased. His heart rate amped up. "You going to look in the bag?"

"I'm not in the mood for dessert."

Determined to get rid of the tension in the air, he crossed the kitchen, which really was just a matter of taking a few steps. "Do you have a fork, then? It's chocolate-caramel pie from Dario's, and I'm addicted."

For a second, she said nothing, and then slowly, a smile lifted her lips, her eyes brightened, and she laughed. Pleasure filled his chest at the sound. She was always gorgeous, but when she laughed, she was adorable. Those expressive eyes brightened, and her cheeks rounded with happiness, her rigid stance relaxing.

She tilted her head to one side. "Shouldn't you tell me to put it in the fridge for later?"

Making a face, Chris shook his head, opened the bag, and withdrew the take-out container. "No way. You don't put food this good in the fridge for later. There are rules about these things."

A strange expression he couldn't decipher passed over her features. He almost asked if he'd said something wrong.

She held out her hand. "Then I changed my mind. I want it."

His breath stumbled in his airway, and he made a noise somewhere between a gasp and a groan. Chris could write a freaking book on what he wanted. And couldn't have.

"That seems fair. It is your birthday, and I did bring it for you."

She took it from him, her hand reaching out cautiously as if he were dangerous. *Ha. The only dangerous one is you, Everly Dean.* She was the kind of woman who could distract a guy from a well-made plan.

"Thank you."

"I'm sorry your birthday sucked."

She shrugged, dug a spoon out, then popped the lid of the container. "Most of them do. Not always this bad. At least it's almost over."

No one should feel that way about their birthday. What happened to make her feel that way? He spent too much time thinking about Everly—what *her* favorite dessert was, why she'd become a producer, why she lived in San Verde when she could work anywhere, what it would feel like to kiss her, to see if she had more than just those few freckles dotting her nose or wake up in her bed.

She's your employee. And not a short-term fling.

"Is the station phone going nuts?"

Now he shrugged. He didn't want to talk about work, which in and of itself was strange. His gaze was fixed on the spoon with the bite of creamy rich chocolate heading for her mouth. She licked her lips before opening them, and Chris's stomach tightened, his breathing shallowed. He could imagine, vividly, how she'd taste. The chocolate covering a hint of caramel with whatever would be uniquely Everly. When her eyes drifted shut, her mouth closing around the spoon, he curled his hands into fists, fighting the urge to lean into her. Inhale her. Taste for himself.

Her eyes fluttered open, locked on his. "Delicious."

Yes. Yes, she was. He needed to get back to work.

"I should go." It might have come out a little sharper than he'd intended, but *come on*, he was hanging by a thread here. Between wanting to hug her, kiss her, comfort her, and have a strongly worded conversation with her ex, Chris's emotions were on overload.

Tilting her head to one side again, her hair swung to the left, giving him the scent of vanilla. Pursing her lips, she studied him. "Why did you bring this? You don't even like me."

Shock silenced him. His heart beat an uneven tempo beneath his ribs. That's what she thought? *I like you too much. I think about you all the time, and it distracts me. You make me think about coming home to a tree-lined street in a quiet neighborhood. You make me forget why I'm here.*

"That's not true. At all," he managed, voice gruff.

Her eyebrows arched up. "Really? Evidence would suggest otherwise."

What *evidence*? He was always polite and professional with her—he made sure of it. It took a tangible amount of energy to not clue her in to how he felt. Usually, he walked away from an interaction with her feeling like he'd run a race in jeans.

"I'm not sure what you mean or why you think that," he admitted. "But I promise you, it isn't true." What else could he say?

Fighting to stay still, not shuffle under her watchful gaze, he wished he could think of something else to say to erase her look of doubt.

"Well . . . thanks."

Shoving one hand in his pocket, he retrieved his keys, closed his fingers around them tightly. "No problem. See you tomorrow."

He let himself out, nearly flew down the stairs in his efforts to get some fresh air. His phone rang the minute he got back in his car.

His chest still felt tight. "Hello?"

"It's me," his father said, his voice booming through the Bluetooth.

"I secured two new sponsors today."

He didn't expect applause or even a "Good job." He knew better.

"Your sister was listening to the show this morning."

Chris bit back his groan. He loved his sister. He truly did. But she was the only girl in a family of boys—extended family included—and she was the epitome of indulged. Particularly by their father. At thirty-three, she'd yet to hold down a job long term because she was too busy "finding herself." Ari spent her days searching for her chakras or chi or whatever it might be at the moment. Usually, she found them at star-studded parties or all-inclusive spas.

"I don't need to tell you how bad dead air is for a radio station, do I?"

Nope. But he would, anyway. "It was seconds."

"Seconds following an unprofessional outburst from your producer. I told you to boost ratings, not find ways to tank them."

"Dad." He could already see where this was going. The back of his neck prickled.

"Ari's been thinking about hosting a show. Something tied into her love of fashion."

There it is. He dropped his head to the steering wheel. It was bad enough to have his dad checking in with him constantly. Weekly phone calls, Skype sessions, memos with suggestions. Chris did not want his older sister underfoot for his final few months. He definitely didn't want to be her boss—knowing she wouldn't listen to anything he said—for the brief slice of time she'd explore this new adventure.

Besides, that spot was currently filled with two very capable employees. The ratings weren't great, but they weren't down by much in comparison to the other slots. The station was doing better than when he'd arrived. After having gone through several management changes over the last few years, the staff who'd been there awhile were tentative about Chris's arrival. He'd overheard them on his first day, commiserating about the new owner, how he'd emailed a list of expectations and policies. Not wanting to set himself back before he even got his feet wet, Chris hadn't mentioned he was the owner's son. Seemed safer. Ari had no desire to have people like her if telling them who their father was got her where she wanted to be quicker.

"This isn't something someone just does for fun. These people go to school. They intern, pay their dues. They're passionate about it. It's a career, not a hobby." This felt like another test. "The station is under my control, Dad. Things are going well, and today was nothing more than a hiccup."

"My guy keeping an eye on your numbers says you're not even rated as one of the top stations in the state. You've got a long way to go and not a ton of time to do it. Maybe it's more than you can handle." The words sat between them like concrete. Working for his dad felt like being on a reality show like *Survivor* or *MasterChef.* The contestants got in the groove, and all of a sudden, the host throws a wrench into things, making winning feel impossible.

His dad cleared his throat loudly. "You remember the deal, right?"

Chris started the car and put it in Drive to head back to the station. *It's on my mind 24-7, so yeah, Dad, I remember.* Eighteen months turning around this off-the-map station, almost twelve of which had passed. At the end, Chris's dad would let go of the reins. *Feels more like a vise.* Chris would be head of communications for all his father's companies. He had plans to unite the divisions of each company. It was exciting. Or would be. The best part, and most ironic, was that he'd have far *less* communication with his father. And maybe, though not likely, earn a drop of his father's respect. He knew he was a lucky man to have the opportunities he did. But they didn't come free of charge.

"These things take time, " Chris said carefully. The ratings *were* improving in some areas. After they'd narrowed their demographic and played to it, they'd seen a large spike.

"Along with strong leadership. The 10:00 a.m. show is the lowest ranked and the quietest spot of the day. Letting Ari try her hand won't hurt anything."

"You can't just fire two people because your daughter woke up wanting to play deejay today."

"That's not the only reason, Christopher. It would serve you well to remember who you're talking to. A good leader knows when to cut his losses, and I personally think you should cut the segment. People want music, not chitchat. Get rid of them. Both of them. The producer and the deejay."

[4]

Everly was considering how many episodes of *Veronica Mars* in a row qualified as too many when her phone buzzed on the coffee table.

Trying to move as little as possible while reaching for her phone, she half slipped off the couch, managing to stop herself from falling by bracing one hand on the table. One more reason to live alone. She glanced at the screen as she righted herself back into her comfy position.

STACEY: Backyard. Bring the list.

Head resting on the arm of the couch, Everly smirked and typed out a response.

EVERLY: Clarify.

STACEY: Get your ass out here.

EVERLY: My birthday. Can't go out. Rules are rules.

STACEY: Don't make me come in there. Bring your damn rules. Or I'm going to invite a bunch of my fun friends to your house now.

Everly sat up, laughing out loud, while typing.

EVERLY: On my way.

STACEY: Atta girl.

EVERLY: No one says that, dork.

STACEY: Just did.

The grounds of the house had been expertly manicured to create a community garden in the fenced backyard. When Everly went through the gate, her throat thickened and she stopped on the concrete path to stare.

Stacey had tied purple and black balloons to one of the wrought iron bistro set chairs. A pink bakery box from Baked—home of the best chocolate ganache cupcakes on earth, owned by one of Stacey's friends—sat in the center. A gold, dress-up tiara sparkled on top of that box, the late-evening sun bouncing off the fake jewels. It took her a while to open up and feel close to people, but once she'd let them in, the nerves took a back seat. Every now and again, even in a close relationship, they snuck back, overwhelming her with the reminder that she was not as isolated as she sometimes believed.

"Are you coming over here or not?" Used to her, Stacey stood, hands on her hips, smiling. Her blond hair was loose and wavy, like she'd just let it out of one of her haphazard buns. She'd changed from this morning and now wore a pair of cut-off jean shorts and blue T-shirt that read: SARCASM LOADING.

"Seriously. You are really bad at this," Stacey said, walking over and taking Everly's arm, pulling her toward the table. She yanked out a chair, nudged Everly—not so gently—into it, and sat across from her. A car drove by, music pumping loud, breaking into the quiet.

Everly worked on not bursting into tears. Growing up in a house where emotions swung like a pendulum, she'd learned to hold back her own. Weigh and carry them before deciding whether it was worth sharing them. She knew that part of her problem getting close to people—*men* in particular—was a defense mechanism. Expecting nothing was infinitely safer.

"You didn't have to do this, Stace." Her voice came out rough. She felt bad when people did nice things for her. She could never wrap her head around the idea that she deserved it. *Stacey would kick your ass for thinking that. You deserve whatever you're willing to give, and you'd do this for her.*

Stacey picked up the tiara, inspected it closely, tilting it so the sun bounced off the fake jewels. Then Stacey placed it firmly on her own head. Everly burst into laughter instead of tears.

"You're awesome," Everly said, noting the gift bag on another chair.

"I know. And before you complain about any of this, you're thirty, it's your birthday, and just because it started out shitty does not mean I'm okay with letting it end that way. Everyone deserves cake and presents and a little spoiling on their day. You'd do the same, and have, for me."

Swallowing around the lump in her throat, Everly could only nod. Stacey reached out a hand, reminding Everly that she still held her notebook.

"Give me that. You have cake. Tara made it special for you. I won't sing," Stacey said with a smirk playing on her lips. She held up her hands like she was swearing on a Bible.

Handing over the book, Everly flipped the top of the box open and stared down at a beautiful miniature cake. Shaped and decorated like a present, it had polka-dot wrapping paper and a thick bow. A white tag read *Everly.*

"This is stunning," Everly said.

Stacey glanced up. "Yeah. Tara's the best. I told her it was too pretty to eat, and she said cake is always meant to be eaten."

"Thank you."

"You're welcome. Want your gift?"

Everly eyed the bag, nerves dancing in her belly again. "I don't know. Do I?"

Laughter shone from her friend's eyes. "Oh yeah. But maybe you should save it for later. You have batteries, right? I mean, it came with some, but it's always good to have backup."

Even in the quiet of her own backyard, with no one else around, Everly's cheeks warmed. "You did not." *Of course she did.*

"Babe, you're thirty. They say this is the friskiest time of your life. I think you should add *sleep with a younger man* to this list." She tapped her index finger on the page.

Everly rolled her eyes. She held out her hand. "Give me back my list."

Stacey shook her head. "Nuh-uh. Eat cake. This needs work."

Everly picked up one of the two forks beside the box and dug in. She might end up in a sugar coma later, but it'd be worth it.

"You're not helping with the list," Everly said around her first delicious bite.

"Uh, *yeah*, I am. This is boring. You turned thirty, not one hundred. I love the work one. I told you six months ago you needed to pitch that podcast idea. Other than that, though, let's see . . . Find your happy? I brought you your happy." Stacey pointed to the gift bag, and Everly almost choked on her bite of cake.

Her friend set the journal down and reached under the table, dug around a moment, then pulled up a bottle of wine and two glasses.

Everly peeked under to see what other magic tricks she was hiding. "You're like a dirty Mary Poppins."

Stacey laughed as she opened the wine and poured them both some. "I like that. Mary Poppins with sass."

Everly had the glass to her lips when Stacey raised her glass. "To you. To being one of the best people I've ever met. And to thirty being the year you realize just how kick-ass awesome you really are."

Everly clinked her glass, determined to take her friend's words to heart. "To you being a great friend and a lousy singer."

Stacey tilted her head back and laughed. Everly noticed the curtains on the bottom-left unit flutter open. Lexie pressed her face to the glass, smooshing her nose and waving. Everly waved back, and Stacey turned to do the same.

"Okay, for real. I think this list is a great idea. But we need to spice it up."

"It's not a bucket list, Stace. It's a guideline for getting what I want out of life. Starting this year."

Stacey sipped her wine. "Okay. What do you want?"

Everly's stomach tilted when she realized she didn't really know. "I feel like I have a better idea of what I don't want."

Her friend gestured with her hand for Everly to continue, then picked up the other fork.

"I don't want to date guys I don't connect with anymore. Maybe they don't all cheat, but it never goes anywhere, which I think I've been doing on purpose. I don't want people to think I'm a snob just because I have a hard time talking to them. I don't know that I want a different spot at the station, but I hate feeling like I'm too scared to push past my safety net. At work and in my personal life."

Stacey nodded, swallowing down her cake. "Okay. Good. We can work with this." She reached down to her purse, which was beside her on the ground, and pulled out a pen. She wrote something in the book.

"Hey!" Everly reached for the journal.

Stacey batted her hand way. "I'm helping. It's not like you can't change it back. I'm just adding a couple of things. You have room. Also, the title needs to go. This isn't just about thirty. It's about you seeing how truly awesome you are and opening yourself up. Even, maybe especially when, you're scared. Until you wrap your head around that, you pretend."

She sipped her wine before responding. "Are you dropping clichés on me now? Fake it 'til I make it?"

Stacey shot her a sassy grin and nodded. "You got it, babe."

Everly sat on the edge of the chair, waiting, worrying her bottom lip while Stacey scratched the pen across the page. Staring beyond her friend at the houses in the neighborhood, she thought about what it'd be like to have her own place . . . an actual home of her own. Did she want that? Yes. And though she wouldn't say it out loud, not even to Stacey, she also wanted to share that home with a husband and family. All while having a job she loved and excelled at. *Maybe you do know what you want.* But so far, she'd taken the wrong path to get it, because as great as it was to have a friend like Stacey, she was sitting in the backyard of a rented home, feeling restless, and tonight, she'd go to bed alone.

Everly glanced at the gift bag and couldn't help but laugh.

When Stacey passed her back her book, Everly stared down at her list. Stacey had added more than ideas; she'd included funny little notes with arrows pointing at a few of them and a smiley face beside the last one.

~~The Rules for Turning 30~~

Ten Rules for Faking It

1. *Focus on the good.*

2. *No hoarding—animals or otherwise.*

3. ~~Stay home on birthdays~~. *Do something you enjoy on your birthday.*

4. *Try one new thing each month outside of your comfort zone.*

5. ~~Do something bold to gain notice at work~~. *Pitch*

and push the podcast idea at the next meeting. End goal: getting our pick of time slots.

6. ~~*Do something exciting. Even if it gives you hives.*~~ *Be bold. Even if it gives you hives.*
7. *Figure out what makes you happy and grab on tight. No more holding back.*
8. *Date men who make you feel things. (And no, I actually don't just mean those things. Stop hiding, Everly.)*
9. *Believe in yourself, in your value as a friend, lover, girlfriend, daughter, producer, and all-around great human.*
10. *Make the first move. (A real move. Lip-locking, hand-grazing, sultry-look giving. You choose.)* ☺

Her stomach only wobbled a little, but Everly convinced herself that was from eating too much cake and not because she was scared. *If you're scared and doing it, anyway, that counts as something from the list.* She inhaled deeply, feeling her chest expand before she let the breath out slowly. Maybe it was time to make some changes. For herself.

[5]

Chris rarely worked from home. It made him stir-crazy. But today, he couldn't face Everly, he couldn't deal with being at the station, looking at her and Stacey, knowing he didn't have an answer for how to save their jobs.

Why did he put up with his dad's garbage? Was it really going to get him where he wanted to be?

"Knock off the pity party," he muttered, bringing his coffee to the small table by the patio that overlooked a busy street.

His phone buzzed with the group text he and his brothers had started so long ago, he'd probably never find the beginning. Chris had updated them on Ari's new plan, and the three of them were alternating between coming up with ideas to distract her and complaining about their father. *Totally productive.*

NOAH: If you boost the ratings, especially during that time segment, Dad can't fight you.

CHRIS: Thanks, genius. I hadn't thought of that.

NOAH: That's why I'm here.

WESLEY: The numbers really aren't that bad. I played with some of the data, and it looks like when you targeted ad space and music to a specific demographic, your ratings improved.

NOAH: Do you ever get tired of talking like that?

WESLEY: Like I know what I'm doing? No. But I get why it would be hard for you to understand. Most things are.

Chris laughed. This wasn't helping, but it was improving his mood. Opening up the laptop, he logged in to the station's site, his heartbeat accelerating with every ping signaling a new message. People were commenting on Everly's overshare yesterday. They were . . . invested. Opinionated. *And mostly on her side.* He'd changed the password on the email because he didn't want her to have to deal with it. As station manager, it was well within his job description to take this on. He told himself that was the only reason he'd done it—that he'd do it for any one of his staff—but he knew he wanted to save her from having to see possible criticism.

NOAH: What about giving away a trip during their segment?

CHRIS: Trying to save money, not spend it.

WESLEY: Get sponsors. That's how most stations do it.

NOAH: I say we ship Ari off to Bermuda. She's terrible with directions, so she won't make it back.

Chris laughed out loud. They all loved their sister. They weren't as close to her as each other, but when the four of them were in the same room, the bond was undeniable. Just because she bounced on their nerves like a kid on a trampoline didn't mean they loved her any less. But seriously, Chris needed to find a way to push her interests elsewhere.

WESLEY: Too bad she didn't get picked up for The Bachelorette. That would have kept her busy for several months.

NOAH: WHAT?

Chris frowned at his phone screen. When the hell had she applied for that, and *why*?

WESLEY: She wanted to apply, so she asked me to help her with her audition tape.

CHRIS: You helped her? What the hell?

NOAH: Not cool, man. She's a pain in the ass, but we don't feed her to the wolves. Or sketchy singles, in this case.

CHRIS: Dad would have lost it if she got in.

NOAH: He wouldn't have let her.

WESLEY: It's all staged. It didn't seem like a big deal, and she didn't get chosen.

NOAH: I would have kicked your ass if she did.

WESLEY: Ari has a better chance of that than you.

Chris kept one eye on the phone, but his attention kept getting pulled to the subject lines of the emails that would not stop pouring in. Men and women alike were offering Everly advice, compassion, and, his least favorite, dates. *You really need to get over this crush or whatever this is.* He wanted her to be happy, definitely wanted her to date someone better than Simon the Snake, but thinking about her with anyone made his heart feel like it were caught in a vise.

WESLEY: I have to go. Some of us work.

NOAH: Same. You want to grab a beer later?

Chris felt a twinge in his chest. He missed going out for beers with his brothers. They were both in Manhattan, and though any of them could easily hop on a plane, they all worked too many hours to just drop everything. *You'll be back there soon enough.* Definitely something he was looking forward to.

WESLEY: Sure. Too bad you can't join us, C. Maybe when Dad lets you out of exile.

Chris smirked and typed back his response. It wasn't polite.

***

He'd need to hire someone just to deal with the emails and social media if the response to Everly's rant didn't die down soon. Chris had spreadsheets littered across his table. He'd spent the last several hours going through numbers and research. Popping the top on a beer, he took a long swallow and went out to his patio. The sun was setting through the light film of hazy smog. Traffic moved below, music from someone else's apartment filtered through the air. It was a perfect California night. Chris sighed heavily and leaned his forearms on the railings.

The thought of how many guys offered to take Everly out not only blew him away but pissed him off a little. Did these guys actually think they could email a "Hey, baby, I'll take your mind off your troubles," and she'd be all over it? What kind of idiot was Simon? The kind who had a woman like Everly—smart, funny, shy but sarcastic, hardworking, and so pretty it could drop a man to his knees—and blew his chances. She deserved someone who would bring out that cute smile—the one she got when Stacey said something funny on-air and she was trying not to laugh. She deserved a guy who would remind her every day that he was damn lucky to be with her.

You are not that guy, Chris reminded himself before taking another long swallow of beer.

He had four to six months left in this so-called exile. For as long as he could remember, he, Wesley, and Noah had been jumping through hoops their dad pulled out of nowhere like restless whims. The three of them had considered working elsewhere, but loyalty always won. That and a desire to prove to their father that all three of them could earn his respect. His pride.

***

Chris wasn't giving up on the station. Unlike his dad, when he was in, he was all the way in. His father bought businesses like bags of chips, tossing them out if he didn't like the flavor. Chris knew there was a way to build 96.2 into something bigger than his father imagined it could be. Chris trusted his own vision and his own gut. He could turn things around and wasn't walking away until he did. His way. Maybe he couldn't do anything about the guys Everly dated, but business was his . . . Chris lowered his hand, jolting when the glass bottle clinked against the metal railing. An idea swirled in his brain, making his heart pump heavily. A *good* idea. It could save the segment, boost the ratings, pull in even more listeners, and open up his dad's eyes to the fact that Chris had a knack for taking something that was crumbling and rebuilding it into a work of art. This was the kind of thing his grandfather would call *inspired*. It was risky, but the payoff was huge.

Going back inside to his computer, he saw the fifty new emails that had popped up in the time he'd taken a break, and he knew he was onto something. This could be the key to getting what he'd been working his whole life toward: proving to himself, and his father, that he had a head and heart—though his dad always said there was no room in the corporate world for feelings—for business. He'd be able to move on to the next step, up and away from his father's control. *Still in his company, but not under his thumb.* That had been the ultimate goal from day one, and even if it killed him to watch it play out, there might be the unexpected bonus of helping Everly find happiness—if that's what she was after.

Win-win. Mostly.

[6]

Everly hitched her canvas bag farther onto her shoulder and walked toward the back entrance of the station. It felt like she'd just left, and now she was back. The day after her birthday had been a gong show—according to the morning show deejay, she'd broken the internet—or at least the station website.

They'd had tech guys scrambling to fix things because there were so many visitors to the site, their social media had blown up, and Everly couldn't log on to the email. It was . . . overwhelming. It made it that much harder to avoid thinking about what she'd shared over the airwaves. It did keep her distracted from the chatter and teasing bouncing around the break room and the media booths.

"Hey," Stacey called out. She was hurrying over from where she'd parked her car. Dressed in a gorgeous blue sundress, she personified the term *California girl*.

"Hey. How was your date last night?"

Stacey grinned. "Yummy."

Everly laughed at the way her friend waggled her eyebrows. "You let him stay the night?"

Stacey narrowed her eyes. "You have your rules, I have mine. No sleepovers. I don't need to be tied down. Well, actually—"

Everly laughed and lifted her hand. "Don't. I don't want to know. How come we're being called in early?"

Stacey unlocked the door and shrugged. "Don't know. Chris said he wanted to talk about our segment."

Everly's skin itched. What about it? Maybe he was pissed they'd turned the other morning into a *Maury Povich* episode. He'd seemed okay when he'd brought her dessert, which, in and of itself, was strange to wrap her head around. Why had he? *Pity brings out kindness in people.* She didn't want it to mean anything more than what it clearly was: Her boss brought her something to ease the sting of a fantastically bad day. Maybe he wanted to be friends. *Maybe he was softening you up to fire you.* Though, firing really called for more of a good shiraz than sweets, but maybe he didn't know that.

"Your negative thoughts are making *my* brain tired," Stacey grumbled, bumping her shoulder against Everly's.

"You're tired because you didn't sleep all night. You're not so young anymore. You need more sleep."

With another cheeky grin, Stacey bumped her hip this time. "You need someone who makes you want to lose sleep."

Rule eight: *Date men who make you feel things.* She didn't *need* a guy, or particularly want one right now. Next time, though? *It won't be the same old, same old, make me laugh and come out of my shell so I can avoid digging deeper and figuring out what I want.*

What she *wanted* was to know why Chris hadn't shown up for work yesterday and why, though she didn't mind and often did, they were coming in early.

"Jesus, I can *feel* the worry vibrating off your skin. Chill, Ev. We're fine."

"He probably just wants to talk damage control," Everly said.

"Damage control? You blew up the internet. He probably wants to thank you for putting the station on the map."

Rolling her eyes, Everly opened the door and held it for Stacey. "I wonder what would have happened if you'd gotten to sing on-air. Today could look very different for both of us."

"I would have been discovered as the next sexy pop sensation, and you'd have to do the show alone," Stacey answered, taking the stairs ahead of her.

"I'm sure. They'd do a special on you about how you were wasting your amazing ass . . . ets and talents in a deejay booth."

Stacey glanced back over her shoulder, completely into the idea. "Some people would have suspected because my speaking voice is already so sexy."

"Lucky thing I spoke in time to stop that from happening," Everly said.

"Destined to be together. Hey, you can pitch the podcast idea today." Stacey held the door at the top of the stairs open.

Everly bit back her groan. "One thing at a time. How about that?"

"*That* would be boring."

The small lobby of the station was quiet at this time of the day. Their receptionist wouldn't be in until later in the day. Awards from long ago filled one portion of the wall beside the window that looked out on the parking lot. To the right was a large sunshine logo with the station numbers inside. They could definitely use some brand updating, but she hadn't mentioned that idea to Chris because she was usually too busy trying not to get tongue-tied around him. *You could mention it to the whole group. It could be the new thing you try.*

Everly spent many of her off hours at the station, working on programming, contacting guests for interviews, or updating social media. That way, when she and Stacey had their weekly meetings, they could focus on the content of the show.

Maybe Chris just wanted to switch some things up, build on the momentum of a wider audience from her . . . *Hmm, let's call it* the Unfortunate Incident. TUI *in close circles.*

Stacey paused. "Did Simon phone?"

Everly shook her head. "Nope. I doubt he will. I think the coffee and bagels all over the floor made things clear."

"You do anything last night? Maybe add something fun to that list?"

Everly laughed, gesturing to the door. "Hung out. Looked up kittens."

Stacey's eyes widened, but she opened it. "Careful. No hoarding."

"One is not a hoard." The door drifted shut behind them.

"That's how it starts."

Stacey pushed through the swinging door that opened up to the hallway, which led to the control room.

The early-morning deejay, Mason Hearth, waved as he spoke into the microphone.

"Sorry about our internet being down, folks. I'm going to make it up to you with a no-repeat, thirty-minute hit list."

Everly winced. *Yeah. Sorry about the whole internet thing.* Mason's producer, Mari, had her head down in her own booth. Passing the meeting room, a storage room, bathroom, and a couple of smaller rooms, Everly and Stacey went into Chris's office together.

Chris sat behind his desk, looking through a stack of paperwork. When his head popped up at their approach, Everly was surprised he looked tired. His hair was mussed, his tie off, and his suit jacket hung across the chair in front of his desk. He looked . . . sexy. *Note to self: Boss is hotter when he's frazzled. P.S. on note to self: Do not notice things like your boss being hot.*

"You look like you've been here all night," Stacey said, taking the chair that didn't have his jacket.

Chris stood up, his gaze, which *felt* intense, on Everly as he moved around the desk. "I have. I came in late last night." He moved his jacket and gestured to the chair.

Unease poked at Everly's insides. Why was he watching her like that? Did he regret bringing her chocolate pie? She didn't regret eating it and wished she had a large slice right this minute. Something to do with her hands. Something to focus on other than his stare. This had to be about the backlash over TUI. Chris leaned against his desk, crossed his arms over his chest. Had his chest always been so wide and sculpted? *No, Ev, he worked out extra hard last night and now he's all muscle.* He'd rolled the sleeves of his dress shirt up, and she got stuck staring at his forearms. *Okay, okay. He has nice arms. Big deal. Didn't you just swear off men? No. Maybe you should have. Just some men. Like guys you don't connect with and bosses.* She'd swear off those men.

Letting her gaze wander up, she felt a jolt of something she couldn't put a name to zip through her veins. Why the hell was he looking at her like that?

"What's going on, Chris? You're staring. It's making Everly nervous," Stacey said.

Everly widened her eyes at her friend. She wasn't wrong, but *still.* "I'm fine."

Chris looked over at Stacey and smiled. When his gaze returned to Everly, he sighed. *Ahhh, Everly Dean. Making men everywhere sigh in frustration.*

Rubbing a hand over his face, he moved back behind his desk. This time, when he met Everly's gaze, there was the familiar layer of detachment. Cool professionalism.

"Sorry about that, Ms. Dean. I haven't had much sleep."

Seriously? The man brought her chocolate pie and now they were back to last names? And not even in the cool jock-style way. Everly shared a "what the heck?" glance with Stacey, who shrugged.

"No harm, *Mr. Jansen.*"

Stacey snorted. "Jesus. You did not wake me up at the crack of stupid so I could witness you being weird. What are we doing here?"

Chris took a deep breath, and Everly realized that he was nervous. Which was incredibly strange and had the added bonus of making her feel more of the same.

"We've had over a thousand phone calls in the last two days, regarding your . . . incident," he told Everly.

There were only so many times she could sink into a pit of

shame. *Not your fault. None of it was on you.* That didn't make the mental replays of each of the events feel any better.

"I'm calling it *the Unfortunate Incident* in my head," she said. *Did you need to tell him that?* "Sorry."

Chris's lips twitched. He waved a hand and then folded both of his on his desktop. "Please, don't apologize. People are livid on your behalf. Our email got so overloaded, the server crashed."

Everly winced. "I heard. Also, I can't log on to the email."

"I changed the password," Chris said.

Everly frowned. "What? Why?" He didn't think she could do her job.

"There was a lot of correspondence, and I figured you didn't need to read through all of it."

"It's my job," she said, stiffening.

His gaze was . . . assessing. Like he was measuring her for something she didn't know about. "It's *my* job, as station manager, to step in when I see fit. To make decisions on behalf of my staff and this station."

She nodded, feeling chastised.

"None of this is her fault," Stacey said.

Chris leaned back like he was growing more comfortable with the conversation as Everly went in the opposite direction. "I didn't say it was. But here's the thing . . . your show hasn't been producing the numbers we need. Then there was"—his lips curving up—"the Unfortunate Incident. Listeners are invested. You wouldn't believe some of the messages and emails. Some have offered to take care of Simon for you."

"Hell, I offered to do that," Stacey interrupted.

Everly glared at her. Now wasn't the time for jokes.

Chris carried on, looking directly into Everly's eyes. "Others have sons or nephews they'd like to introduce you to. Several men called the station to tell you they'd be happy to go on a date with you anytime. Some people left irate messages about fidelity and loyalty. There were over two hundred calls just to wish you a happy birthday."

Everly felt her face flame. Chris got up quickly and moved to sit on the edge of his desk, directly in front of them. The rest of Everly heated up inexplicably.

Stacey, however, bounced in her seat. "Wow. That's wicked cool."

When she looked at Everly expectantly, Everly could only shrug because she wasn't sure which part was cool. She didn't want anyone to take care of anything—she realized this morning that she couldn't have been all that invested if her heart didn't even feel bruised from the breakup. Her pride had been knocked around, but that was different. She also didn't want to meet any of their listeners' sons or nephews out of misguided pity. If she said yes to that kind of arrangement, her dad would be all over setting her up with "a stand-up man" from his law firm. No, thank you. Though the idea that so many people rallied on her behalf was, as Stacey said, wicked cool. And interesting. They worked their butts off to gain an audience and higher ratings. One unforeseen mishap and now they were popular? She could get her own dates. *But you've already acknowledged you need to branch out. Try something new.* Suddenly, pitching the podcast seemed like child's play in comparison to where she thought this was headed. Also, she didn't need birthday wishes from strangers, but that part was also kind of sweet.

Chris blew out a hard breath like he was bracing for something, and that's when Everly's nerves really bit into her skin. He was going somewhere with this.

"The owner of the station wants your segment—wants both of you—cut."

Everything slowed down, and she felt like she was watching from afar, seeing her own jaw drop, feeling the panic coursing through her, easy to see on her face. Beside her, Stacey blinked rapidly.

One hand gripped the edge of his desk, but he held up the other, and his words came out hurried. "Let me just tell you what I'm thinking before either of you freak out." Clearly, they both looked like freaking out was a possibility. "I told him I think it's the wrong move, but he brought up the numbers, the low audience, and he jumped all over the dead air like he was waiting for another reason. I've been here all night because I have an idea that I think will not only blow the ratings through the roof but possibly secure you the coveted morning spot."

Rule five was being dropped in their lap. *You'd have leverage to pitch the podcast.* Her heart was beating too hard in her ears for her to fully process what he was saying.

"You want to fire me over fifteen seconds of dead air?" Stacey's voice went hard.

Chris shook his head. "No. I don't. I'm not going to. Honestly, it's not about that. It's the owner looking for an excuse. I have an idea that'll put you both on the map and make it so you can ask for the moon."

Everly breathed in and out slowly, tapping her fingers against her thigh. Index, middle, ring, pinkie, back. Repeat. "I don't want to be on the map, and I don't want the moon. I just want to do my job."

Chris turned his body so it felt like the two of them were in an intimate and private conversation. Like the space between them diminished into nothing. Her stomach flipped like a fish out of water.

"I know, Everly. But the bottom line is, we have to do something. I think both of you are great, but unless we come up with something, he's going to use the other day as an excuse to can you both."

"He can't do that," Stacey said, crossing her arms over her chest, glaring down her nose at him.

"When you guys signed the new contract, it explicitly stated that he could. For the betterment of the station, numbers, or listener enjoyment. He's a businessman. His bottom line is money."

Of course it was. That was the whole point of owning a business—to profit. She understood that; it's where the line "It isn't personal" stemmed from. She and Stacey were nobodies. *Not to Chris. He's got an idea to avoid this.*

Chris's eyes darkened, darted away, and then back. "Now, will you hear me out?"

Stacey leaned around Chris to catch Everly's hand. "Breathe, babe. Let's just see what he's proposing, and if we don't like it, we'll go and see how he does covering the spot this morning on his own."

Knowing her friend was trying to lighten the mood, Everly forced a small smile, but it didn't settle anything inside of her chest.

"Everly?" Chris looked at her with so much concern, she lost her words for a moment. "Will you hear me out?" That was the second time he'd used her name and both times lowered her defenses, tumbled the wall he usually put between them.

She blinked as she gnawed on the inside of her cheek. Did she really have a choice? *You always have a choice.* She was going to have to add to her list or maybe just put an asterisk at the bottom: *Have a backup plan. For everything.*

"Yes."

[7]

Everly watched the internal debate play out across Chris's features. How had she never noticed how straight his nose was before? Or how, up close, there were little flecks of gold mixing with the greens in his eyes? *More importantly, why are you noticing now?* She did her best to remain patient, but she really wished he'd hurry up and tell them what he was thinking. She didn't want to lose her job. *You won't lose your job. You can't lose your job. Listen to him.*

"The audience wants a fairy tale, and I'm proposing we give it to them. Reality television has a huge market, and with what happened, it got me thinking we could work the audience interest into that framework. On the surface, the idea is simple—listeners will nominate potential dates. You go on three dates a week for four weeks. Each week, you choose the best of those dates, and that guy goes into the final round. In the fifth week, there'll be four men for you to go on a second date with."

Everly's head was spinning. *This* was fairly simple?

Chris's enthusiasm was hard to miss. "You'll drop two that week and in the sixth week, you'll choose between the final two. The entire time, the audience will be allowed to weigh in on your candidates. I'm thinking you do some social media posts about the dates and your feelings on them. The audience already connects with *you.* They're going to want what makes you happy. Either way, the choice, of course, will be yours."

Her tongue wouldn't work. Never mind peanut butter; her mouth filled with concrete, and something lodged in her throat. Maybe her heart. Or her lungs. She tapped her fingers against her thigh, but it didn't help. She pushed her right thumb into her left palm. Hard.

"Ev, breathe," Stacey said, pushing Chris's rolling chair back. She gripped both of Everly's hands and forced her to meet her gaze. "Hey. It's okay. Breathe."

She choked out a breath, shaking her head like she could clear the craziness from her brain.

"Are you okay?" Chris's worried tone cut through her haze.

Stacey turned to look at him, releasing one of Everly's hands. "You just asked to set her up on a bunch of dates as a way to boost ratings. You may have noticed that she has a touch of social anxiety, so maybe you can see why this might have thrown her."

Everly dug deep to find her voice and her professionalism. She appreciated Stacey understanding and having her back. But she *was* thirty and could speak for herself. "To clarify, you think if I select some listener-suggested dates, it'll boost our ratings and make the owner back off?"

Chris nodded, the excitement in his gaze dimming. "I think it's unique and fun and could mean great things for the station but also for you professionally and personally."

His words were careful, making her think maybe this was *his* way of having her back. He wasn't pressuring. He was laying out an idea.

Chris stood and paced behind his desk for a moment before going to stand over by the window. There was something in his gaze when he looked at her, something she hadn't seen before, even when he'd dropped the wall between them at her house the other day. Softness? Caring? *Don't misread a look while you're emotional.*

"Everly, this isn't something you have to do."

She forced herself to breathe slowly. Evenly. He was serious.

He had her back, for whatever reason. Could she do this? Online dating was the norm these days, and she hadn't had any luck with her current methods. It gave her control, which she loved, but also pushed her boundaries, which she didn't like but knew she needed.

"What if I don't?" she asked, curling the fingers of both hands into tight fists.

"We'll put out a press release thanking everyone for rallying around you. Then I'll fight to keep you and Stacey here."

It was a risk. Either way.

A strange calm, almost numbness filled her chest. "Tell me more."

He nodded. "The idea is similar to *The Bachelorette.* We screen possible dates recommended by our listening audience. The station pays for you to eat dinner with these guys. Just a regular first date, no expectations other than the hope that you'll find your Mr. Right. At the end of the six weeks, the choice you make doesn't bind you into anything. You simply choose a man you'd go on a third date with."

Stacey covered one of Everly's fists with her hand. Everly sent her a smile, letting her know she was keeping it together. *This is like your regular segment meeting; just discussing an idea to boost ratings.*

Right. "Define *screening.*"

Chris straightened, his gaze growing more serious. "Extensive screening. Background checks, applications, and security on each date."

She frowned. She liked the safety aspect of it but . . . "That sounds awkward with a third wheel." *Though maybe it'd help when conversation lags.*

"It'll be discreet." Chris sat down across from her again. "I know you're shy. I know you don't love being in large groups of people. Everything will be tailored to suit you, to fit into your comfort zone."

She arched her brows but said nothing. Everyone in this

room knew this was so far out of her comfort zone, it might as well not exist.

Chris continued, "You don't have to talk on-air. Though you could. You have a great voice. You and Stacey can add it to your segment if you feel comfortable. I was thinking you could do a blog post after each date, or we could get a hashtag going. We utilize Instagram and Twitter to give people a rundown. Stacey can be your wingwoman. If you want, and you're comfortable, she can talk about the dates, share what you say on the blog, be the on-air voice. People are going to love this. They want you to be happy. This brought fans out of the woodwork on your behalf. It's powerful."

He really had thought about this a lot.

Her brain was a natural devil's advocate. "You might have heard, but I'm sort of just getting out of a relationship that didn't end so well," Everly said dryly.

His eyes softened, and so did his tone. "You did. I know. I also know you're one of the best producers I've met. Think outside the box here. If it were someone else, not you, what would you think of the idea?"

She'd think it was fun. Entertaining. She wanted to pace. The room was too hot, and her clothes were too tight. Heck, her *skin* felt confining.

"I'll do it," Stacey said.

Both Chris's and Everly's heads turned in her direction.

She smiled. "Why not? I like going on dates. I like people and socializing. I'm happy to let you foot the bill for me to eat at some fancy restaurants. I mean, I don't have to marry the guy. There's nothing that binds us together if we decide to go our separate ways after the six or seven weeks, right?"

Chris nodded, shifting his gaze back to Everly, but she looked to Stacey. Her heart filled with fierce gratitude. "I think I take it for granted how good a friend you are." Stacey would do it, even though she feared serious commitments like Everly did an unannounced party.

Stacey smiled. "I love you. You know that."

Chris cleared his throat, shifted in his seat. "I appreciate you being so supportive, Stacey. And that you guys are so close. Part of what makes you such a good team is your genuine friendship. But that won't work."

Everly nodded. He'd asked her to think outside the box—take herself out of the equation. If the audience fell for Everly's story, they'd want to see it through. Part of her heart swelled with appreciation. The other part shriveled with worry that she knew she was really considering this. "He's right," Everly told Stacey quietly. Her voice was much calmer than her pulse.

Chris scooted his chair a little closer, and their knees accidentally brushed against each other. She sucked in a breath at the unexpected contact and the jolt of electricity that woke all her senses.

"The audience fell for *you*, Everly," he said. "They want you to get your happily ever after."

Hearing him say her name in that soft, almost whispered tone had a funny effect on her heart. It couldn't decide if it wanted to race excitedly or slow to a responsible pace. It didn't help her indecisive heart any that he'd said they'd fallen for her; she didn't feel like she was someone anyone would fall for right at this particular moment. She felt like two people right now—one who thought this idea was great and another who feared having to actually go through with it.

"Can you give us a minute?" Stacey looked at Chris as she stood up and went to the door, opening it.

He didn't answer; he just went through it, closing it behind himself.

Stacey came back and sat across from her, took her hands. "Hey. Look at me."

Everly stared at her friend, who, clearly, had already bounced back from the effects of the explosion.

"This is your chance," Stacey said.

Everly pulled her hands back so she could stand. Move.

Something. She opted to be obtuse. She wanted Stacey's thoughts. "My chance for what?"

"The list. Your rules. Ev, this is perfect. Doing this will check, like, every box." Stacey stood up as well, her eyes bright with excitement. "Try something exciting outside your comfort zone? Check. Finding guys who get under that shell? Check. Awesome new segment? Hell yeah. Be bold? What's bolder than this? Find your happy? Well, my birthday gift for you should have helped with that but, hey, double check. How was it, by the way?"

Everly laughed. "We aren't discussing your birthday gift."

Stacey's eyes widened with absolute delight. "You tried it, didn't you?"

Everly's cheeks felt like red coals. "I didn't say that. Could you focus? We could lose our jobs."

"You didn't have to say it, and I'll say again—you're welcome. We're not going to lose our jobs. You're going to do this. You know you are."

Crossing her arms over her chest, Everly eyed Stacey. "How do you know what *I'm* going to do?"

Stacey pointed at her, the teasing expression gone. "You love your job. If we'd come up with this for someone else, we'd be calling ourselves geniuses. The fact that it comes at a time when you're ready to slip into the driver's seat of your own life is perfection."

Unable to help herself, Everly tipped her head to one side. "According to Chandler Bing, it's *gum* that is perfection."

Stacey rolled her eyes, leaned against Chris's desk. "No *Friends* references right now. We'll get distracted."

Everly looked down at her Converse. "You think I've been a passenger in my own life?"

She saw Stacey's sexy-heel-clad feet step forward before her friend gripped her shoulders.

"I think you don't give yourself enough credit or opportunity to show how badass you are. We're about to kick our little show into the stratosphere. People love an underdog story, Ev. I know you don't like the spotlight, but you deserve to shine. We can play this to our advantage and take what we want, what *you want*, out of it."

Everly pulled away, pressed her hand to the center of her chest where it ached.

Stacey didn't give up. "It's like the universe looked at your list of rules and said, 'I got this. Here you go.'"

Everly turned and stared at her. She was serious. Serious and really, freaking excited. "I can't go out with a bunch of strangers."

"Everyone is a stranger before you meet them."

She rolled her eyes. "What if these guys are crazy? Murderers? Men with strange fetishes? Tax evaders?"

Stacey bit her bottom lip, and Everly knew she was trying not to laugh. "We will write it directly in the contract that all candidates must be screened and their tax histories must be available for review."

Pulling in a shuddery breath, Everly sank back into the chair. "Next year, I am so staying home on my birthday."

***

Hours later, Everly and Chris sat across from each other in his office. She read through the paperwork he'd had the legal department draw up outlining the expectations, parameters, and terms.

She glanced up through lowered lashes. He was typing something into his phone, a look of intense concentration making his brows push together and his forehead wrinkle. What kind of women did he date? *Probably someone like Stacey—outgoing, voluptuous, confident.* Not that it mattered. Despite the fact that they'd talked more today than . . . ever, it was still hard to completely relax in his presence. He'd be another man she could hold back from. Hide from. If she was going to do this, she wanted someone she could connect with on every level. *Which means you have to unlock the doors to all your levels.*

She cleared her throat. "Two dates a week instead of three."

Chris looked up from his phone. "Okay. Can I ask why?"

She leaned back in the chair, rolled the pen she held between her thumb and index finger.

"Three is too much. I'm not an overly social person at the best of times, and this is going to be taxing on my . . ." Her what? How did she tell him that too much time around people, even though she could hold her own, was exhausting? That even though the idea of going out and having fun sounded good in *theory*, when it came down to actually *doing* it, she was less likely to back out if there wasn't such a demand? It was one thing to have a busy week, but he was asking her to be busy for up to *six* weeks.

He set his phone down, not waiting for her to find an appropriate word. "No problem. I'll have them change it. Anything else?"

"Three weeks instead of four. A total of six men. Going into week four, there will be three bachelors left. Listeners can vote for their favorite of the three, I'll choose the second and that way, I'll have two second dates in week four. Week five will be the announcement of which one I choose. Less stressful." *Sort of.*

He considered this a moment but she didn't back down. She absolutely could not go on four second dates in one week and six weeks was a really long time. Longer than her relationship with Simon she had scheduled dates.

"Sure." He gestured with his hand to keep going.

"I pick the places."

"Done."

"I have final say on the candidates."

"Of course."

"I only meet people at the chosen places. No one picks me up at my home."

Chris folded his hands on the desktop. "Your safety will be

the number-one priority. I want you to be as comfortable as possible, and I know the situation kind of pushes against that, but we'll do whatever you need to make it work best for you. You're the priority."

There was something about the way he said it, his gaze on hers like there was an invisible string locking them together. She wanted to make a flippant comment about the ratings being the top priority, just to smooth out the jitters setting in. She didn't, though, because the way he spoke, the way he looked, she knew that he meant what he said. Why the idea of him caring so much, so genuinely, made her feel light-headed, she did not know.

"I'm sorry that the other day complicated things, but I really believe this is going to be a win for all of us."

"Especially if I don't get fired," she said, lifting her lips in a small smile.

"I don't want to fire you. You're excellent at your job," Chris said.

Everly blinked rapidly and then looked down at the table, shuffled the papers together. "That's nice of you to say."

Chris's hand covered Everly's, and that flicker she'd felt earlier when just their knees touched seemed more like a flash fire when he left it there. No shields now. His gaze captivated her with its sharp focus, like he wanted to see *deeper*. More clearly. Or maybe he wanted her to be the one who looked a little further.

"I'm not in the habit of saying things to be nice. It's true, Everly. If I've made you feel otherwise, I apologize."

Pulling her hand from under his in hopes of settling the rapid pace of her pulse, she tapped the papers against the table, straightening them. "Thank you. I'm going to take these by my folks'. My father is a lawyer. I'll have him review them and get them back to you tomorrow."

Chris leaned back in his own chair, crossed one leg over the other knee. "A lawyer. Hmm. What type?"

Everly smirked. "Divorce. It'll come in handy one day if my mom and dad ever decide they've had enough of threatening to leave each other for good."

His lips tilted downward, but instead of making an offhand comment about how weird that was, a response she often got, he shook his head. "That sounds hard on you."

Her fingers flexed on the papers. Most people didn't get that it *was* hard on her. "It's not like I'm a kid anymore."

He watched her carefully. "No. You're not. But our parents' behavior can impact us as adults more than we expect."

It felt unsettling that he'd somehow said the exact right thing.

Chris stood up as she did. He pushed both hands into the pockets of his suit pants. He hadn't put his jacket or tie back on, and the somewhat relaxed state was disarming. He *almost* seemed normal. "My father is on his sixth engagement."

Everly's jaw dropped. "Wow. That's a lot of diamond rings."

This time, it was his lips that curled into a smirk. A sexy I'll-see-your-crazy-parents-and-raise-you one. "Yeah. That about covers it. He's only gone through with it three times. Not sure he'll actually marry this one, but she's closer to his age this time."

"Does he live here in LA?" Questions popped into her busy brain. Did he like any of the stepmothers? How old was he when his parents divorced? Was a clean break and moving on better, from a kid's perspective, than constantly reuniting? She worked with this man every day and hardly knew anything about him.

"No. He's in New York. Most of my family is."

"Are you close with your mom?"

The smile, which made the curve of his cheeks and one, small dimple pop, was genuine and warm. It made Everly's insides dance with an unfamiliar feeling.

"We talk often. She likes to travel and prefers tropical islands."

"Can't say I blame her." She glanced at the time. If she left for her parents' house now, she might catch them at dinnertime and swing a meal out of it. When things were good between them, she made it a point to visit. It didn't eliminate the guilt of avoiding them when they were separated, but it gave them less ammunition to say they never saw her. Maybe one day, they'd make the connection between the state of their marriage and her visits. Her stomach rumbled loudly.

Chris's laughter made her cheeks heat, and when he arched a brow and stared at her stomach, she covered it with her hand in response. Like somehow that would hide that the sandwich she'd eaten for lunch wasn't enough.

"Let me buy you dinner," he said.

Everly's breath twisted in her chest, coming out sharply. The words hung between them as she looked up into his dark eyes.

Chris ran one hand through his hair. "We've been going over this for hours. No harm finishing up while feeding you, right? It seems like the least I can do."

The least he could do because . . . what? He felt guilty? She wasn't sure, but she also wasn't sure about being alone with him any more while her heart felt unsettled. It was as if there were an invisible danger sign flashing in the back of her mind. His quiet offer and the way his smile confused her should come with a warning: *This is not the Chris for you.*

She shouldn't even need that reminder. The adrenaline of the day must be wearing off for her thoughts to be so scattered. Most people didn't understand the amount of energy it took to be inside of her own head. She wore herself out sometimes. "Actually, I should get these papers over to my dad. Then we'll be able to sign off tomorrow and start promotion."

When he didn't argue, it was easy to believe he'd only asked out of obligation. "Besides, you'll be paying for enough of my dinners starting soon. You should probably save your boss some money. You don't even know yet if he'll sign off on this."

He nodded, looking *almost* disappointed. *As if. Why would he be?* She shook off the feeling as he stepped aside and gestured to the door. "Let me worry about that. Pitched properly, there's no reason for this not to fly." His tone wasn't brusque, but it didn't have the easy cadence they'd found in the last couple of hours.

You always do this. You make things awkward. Everly tightened her grip on her bag, unsure what she'd said that shifted the atmosphere between them. She'd spend a good portion of her evening replaying everything she'd said, trying to figure it out, though.

His reserved mask slowly slipped back into place. He walked behind his desk, looked down at his calendar.

"Thank you for all your hard work and compromise. If there's anything else you need, just let me know," he said, looking at her again, but something felt . . . off. His gaze had lost the warmth she'd felt earlier.

She pulled her bag onto her shoulder, breathing through the restlessness seeping over her skin. "Okay, well. Good night."

His smile held a hint of regret that she didn't understand. This man was more confusing than most. "Good night, Everly."

[8]

Chris let himself into his condo, juggling the take-out bag and the six-pack of IPA he'd picked up on the way home. The lack of sleep coupled with the adrenaline of a kick-ass idea was catching up with him. Maybe he could blame those things for asking Everly out to dinner. Setting the food and beer down, he shrugged out of his coat, tossed it on a barstool, and opened a beer. Taking a long swallow, he let out a sigh that loosened all the tension from his shoulders.

There'd been a moment there, when his breath had caught tightly in his lungs and he'd hoped like hell she'd take him up on the offer of dinner. Thankfully, she was more sensible than he was.

It would have been a work dinner, he reminded himself. The problem was, he had to *keep* reminding himself of their strictly professional and platonic relationship. When she left, the confusion in her gaze made him hate himself, but it was better that she think he was a hot-and-cold jerk of a boss than know how very much he would have liked to take her out.

Stop it, he demanded of himself. He had a lot to celebrate.

Overall, it had been a damn good day. Transferring his tandoori chicken to a plate, he took his beer, his food, and his phone to the couch. The apartment was more than he needed. The kitchen and living area were one large room with high ceilings and lots of windows to let in the California sunshine. He had a couch, coffee table, and big-screen television with surround sound. The basic necessities as far as he was concerned. He had a king-size bed and a dresser in the master bedroom. Other than that, he hadn't bought anything. No point when he was heading back to New York.

He liked California. After living on the East Coast all his life, it was sort of a culture shock. It wasn't hard to get used to the sunshine, though. Turning on the news, he muted it and dialed his brother's number, putting it on speaker.

"Hey. How's it going?" Noah asked, his voice filling the room.

Chris spoke around a mouthful of chicken. "Not too bad. You?"

"Same old. Just purchased a couple of warehouses in the Heights. I planned to turn one into apartments and the other into a community center. Gramps would have loved them, and it's time to give back to the community."

"It's a great idea." He thought of Everly's apartment. Their grandfather had been born in New Jersey and would have loved the concept. "Renovating it into something else keeps the original charm but brings new life." Unfortunately, he knew how this story played out. "Which part did Dad squash?"

"What the hell is the point of him giving us the lead on projects just to tell us no?" There were muffled sounds of his brother moving around as he spoke through his irritation.

Swallowing his bite, he took a quick sip of beer before attempting an answer. "I'm sure, in his mind, the reasons are plenty. My guess is the only person he likes to give back to is himself. You off-loading the warehouses?"

"Probably. Maybe I'll keep them. I have my own money, so it's not like I can't buy them, but it pisses me off that he won't let us put our own spin on things. It's time to branch out. Do more." He hated the frustration in Noah's voice. "It's such a waste. Whatever. Same old. What's going on with you? How's life in radio? You figure things out?"

"Actually, you guys gave me some ideas. I need you to talk to Ari, though."

"How long you think Dad can pretend she's not old enough to get her act together?"

Chris stabbed another piece of chicken. "Not sure. But I need you to run interference for me. Send her on a spa week, something. Anything to distract her. I need time to get something in place so I can show him there's no room for Ari to step in." Though it wouldn't surprise him if Ari just dropped the idea and moved on to something else. All the more reason not to let her inside his station.

"Good luck with that. Dad listens to me about as much as he does you. I'll try, but I can't promise anything. Once you're working alongside him rather than *for* him, you aren't going to know what to do with yourself."

Chris laughed. "A problem I welcome."

Noah murmured in agreement before asking, "What do you have planned?"

After outlining the basics, he added, "She's shy. More than just shy, really." He didn't want to say more. It wasn't his place. But it would impact the outcome. "That makes her a wild card. Once she relaxes a bit, though, she opens up and is amazing to talk to. She's funny and sarcastic and really smart."

"Sounds like you want her to have your babies, little brother," Noah said, laughing.

Chris nearly choked on his next bite. "Screw you. She's a nice woman. And an employee. One Dad wants to screw over just because Ari has another harebrained idea."

"You know, I could use some sunshine and a visit. I'll talk to Dad, but I'm going to clear my schedule."

Chris was all for seeing his brother. It had been way too long. "Let me know if you're coming. I'll order another bed."

His brother's laughter filled the room, almost like he was there. Yeah, it'd be nice to see him.

***

After a long, hot shower, Chris dressed in lounge pants and a T-shirt and brought out the paperwork again. Once Everly had looked at the idea as a promotional tool, she'd really gotten into the planning. He loved watching that cloak of quiet slip off as she became more comfortable. *And then you made things awkward.*

He worried that once she put herself in the position of having to select candidates, she might shut down. When he'd presented the idea, he'd expected her to refuse. He'd sort of thought Stacey would tell him to do unpleasant things to himself. He shouldn't have underestimated them.

Still, he planned to make sure they had everything ruthlessly organized so it would be as easy a process on her as possible.

His hand hovered over his phone, and he toyed with the idea of calling her. *To what? Invite her over to share your leftover tandoori chicken?* Chris opened his laptop. He didn't need to phone her. He'd see her tomorrow. And the next day. And the one after that. And soon he'd be keeping tabs on the men she was dating. *That's going to suck.*

"But it's for the best." He cared about Everly. "All of them. You care about all of them." Which was unusual. Most of his father's companies, the ones he'd spent time in, had a more corporate, serious feel. This one felt like more than a workplace. It was fun. He'd been intrigued by Everly the second he'd seen her. That had notched up to interested the first time she laughed with abandon, then blushed because of it. Over the last twelve months, he'd begun to care more than was wise. Differently from the others. None of his other staff made him feel like he'd swallowed his tongue when they walked in the room. He didn't want to be the reason any of the others laughed. "You're not the right guy." Not for anyone, which meant this was an excellent opportunity to help a *friend* find happiness before he moved back across the country. *Where you won't have to witness her falling in love.*

Pushing away from the laptop, he leaned back on two legs of his chair. He was restless. He hated feeling that way. Dropping the chair back to all fours, he scrolled through his phone, his finger hovering over his mom's contact. Chris had surprised himself, opening up to Everly today. The words about his father had just tumbled out of his mouth. He hadn't talked to his mom in a couple of weeks, but before he could text, someone knocked. Leaving the phone, he went to the door and opened it. Rob, one of his neighbors who'd become a friend, smiled at him.

"Hey, man. What's up?" Chris stepped back.

"Not much. Thinking of going out to grab a drink, thought I'd see if you were around. Didn't know I'd catch you in your jammies," he said, laughter in his tone.

Rob was a big guy, a couple of inches taller than Chris's six feet. He owned a couple of gyms and had the arms to prove it. He took advantage of his own equipment and the roster of classes his places offered for mixed martial arts, yoga, and kickboxing. Chris went to a class now and again but usually preferred running to clear his head.

"I was going to offer you a beer," Chris said, shutting the door.

Rob laughed. "That's okay. I can get my own." Detouring past the fridge, he did just that.

Chris sat down on one end of his couch as Rob sat at the other, cracked open his beer, and took a drink.

He gestured with the can. "Heard the show the other day. Was all excited to hear Sexy Deejay sing when your producer cut in. You kick the guy's ass for her?"

Laughing, because Rob *knew* Chris hadn't gone after the guy, Chris shook his head. "Stop calling her *Sexy Deejay*, man. Her name is Stacey."

Rob shrugged, then looked down at his beer. "No disrespect, man. That voice just gets me. It's like when you hear a singer you love, you know?"

Chris tilted his head and gave his friend a mocking grin. "So, you're in love with her, then?"

Rob chuckled. "Screw you. You know what I mean. When are you going to bring her down to the gym?"

"Right after never. The staff goes out as a big group now and again, but it's usually to grab a drink, not get a workout." The couple of times he'd grabbed a beer with them, Everly hadn't joined, and he'd felt like an idiot for being disappointed. Once, he'd gone with the plan to tell them who his father was, but that was the same week his dad decided to audit Chris's performance. He'd sent a damn accountant from New York to check up on him. Chris had been too pissed off to want to be associated with his father. Maybe he should consider putting together a staff event. A night out, a ball game. Something to unite them while showing he cared about them. *A goodbye-to-you party?* A sharp jab in his chest surprised him. It was a good idea. They'd be going through more upheaval before the year was out.

"Worth a shot. I'll just give you some more free passes. You can give 'em away on the radio as long as you make sure she gets one."

"Whatever." He chuckled. Rob had no trouble finding dates, but he had a thing for Stacey despite having never met her in person.

Setting his beer down, Rob clapped his hands together once and rubbed his palms back and forth. "I have a favor."

"Shoot."

"I want to do an anniversary party at the East Side gym. We're coming up on three years. I'd like to announce my plan to work with the San Verde School District to offer discounted and free classes to students, and I was wondering if the station could do another on-location event?"

They'd done it before with the gym, and it was standard to participate in community events. Chris considered logistics and who would be up for covering the spot. Getting out in the community was always a great idea, and with his plans for Everly, it might be a way to further promote their show.

"Send me a quick email with the date you're thinking, and I'll take a look when I'm at work tomorrow. I'm positive we can. Just need to look at the timing. We're going to be doing something different in the next couple of months, so I think it would tie in well."

"Something different how?" Rob leaned over and picked up his beer again.

He told him about where Everly's public confession had led, burying his own discomfort over the idea of his producer looking for love with a bunch of random listeners. *We'll have measures in place to make sure they're stand-up guys.* He wished the security was the only thing making him unsure of the idea.

Before he could think too much about what *did* bug him, Rob asked, "Everly's on board? Didn't you tell me she was super shy and didn't really like crowds?" Rob's skeptical look matched his tone.

"She's willing. As a producer, she sees the positives."

"As a producer. Hmm. Interesting. Maybe I ought to submit my profile," Rob said, his grin widening.

The growl left his throat without permission. "Maybe we're busy the day you need us on location."

They stared at each other a beat, and Chris fought the urge to look away before his friend saw too much.

"Man. Why don't you just ask her out?" Rob said, his smile shifting to something different. Something knowing.

Too late. "I'm not staying. You know that."

Rob shook his head and picked up his beer again. "Not sure if you know this, but you can go out with a woman without marrying her or turning it into a long-term commitment. You like this chick. Take her out. Have some fun."

Chris stalked to the cupboard and pulled out a bag of chips. "Everly isn't a fun kind of girl."

Rob snorted. "Then definitely don't ask her out."

Chris shot him a glare over his shoulder, then dumped the chips into a bowl. "Shut up. You know what I mean."

"So, you have no problem with her dating a bunch of guys who have to find their dates online?"

The bowl almost bounced against the countertop when Chris set it in front of his friend. "Online is where *most* people meet their significant others. Why are you being a jackass about this?"

Rob picked up a handful of chips. "I'm not trying to be. But you like this girl. You've liked her since you got here. Seems stupid not to ask her out. Especially if you're going to be jealous of her choices."

Chris picked up his beer but didn't drink. Nope. He just needed something to clench his fist around. "It's going to boost the ratings." *What a freaking cop-out.*

"Sure, man," Rob said around a mouthful of chips. "That's what matters here. Keep telling yourself that."

I will. There are no other options.

[9]

I genuinely want to know," Stacey said into the mic. "What is the huge fascination with avocados? They're mushy. I just don't trust anything green, you know?"

Everly rolled her eyes and pressed the button that let her speak through the booths without interrupting the show. "Get people to interact. Ask them what they hate that other people love."

Stacey gave her a thumbs-up. "This is why Everly is the Watson to my Sherlock. She wants to know what popular foods you dislike that other people rave about. Phone in, tweet us, or post a picture on Instagram and tag us."

It had to be her voice, the infectious way she put life into everything she said. The phone started ringing immediately. Stacey winked at her through the booth window.

***

Everly hung up the phone, wrote down the caller's name and request, and then turned up her mic to hear Stacey.

"I love that song. It's one of my favorites. I saw them last year, and it was the best concert, hands down, that I've ever been to," Stacey shared. Her eyes connected with Everly's, making Everly's stomach do a nervous jump. The routine didn't settle her heart, because she knew what was coming. They were ready to launch the contest. They'd all been working overtime this week to get things in place. When she was busy, she was able to put it out of her head, even if what she was busy with was organizing her own version of *The Dating Game*.

Here we go. She tilted her chin down, then up, in slow motion. A nearly imperceptible nod, but Stacey saw it. Understood it.

"Concerts make for a great date night. We've been thinking a lot about dating here at 96.2 SUN. Many of you heard my girl Everly's dating woes last week. On her birthday, no less. What you might not know is, after she accidentally shared on-air, and after I convinced her not to kill me and hide the body for doing that to her, thousands of you called, emailed, and tweeted. She was blown away by your support. We all were. And it's still coming in! Sometimes the best ideas come from the worst moments in your life."

Everly rolled her eyes. She'd written out an introduction to the dating series, but as usual, Stacey was doing her own thing. She saw Chris outside the booth, their eyes locked, and her stomach did another strange tumble. Different from the last one but no less unnerving.

"We have some exciting news, and you guys are the reason—96.2 SUN is going to host its own version of *The Bachelorette* featuring my wonderful producer, Everly, and *you*, our worthy listeners."

Everly rubbed her palm against her jeans, up and down, applying pressure as Stacey continued to explain.

"Let's be clear, folks—we're looking for a *good* man. Not some fairy-tale version of Prince Charming where he's all perfect and dashing—though there's nothing wrong with dashing. Am I right, Ev?" Stacey looked her way.

Everly arched her brows and frowned. Stacey knew the look and got back to it. "Right. As I was saying, a real-life prince for my girl is one who has a steady job, a sense of humor, isn't hard on the eyes. Someone who is nice to their family and has a cool group of friends."

She paused, looked at Everly. "Did I miss anything?"

Everly didn't pipe in often, but she'd been known to now and again in an organized, scripted, and planned way. "Not that I can think of, Stace. Though all contestants will need to go through the screening process."

"Right," Stacey said as she jotted something down in front of her. "We're taking your thoughts on Everly finding her happily ever after seriously."

Everly rolled her eyes and dramatically dropped her head down to her folded arms. Stacey laughed on-air, and when Everly looked up again, her eyes locked on Chris, who was smiling and staring her way.

As Stacey gave the listeners details on how to apply, Everly scratched out a message on her small whiteboard and held it up for Stacey to see.

It read: *Happily ever after? You're asking for it.* Everly shook her fist mockingly through the glass and saw her friend try to bite down on a bark of laughter.

Amusement colored Stacey's voice. "Everything you need to know is up on our website. Candidates have to meet all the requirements to be considered. I'll be answering questions throughout the day. But right now, let's get back to doing what you all came for. This next song is an old-time favorite."

The music played, giving Everly at least seven minutes' reprieve. Chris came through the deejay booth to see her, opening the door and leaning on the jamb.

"We're good to go," he said.

It had been a week since she'd signed the contract. Her parents thought it was the best thing ever, and she'd had to make her dad go back and read the fine print to be sure her ass was decently covered. For two people who couldn't decide whether or not to take their marriage seriously, they certainly wanted to see her partnered up. It had irritated her more than she'd wanted to let it.

Pulling in a breath she hoped didn't sound shaky, she faked

a smile. *Rule six: Be bold, even if it gives you hives.* Which reminded her, she needed to pick up some calamine lotion. "Excellent. Now, it's just wait and see. I'm not sure how many applicants we'll get."

That was just one of her worries. She had a list longer than her rules. She didn't want the online equivalent of throwing a party and having absolutely no one show up. *Oh my God. What if absolutely no one applies? What if people apply because they feel sorry for me? What if*—Stacey popped her head around Chris's shoulder, her hand on his arm. Everly wished she had even a tenth of the ease her friend felt around others. *It just takes you longer to warm up. There's nothing wrong with being cautious.*

"As if. We're probably going to blow up the website with all the traffic. You're hot, babe."

Chris chuckled and stepped into the room. Pulling a chair over, he sat closer than he needed to, but oddly enough, she liked his presence, even when it was one of the reasons for her uneven breathing.

"It's going to be great. That's something I wanted to talk to you about."

She tilted her head and lifted one side of her lips. "Which? Me being hot? It going great? Or the two together breaking the internet?"

It was interesting and a little amusing to see the way his eyes widened and color blossomed on his cheeks. Most guys didn't blush.

***

Stacey hurried back to her spot, and Everly was left breathing in the scent of Chris's cologne or soap or whatever it was that made him smell so precisely *delicious. Nope. Take that back.* Chris was not on the list of possible candidates for several reasons, the most important of which being he was her boss. There were plenty more she could easily think of—he only just started talking to her and acting like she was there. He made her close up and have trouble breathing when she was looking for a man who'd help her be more open. She wasn't entirely sure whether he liked her. If she was the Queen of Quiet in the office, he was the King of Mixed Messages. If she was doing this, she was doing it right. Or different from how she'd been making her choices so far. Which meant Chris and his on-again, off-again smile was off-limits even if he wasn't her boss. *Which he is! Okay, don't yell at yourself.*

"Everly?"

Right. Conversations required paying attention. "Yes? Sorry. I was just messing with you. Sorry. What were you going to say?" They were better on professional footing.

"My brother develops software. It's one of his things."

She leaned back, impressed. "*One* of his things?"

His smile made that dimple appear, and Everly did her best to ignore the impact on her pulse. *Just nerves. Always nerves.*

"He's a tech geek," Chris said with an easy-to-hear affection. "He has something for us to try. I'm going to take all the applicants as they come in, screen them, make sure they've checked all the boxes, and then send them to him. He'll upload them to this app, and it'll be like your personal version of Tinder."

Tinder? Like swipe right and heart me? The phone rang behind her, but since her lungs weren't working, she let it go.

Chris continued, excitement shining in his hazel-ish eyes. "You'll be able to go through the screened options and choose ones you'd consider. Once you settle on two for the first week, we'll announce. Those profiles will go up on the website. We have the choice of taking applicants over the next few weeks, or we can choose a cutoff date within the next week or so. That gives you the option of knowing all your choices well in advance. I was thinking that with your anxiety, that might be a better way to go."

Just like that, the room shrank. Oddly enough, her lungs started working again. Pushing back from her seat, she stood, brushing his arm with her hip. She went to her bag and pulled her water out of it, took a long drink, letting it soothe her dry throat. There'd been absolutely no judgment or condescension in his tone. *With your anxiety.*

"I'm sorry. Did I say something wrong?"

She turned, tried to keep her emotions from taking over. "I just . . . Most people don't mention my anxiety as if it's one more characteristic to describe me. Like, 'Oh, well, with your red hair, the color is all wrong.'"

His brows furrowed. "You have brown hair."

Her lips fought the smile, because it was ridiculous to feel so much appreciation that she wanted to beam. She closed her eyes, pushed the feelings down. "Never mind." Now wasn't the time to tell him how good it felt to have someone say it like it was just an acceptable piece of her—something that could be easily accommodated, like inviting a vegetarian for dinner.

Her parents, former friends, and exes had called her many things: neurotic, fussy, anal, bitchy, uptight. But they'd never once worked to understand the feelings that came along with having anxiety. They'd never made simple adjustments to plans to take her feelings into consideration. They'd downplayed most of her feelings until she'd questioned whether she felt them. People didn't understand that she didn't *want* the extra stumbling blocks her worries threw into her path. They just happened, and navigating around them was exhausting. The fact that Chris was taking everything about her into consideration made Everly feel too much. Which made her anxious. *Because, of course.*

"Continue. Please."

Chris folded his arms over his chest. "Okay. You'll go through the app and pick your dates. We'll set things up, but I think the initial contact would be best if made by you. You'll be able to text through the app, which I think is one of the best parts. You can go back and forth a little before you talk on the phone or meet, without sharing your actual contact information."

A halo of questions seemed to vibrate around her brain. "Will there be time for all of that?" Two dates a week, two guys. Twice the communication and interaction. She'd talked to her ex only a couple of times a week by phone. They texted most of their plans because she hated being on the phone. Now, she'd have to ring a couple of guys up every second day and be all, "So, you want to take me out, huh?" Everly laughed at the thought of even being able to say that out loud.

"Are you okay?" Chris stood and walked into her space. He took the water from her and set it on the desk. "Seriously, Everly. You can still back out. If you're not okay with this. If—"

"I hate talking on the phone," she blurted.

His mouth formed an *o* at her interruption and the realization of what she was worried about. Then he smiled, and it felt soft and intimate like a hug. One of those ones where the person pulls you right in and smooths their hands over every part they can touch.

"Of course. Texting is okay, right?"

She laughed to cover the awkwardness she felt. "Yes. It is. And so is being on the phone when I need to. I just . . . I've never dated two men at once. It's all new to me." *Way to put it mildly.*

Pushing past him, she went back to her seat. "I'll be fine. Once we get going, I'll settle in, I'll know more about what to expect."

"Then you're sure?" He spoke from behind her, and she swiveled again to face him.

"I think we're out of options at this point, boss."

Chris scrunched his face at the word *boss*, which made Everly smile. "It's easy to feel like there's no way out, but we always have options. I won't make you do anything you don't want to."

Everly pulled in a deep breath and took her time letting it out, feeling her body relax with the exhale. "No. You won't, and you're not. I chose to do this." *It's an opportunity to take control in several areas of your life.*

She turned back to her computer, ready to bury herself in work and the rest of their segment.

"Everly?" His voice was husky, nearly whispered. Sensations rippled over her skin from the three syllables, taking their time and leaving a mark. *What's that about? Need another reminder he's your boss? Maybe I'll put it on a whiteboard and keep it where you can see it.* She couldn't focus on her work if her pulse was going haywire.

"Hmm?" She wrote things down in her notebook that she wasn't sure would make sense.

"Why don't we chat after your segment?" He walked to the door, and she was just about to agree but remembered what she had planned next.

She let out a groan and leaned back in her chair. "I can't," she said, meeting his gaze.

"Because?"

She sat straight, stiffened her shoulders, and gave him a lopsided smile. "I'm going shopping."

Chris stared at her. He didn't get it. "Oh."

"*Oh* as in, you'd like to join us?"

He rubbed a hand over his chin. "Us?"

She grinned. "Yup. My good friend Stacey and I are going to"—she put her hands up to use air quotes—"find me a single, about-to-be-wooed-off-my-feet wardrobe that will revitalize not only my closet but my life."

His hand covered his mouth, and she knew he was hiding a grin. Clearing his throat, he dropped his hands, slipped them in his pants pockets.

"Stacey's words?"

"Obviously. She's quite enjoying her opportunity to play the gal pal to my real-life heroine of a rom-com. According to her, this means a fashion montage, which I will, apparently, begrudgingly enjoy."

Chris chuckled. To his credit, he didn't outright laugh. It

was a dignified, reserved, wow-that's-rough show of humor. "Sounds like she has you covered."

"She will. As of this afternoon, she'll have me covered from head to toe."

Did his eyes just flare? Heat up?

Stacey knocked on the window between them. She'd written on her whiteboard: *Need food. Feed me. I'm fading fast.* She'd let the word *fast* trail off the board.

Chris and Everly both laughed, but it was he who answered, "I'll order something in. We've got a few longer days ahead of us."

When he left, making it so she could breathe properly, Stacey put the whiteboard up again. This time, it read: *Cannot wait to go shopping. You excited yet?*

Everly picked up her board and jotted down a response. Everyone was part of making this a success, and she wasn't about to play woe-is-me simply because dining with strangers rated just below drinking milk past the expiration date.

She turned her sign and felt okay with what it said; it was partially true. In her own way.

Can't wait.

Stacey's grin was huge. She gave Everly a big thumbs-up and then pressed a button to switch from music to talking.

"It's a happy day here at the station. I want to know what makes *you* happy. Let's do a Sun Tweet Fest. Tell me what makes you happy using the hashtag #sunfun. I'll randomly give out some passes to a local gym to one listener before Ev and I sign off for the day. Come on, people, get us trending."

Everly shook her head and pulled up Twitter on her computer. If nothing else, Stacey was good at keeping her distracted from her own thoughts.

[10]

The app his oldest brother, Wesley, created was awesome. Chris looked through the data Wes had compiled. Just like other apps, the user swiped through the candidates, but these guys were all ones who'd applied for the chance to date Everly. When their image was pressed, a small bio came up, and there was even a link to a video recording. It wasn't a requirement, but several of the applicants had done a quick intro clip. Chris had been up late most nights compiling information, sorting through candidates, and triple-checking background reports, criminal record checks, work histories, and anything else he could find out about these guys. The nice part about Wes's app was it did a background screen before uploading the candidate list. Sort of like a final red flag checker.

In moments like these, it helped that he had connections and could call in favors. It also didn't hurt that he had his own money to hire an investigator. The station could have covered it, but without his push and personal weight, the process would have taken longer, and he didn't have the time to waste. Everly would be safe, and his father wouldn't have time to question any of the process. Tonight, they'd choose the first two.

Putting aside the fact that the whole idea of Everly going out with *anyone* made him slightly ill, everything was progressing perfectly. His phone rang, interrupting his perusal of bachelor number four. His dad's name popped onto the screen.

Chris bit back his sigh as he swiped. "Dad."

"Are you serious about this? I thought you were trying to one-up your sister, but you're actually going through with it?"

I'm fine. How are you? "People are already invested. We're selling promo spots quicker than ever. We've had 450 entries for possible dates in the last two days."

There was a slight pause. "Excellent. You took a risk, and you're lucky—*so far*—that it's working. I want you to keep me in the loop, and I mean it this time. Don't fill me in after the fact. You get those numbers up, and we'll be able to up my asking price."

Chris's breath caught. "What?" The station—the staff—didn't need to go through another turnover.

"We'll see. Hard to turn down profit, son. What's the point if we do?"

Granddad would have a far more concise and impactful answer than Chris could muster at the moment. His father didn't truly listen to any of them. *But you have to try.*

Chris stood up, paced back and forth in front of the windows. "Why turn it over if it's making a profit? It doesn't hurt to have these holdings." Any more than it would have hurt to keep the warehouses Noah was attached to. *Why do you care? You won't be here.* It didn't sit right, though. In fact, it made his stomach clench.

Sometimes his father reminded him of a child who couldn't choose a favorite toy, so he grabbed them all before anyone else could, then decided he didn't want any of them.

"I'll think about it. Not really your concern. This goes the way you want it to, you'll be home in no time doing exactly what you've wanted. Now, I want you to take a closer look at the subsidiary companies. I think we should off-load them sooner rather than later."

Frustration rolled through his body. "You have enough going on that you don't need to micromanage any of us. I've been here for almost twelve months. I'm doing what you asked, including looking into our sister companies. Can you just let me do my job, Dad?"

"Be happy to," his dad said, laughter in his booming voice. "As long as you don't mess it up."

The buzzer signaling a visitor sounded. "I have to go."

His father's low rumble sounded in his ear. "Updates. Don't forget."

Check the damn website if you want to know what's going on. "Of course. Good night."

He pressed End before his father could reply, shoved his phone in his pocket, and raked both hands through his hair. He was tired of pandering to his father's whims.

Pressing the button by the door, he said hello.

"It's Everly."

Two words in her soft voice and his skin felt too tight. They'd arranged for her to come by, check out the software, and choose the first two candidates. Now the idea of having her in his home, his *space*, didn't seem like the best way to keep his distance. He buzzed her in, waiting by the door.

"You need to set up a couple of dates of your own," he mumbled to himself. With someone who didn't work for him. Preferably in New York, where he'd actually live.

Pulling the door open, he watched her get off the elevator. Her hair was down, soft brown curls framing her face. She wore a pair of jeans, bright blue Converse, and a thin sweater. His heart bounced; the sensation surprising him.

Everly held up a brown paper bag. "I brought payback," she said, coming into his apartment.

As she walked by him, he inhaled deeply, catching the sweet, flowery scent of her hair. *Your whole place is going to smell like Everly.*

He shut the door behind her. "You didn't need to pay me back," he said, his voice a bit gruff. *Pull yourself together. You've never crossed a line or led a woman on. You haven't even told her you're moving across the country in six months. Stick to the plan. The ultimate goal. This contest is going to be the proof Dad needs that you're ready to move forward.*

All good reminders that shifted his focus, realigned his priorities. "What are you paying me back for, anyway?" He couldn't think of anything he'd done for her.

"You brought me chocolate pie. That definitely deserves payback." She stood by the door, glancing beyond the entryway. "Nice place."

Maybe don't stand here just staring at her?

Chris smiled. "Thanks. Come on in."

He gestured toward the kitchen, and Everly set the bag on the counter before pulling out two take-out dessert containers.

"I brought two," she said, smiling at him over her shoulder.

"Pies?"

Turning back to her task, her hair fell forward, and he got stuck staring at the graceful curve of her back and neck.

"Nope. You brought me your favorite. It's your turn to taste mine."

Swallowing down his groan was painful. She turned and handed over one of the containers. Their gazes held, and he forgot to move, to take the offering. To breathe.

"Your life is about to change irrevocably. Do you understand that?"

His throat went dry. "Pardon?"

Everly grinned, and his stomach twisted in the most delightful way. "Once you've had my friend Tara's cannoli, you'll never be the same. They are the best."

Pulled back into the moment by his New York roots, he eyed the container skeptically. "You know I'm from New York, right?"

She nodded, her lips flattening. "I try not to hold it against you, though."

A laugh burst from his chest, and he took the box and fork she handed him. "Let's go sit in the living room."

They sat down with almost a cushion between them, angled toward each other, and took the lid off their desserts. Before she could dig in, he plucked the fork from her fingers.

"Rookie," he said, shaking his head as he set both of their forks on his coffee table.

Everly laughed, arched one brow in curiosity laced with challenge. Chris picked up the rolled dessert, the scent of lemon filling his nostrils and making his stomach growl.

"You have a lot to live up to, little cannoli," he said, making her laugh like he'd hoped to. He could get high on Everly's laugh. He bit in, enjoying the sugared crunch followed by the delicious mix of lemon and white chocolate flavors on his tongue.

Everly straightened her shoulders and sent him a smug look. "Well?"

All he could manage was, "Mmmm." He finished it in three bites and wanted another. When he eyed hers, she laughed and pulled the box to her side.

"Not likely, pal," she said through laughter.

Pal. Friends. They could be that. It was a hell of a lot better than nothing. *Keep it light. Easy.* As the youngest of four kids, he had an arsenal of puppy-dog expressions. Leaning forward, he gave Everly one that always worked on Ari.

Everly leaned back even more, her laughter escalating. "Oh my. Does that look actually work on anyone?"

Pretending to sulk as he straightened in his seat, he rested one arm along the back of the couch. "My sister. Well, it used to. Not much works on her now."

Everly picked up her cannoli and brought it to her lips, and all the humor fled from Chris's being. She was sexy without even trying. When she took her bite, a little bit of the cream filling remained on her cheek. He pointed to it, wanting to swipe his thumb across the spot more than he wanted another dessert.

Laughing, she went from sexy to sweet in seconds. "Oops,"

she said, picking up a napkin. She whisked the spot away and took another bite. She had one-third left when she looked at him through lowered lashes. She held it out to him.

"For real?"

"Yeah. I have a hookup. I can get more."

Maybe there was something wrong with his brain. Maybe it short-circuited. What else would account for the fact that instead of taking it from her hand with his fingers, he leaned in and opened his mouth. Her brain must have been on the fritz, too, because despite her slight inhalation of a breath, she brought the pastry to his lips, feeding it to him. Their gazes were loaded missiles locked on one another, ready to detonate. His peripheral vision narrowed and his hand came up to loosely circle her wrist. It was Everly who touched her index finger to his mouth, to his tongue. *Jesus. She tastes better than the damn cannoli.*

Everly gasped, and the moment broke. She jumped up from his couch, knocking her container to the couch. "I'm sorry. Oh, shit, did I get anything on your couch?" She swiped at it, somewhat madly, with a napkin.

"It's fine. There's nothing there," Chris said, his voice like gravel sliding over concrete. What the hell had he just done? *Sucked the finger of the woman you can't stop thinking about. Thanks, Captain Obvious. It was a rhetorical question.* Maybe there really was something wrong with his brain. He was talking to himself. *Since you're at it, how about you calm down your employee who's going to wear a hole in the fabric of your cushion?*

Chris covered her hand to stop her movements. "Ev."

She jolted at the nickname. It'd come out of nowhere and, sadly, felt right. "I'm so sorry," she said, looking down.

"Please don't be. If anyone should be sorry, it's me."

Straightening, she looked past him and asked, "Can I use your washroom?"

She needed a minute. Good. He could use one, too. "Down the hall, second door on the right."

When she walked away and he was sure she was out of sight, he let out a heavy sigh and flopped back against the couch. "What the hell?"

He only gave himself a second to shake it off. He could fix this. It was a moment. They were *friends*, sort of. It was nothing. Scooping up both of their containers, he took them to the kitchen and recycled them. He grabbed them a couple of waters, debating whether or not to offer her wine or beer. *That's a great idea. You two could knock back a few and forget all about setting her up on dates.*

Chris groaned again and dropped his head to the front of the fridge, the cold surface soothing his heated skin.

She'd go now. She'd come out and tell him she couldn't do this, that finger sucking had not been on the menu. Everly would storm out, tell Stacey, who would, rightfully, kick his ass. He'd spend the next six months hiding in his office while Everly went on dates and laughed about her creepy boss who had a thing for sucking fingers.

"It's not a *thing*," he said, feeling the need to defend himself. It was a damn moment, not a fetish.

The bathroom door opened, and Chris pushed off the fridge and turned, water in hand, his stomach sinking at the thought of her leaving. For all his education and experience in communications, when she appeared in the doorway to his kitchen, he couldn't think of one sensible thing to say.

[11]

Everly's heart was trying its very best to burst right out of her chest. She wouldn't run. Ten Rules for Faking It were already in play, and she was done chickening out over everything. It was nothing. *Nothing doesn't involve sticking your finger in a man's mouth. Your boss's mouth.* Oh God. Was it possible to actually panic herself to invisibleness? She pressed her nails into the fleshy part of her palms. She would not run. It was a momentary lapse of sanity, and now she'd play it off. They'd get it on . . . *Holy hell, Everly! You most definitely will not get it or anything else on with him.* She meant *get on with* their night. Their work. But apparently, her brain was broken.

Chris lifted his head from the fridge. She wasn't sure what he'd been doing, but maybe he felt as stupid as she did. *People never feel the way you do. You can't know that.* He stepped forward, and her breath got caught, tangled in her throat. A weird, garbled sound left her mouth. Of course. *Because things aren't awkward enough, you need to add strange noises.*

"Are you okay? I truly apologize," Chris said, his eyes searching hers as if they held some secret.

He was sorry? He hadn't stuck his finger . . . *Don't. Just don't.* "I'm sorry," she whispered. She wasn't leaving. Rule six: Be bold, even if it gives you hives. She scratched at her stomach. Staying was brave.

"I respect you and didn't mean to cross a line. You're an employee, and I hope I haven't made things unbearable. I understand if you want to leave."

Does he want me to leave? Wait, what was unbearable? My finger? It tasted like cannoli. That's hardly unbearable. I can't leave! I'm being brave.

"But I hope you don't," he said, passing her the water.

Pasting on a smile that probably made her look like someone was pinching her, she took the water. "Not leaving. Sorry about the awkward moment. If we could avoid talking about it for the rest of ever, I'd truly appreciate it."

He gave a curt nod. "Done. Absolutely."

Okay. She could do this. *They* could do this. When his lips curved into a more relaxed smile, Everly's brain brought up the memory of how sexy his mouth felt wrapped around her index finger. *My brain hates me.*

Chris's eyes narrowed. "You good?"

"Awesome," she said with way too much enthusiasm.

They made their way back to the living room. When they sat in the same spots on the couch, nerves washed over her again, threatening to buckle her knees.

"Again, I'm so sorry, Everly."

The tone of his voice caught her off guard. He was *really* sorry. Was it because of her? Would he have been sorry if he'd accidentally sucked Stacey's finger? *Ew.*

"The app?" Easiest way to get over something was to avoid thinking or talking about it. Said no therapist ever. Whatever. She was a producer, not a shrink.

Chris cleared his throat and pulled his phone over. His coffee table also held some remotes, his laptop, and a lot of paperwork. What did he do besides work? Outside of work? The next man she chose was going to be able to balance personal and professional. *Like you?* That was a bit of a pot-kettle situation, but she was working on it. She was here, ready to map out her dating life.

***

"I have some rules."

Chris scrolled through his phone, pulling up an app. She couldn't see it but didn't want to lean in closer. He glanced at her from the side of his eye. "For dating?"

She gave a low laugh. "Dating. Life. Getting through birthdays." Everly took a deep breath. "I actually meant for possible guys. No face tattoos, unkempt or abnormally long beards, weird fetishes, or nose rings."

Chris set his phone down on the couch between them and gave her his full attention. "Define *abnormally long*."

She thought about it, then gestured to her shoulders. "No farther than the shoulders, I think."

He nodded, and she felt like he was holding back a grin. "Weird fetishes could mean any manner of things."

Like finger sucking. *Oh. God. Get out of your own head.* "Just . . . nothing too out there."

"Those all seem reasonable enough."

She wasn't sure if he was on the brink of teasing her, but the way his lips almost curved made her head feel light. "I'm not done," she said. "He should be outgoing. Bold. Like to try new things." *Basically my opposite.*

Chris nodded. "You've given this some thought. Those are very specific."

Her shoulders stiffened. If she was doing this, she wanted what she wanted. Why not? It was her dating show. Or whatever. "They are. I've had some lousy luck so far with men, so I might as well be up front about what I want."

Was it her imagination, or did his eyes flash fire? He looked down at his phone.

"Everyone has their hard lines in the sand."

He didn't make her feel judged. He just smiled and nodded again, his fingers tapping the phone. "Anything else you *do* want?"

Hmm. She bit her lip and gave it a moment of thought, appreciating that he didn't rush her in any way. "Outgoing. Maybe someone artistic? Someone with a sense of adventure. Someone funny, but how do you know? I mean, anyone can write anything down on these things, and then you find out nothing is true."

Chris started to stand but paused and looked her way. "We're going to do everything we can to make sure that everything is verified. We'll have security nearby on all dates, so if it turns out the man who said he was a funny, outgoing artist is actually a long-bearded, face-tattooed guy, we'll end it."

She smirked, biting her lip so she didn't laugh. "Thanks."

"My pleasure. I'm going to plug this into my television," he said, walking toward the huge screen. He did whatever he needed to do to get it set up and then grabbed one of his many remotes and turned the TV on. The screen was a deep purple with a black logo of an *E* curling into a heart. To the right, it said *Ever Love.*

Everly's mouth dropped open, and she stared at Chris.

He shrugged. "My brother tailor-made it for you." Her eyes were drawn to his throat as he swallowed and then turned back to the screen. Everly forced herself to turn her head in that direction, too.

"Okay, so we'll go through the candidates. They've been uploaded, sorted, and categorized according to things you've told me. We narrowed the age bracket and basic physical requirements based on the questionnaire we had you fill out. Each guy will pop up, and you can see him and read his bio. Several of them uploaded a video message."

"Really?" Everly leaned forward.

"It's a great feature. You can get a sense of them that way, I think."

He handed her the remote, and nerves hopped around like bouncy balls in her stomach. She was doing this.

After showing her how to move through the candidates and

"like" one, he leaned back and let her look through without commenting. The screen had their images on the left, a list of who they were, age, occupation, interests, and an optional one-line comment about why they were doing this. If there was a video clip, there was a small, sideways triangle on the bottom of their picture.

She wished Stacey were here with her, but she decided her friend would have too much to say.

Matthew Fortin
33
Carpenter
Building furniture, long walks, sunsets, coffee
To meet my soul mate

"Pass," she said, pressing the arrow.

Chris laughed. "The passes might be easy. Too mushy with the soul mate thing?"

Everly turned her head and smirked. "Sunsets aren't an interest."

Chris picked up his water and took a drink. "Good point. Onward."

Brad Corden
30
Airplane mechanic
Flying, driving, traveling, swimming, motocross
Seems like a fun opportunity

Everly pressed the Play button.

"Hey, Everly. This feels a little weird, but okay. My name is Brad. I figured I'd throw my hat in the proverbial ring because you deserve to go on a date with a man who isn't a loser like your ex. I like to have fun and try new things, and I'd love the chance to take you out, make you laugh, and get to know you."

Everly pressed the little heart icon.

Chris shifted in his seat. "Look at that. First one already."

When she looked over, she noticed his jaw seemed tight, and his arms were crossed over his chest.

She clicked the remote. Pass. Pass. Like. Pass. Definite pass.

Thirty-nine-year-old John Ringer, the self-taught artist, who liked camping and swimming nude, got a pass.

Jeff Tosi, the twenty-seven-year-old guitar player who liked rock and roll and hot chicks, also got a pass.

Chris wandered off, and Everly continued to press the buttons. It was a little weird scrolling through her own personal catalog of possibilities. She wanted someone whose image and words made her stop and think, *Wait, tell me more.*

When Chris sank down on the couch beside her a few minutes later, he had a large bowl of popcorn. He grinned at her.

"I like popcorn," he said sheepishly. He tipped the bowl her way, and she laughed, pulling her feet up under her before she grabbed a handful.

"Juggler?" Everly's popcorn nearly lodged in her throat. "Is that a real profession?"

Chris kicked his feet up to his coffee table. "Maybe if you're good enough. Press Play."

When she did, Aran Kirk's voice came through the speakers *loud* and clear. "Everly. I can't wait to meet you. I have many things to teach you and learn from you. Our journey will be a unique one, but fear not," he said, pausing to lean off-screen. When he came back, he held three orange balls in his hands. He started to juggle before speaking again. "I am used to the unexpected. Are you?"

Everly groaned. "Why would he end it with a question?"

Chris turned his head and stared at her.

"What?" Did she have popcorn in her hair?

"The question at the end was what you found odd?"

Everly laughed, then gave him a mock frown. "Juggling is a lost art."

His brows shot up, and he sat forward, setting the popcorn bowl between them. Selecting three pieces, he tossed them up in the air and tried to catch them, missing all three.

Everly bit back her laugh and pointed at the screen. "He's not right for me, but maybe he gives lessons."

Chris scowled at her and picked up the stray popcorn, tossing it onto his coffee table. "Pass," he muttered.

Laughter burst from her, and she snuggled farther into the couch, not even realizing she'd put her nerves away. "Damn right it's a pass. All the way around."

"Amen," Chris said, scooping up some more kernels.

Pass. Pass. Pass. *What the actual what?* Pass. Pass. Everly's eyes were gritty. She set the remote down to take a long drink.

"You okay?" Chris asked.

His soft voice broke the reverie she'd been stuck in, thinking about how she wasn't going to find anyone.

"I guess. I've only liked three out of thirty-seven." Those were some pretty bad odds.

"There's plenty more," he said, smiling at her. He reached out like he might squeeze her shoulder or touch her reassuringly but pulled back. *He's probably worried you'll try to stuff another finger or your arm in his mouth.*

Everly turned back to the screen, pressed the button to move the choices forward.

"Owen Baston, thirty-one, craft brewer. That's interesting," she said.

"You like beer?" Chris picked up his water, not looking at her.

"Not particularly, no. But it's different, and I want something different."

He had reddish-brown hair and a happy smile in the picture. He was handsome but in a rugged sort of way. She'd never really dated anyone *rugged.*

She pressed Play.

"Hi, Everly. This feels a bit strange. I've never even taken a selfie," Owen said to the screen. Everly laughed out loud. "This isn't the usual way I go about getting dates, but it felt like it was time for something different. When I heard you on the radio, aside from feeling mad on your behalf, I thought, 'Man, I wouldn't want to piss her off.' I was immediately intrigued. Regardless of who you choose, good luck. You're better than Simon."

She was smiling when the clip ended.

Chris huffed out a breath. "I should get you a shirt that says that, in case you forget."

Turning, she stifled a yawn and asked, "What?"

His eyes went darker. He had such long, enviable lashes. "You're better than Simon."

She smiled and, without thinking, reached for his hand. "Thank you. I'm okay. I realized I felt nothing when we broke up, so that was a pretty good indication it wasn't important to me."

Chris removed his hand from hers, and she had to fight against cringing. *Right. Don't touch his hand. Don't touch him. He doesn't like it, and the guy has been pretty accommodating about your handsy behavior.*

"Still sucks for someone to treat you like he did," Chris said.

Everly looked back at the screen. "Yes. It does. I like Owen for date one."

Chris sucked in a breath and started to cough. Everly didn't know what to do, so she handed him his water and just waited nervously to make sure he was okay.

"Sorry," he said, his voice scratchy. He took the water. "You sound so sure."

Giving him a wry smile, pushing down the tornado of thoughts in her head, she said, "It gets tiring to be so unsure all the time."

His face was red and his eyes were a bit watery. "Okay, then. Owen, you have yourself a date."

For the moment, she could smile. She was a great plan maker and often dreamed of traveling, heading out to a club to go dancing for a night, joining bingo—it wasn't just for old ladies—but she always stopped short and canceled her plans. No canceling. She was doing this. Maybe doing things completely backward of what made her comfortable would help her figure out exactly where she was meant to be.

Or she'd have a panic attack, get hives, and stand Owen up. Time would tell.

[12]

Everly lifted the water bottle to her lips, grateful she was alone in her apartment so no one could hear the glugging sound of her swallowing. It was like she'd run a marathon in the heat, weighted down by blankets. She was sweating in too many places. Maybe there was something wrong with her. Sweating could be brought on by medical conditions. She just couldn't think of which ones. *Stop.* Everly set the empty water bottle down. She pulled in a half breath because that's all her lungs would allow. *One. Two. Three. Four.* She imagined her hand slipping out of Owen's because of sweat. *Stop. One. Two. Three. Four. Five, six, seven.* She leaned against the counter, her lungs expanding. She'd been on dates before, so the level of anxiety pumping through her was unexpected. *This one comes with a hell of a lot of pressure.*

She went back to the bathroom, closed the door, and stood in front of the full-length mirror. Once she made it clear that she wasn't wearing anything low-cut, see-through, sequined, or with *any* type of feathers, Stacey had taken the shopping seriously.

Which was why she at least felt good about her appearance. She'd gone with a pair of dark gray pants and a thin, pale, pink sweater with a wide neckline. She'd have preferred black or gray, but Stacey wouldn't negotiate on that one. The top hung from her slight frame nicely, enhancing what little shape she had. Stacey—who favored the curvy side—always lamented Everly's slender shape, but there were plenty of times in her life that she'd have liked to fill out a top the way her friend did. *Grass is always greener.*

Her phone rang. She looked down to where she'd set it on the counter. Of course Stacey would FaceTime her. She pressed Accept.

"Let me see," Stacey said, her face filling the screen.

Everly turned and faced the mirror so her friend could see.

"Good. Hair looks great down. You should wear it that way more. Subtle makeup. Add a bit of that gloss before you leave the house, and don't chew it off. That sweater looks kick-ass on you. Your boobs look hot."

Because I'm sweating everywhere. Everly smirked. "If only it were you I was trying to impress tonight."

"Too late for that. Besides, you don't have to impress anyone. Just be yourself."

"I'm going to try to be a little less myself than I am right now," Everly said, leaving the bathroom.

"Hives?"

"Not yet. Too much sweat."

"It doesn't show." Stacey scrunched her brows on the screen. She was *really* looking.

"Nerves, one to ten?"

"Twelve. I might be sick." She touched her hand to her stomach.

"Look at me," Stacey said, her tone sharpening.

"Stacey. I'm literally looking right *at* you."

Undeterred by Everly's sarcasm, she nodded. "That's right, now listen to me. You deserve to have a bunch of good-looking, fun bachelors take you out and treat you right. This doesn't have to go anywhere. Focus on tonight. Just tonight. The very worst thing that will happen is you won't enjoy the evening, so you don't go out with him again."

"Wow. You really have not considered all the other terrible things that could happen."

Stacey sighed, but not in exasperation. "Give it to me."

"Okay. He could be a pervert, a weirdo. I said no face tattoos but he has other ones and might just be waiting for the right moment to shave his head and get his skull inked. He could have a girlfriend, a wife. Both. A slinky underwear fetish. You know I hate thongs. He could be duller than my Broadcasting History course was even though his hobbies included zip-lining and hiking. Oh my God, he could want to go zip-lining."

Her friend held up one hand. "Stop. I get it. Jesus, your brain is like an overpacked freeway in the middle of rush hour." Her tone was soft and so . . . accepting, Everly's eyes watered. "Sweetie, you've got this. Get out of your own brain. Breathe."

"I have to go." She couldn't talk about it anymore.

"You've got this. The Facebook post looked great and has hundreds of comments. You heard his on-air interview. He's funny and sounds sweet. The whole city is rooting for you."

No pressure. After Everly chose two guys—well, she'd actually chosen them all—they'd decided to interview each man and play clips as part of their promos. They'd also gone with Facebook posts that allowed more interaction than a blog. Everly was keeping notes in her rule book just because sometimes her anxiety ramped so high she forgot things.

"Hopefully, I won't let them down."

"Okay. You know what?" Stacey said, her tone rising.

"What?" A stitch tugged at Everly's side. Did Stacey think she should change? Maybe gray would be better. Maybe . . .

"I'm adding a new life rule. Not for your list but just so I don't have to kick your ass. Believe in yourself. I mean it. You have faith in everyone else. Have some faith in my best friend."

Surprise, and a bit of amusement, pulled a smile from Everly. "That's like a teacher tone you've got going on there."

Stacey nodded. "I didn't like it, so don't make me use it again."

They were both smiling when Everly hung up the phone. *Believe in yourself.* Interesting concept. *There are 457 applicants to date you. Maybe you should have a little faith.*

It wasn't really a world full of strangers she was worried about; it was her job and Stacey's. This contest had already started bringing more money into the station. More companies were willing to pay premium prices for the advertising spots on their show than even a week ago.

She'd just gotten in her car when her phone rang again. She pressed Accept through the steering wheel so she could get going and *not* be late. *He could be late.*

"Hello." She swung out into the post-rush-hour traffic.

"Hey. It's Chris."

Her body relaxed. "Hi. Everything okay?"

"Of course. Just wanted to check on you."

She stopped at the light at the end of her street. "I've been on a date before. I'm good." *What he doesn't know . . .*

The silence made her think maybe she'd lost the call. She turned right and headed toward the restaurant she'd picked out.

"You don't have to pretend this isn't hard for you. I just wanted to tell you that no matter how it turns out, I admire you."

The words warmed her in an unexpected way. She tended to err on the realist side of things as opposed to being warm and fuzzy. But something about the soft cadence of his voice and the fact that he'd called her on her false bravado boosted her confidence. She thought of making a joke about the admiration piece, but she knew it was because of her nerves, and it felt nice to have someone—other than Stacey—acknowledge that they were real, that even if she was overreacting, she was allowed to feel how she felt.

"Thank you."

"Talk later?"

She nodded, then remembered he couldn't see her. "Sure."

When she hung up, she realized she was now looking forward to the evening. Or at least the end of it.

***

Owen Baston was waiting for her by the hostess station. His leather jacket and slightly too-long hair looked less intimidating in person, but butterflies still unfurled in her gut. His eyes caught hers immediately, giving her no time to prepare or take a moment to get her breathing under control. His brownish-red hair was messily styled. Or maybe he woke up that way. He didn't look like he cared about how his hair looked. His eyes crinkled at the corners when the smile moved all the way up his slightly stubbled cheeks. He wore a black sweater under the leather bomber with dark jeans. Some of those butterflies batted their lashes. This man could be a poster model for their contest. *Want to find the one? Find it right here on 96.2 SUN.*

Everly pressed her fingernails into her palm, acknowledging the increase of her pulse and waiting for those other telltale signs: quivering heart, somersaulting belly, that quick rush of adrenaline. Maybe this was why she had so little luck in love—the feelings of panic and attraction were incredibly similar. How was she supposed to know the difference?

"Everly?" Even his voice was nice.

What was wrong with her? *You're guarded. Just breathe. Or at least talk. Try talking and breathing.* "Yes. Owen." She didn't make it a question.

He leaned in, one hand on her shoulder. Everly didn't know if he was going to hug her or kiss her cheek or squeeze her arm. Like she'd spiked her water with Red Bull, she tried to accommodate all three: stepping into him, lifting her arm a bit, and turning her head, which she then smacked into his chin.

Owen laughed and stepped back, rubbing his chin while Everly pressed her feet firmer to the marble lobby floor and counted silently to stave off passing out. *Awesome.*

"Off to a good start. Sorry about that," he said.

She flinched. "No. I'm sorry. I tend to be awkward in new situations. Which I probably shouldn't say, but I made it pretty obvious, so it seems better that you know, I know. That I'm aware of it. I'm not oblivious or anything. Honestly, you can run if you want."

Could she turn around and just walk out? Owen took it in stride, laughing at her rambling, earning him about a dozen checks in the pro column so far. The hostess smiled at them.

"Oh, good. Your party has arrived. Come this way," she said, turning to walk through the rows of tables.

"I'm rarely ever called a *party* all by myself," Everly muttered jokingly. The hostess didn't hear, but Owen clearly did. His lips twitched, and she shrugged. "Just don't want you to get your hopes up." Owen's hand came to her elbow, not grabbing or holding. Just guiding. He leaned down just a little. "I'll try to keep my expectations realistic."

Everly laughed, surprised and a little relieved. Maybe this would be okay. They stopped at a booth at the back of the restaurant. Tiny votives were arranged in a circle in the center. Everly's breath came easier. She'd already gotten the make-a-fool-of-herself portion of the evening out of the way. They were set apart from the busier part of the restaurant, and she couldn't help but wonder if Chris had requested that. To anyone else, it would seem romantic, but for her, it helped her relax.

"Your waitress will be with you in just a couple of minutes," their hostess said.

To his credit, Owen waited for her to slide into the bench seat before he sat across from her. A gentleman. A handsome, easygoing one. Not exactly a hardship. She looked around, noticing how busy the restaurant seemed and again wondering if Chris had gone the extra step to ensure her comfort.

"Are you okay?" Owen shrugged off his jacket, tossing it on the seat beside him and leaning back against the padded booth.

Soft music played from the speakers, dishes clanged

somewhere beyond them, and the scent of bread and flowers wafted through the air. She focused on those sensory things for a moment, tapped her fingers against her thigh.

"I am. I'm sorry. I get pretty nervous. I just . . . well, this is all a bit overwhelming." Honesty worked. They were adults.

"I get that. A couple of the guys at my work told me about the contest. Three of us from the company entered. I was pretty stoked when I got chosen. But I was nervous, too."

It was strangely soothing to know he hadn't been 100 percent worry-free. Not that she wished nerves on anyone, but clearly she wasn't alone. If she shifted how she approached this—treated it more like a work thing—maybe she could get to a point that she relaxed entirely. She did preinterviews for the station all the time, and it's not like she was totally inept at talking to people. She just froze under pressure. Around strangers. In large gatherings. *Stop.*

Everly smiled brightly. "You work for a brewery?"

He nodded just as the waitress approached. Red hair tied back from her face, she smiled at both of them and placed ice water on the table.

"Good evening. Welcome to Antony's."

She went through the specials at Mach speed, but they went with items off the menu—linguini for Everly and seafood manicotti for Owen. He ordered a wine, but Everly stuck with water. Leaving them with bread to snack on, the waitress promised to put their orders in right away.

Owen waited a beat before he returned to their conversation. "I'm senior manager of product development. I've been there since I was nineteen. I interned before I ever got hired. How about you? What's being a producer like?"

She found her footing and settled into the evening. There were a few moments where she was able to drop her guard enough to laugh and have fun. The meal was delicious, and Owen was funny and charming. Could she open up to him? It was the first date in a long time that she enjoyed. That was something.

The one time their fingers touched over the bread, she felt a small spark of warmth—like putting her hand too close to a match. Not that bread was an aphrodisiac or anything, but it was a good sign. She wanted that moment, that pause where her heartbeat sped up. Like when she was a kid and she had a crush on Jamie Steiner. They'd had to hold hands in square dancing, and her fingers shook before he'd even slid his sweaty palm into hers. Her heart had stuttered.

So, basically, you're waiting for a man to make you feel like you're thirteen again? No wonder you can't find happiness, Everly. Give it time. You expect too much, too fast.

"Your bill and gratuity have been taken care of," the waitress said when she returned after clearing their plates.

Owen walked her out to her car, and there was a moment she thought he might lean in to kiss her, and her body braced, readied for impact. Her breath froze in her lungs, and she had an image of not being able to breathe right at the moment their lips would touch. It surprised her when Owen stepped back with a half smile, giving her space as if he realized she needed it. The gesture made her *want* him to kiss her—almost. It definitely made her curious about what it would be like to have those very nice-looking arms pull her close.

"Guess I'll know how it went when I read Facebook, huh?"

Everly laughed, running her fingers over her key chain. "I had a really good time. You're easy to talk to and spend time with."

"Same with you, Everly. It was a really good night. For the record, I'd like to kiss you, but I should probably give the other guys at least half a chance, right?"

She liked his confidence and that he could make her laugh. "It's not a bad idea."

"One more thing?" He stepped closer, and Everly's breath caught in that way it did when she was anticipating something good.

"Hmm?" *Thank goodness you didn't have garlic. Wait. He did.* Her mouth went dry.

"Your ex was an idiot." He stepped away again.

She didn't know what to say, so she got in her car, waved once more, and drove home.

She thought of phoning Stacey on the way home, but she wasn't ready to break down the evening just yet. The nervous energy that had fueled her through the evening began to dissipate, and by the time she arrived home, she wanted pajamas and a glass of wine. She'd earned them.

It wasn't until she was heading up her walkway that she saw Chris. He was sitting on the top of the four stairs that led up to the entrance. He'd clearly run his hands through his dark hair several times. He wore a pair of jeans and an NYU sweater that was tattered at the sleeves. Well-worn sweaters were the best, and his looked like an old favorite. Chris's gaze roamed down once, back up, stopped at her eyes. Everly's heart stuttered. What was he doing here?

"Hey," he said.

Her words got caught in her throat while her fingers tap, tap, tapped against her purse. Taking a deep breath, Everly sat beside him, her thigh touching his. Her fingers shook. She pressed them to her legs.

Act normal. Like, other people's normal. "Hey."

They sat there, the stars and nearly full moon above them, breathing in the crisp air, saying nothing. The moment couldn't last. The best ones never could. Everly knew that. This new *thing* between them couldn't become something more. She knew that, too. But it was the best moment of her night.

[13]

Chris had no right to be there. None. Yet sitting with her in the quiet of night, the stars peeking at them from behind pockets of clouds, Chris didn't want to be anywhere else. There were a lot of things he wanted, though, and he'd learned early on in life that if he had an end goal, frivolous desires did nothing but get in the way. Knowing that didn't push him to leave. It was too rare, in his life, to be exactly where he wanted to be. The thought made him frown, so he pushed it away.

Turning his head, stopping himself from breathing her in—or, worse, leaning into her—he asked, "How was the date?"

Her smile flipped the want switch inside of him up to full blast. "It was actually really good. I had fun."

Not the answer he'd expected. His stomach reacted like she'd punched him. *You want this for her.* He'd come here to let her talk it out, to support her, to be there for her even though she would never ask. He wasn't one of her *people.* Okay, he wasn't Stacey. He was invested, though, and there was nothing wrong with letting her know he had her back. They could be friends in addition to coworkers.

Happiness shone in her eyes, and she didn't look tense. He hadn't considered that—her having fun. *This is a good thing. Damn good. Might speed up the whole process and make the ratings soar.* He pictured the headlines: RADIO SHOW PRODUCER

FINDS LOVE IN ROUND ONE. His heart slipped like a lead weight down to his stomach.

Everly's accelerated breathing brought him back to the moment. Their faces had moved closer, and she was looking at his lips, which made him look at hers, and that want twisted hard into outright desire. *Friends. You want to be friends with this woman.*

"Did he kiss you?"

She sucked in a breath.

Chris stood up. "Sorry. None of my business." Shoving his hands into the pockets of his jeans, he tried to come up with an excuse for being there on her doorstep. *Like a teenager with an unrequited crush.* Pathetic. He really needed to get his head on right, and standing on Everly's walkway wasn't doing it.

Everly stood up and walked to him, looking up at him with a new curiosity he absolutely could not explore. She opened her mouth to speak, and his heart glitched. Short-circuited.

"I just . . . I don't know why. I was curious. Sorry. I was worried about you and thought I'd drop by. I hope that's okay?" *You should babble more, man. Sound more incoherent.*

"Of course it is. It's nice that you did. You're welcome to anytime. Especially if you bring treats."

An open invitation. He wasn't sure if that was a blessing or a curse. Now what? "Listeners will be curious about how it went. No pressure, but the sooner you get your date recap on Facebook, the happier they'll be." Falling back on work conversation was always his go-to. "I'm glad it went well, but you've still got another date this week, so no falling in love after one pasta dinner."

Whatever he thought he saw in her gaze seconds earlier shuttered. She brought her hands together, twisting them in a rubbing motion. He'd made her nervous, put her on edge. He hated that. Chris reached out to touch her shoulder, but she stepped back.

"I'll get the post done tonight. I wanted to ask . . ." She trailed off, inhaled deeply, let it out slowly.

Anything. His heart puffed up. "What?" Did his voice crack? Jesus. He really was reverting to a teenager.

"Did you ask the restaurant to put us somewhere removed from the crowd?"

Chris shoved a hand through his hair and looked up at the moon, then down at the ground. "I just thought it'd make things easier on you."

She nodded, giving nothing away. "It did. Thank you."

She turned and went into her building. Didn't even say good night. Chris stood there and watched her go, a little piece of him waiting to see if she'd turn back. She didn't. Then he went home. He had work to do. It was a success; things were good. *This is exactly what you wanted.*

***

He avoided Everly most of the next day, which was cowardly but necessary. Her Facebook recap was charming, and even though he'd made sure to schedule his meetings off-site for her in-office hours, he'd still tuned in to the show. Sitting in his car, between appointments, he listened to the end of Stacey's playlist.

"That was Old Dominion, in case you didn't know, with their newest single. Speaking of newly single," Stacey said, letting the word hang.

Stage laughter cut in, and Chris smiled, knowing that his deejay was messing around with the soundboard.

"Uh-oh, the daggers my producer is shooting me through this glass makes me glad it's triple pane. *What?* Oh. She's shaking her head. It's not. Which means I'd better not make any corny jokes."

Chris could picture the look on Everly's face. He closed his eyes and leaned his head against the seat.

"No more joking around. Thank you, SUN listeners, for

sending in your very worthy bachelors for my best friend. You may have read on our Facebook page that date number one was a success. She doesn't like to talk much on the air, so I had to get her preapproval for this, but Everly's going to answer a couple of questions. You ready?"

Chris's eyes popped open as Everly's "Yes" came through his speakers.

"Can we rate the dates from one to ten?" Stacey asked.

"No."

"Would you date Owen again?"

"It would be cheating to tell you," Everly said, her soft voice sending a jolt of energy over Chris.

"No cheating. That's what got us here in the first place."

"Stacey," Everly's voice warned.

"My bad. Sorry. What's the most important quality in a man?"

Chris sat straighter.

"Honesty. Transparency."

"Good answer. I totally would have gone with *abs*, but yours is nice, too."

Stacey went on to share some of the highlights that Everly shared and then read a series of Twitter questions from listeners. Chris turned off the radio and grabbed his phone from the passenger's seat. Opening the social media app, he typed in the hashtag everlyafter.

@962SUN I went to high school with Owen. He's the best. You should totally date him again. #everlyafter

@962SUN My nephew is single and better-looking than the guys you chose this week. DM me #everlyafter

@962SUN Simon sucks. Team Everly. #everlyafter

Chris nodded in agreement and scrolled through a few more. They'd had over five hundred new followers on Twitter alone. He'd hired a remote social media person to work specifically on the traffic brought in through this. He hoped Everly wasn't scrolling through this stuff. There was a lot of positive, but there was negative as well, and she didn't need the extra stress. What he hadn't anticipated was the way it would play out for the selected bachelors.

Even if this Owen guy wasn't the one Everly chose, he'd have no trouble getting dates in the future. None of the candidates would. This was, in a sense, giving a lot of guys their fifteen minutes of fame. *What's it giving Everly?* Hopefully, everything she deserves, including a good guy.

And no, that doesn't get under your goddamn skin because this is exactly what was supposed to happen. His phone rang, saving him from his own thoughts.

"Hey," he said. He started up his car and pulled into traffic.

"You there yet?" His brother wasn't known for patience.

"Just about. I got tied up in meetings. I thought you were going to fly out here."

Something rattled in the background before Noah replied, "I am. But I just want your opinion first. See if, on first glance, it's worth taking my time to check it out."

Noah wanted him to take a look at a run-down mansion that was rumored to have been owned by a deceased Hollywood starlet. It was on the water, which, despite the fact that he lived in California, Chris didn't get out to enough.

Taking the exit for Harlow Beach, they talked more about the property. His brother was looking at a few different ones, trying to decide if he wanted to step away from their father's empire and forge his own way. Chris understood the thought but had worked too hard to jump through all his father's hoops to give up when he was this close. About twenty minutes later, Chris pulled up in front of a sprawling estate. That was the only word for it. The house and the grounds, both overlooking the ocean, were massive.

"I don't think anyone's lived here in a while," Chris said

into the phone, getting out of his car and leaning on the back of it. High, wrought iron gates let him see through to the overgrown yard, the worn, cobbled path that led to the house.

"Is it big?" Excitement shook his brother's voice.

"You've seen it. Of course it's big."

"You say that to all the girls."

Despite rolling his eyes, Chris laughed. "Jesus. What are you? Fourteen? It's what I saw online. Overlooks the ocean, the exterior needs a ton of work, and the yard is a mini-jungle. But it's got potential, bro. Serious potential."

"You think I'm a fool?"

Chris pushed off his car and walked closer to the edge of the embankment, stared out at the water, breathed in the salt air, and let go of his own worries. He'd sat on Everly's stoop, waiting for her to come home last night. What did he know about being a fool? A *lot*.

"You've got other places to look at, so I say you take your time to choose. You're sure about branching out to the West Coast?" *It'll suck if Noah ends up here just as I head home.* He wouldn't negatively influence his brother's thoughts, though. That was their dad's job.

"I feel restless and trapped. I don't know what I need or what I'm looking for just yet, but I need to strike out on my own, Chris. I'm tired of him turning every idea I have into either his baby or something entirely different from how I'd envisioned."

He nodded even though his brother couldn't see him. "What were you thinking? Buying and flipping for yourself?"

There was a pause, and Chris realized, in the quiet, he missed his brothers, his mom, and even his sister. He needed to reconnect with them soon.

"I'm thinking of a luxury bed and breakfast. Or something like that."

Chris smiled. "Really? Hospitality isn't the same as real estate, bro. Way longer to make a profit, and you have to basically wait on people's whims. We're only an hour from LA here. You could make good money off this buy if you fix it up. Even with the costs of hiring a crew and renovations."

"Now you sound like him. Buy, fix, sell. I want to build a legacy. My own. I think. Something he can't get in the way of. Something that, even if it crumbles, will tell a story a hundred years down the road."

"Like this house."

"Exactly."

The drive back gave Chris time to think about what Noah said, about building his own legacy. He believed he'd be doing that very thing. Once he took over as head of communications for all his father's companies, he had plans that would unite and strengthen every one of them. His brothers pushed back more with their father than Chris did. Mostly because he worked better if he had a tangible goal set in front of him to reach. He was almost there.

Switching on the radio, thinking about what he could grab for dinner that would be quick and filling, he pressed the button for another station. He liked to see what the other guys were up to.

Ads. Ads. "You're listening to 102.9 CALI. Up next, we're talking to Simon Westwood of Westwood Paper Products. Some of you might know him from his store, which is having a massive blowout sale this weekend. Any kind of paper for all your paper needs."

Chris's fingers tightened on the steering wheel. *Is that . . .*

"Some of you might know him as the jilted former lover of one Miss Everly Dean of 96.2 SUN. Did you guys hear her outburst a couple of weeks ago? Smart people that we are, one of our deejays recorded the audio before they took it off their website. Listen to this."

Everly's voice filled the interior of his car like anger filled his gut.

"I found Simon in bed with his personal assistant this morning. You do not want to know how she was assisting him." Background

sound effects cut in and then, *"If you happen to find a man who looks like Chris Pine, acts like Chris Hemsworth, smiles like Chris Pratt, and has a body like Chris Evans's, I'll rethink things. But until then? I am officially off the market."*

The deejay came back live. "All I can say is, 'Poor Simon.' I mean, this guy gets his life aired out in the most public of ways without being able to share his side of the story, and then his ex announces she's done with men only to turn around and become the star of her own dating game show. Well, we've got Simon's back, and he's telling his side right after this next music break. You can count on us to give you the goods and the tunes."

Chris smacked the steering wheel. "Son of a bitch."

They'd had a contingency plan for Simon worked out with the legal department so he couldn't come at them for defamation. Everly had not said his last name, which was a huge saving grace. Chris hadn't considered the loser would not only find a way to make the public feel sorry for him but use the momentum of the contest to pump up his own business. His jaw tightened. "You should have." He definitely should have thought about the guy striking back. *Shit.*

He also hadn't considered anger he'd feel on Everly's behalf. As if the jerk hadn't already embarrassed her and treated her poorly, he was still using her for his own personal and professional gain.

The car ahead cut him off, making Chris slam on the brakes and jolt forward. He swore even as he forced his breathing under control. He might not have anticipated this move by her ex, but he'd be strategizing *their* next ones. *If* that was what she wanted. He needed to see her and talk to her, because there was no way he'd put ratings above her mental health. If there was any chance of her letting Simon get under her skin, he'd call the promotion off and just deal with the consequences.

[14]

Everly had emptied her entire closet. Every article of clothing she owned was scattered around her small bedroom. Lifting the bottle she'd set on her nightstand to her lips, she finished off what was left of the cranberry vodka cooler she'd opened. It tasted bitter and warm.

"I see you've been busy," Stacey said, walking into Everly's bedroom.

She'd heard the door open, so she wasn't surprised to see her friend stroll into the room. Why had she given her a key again? Oh, because someone should have access to her home in the case Everly slipped in the shower and couldn't get to the door. In the event she got a cat and needed someone to feed it. *Right. When you're out of town on all your spontaneous adventures?*

"I'm minimizing." Hands on her hips, she stared around the room, wondering where to start. That was the "in" thing to do, right?

Stacey gestured with her chin toward the two empty bottles on her table. "Looks like you're drinking."

Everly shot her a look and went to the pile in the middle of her bed. Her preppy phase. Collared shirts, pleated skirts, and pale cardigans. She scooped it all up and carried it to the corner of her room. The over-and-done pile. That pile was going to be huge.

She sank onto the side of the bed. "I'm cleaning out my

closet and actually getting rid of things, rather than convincing myself I'll wear them one day. I deserve a drink or two." She crossed her arms over her chest and stared at Stacey, giving her what she hoped was a cheeky smile. "The new me. This is the thirty-year-old me."

Stacey chuckled, leaned on the doorjamb. "Amen, sister. As long as your thirty-year-old, independent self isn't drowning some misplaced sorrows over your asshat ex rehashing your dirty laundry—no pun intended—while reenacting *The Purge* on your poor wardrobe."

Eyeing a very unique pile by the closet door, Stacey crouched down. "What the—?" She lifted crocheted cardigans—or what were meant to be cardigans—shawls, and scarves. She arched her brow so high it almost disappeared into her hair. "What were you thinking?"

Everly giggled as she stood up. "Dad wanted to buy a boat, and it pissed Mom off. She hates the water. So she took up crocheting. It was a dark time that resulted in all of that. I should hang on to those and give them to you on special occasions."

Stacey stood up. "You're a mean drunk."

Everly's phone buzzed on her nightstand. She spun a little too fast in her attempt to look at it. Okay, maybe she didn't drink all that often, and maybe she'd started today because Simon the Snake had slithered even lower than expected.

CHRIS: I need to drop by and talk to you. Is that okay?

Everly picked up her phone and typed:

Why not?

He might as well join the party. She set the phone down and turned again, slower this time. She looked at the mess in her room and sighed, frustrated with herself. "You know, I never wear this stuff. Why do I even have it?"

Moving into the room, Stacey went to the new-and-improved pile that they'd mostly purchased last week for her dates. "Because it's hard to let go of things and say good-bye to them even when we should? Because each of them represents a stage in your life? A little piece of who you were, even if you don't want to be that person anymore?"

Everly snorted and walked to the bed. She curled up in the middle of it, her body curving around the pile Stacey was admiring. "You're pretty philosophical about my spring cleaning."

Stacey lifted an armful of the garments and walked to the open door of the closet. She began hanging things back up. "It's summer. Too late for spring cleaning."

"Or really early," Everly said, her tongue feeling thick.

"Simon is a dick."

"Agreed."

Stacey walked back to the bed, tilted her head, and stared at Everly, whose eyes were feeling kind of heavy. "You're such a lightweight, Dean."

She nodded, her cheek brushing up and down against the softness of her pillowcase. "Lightweight loser in love."

"You weren't in love with him."

Everly rolled to her back. "I wasn't. Thank God. But I never am. I'm no better than my parents, Stace. I can't make a decision and stick to it."

Stacey sank down onto the bed, more clothes draped over her arm. "Bullshit. You're nothing like your parents. And when you actually meet the one, you'll stick. You haven't ditched me."

Moving just her eyes, she looked at her friend. Blond hair fell over her bare shoulder. Stacey always seemed so *sure*. What was that like?

She poked Stacey's arm. "You'd just hunt me down."

"As long as you know it. Don't let him get to you. It works in our favor." She got back up and worked on returning Everly's clothes to their rightful place.

"My mom called. She heard Simon's side of things. 'Men make mistakes,' she said. 'Love is hard. Impossible if you're going to give up without a fight.'"

The hangers clattered together. "Then let your mom date Simon on one of her breaks from your dad."

Everly laughed, pressing a hand to her stomach so it didn't jostle around inside. She *was* a lightweight. "That's gross."

The buzzer to her apartment sounded, and she rolled to her side too quickly, which made her groan. "Forgot to say Chris is dropping by."

Stacey bounced up. "Perfect. Any more than two and it's the start of a party. Your favorite. I'll get it. You get up and help me put this shit away."

"Yes, Mom," she called, throwing her arm over her face and not moving.

She wanted to have a little nap. Stacey and Chris could figure out what to do about Simon. She'd just follow their lead. *God, wouldn't it be great if I could actually release control like that? You don't need to let go of the control—you need to take it.* She sighed. Her mildly drunk self was right. She needed to be in charge of what came next. Other than putting her clothes away and figuring out something for dinner.

"Spring cleaning," she heard Stacey say.

"It looks like spring threw up. I've never seen you in anything other than black and gray."

That wasn't entirely true. He'd seen her the other night after her date.

Everly slowly uncovered her eyes, her stomach rolling for an entirely different reason now. One she didn't want to examine right this minute.

Chris's voice was thick with amusement. "Who knew you had this much color in your wardrobe."

"Hi."

Chris stopped where Stacey had, in the doorway of her bedroom, surveying her space. His hair was windblown, and he wore a dark T-shirt and jeans. He looked good. He looked relaxed, but he must be here for a reason. *Why are you not freaking out over what the reason could be?*

"Hi." Their eyes met and held. A shiver zipped through her body like lightning. There and gone in the blink of an eye. She didn't blink. She just stared.

"Fascinating conversation, but I'm going to go make Two Drinks Max here some coffee."

Chris chuckled, and Everly's eyes moved down to his throat to watch the way it moved with his laughter. She liked the sound of it. Had she ever noticed that about a man before? She thought about Owen's smile from the other night. He'd had a nice laugh, hadn't he? Or had she been too nervous to realize?

"Wouldn't have pegged you as a lightweight," he said, moving farther into the room.

Like the earth jolted a little, Everly's head spun, and it wasn't the booze. There was something surreal, almost dreamlike, about Chris Jansen, Mr. Suit and Tie, who'd barely spoken to her over the last year, standing in her bedroom. More incredible? She wasn't panicked. When had that happened? She continued to stare, waited for the bubbles of anxiety to hit the surface. All she felt, though, was disappointment that she probably looked like a bigger mess than her room. She realized too late that all her clothes were on display, and some of them were not ones she wanted to share with this man.

As if he'd read her mind and had a sixth sense, his eyes flitted about and landed on her Care Bears T-shirt. The one that read GRUMPY IN THE MORNING—LOVE-A-LOT AT NIGHT. The two respective bears sat with their backs to each other. Chris bit his lip, but it didn't hide his smile.

She jackknifed, pulling herself up, and reached out to snag it from its pile.

His laughter did funnier things to her stomach than the vodka. *Not unpleasant things.*

"Cute," he said, grinning at Everly.

Everly stood up, hoping her cheeks weren't blazing pink. It *was* a cute shirt, and it was cozy. "What are you doing here?"

Chris frowned. "Could we have this conversation in your living room or kitchen?"

Everly nodded and then followed behind him, wondering why she'd never noticed how good he looked in jeans before.

He doesn't wear jeans to work, and you generally resist staring at your boss's ass. Not just because he was her boss either. Memories of the other night came back to her, and her cheeks felt like they caught fire. Good thing she'd capped her list at ten or she'd have to add: No lusting after off-limits men who make you feel off balance, especially when they are in charge of your career. Without a limit, it would have been a very long list.

She *was* a wimp. Two coolers and now she was all brain-fuzzy over Chris Jansen? Good thing she had another date coming up tomorrow.

Still holding her Care Bears shirt, Everly took a seat on her couch. Stacey was curled up on a chair. Chris walked to the window and looked out, his square jaw set tight. *Did he hear Simon on the air? He must have. Was he mad? I didn't do anything!*

"Coffee is almost ready," Stacey said.

Everly's manners kicked in belatedly. "Chris, do you want a cup?"

He didn't look at her when he declined. When he shared a look with Stacey, she felt like she'd taken a punch to the stomach. What were they communicating with unspoken words?

Had Simon screwed things up for her? The interview with him sucked, but it wasn't that big a deal, was it?

The website and all their social media were still going crazy with the contest. Companies and corporations were contacting them for ad time and upping the prices they were willing to pay. They were bringing in more corporate sponsors than any of them had imagined. She had no reason to worry. *That doesn't always make it go away, though.*

She braced her back against the softness of her couch, let herself sink into it. Stacey got up and grabbed some coffee. Whether she was just being a good friend or giving them a moment to talk, Everly didn't know. What she did know was she owed Stacey a dinner or a bottle of expensive wine. Something to thank her for how awesome she'd been.

Stacey came back with two mugs and handed one to Everly before returning to her seat.

Everly sipped. Waited. Sipped again. Patience was not her strong suit. "What's going on?"

Chris met her gaze finally. "I wanted to talk to you about calling off the contest."

Everly jolted forward, sloshing coffee over the rim of the mug and on her hand. "Damn it."

Chris rushed forward, took the cup from her. "Did you burn yourself? Are you okay?"

"I'm fine," she ground out, shaking the scalding liquid off her fingers.

Stacey stood as well, going to grab a cloth, she hoped, and Chris took Everly's wrist to examine the burn. "You need to run cold water on your hand."

Shaking him off, his touch seeming hotter than the coffee, she stood and walked ahead of him, ran the water. "I'm fine. I'm fine." But the water stung as she slipped her hand under the spray. Looking at him over her shoulder, she saw his brow was furrowed in worry. "What do you mean, call it off?"

"Yes, explain yourself," Stacey said, joining them in the kitchen. She tossed the cloth she'd used in the sink. Everly would put it in the wash later. Right now, she needed to hear what Chris had to say.

Stacey pointed at him. "We aren't quitters."

Chris gave an exaggerated sigh, placed his hands on his hips, and stared down at the floor. When he looked up, he pinned Stacey with a glare. "Do you *ever* remember that I'm your boss?"

Stacey rolled her eyes. "Sorry. Explain yourself, *boss*."

Everly bit her lip to keep from laughing, because it didn't look like Chris found her all that funny. She turned off the water, which brought Chris's attention back to her. He grabbed a tea towel from the bar on the stove and came closer, taking her hand in his. Her heart galloped, and she told it to chill out. Then she focused on keeping her body stiff so she didn't do something stupid like lean in and rest against him.

"It's still red," he commented, brows furrowed.

She tugged her hand away, drying it with the towel. "It's fine. Can you please answer the question?"

"Your ex is using this as a promotional tool to turn the spotlight on himself," he said.

"Uh, yeah," Stacey said.

Chris stayed focused on Everly. "I don't want you to feel stuck. We can take a different approach. I won't have him sullying your name all over town."

She didn't even feel the smile sneak up on her, but she felt it in the way her cheeks stretched. She probably looked like a fool. "Sully? What am I, a heroine in a historical romance novel? Are you worried I won't make a good impression on high society?"

Stacey cracked up but tried to look serious. "Perhaps you could challenge Simon to a duel."

"At dawn," Everly added.

Stacey rolled her eyes. "Duh. That's the only time you can challenge someone to a duel."

"I don't think it is. I'm pretty sure you can do it at sunset, too."

Chris made a growly sound of impatience, which sent a shiver running over Everly's skin. "As funny as you two are, I'm being serious. I didn't anticipate he'd try to tell his side, and I should have. You don't need to feel boxed in by his actions or this contest."

Rubbing the material of the tea towel soothed her fluttering heart. Mildly. "This is what I signed up for. We're using what happened as promotion, so it doesn't surprise me that he would as well. I'm not backing out or giving up." She thought of her list. Rule six: *Be bold, even if it gives you hives.* She could do bold. She paused. *No hives.* "I said I'd do this, and I will. If he wants to paint a different picture, that's on him."

Running a hand through his hair, Chris stared at her like he expected her to change her mind. She and Stacey exchanged a glance. Stacey shrugged.

"Despite the security, this could draw the wrong kind of people in. His stupid interview could have people trashing you online instead of supporting you."

"That could happen anyway. One of the guys she dates who doesn't get pushed through to the next round could say things online. We've thought of this," Stacey said.

Chris caught Everly's eye, and it struck her that she wasn't as nervous with him in her space. The first time he'd come, she'd had trouble catching her breath.

Stacey waved a hand. "This doesn't change anything. Promo and ad space interest are through the roof. Our social media people are working overtime to keep up with the number of messages and emails. People would go crazy if we stopped this."

Everly nodded, and Chris moved closer.

Her fierce friend paused, and Everly smiled at her. "Can you give us a minute, Stace?"

Her friend's brows arched up, her forehead crinkling. "Okay," she said, drawing the word out longer than necessary.

Everly's heart rhythm tripled. Being alone with Chris was enough to sober her all the way up. So much for the whole I-can-breathe-around-him-now theory. She clenched the towel between her hands, playing a one-woman version of tug-of-war with the two ends.

"I'm worried that this will get out of hand. That I cornered you into this," he said, his voice lowering.

His arm brushed against hers, but she didn't step back. The warmth of his body and the heat of his gaze made her want to step *forward*. The alcohol had pretty much worn off, and she felt hyperaware of . . . everything. Like that chick in *Twilight* after she turned. *What is wrong with you? Finish having a normal conversation with your boss. Pretend you've got this.*

"We can't go backward because Simon is a jerk. The whole reason I'm in this mess is because he's an idiot. Well, and also because my best friend is a bit of a wild card." Also because of a list she'd decided to make and see through, but there was no way she was letting him in on that little secret.

His gaze snapped back to hers. "I should have expected retribution from him. I let you down, and I don't want you to feel uncomfortable."

Without meaning to, which surprised her because she was usually very purposeful with her touching, she pressed a hand to his chest. A charge of electricity zipped from her hand straight up her arm and burrowed right into her chest. Into her heart. Letting herself acknowledge the feeling wasn't smart. He'd been very clear the other night that she was an employee. End of story. *He's helping you find a man for goodness' sake.* She knew he cared for her, for all of them. She didn't need to mess up this tentative foray into friendship by misinterpreting his feelings or her own. Her thoughts, *and feelings*, were reserved for the five remaining men she had scheduled dates with.

"I'm thirty years old and single. I want forever, but I'm scared to find it. It's time for me to get a little uncomfortable."

The moment held, froze, and spun out. Her hand on his chest absorbed the steady thump of his heart so it felt like her palm had its own heartbeat. She physically fought the urge to curl into him and fit her body to his.

"What are we doing here, people?" Stacey called from the other room.

The moment snapped like a twig underfoot, and Everly all but jumped back.

"Moving forward," Chris said, his voice rough and his gaze sharp, focused. On her.

Stacey appeared in the doorway. "Yay. Can we do it with food? I'm starving."

Everly rolled her eyes, stepped around Chris and out of his personal space. Her lungs loosened, and she pulled in a deep breath.

"Yes. You order something. I need to put my clothes away and figure out what I'm wearing tomorrow night on date number two."

She walked away, back to her room, resisting the urge to curl up with her clothes again. If the effects of the alcohol had already started to wear off, why did she feel so very intoxicated?

[15]

A strange kind of energy pulsed through Everly's body. It was an I've-got-this-screw-Simon-and-the-girl-who-rode-him type of enthusiasm. Tonight's date *would* be a success. Every bit as much as the last one. Rule seven: No more holding back. She was a smart, fun, *funny* person who could handle a second first date in the same week. With that reminder, she pulled the door of Mocktails open. Despite its moniker, it did serve alcoholic beverages. She'd checked. Just inside the door, waiting to the right of the hostess station by a few other people, was her date. Corbin Brown, thirty-four years old, owned his own house-painting business and liked animals, sailing, and hosting parties. The party thing made her shudder, but Everly reminded herself she was doing this to become more of the person she imagined herself to be. Someone who didn't feel like she was going to throw up if they had to hang out with more than three people.

He caught sight of her, his dark eyes widening and a smile taking over his angular face. As he walked toward her, she realized that he was well over six feet, with shoulders like a linebacker.

"Everly," he said, his voice softer than she'd expected from such a large man. He pulled her into a hug before she could set any boundaries.

Her surprise was muffled against his chest, and he let go of her before she could say a word. "Sorry," he said, looking down at her. "I'm just so glad to meet you."

That's nice. "Thank you," she said, somewhat stiffly. She held out her hand. "It's nice to meet you, too, Corbin."

His wide mouth turned up in a one-sided grin. He shook her hand and said nothing, but she sensed his amusement.

"We have a reservation under your name, right?" He gestured for her to go ahead of him.

The young woman at the front had her hair pulled back and a happy smile on her face. "Welcome to Mocktails. Do you have a reservation?"

"We do," Everly said, her voice catching. "Sorry. Yes. It's under *Dean*."

She spotted the security detail eyeing her from the corner of the waiting area and gave a half wave. Corbin's eyes followed her gaze even as the hostess said to follow her.

"You bring a backup date in case this one doesn't go well?" he asked.

Everly laughed. "Not exactly."

They were brought to the second floor—which was more of a raised seating area than an actual second story. Low lights lit the way, and laughter, clinking glasses, and music set the mood as relaxed and carefree. The mood of the room. Not Everly. She willed her heart rate to slow down as she slid into the chair Corbin held for her.

"Your waiter will be with you in one moment," the hostess said and left them.

Corbin beamed at her across the table. Everly tried to smile back but couldn't settle facing the entire room. They were in a corner, so she could see everyone and they could see her. *They aren't looking at you.*

"You okay?" Corbin asked.

Everly saw the security guy take a seat at the bar. What even was her life right now? She was on a date in a crowded place with a stranger and a bodyguard. She'd rather be home watching

Veronica Mars, texting Stacey, and eating cookie dough. *But you're not, because you turned thirty, not thirteen. So, get your head in the game, Dean.* Rule number one: Focus on the good.

"I'm fine. I just get a little nervous staring out at the room."

The waiter approached even as Corbin stood. "That's an easy fix. Have my seat."

"Oh, everything okay here, folks?" the goateed waiter, who looked too young to serve anything *but* mocktails, asked.

Everly's pulse skittered, and she stood up. *People aren't staring at you guys. You're not making a commotion. He's being an absolute gentleman.*

"Everything is great. My girl just wants to sit on the other side of the table."

Corbin switched spots with her, and the waiter took their drink orders after telling them the special.

My girl? Stop. Focus on the good. He's thoughtful, and what was he supposed to say? "My blind date that I applied to a radio station for is being weird and wants to switch spots"? He simplified it. You should try that.

"Better?"

"Yes." Everly nodded, reminding herself of her earlier energy. *I've got this.* She pushed aside all her nerves, drawing on the inner strength she used when she had to attend a work function or one of her mother's parties. "Everything is great. Sorry about that. Do you want to look at the menus first?"

"For sure," Corbin said.

They glanced through, and after declining to share an appetizer, Everly chose the grilled salmon with baby potatoes. Corbin ordered a steak with onion rings, fries, and a side salad.

He shrugged when the waiter left their table the second time, picking up the beer he'd ordered. "I require a lot of fuel."

Everly smiled, her shoulders loosening. "I guess so."

"I don't get it," Corbin said.

"What?" Everly paused with her wineglass halfway to her mouth.

"Gorgeous woman like you? I don't understand why men cheat, anyway, but when you've got the deluxe model at home, what the hell was he thinking?"

She grinned, but she wasn't entirely sure if she considered it a compliment. She decided to sidestep the conversation entirely. He pulled his phone out of his pocket as she asked, "You own your own business. What's that like?"

Corbin checked something on his phone, then glanced up. "I love it. I've got a crew of guys who work under me, so I can work whatever hours I want. My mom takes care of the paperwork, and I can take Scooter with me everywhere I go."

"Scooter?" *He drives a scooter?*

He picked up his phone and swiped his thumb across it, all while bumping his chair over so they were closer and she could see.

"My dog. He's just the sweetest thing ever. I can't wait for you to meet him."

Everly's stomach dipped like she'd just fallen flat on her ass on a hard surface. She stretched her lips wider and hoped she looked like she was smiling and not panicking as she looked at the pictures.

Oh, the pictures. There were so many pictures. By the time she'd seen his Lhasa apso in a pumpkin costume, a dog-size Green Bay Packers jersey, and Christmas pajamas, she needed a refill for her drink.

"He sleeps on my bed. My last girlfriend didn't like sharing her pillow, so I've trained him only to use mine," Corbin said, setting his phone down and winking at Everly. "So that'll never be an issue if you don't like to share."

I'm guessing that wouldn't be my issue, dude. If she smiled any wider, her lips would crack. Glancing around, she saw their waiter. "Our food!"

Thank goodness she'd switched seats because she just *knew* people were looking their way. Her cheeks burned when she realized how loud she'd been. Corbin let loose a deep chuckle.

"Hungry girl."

They were partway through their meals when he committed the cardinal sin. Sharing was fine if you were both on board with it. It was a deal breaker, in Everly's world, on a first date. Sure enough, he reached across with no warning and scooped up a potato, popped it in his mouth.

"Delicious. You want an onion ring?"

"No, thank you." *Don't be so uptight. He's comfortable in his own skin. You can't say the same. I mean, he's a lumberjack of a man who dresses up his dog. He has to feel pretty confident to show those pictures . . . wait. What if he and the dog have matching costumes?* Her brain flashed to Scooter and Corbin in matching pumpkin outfits, and she choked on her bite of salmon.

"You okay?"

She nodded, her eyes watering. Taking a long sip of water, she forced herself to think of something else, but matching costumes kept coming to mind. Corbin in a Santa outfit, Scooter as an elf.

"You've got a great smile," he said, reaching across the table to cover her hand with his.

His phone rang, and though he looked sorry, he answered it. Everly used the moment to regain her focus so she wouldn't get a case of the giggles.

"He probably just misses me. Put him up to the phone," Corbin said in a loud whisper.

Everly's eyes widened. *No way. He wouldn't.*

Corbin's shoulders curled forward as he pushed his plate away and spoke into the phone. "I'll be home soon, buddy. You miss me? Aren't you having fun with Grandma?"

Everly glanced around. No one was staring at them.

"Who's a good dog? I love you, buddy. I'll be home soon."

Keeping her eyes on her plate, Everly picked at her salmon.

"Sorry about that," Corbin said.

She looked up again, hoping her eyes were judgment-free. *Focus on the good. He loves his dog.*

"No problem. Everything okay?"

The happy light in Corbin's eyes had dimmed. "It is. We're not apart often. I spoil him a bit, I guess. My mom says hi."

Everly had no words. She shoveled the salmon into her mouth and nodded as she chewed.

"Might have to cut it short," Corbin said a few minutes later, glancing at his phone again.

Everly said a silent thank-you. "Sure. If you need to."

Because she definitely wanted to.

***

"You're lying," Stacey said into the phone as Everly crawled into bed that night.

Part of her had wondered if Chris would be waiting for her on her stoop again, but he wasn't.

You're not disappointed, she'd told herself as she let herself into her home. When Stacey phoned, just as she was heading to bed, she lied to herself again and said she hadn't wanted it to be him. She wasn't quite sure what was going on in her head and her heart where he was concerned, but it felt like they were dangerously close to establishing a friendship.

Everly refocused on her conversation. "I wish I were. In the end, he didn't finish his meal. He boxed it up for Scooter." Might as well tell her everything. "Then he ordered a chocolate-free dessert for the dog to make it up to him."

The line was suspiciously quiet.

"Are you laughing?" She grinned and leaned against her headboard.

Stacey cleared her throat. "Of course not. So, what were you thinking for hashtags?"

Everly smiled. "How about *hashtag no matching outfits?*"

Her friend didn't hold back this time as she snort-laughed and tried to speak around it. "That's good. What about *hashtag love me, love my dog?*"

"*Hashtag man's best friend and more.*" Everly ignored the text coming in.

"What about *hashtag TMI about my dog*?" Stacey got her laughter under control. "Why does he even need a date when he has Scooter?"

"Not all restaurants allow animals, you know. The man likes his food."

"I'm sorry, Ev," Stacey said, her tone evening out.

"No reason to be. I'll figure out a way to write it up nicely, but I bet you can guess who wins this week's round."

This was good. She could laugh about it and the evening had taken such strange twists and turns, she wasn't even obsessing about anything she said that might have come across as wrong or dumb or embarrassing.

"Owen sweeps the week," Stacey cheered.

"Paws down," Everly agreed, both of them breaking into laughter again.

When she hung up with Stacey, Everly saw that Chris had texted.

CHRIS: Night go okay?

EVERLY: Don't you want to wait to read about it on Facebook?

CHRIS: I'd always rather hear it from you.

Now, why did that sentence do something funny to her belly? She really needed to pull herself together. Between turning thirty, worrying about her job, breaking up with Simon, and starring in a one-person dating drama, her thoughts were jumbled.

EVERLY: He loves his dog. A lot.

CHRIS: That's . . . good?

EVERLY: Took him home dessert to apologize for being out.

A gif came through of Ryan Reynolds face-palming, and Everly laughed. She loved a good gif.

EVERLY: Exactly. Owen wins this week.

CHRIS: Clearly. Night, Everly.

EVERLY: Night.

She lay awake, staring at the ceiling, the breeze wafting into her room from the open window. Taking stock of how she felt, she realized that despite the date tonight, she felt *good.* She was going to sleep smiling rather than cataloging the things that went wrong tonight. Maybe there was a chance for her to find her happy through all of this. If nothing else, it could be a chance for her to nail down what she didn't want out of life while, maybe, giving her the courage to go after what she *did* want. *You just need to figure out what that is.*

[16]

Rule four: *Try something new each month. Rule six: Be bold, even if it gives you hives.* It didn't seem to matter which of her rules she recited in her head, Everly couldn't make herself get out of the car. She hated going to the gym. Okay, she'd never gone to a gym, but the idea of sweating near strangers or listening to big, bulging men grunt through weight lifts just weirded her out. In her head, all gyms were sort of like a bad eighties flashback—teased hair, spandex, and Jane Fonda bodysuits. *If you go in, it's a twofer: two rules, one activity.*

She gripped the steering wheel, wondering what she'd been thinking. *You were thinking of doing something for yourself.* A couple of listeners had come into the station to pick up their free passes to a local fitness center and raved about the place. Everly entertained the idea of checking it out, telling herself it would be a great way to meet people and get outside her Boring Comfort Zone, which Stacey referred to as her *BCZ.* To be fair to herself, she'd already pushed the boundaries of her comfort several times lately. She'd gone for sushi—which wasn't her favorite—on the latest date with her first like on the app, Brad. Total boundary pushing. *So what's one more?*

"Yet you're still sitting in the car." She looked through the windshield at the quaint, rectangular building. She'd watched several people go in and out. The kickboxing class she'd looked up online, one of the ones recommended by the listeners, started in ten minutes. Everly was intrigued by the idea of kicking and punching a heavy bag as a way to expel stress. Every woman wanted to be able to go a little Black Widow now and again. Black Widow kicked some serious ass and probably never sat in her vehicle wondering if she should go for it. "Consider it work. This way you can verify whether or not this place is as great as their ads say."

That bolstered her courage a bit, enough to get her out of the car and into the gym. It was different from how she'd expected . . . more sedate, with less spandex and fewer mirrors. A woman dressed in athletic wear similar to her own—yoga pants and a tank top—greeted her with an easy smile. Her red hair was pulled into a side braid, and she didn't *look* like she lived and breathed weight training. *See? Not so intimidating.*

"Welcome. Are you joining us for a class tonight?"

As she walked toward the reception desk, some of her unease loosened. "I am. I haven't been before. I was hoping to drop in on the kickboxing."

The woman typed something into the computer. "Awesome. I'm Misha. That's one of my favorite classes. The instructor is great for all levels."

Misha asked a few questions, charged a reasonable amount, and led Everly through a state-of-the-art fitness center. It was busy with people on treadmills, ellipticals, and other machines. Everly kept her gaze on the receptionist's back so she didn't accidentally lock eyes with anyone. One night. Forty-five minutes of cardio. She could handle that in a roomful of strangers who would never see her again. *Unless you love it—then you could be a regular; you could get a membership.* An image of herself as Black Widow kicking ass popped into her overactive brain. It made her smile. One step at a time. Music buzzed quietly through ceiling speakers, and the news played on low from a television in the corner. There were rooms off the central fitness area with blackened windows, which increased her comfort level. Everything was better when people weren't staring. Misha stopped in front of one of the far rooms, and Everly heard conversations coming from within. Laughter rang out, and different music played. *You can do this.* She felt like she was getting her cardio just by showing up and getting to the right room.

"Did you want me to introduce you to Rob, the instructor?" Misha smiled at her.

"No, thank you. I'll just find a spot at the back."

When Misha left, Everly continued standing just outside the room, pressing her fingers into her thigh. Things that could go wrong: She could fall flat on her face, she could kick someone, someone could kick her, she could get a concussion, she could sweat right through her clothing. *Way to think positive.* Okay. She could do positive. If she did sweat through her shirt, it wasn't white, so there was that. She could pick up some cool moves and feel more confident when she was walking alone. If she sucked or made a fool of herself, no one would know.

"Everly?"

She spun around, her heart jumping into her throat. Chris stood before her dressed in athletic shorts and a plain gray T-shirt that hugged his chest and revealed surprisingly sculpted arms. His hair was a little sweaty at the sides, making it look darker, and he was breathing faster than normal.

Her tongue worked itself into a knot.

Chris leaned in, and Everly caught the hint of sweat mingled in with his regular scent. *That should be gross. Sweat is gross.* Only he didn't look or smell gross. Nerve endings went haywire along her skin, surprising her into stepping back.

"What are you doing here?" Chris's eyes roamed over her once, then locked on her own.

Find your words. Hello, tongue? Now would be an excellent time to remember how to speak. The music in the room behind them swelled, pumping out a heavy beat. It matched what her heart was doing in her chest.

"Do you usually work out here?" A slight smile tilted his

lips, and his gaze softened, narrowed so it was like she was all he could see.

She shook her head. "Kickboxing. I'm going to try it." *Awesome job, Yoda. You can speak.*

Chris looked around her into the room and lifted his hand. Who was he waving at? Did *he* work out here regularly? The shape of his chest and arms suggested this wasn't *his* first time in such a place. He focused on her again. "Is there a reason?"

She forced her eyes upward. "Pardon?" Why was her mouth so dry?

He arched a brow. She didn't blame him. Her inability to string words together was brow-lift-worthy.

"Kickboxing. You just trying it for fun or . . . do you feel like you need a way to defend yourself for a particular reason?"

Her pulse settled at the light undercurrent of worry in his voice. Her heart quivered once and then settled to an acceptable pace. She waved her hands, dismissing the notion. "No. Not at all. I . . . well, I . . . I'm just trying something new. We always offer passes to this place, so I thought I'd give it a go." She probably looked completely out of place. *Don't think like that. I could be a kickboxer. Show some damn spine, Everly. Look like you belong. Be bold.*

She straightened her back, squared her shoulders. "I should get in there. I don't want to miss anything."

Not waiting for a reply, she went in and was happy to see there were only a half dozen other people, not including the instructor.

"Welcome. Come on in," the tall, dark-haired guy greeted. He had pretty big muscles, but Everly wouldn't call them *bulging*. He didn't look like he made odd, creepy noises when he lifted weights. *See? You always imagine it will be worse than it is.* "Okay, everyone, welcome to kickboxing. I'm your instructor, Rob. I see a couple of new faces. Don't be shy. Don't be hesitant. This will be a combination of cardio and strength building. We'll do some stretches to start, go through a few standard moves, and then we'll break into partners."

Everly's heart clutched. She'd have to partner with the instructor. It was gym class all over again. Last girl standing partnered with the teacher because no one else wanted to join up. She tapped her fingers against her thigh and inhaled deeply. Her breath caught on a familiar scent, and she turned her head when someone stepped close to her side, shoulder brushing hers.

"What are you doing?" she whispered to Chris, relief that it was him pumping through her blood.

"Kickboxing. Thought I'd give it a try." He grinned at her and then turned his head, waving back to the instructor, who was waving at him.

Her stomach pitched like a boat caught in the rapids. *You can do this. Pretend he's Stacey.* She side-eyed him. They talked every day now, in person or via text. Sometimes on the phone. They were officially friends. *Friends don't sweat in front of friends.* This was supposed to be easy. Try something new.

Chris's baby finger brushed against hers, and a spark shot through her like a jolt of electricity restarting an engine. "Breathe," he whispered.

Oddly enough? She did. *You've got this. Even if you don't, pretend you do.*

"Okay," Rob said after he'd led them through a series of yoga poses. He was surprisingly agile and flexible for such a big guy. She didn't know if Chris was because if she wanted to not fall over in front of him, she needed to keep her eyes glued to the instructor.

"Feet planted shoulder-width apart. You want to keep your core tight but your body loose." Some of the words were drowned out by Everly's heartbeat as it picked up its pace, beginning to thunder in her ears. *Breathe. Just listen to the instruction. Just listen to his voice.* Every time she inhaled, she caught a hint of Chris, and it wrecked her focus.

Rob walked them through a cross punch, a hook, uppercut, and jab. He made the movement look fluid and easy, but Everly felt clunky.

"You're doing great," Chris whispered from beside her, following the motions with the ease of someone well practiced.

She glanced his way, stared at his profile for a minute, missing Rob's instruction for combining the moves.

"What relaxes you?"

"What?"

He stepped closer, still punching the air. "Think of something that relaxes you. There has to be something you can think of that settles you the way tapping your fingers does. Picture that. Forget about everything else."

Wait. What? How did he know about her tapping? Rob continued to model the movements, increasing the pace. When he began walking through the classroom, Everly focused all her attention on what she was doing.

Right, right, left. Step forward, uppercut. Rob nodded when he approached.

"Nice job. This guy distracting you?" He grinned at them, giving Chris a friendly shove.

Chris blew out a noisy breath. "Shut up, man."

Rob ignored him. "Because I could show you how to drop him to his knees with just a couple of moves."

Despite the fact that sweat was starting to drip down her back, her heart was going too fast for what she was doing, and she was ultra-aware of Chris beside her, she laughed. "I'd like to learn that."

"Hey!" Chris stopped punching and stared at her.

Everly's mouth dropped open. She dropped her own fists, bringing one to her mouth to hide the grin, then gave up. "I didn't mean for you, necessarily."

Chris stared at her, his lips twitching with amusement. "Really?"

Feeling an unexpected wave of bravery—maybe from endorphins—she put her fists back up and smiled at Rob, then looked at Chris. "Not unless you make me mad."

Rob laughed. "I like her. She's feisty."

Everly's breath caught. She was? *Feisty* wasn't a word she applied to herself. She liked it.

"If you really want to kick his ass, or anyone else's, let's adjust your stance. Another time, we can work on disabling a guy for the hell of it."

Rob corrected her position, telling her to angle her hips in a slightly different way, how to stabilize her feet, then moved back to the front of the class.

"Okay, we'll work through some kicks, put it all together, and then we're going to work on sparring." His voice easily carried over the music.

"You know him?" Everly asked, enjoying the thrum of energy vibrating through her body.

"My neighbor and friend."

Ahh. Likely the reason we get so many free passes given to the station for doing a live event.

The kicks were more fun than she'd expected, but the combination of jab, jab, cross punch, kick, kick took more work. By the sixth time, she got it down and felt a burst of satisfaction pump through her blood.

"Nice job. You're a natural," Chris said, wiping his forehead with the back of his forearm.

She snorted out a laugh and was breathing too heavily to feel embarrassed by the sound. Instead, she gave herself a moment by grabbing a drink. She could do this. *You are doing this.* She hadn't made a fool of herself at all. Maybe she'd come to another class. Stacey would love this.

When she came back to the mat, she even smiled and nodded at one of the guys looking her way. That rock-star rush of exhilaration vanished with Rob's next words.

"Okay. We're going to do some sparring. It's a little more up close and personal, so you'll have to adjust your moves to your partner's comfort level. If you don't know the person beside you, introduce yourself now, because you're about to try to kick their asses."

[17]

Chris nearly swallowed his tongue as Everly stared at him, wide-eyed like a frightened doe. She'd been fine—great, even—a minute ago. Now that they were going to spar, though, he watched as her nerves visibly pushed forward. Sparring with Everly. Just the thought of it—*Don't. Don't think about it.* If he did, he'd be wishing he'd worn something more constricting than loose freaking athletic shorts.

He loved that she was here, trying something new. Was this her first time here or just her first kickboxing class? He didn't come often enough to know if she frequented the place.

He'd been on the elliptical when he'd seen her walk in and nearly lost his damn footing. He hadn't planned on taking kickboxing but couldn't *not* follow her in. Belatedly, he'd wondered if it would make her uncomfortable and had almost turned around to go, but she'd seemed to calm a little when he'd suggested she breathe. It wasn't a class he imagined her taking. *You're not supposed to be imagining her at all.*

Now, he was happy he did, because he sure as hell didn't want some other person, man or woman, and definitely not Rob, throwing punches at her. He was impressed with her ability to seize new opportunities even though he knew it scared her. Damn, he liked her. Too freaking much. Add admiration to how he felt and he was walking a dangerous line. *As long as you veer to the friendship lane, you're fine.*

"Okay, so we'll work on not reacting, not flinching. Your partner isn't making contact, but the jabs should be fast, repetitive."

Rob wandered over and grinned at Chris. "I'll model it for you with my pal here."

He took up the stance, and Chris ignored the discomfort of being on display like this, particularly in front of Everly. It wasn't his first kickboxing class, so he was easily able to deflect and block Rob's punches. While they danced around each other, Rob talked about stance, keeping his body loose and his core tight. From the corner of his eye, Chris saw Everly's attention fixated on them. Warmth suffused his body and, yeah, maybe added a spring to his step.

"Nice blocking," Rob said, still giving him that all-knowing smile that made Chris want to punch him for real.

Rob gave a few more instructions, and then Chris and Everly, like the other partners in the room, turned and faced each other, adjusted their stances, and got started. At least the other partners began.

Everly's hands hung by her side, but she wasn't tapping. Why had it surprised her so much that he'd noticed? He'd seen the look of surprise on her face.

"You want to punch or block?"

"Whichever you prefer."

She wouldn't choose. So, he did. "You punch, I'll block. Isn't this every employee's dream?"

Her low laugh distracted him, but he put his hands up to block, smiling when she moved into position, started sending slow, easy jabs his way.

"Maybe if they hate their boss," she said, her quiet smile tamed by her intense concentration.

"Loosen your shoulders."

She did.

"There you go. Increase your pace."

She did.

As she let go of the fact that he *was* her boss, she got more into it, her movement coming quicker, more naturally. When she connected with his hand, she stopped, eyes wide, and dropped her hands.

"I'm sorry."

"For what? If this were real, you'd want to hit the other person," Chris said.

"I wasn't actually planning on getting into a fight," she said.

Rob showed up at their side. "Not many people really plan it. I'm Rob, by the way. This guy is my neighbor and friend, but I think he's pretending not to know me so he doesn't have to introduce us." He held out his hand.

Everly shook it. "He told me who you were. He didn't even try to hide it, so I think you're good. I'm Everly."

Rob's eyebrows moved up. "Everly as in Everly Dean from the station?"

She nodded, glanced at Chris. "You listen?"

His friend nodded. "Every day. How's the dating game going?"

Chris didn't want her to feel put on the spot. "Aren't you supposed to be instructing a class?"

Rob winked at Everly. "Someone needs to loosen up. Don't apologize again if you accidentally hit him." Rob made air quotes around *accidentally*.

When he walked away, Everly laughed, and Chris sucked in a breath at the sight of her face filled with genuine happiness.

"It's nice to not be the one told to loosen up for once," she said, wiping her brow.

He started with slow, pointed jabs, pleased when she immediately raised her hands to block him. "Do people often tell you that?"

She nodded, stepped to the side, and jabbed again. "Yup. My favorite is *relax*. When someone tells me to do that, I just want to say, 'Oh, thanks, why didn't I think of that? All better now.'"

Chris laughed, but it didn't seem funny that people dismissed her feelings. "It's always easy to tell someone else how to live their life." He wasn't referring to his own life, but the minute the words left his mouth, he thought of how often his father told him what the right steps were.

Everly executed a great cross and increased her speed. "You sound like you're speaking from experience."

Choosing not to answer, he focused on moving with her, blocking her punches, and then they switched. When Rob called time and dismissed the class, Chris walked out with Everly, avoiding his friend's curious look.

"You don't have to walk me to my car," Everly said. She waved to the receptionist.

He glanced at her from the corner of his eye. "One class and you're a tough guy?"

That brought out her laugh, the one where her eyes lit up. "That's right. Maybe I should walk you to your car."

"My hero," he teased.

The night had cooled off. It was his favorite time of the day. The remnants of sunset touched the clouds like watercolor paintings, and the air felt lighter.

"Will you come back?" he asked when she stopped in front of a four-door Honda Civic. He smiled at the car. Safe, reliable. Very Everly.

Her face scrunched, and he loved the fact that she considered the question so seriously. "I'm not sure. I liked it. I just don't love crowds. Sometimes, though, like tonight, I can forget they're surrounding me. Do you work out there a lot?"

Chris looked back at the building, then at her. "Now and again. I was feeling restless tonight, so I thought I'd work that out." Which sounded a lot better than *I'm thinking too much about you and needed to get out of my own head*.

She shifted from one foot to the other.

Don't do it, he told himself. "Do you want to grab a drink?" He did it. *Shit. You have no self-control.*

Her eyes widened. "Oh, I should," she started, looked down at herself. "I'm sweaty, and I have—"

Chris cut her off. He was sweaty, too, and spending *more* time with her wouldn't help him get her out of his thoughts.

"No worries. You've got lots going on." He didn't want to say good-bye and felt like an idiot for it. Which was the only reason he could think for why he'd blurted out the next part. "I was thinking about planning a staff get-together. I feel like a lot of the employees just pass each other at shift change. It'd be fun to hang out together. Get to know each other." *Before I take off.*

Surprise flashed in her eyes. Clearly more comfortable, Everly nodded. "That'd be nice."

"Would you come?"

She tilted her head. "Why wouldn't I?"

He stuck his hands in his pockets, refusing to shuffle his feet. "You don't like crowds."

One side of her mouth tilted up, and his gaze caught there for a minute.

"No. But a work event is different." She nodded, like she'd decided something in her own mind. "It would be good to do a work thing. Everyone already thinks I'm a snob." She leaned against her car.

"Who thinks that?" Was the staff being hard on her? Their weekly staff meetings were pretty chill, and all of them seemed to get along, but maybe he was missing something.

She gave an atypically sassy grin, and he felt the impact in his gut like a hard kick.

"Uh, everyone? I'm not exactly Chatty Cathy."

Chris shrugged, wanting to tell her she didn't need to be anything she wasn't, but before he could say anything, she pushed off the car and unlocked it.

"I should go. I'll see you tomorrow."

"Oh yeah. Okay. Have a good night."

"You, too." She lifted her hand and gave him a small, shy wave.

Ignoring the sounds of footsteps and people calling out to each other in the lot, Chris watched her drive away.

"Aw, you look like a lost puppy," Rob said, coming up beside him.

"Shut up. I walked an employee to her car. Nothing more."

Rob laughed, clapped him on the shoulder. "Sure. I'll buy that if you're buying the beer."

His gut reaction was to say no, but he realized it was exactly why he'd come out tonight—get away from his own thoughts, hang out with a friend, release some energy.

"One round," Chris said.

"I'll take what I can get," Rob answered.

Chris chuckled. "Story of your life?"

Rob glanced over his shoulder at where Chris had been standing, then looked him dead in the eye. "And yours, it appears."

[18]

Everly lifted her hand to knock, then lowered it. Stupid to be anxious about visiting her parents. Stupid or not, a nest of bees woke up in her stomach, making her palms clammy and her breathing hitch. It was her mom's birthday, and celebrations in the Dean household were wild cards. *Your parents are wild cards.* How she'd ended up *not* being more like them, no one knew. One thing she was sure of, though, when her parents threw a party, anything could happen.

It's not a party. It's dinner with your parents, who love you, you chicken. The last couple of weeks had given them an arsenal of over-the-table conversation topics that Everly wanted to avoid. Tomorrow night was date four out of six. She was halfway. Her mom texted more than ever, asking about the "future son-in-law candidates." *No pressure.*

Forgoing the knock, she turned the handle and let herself into her childhood home. A faint chime sounded when she opened and shut the door. A mixture of comfort and chaos swirled in her chest. The scent of chili and fresh bread hit her hard, making her stomach growl. Music pumped through the house. Her dad was a nut for wireless anything, and Everly was pretty sure most of the rooms in their home were smarter than she was. She couldn't even figure out the lights.

"There she is," her dad greeted, coming out from the kitchen. He held his arms open, his smile genuine and wide.

Everly walked into the hug and smiled against his chest, being careful not to squish the gift bag between them. He smelled like spices and home. Running a hand up and down her back, he pressed a kiss to her head.

He leaned back, looked at her with thick, furrowed brows. He either hadn't gone gray yet or was too vain to let it happen. She suspected the latter since his dark hair only got darker each time she saw him.

"You're too skinny," he said, frowning.

"Don't start, Dad. I plan to eat my weight in chili and bread, so it's not from lack of trying."

He chuckled and shifted so his arm was around her shoulder and guided her toward the deliciousness coming from the next room. "We're enjoying the sunshine in the backyard. Your mother and I invited a few extra guests," he said.

Everly stopped in her tracks at the entryway to the kitchen where she'd eaten breakfast every morning until her teen years when she'd decided it wasn't the most important meal of the day. "Define *extra*," she said, the hair on her arms bristling.

"Come on, Evie. You know more is merrier," her dad said.

So not her motto. As if he'd cued them, a group of people shuffled through the open double doors of the kitchen that led onto a patio. *Oh God, that's a lot of extra.* Through the glass doors, she saw the yard was full of guests. Everly recognized a few of the ones greeting her in the kitchen, and her dad introduced her to the others.

Focused on breathing, their names slipped through her brain the moment the next person said theirs. *Nod and smile.* Why did they do this to her? She kept a viselike grip on her mom's present, wondering why she'd agreed to come. A *small family dinner. They promised.* When did they ever do exactly what they said they would?

"There's my beautiful girl," her mom said, coming into the house, an empty margarita glass in her hand. On her way to hug Everly, she sent a quick glance to her husband, passed him her glass. "Did you tell her?"

"I was about to," he said, smiling down at Everly.

Her chest and stomach seized at the same time like the cogs of a wheel that got locked together. Her mom wrapped her arms around her and held on tight.

"I know it's my birthday, sweetie, but we wanted to do yours up right."

No. Please, no. Why? "What did you do?"

Stacey's unmistakable belly laugh tumbled into the air, and Everly felt equal parts anger and relief. Her best friend was here, which would lessen the stress, but that meant . . .

"We're throwing you a party. A joint party," her dad announced like he'd just said she got to be queen for the day.

"Let me take that," her mother said, taking the gift bag from her hand and putting her arm around her shoulder. "Come on. We had Stacey help us with your part of the guest list, but I have to say, you don't have a lot of friends, Evie. Hopefully, you'll make some new ones tonight. Your cousins are here. Did you know Sam is engaged? He's six years younger than you. It's not typical for a man to want to settle down that young, but he's always been an old soul."

Despite her head wanting to implode at her mom's steady stream of updates, Everly's feet moved and she found herself outside in her parents' backyard. Landscaped to perfection, thanks to a pricey gardener, the yard looked lovely. It was edged by sculpted shrubs and flowering bushes. Little lanterns hung from the pergola over the porch, lit but not standing out just yet. They would later, when the sun went down. Everly used to love sitting on the back porch with the lights, the moon, and the stars keeping her company.

She waved to cousins and acquaintances, hoping her smile didn't come off as stiff. There were more unfamiliar faces than familiar. Pop music played, guests laughed and drank while snacking on food. Several called out greetings and happy birthdays.

Everly smiled and nodded. She could have majored in the smile and nod if there'd been that option at the university.

On Everly's levels-of-hell scale, this was fourth. Surprise parties were worse than the idea of moving back in with her parents. Scanning the yard, her gaze landed on Stacey, whose grin belied her guilt. *Yeah. We'll talk about the friendship code later.* How could she not have warned her? Beside her supposed-best-friend stood their mutual friend Tara, her coworkers Mari and Mason . . . and Chris.

They'd invited her boss? *He's more than that now. You're closer to him than Mari and Mason.* Something swinging in the light breeze caught her eye. Hanging from the oak tree, the same one that had witnessed the great piñata massacre of her seventh birthday, was a donkey-shaped piñata. *They bought a stupid piñata? How have they not figured out how much I hate them after all these years?* Everly's mouth dropped open, and the noise of the party faded against the buzzing in her ears.

"Why? Why did you—"

Her mother cut her off with a shoulder squeeze and a nudge forward. *Maybe it's just for show.*

"Let's mingle," her mother said, oblivious to the fact that her daughter's skin was heating up enough to start a damn forest fire.

Stacey appeared at her side, tension simmering off her normally easygoing friend. "Hey, birthday girl. Let's get you a drink. I've got her, Mrs. Dean."

Everly let herself be led, mostly because she needed to be somewhere else—at home would be her preference, but for now, she'd take across the yard, away from her mother, who looked entirely too proud of herself.

"How could you not tell me?" Everly's whisper held a jagged edge.

"I'm sorry. They sprung it on me. It was a last-minute idea, and I figured they were going to do it, anyway, so it was better to show up and have your back than send you in alone."

Everly kept her head down but angled it toward Stacey. "If you'd told me, I could have skipped out altogether."

Stacey stopped moving and looked Everly in the eyes. "Come on, Ev. That would have hurt them. They just wanted to do something nice for you."

Awesome. On top of being a social moron, you're ungrateful. Gratitude and resentment battled inside of her, staring each other down in their own corners. She didn't *like* things like this. Why wasn't that allowed without having to feel guilty? *Thoughts for another time.* Fixing a smile on her face, she nodded, and they walked over to their friend and her colleagues.

"Happy birthday," Tara said, leaning in for a quick hug. "I made your favorite cake, if that helps."

Everly laughed, squeezed her back. See? Tara wasn't even her best friend, and she knew how she felt about parties. *Thank goodness she also knows cake always helps.* "It absolutely does. Thank you."

Mari lifted her beer. "Happy birthday." The woman towered over Everly, and her smile was a little forced. *Like you're one to judge on that score?*

"Thank you."

She repeated herself when Mason said the same. When her gaze made it to Chris, his quiet smile did something to the heaviness in her chest. Lightened it? Loosened it? She didn't know, but her breath whooshed in and out.

"Hey," she said. Stacey still had her fingers gripped around Everly's wrist.

"Hey," he said. He didn't say *happy birthday,* and something about the way he was looking at her made her feel like it was intentional. Like he knew she didn't *want* to hear it again. Whatever the reason, she could have kissed him for it. *Whoa. Nope. No kissing the boss. That's right up there with sticking your fingers in his mouth.*

"You post about your last date was awesome, Everly. Three

down, three to go, right?" Mason asked, taking a drink of his beer.

The shade of the oak tree coupled with the light breeze was enough to send a shiver on Everly's skin. Or maybe it was the topic of dating. While at a party she didn't want. While standing with people who were sort of her friends but not. And her boss.

"I need a drink," Everly said, then grimaced. "Sorry. Yes. Halfway. It's been . . . interesting. It's teaching me a lot about what I'm *not* looking for in a man." They all laughed, and she relaxed further. "I really do need a drink, though."

"I'll get it for you," Chris offered, hands in the pockets of his jeans. The wind flitted through his hair, ruffling it, and though her fingers usually felt the urge to *move*, Everly was surprised by their desire to straighten his hair. To reach out and run her hand *through* it. She thought about how it looked when it was damp at the gym, and her stomach tightened with need. *Hello, thirty. Thanks for bringing the inappropriate lust aimed in the wrong direction.*

"I'll go with you," Everly said, extracting herself from Stacey's grip.

They went to the row of coolers near the table that was laden with chips, veggies, fruit, dips, and an assortment of other snacks.

Chris crouched and dug through the ice for a bottle of water. He glanced up, and the way the sun hit the ground just behind him made him appear almost angelic. Jesus. She was losing it. Slipping right over the edge. She wanted to hit it off with one of her potentials. Her mind and her heart were surprisingly open. Date three with Brad, who'd been her first 'like' on the app was surprisingly nondescript. She couldn't say anything she truly enjoyed or disliked about the date. Or him. But if she were choosing right now, between Brad or Owen, it would be Owen all the way. She should focus on that. On him.

Not the strange tumble of feelings she tripped over when she was around Chris.

Chris pulled up a bottle of fruit-infused vodka, the one she'd had at her place the night of her 'spring cleaning.' "Will this work?"

Had he remembered? He paid attention to little things. *Which is a nice quality, but he also makes you clam up, and you're looking for a man you can be yourself with. Your new self.* She nodded, and he stood, twisted the top off. She accepted it and took a drink, but it tasted sour in her mouth. Apparently, she wasn't good at hiding anything, because he smiled, took the drink from her, and replaced it with his water.

"Better?"

Her eyes burned and she didn't trust herself to speak, so she only nodded. When he took a drink of the vodka cooler, two thoughts crashed into her head: he was drinking it *for* her, which somehow felt romantic. And because her inner twelve-year-old liked to make random appearances, her second thought was that their lips had both touched the bottle, which was practically kissing. *What is wrong with you?*

Her cheeks warmed. "You didn't have to come to this."

His lips tipped up in an easy grin. "It's like your parents planned my staff BBQ for me. I should have brought the others along."

She laughed, the pressure in her chest loosening by small fractions. "But you didn't, so you still need to go through with it."

"Party planning isn't really my thing. Jane is working on it," he said, tipping the bottle up again. She watched his throat as he swallowed. A little hum left the back of her own throat, and she hoped he didn't hear it.

They stood in silence for a good five minutes before Everly realized neither of them tried to fill it. It was so . . . *nice.* For someone who didn't like being *in* the crowd, she didn't mind observing it. Chris seemed to feel the same. When she glanced at him, hopefully covertly, his eyes were scanning the group, his foot tapping to the music. It was strange how a few weeks ago, she couldn't have imagined him outside of the station. He was a lot like Stacey in his ability to just *fit* wherever he went. She wouldn't have suspected that.

Stacey and Tara wandered over and joined them, drinks in hand.

Stacey gave her a contrite smile, paired with puppy-dog eyes. "Your mom was so excited when she called me," Stacey said.

"Mm-hmm. Plus, you never turn down a party," Everly said. Tara shifted beside Stacey. "Tara, you've met Chris?"

They shook hands, saying hello, and Everly sent a mock glare toward Stacey, who shrugged. "What? So I forgot to introduce them. They're both adults. Besides, you showed up, and I was worried you might kill me for not putting a stop to this."

"I still might," she muttered. "There's got to be something in the friendship code for this."

Tara nodded. "I think you're right." Stacey glared at her, making their friend wince and add, "But she showed up and brought reinforcements, so I think the right and wrong cancel each other out."

Chris laughed, and Everly bit her lip to keep from joining in. She had good friends.

Stacey came to her side and bumped her hip. "There are worse things than a backyard party with people who love you."

"Plus, there's food and cake," Tara said, taking a sip of her drink. Taller than Everly but a couple inches shorter than Stacey, Tara reminded her of a sixties' pinup model. Rounded curves, long, flowing brown hair, blue eyes, and a tendency to wear slightly retro clothing all worked together to make her striking in a unique way.

Focus on the good. "Your cake is worth putting up with a party for. Thank you for the one you made on my actual birthday," Everly said.

Standing in a small half circle, listening to the three of

them chatting and trading stories, Everly's skin stopped feeling as if it were shrinking. Her breathing came easier until she stopped thinking about it. She could totally do this. In the back of her mind, she knew she should be mingling, as her mother said, but if they wanted her here, she'd do it her way. She hadn't bolted, so they were still winning.

That thought was short-lived when she saw her father heading her way, his gaze aimed at Chris. His long gait, height, and happy smile always drew attention. Both of her parents enjoyed being the life of the party and often tried to outdo each other with witty banter and over-the-top flirting when they socialized. Everly hadn't inherited that gene from either of them.

"There's my beautiful birthday girl," her dad said, pulling her into another hug and keeping his arm around her shoulder.

Everly tensed. *Please don't say anything awkward to Chris.*

"I'm so glad your friends could join us. I don't believe we've been introduced," he said to Chris. "Are you here with Tara or Stacey?"

"Chris, this is my dad, Grant. Dad, this is Chris Jansen. He runs the station." She didn't need to add more. If she did, her father would find a chink in her faulty armor.

"You're Everly's boss?" He stretched his hand out, and Chris took it. "Nice to meet you."

Chris glanced at Everly. "Boss and friend. It's nice to meet you as well. You have a great home."

Her father's chest puffed up with pride. Of course Chris would be good with parents. "Thank you. We like it. Where did you go to school?"

Everly groaned, and her father looked down at her. "What? I can't ask some questions of your boss and friend?"

Chris chuckled. "It's fine. I went to NYU. Majored in business and communications."

Her father nodded, clearly impressed. Everly found herself wanting to ask for more details. She realized that as much as they'd been growing closer, she didn't really *know* him. Other questions popped into her brain: Did he miss New York? Did he like California?

"Excellent school," her dad replied.

They chitchatted some more about schools and degrees before her father narrowed his focus.

"Do you like running the station? Is this where you planned to be?"

Everly's curiosity tickled her skin. Did he like the station? Was it his dream job? Was it what he'd hoped he'd end up doing? *This is exactly why you have to stop thinking you feel something more for him. You haven't even asked him any of these things.* She felt like she'd been self-absorbed and vowed to find out the answers to her questions. Friends knew things about friends, and he'd learned a lot of little things about Everly. She missed Chris's answer but tuned back in to hear her father's tone change.

"Well, I can't say I'm crazy about this segment you're running with my daughter," her dad said. "As much as we want her to find someone who makes her happy, I'm not sure the last two men are anywhere near her league."

"Dad," Everly muttered.

"If Everly is in any way uncomfortable, I'll pull it," Chris said, matching her father's serious tone.

She was ready for something stronger than water now.

Sensing her discomfort growing, her friends stepped up. "Have you tried Tara's cream puffs, Mr. D.?" Stacey asked, moving toward her dad.

"They're delicious," Tara said, and Everly knew she was boasting for her benefit. Tara was a kick-ass baker, but she was hardly a braggart.

"Come on. You've got to try them," Stacey said, looping her arm through his.

The two women walked off with her dad, letting Everly catch her breath.

"Wow. That was impressive. It was like a tag-team rescue

mission. I feel like I made a narrow escape." He stepped closer, a playful smile hovering as their shoulders brushed.

She laughed before she could count all the reasons she had to be nervous. "They're well trained. The best in their field."

Chris laughed, and the sound caused goose bumps along her arms. "Your parents are very invested in your life."

She nodded, her ribs expanding fully. Some nights, when she got home from social functions, they actually ached from the pressure of standing so still and trying to be invisible. Or worse, from engaging in idle chitchat about things she didn't care about. She realized, as she stood beside him, breathing normally, that it was becoming easier to be around him. To be her own version of normal.

"They are. They mean well, but they have a lot of opinions about how I should live my life and what I should be doing or should have done by now. Mostly, they just want grandbabies, and it sometimes colors their judgment."

He glanced down at her, and their eyes held for a beat. "What do you want?"

Wow. Good question. "To survive the night without any embarrassment."

He nodded like that was a perfectly acceptable answer. They both knew it was a cop-out.

"You?" she heard herself ask.

Chris shoved his hands in his pockets and glanced around her backyard, filled with cousins, aunts and uncles, and acquaintances she'd barely acknowledged.

"To be good at my job," he said.

For some reason, Everly's heart sank. It was a good answer, and she wanted the same thing, but part of her hoped for something more. For him to tell her something that would make her feel like she wasn't imagining the little sparks of chemistry bubbling between them. The sparks that shouldn't, and couldn't, exist but flared up without warning. On her part, anyway.

"You are good at your job," she said, looking away when his gaze came to hers.

"There's always room to do better. I want the station to reach another level. When it does, I'll know I've done what I came to do."

The answer unsettled something inside of her. What he came to do? What did that even mean?

Her mom came over with one of her aunts in tow. "Honey, why are you hiding out in the corner? Hello there. Who is this young man?"

Subtle, Mom. Like a baseball bat to the head. "This is my *boss*, Chris Jansen. Chris, this is my mom, Jessica, and my aunt Jules." Her aunt and mother were practically twins in the looks department but couldn't be more different personality-wise.

Aunt Jules leaned in for a hug, and Everly caught the scent of her floral perfume. She and Uncle Colt had been married two years longer than her parents but spent all that time living in the same household. If Everly was going to aspire to have a relationship, it'd be theirs. It was solid and real. Never in the kind of flux that the outside world could watch.

"Happy belated, sweetie. Heard the day of wasn't so awesome. I'm sorry about that," her aunt said. She shook Chris's hand after Jessica did. "Nice to meet you."

"Yes, *very* nice to meet you," her mother added.

Everly closed her eyes and took a deep breath. When she opened them again, her mother was eyeing Chris in a way she'd rather her mother never look at a man.

"Nice to meet you both as well. If you'll excuse me, I'm going to grab some food. Everly, would you like anything?"

She shook her head, that peanut butter feeling making her mouth sticky. When he walked away, her mother stepped closer. "I had no idea your boss was so yummy."

Every spark she'd thought she felt fizzled like a watered-down firecracker.

"Mom. Ew." Yes, it was a ten-year-old's response, but there

were so many times, in her parents' company, that's how she felt. Being with them transported her back to a time where she had little say over anything in her life. Everly wrapped her arms around herself, tapping her fingers against her biceps, hoping it came off as matching the beat of the music.

"What?" Her mother's jaw dropped. "You don't think he's handsome?"

Aunt Jules chuckled. "I think she was referring more to you commenting on it, cougar."

Everly laughed, appreciating her aunt. "Yup."

Her mom poked her in the arm. "There's nothing wrong with me being able to acknowledge a good-looking man."

As long as that was all it ever was, Everly didn't care. She just didn't want details or to share these kinds of conversations with her mother.

Her mom clapped her hands together. "Let's do presents."

Oh yeah. Let's hit every single circle. Her mother *knew* she hated opening presents in front of people. It completely flustered her even when it was just family.

"Mom. Let's just do yours. Please? I don't want to take away from your day."

Her mom squeezed her shoulders, leaned her head against Everly's. "I don't mind sharing my day with you. Let's do it together."

Everly's stomach swirled, spinning out of control. The sensation reminded her of the little tops that fell out of the piñata so long ago, bouncing into a twirl on the cement below the branch of the tree. She'd watched them spin over and over again, amazed at how they'd created a toy to match the sensations happening inside of her.

Her aunt patted Everly's arm, giving her an understanding smile. "Jessie, let's just do yours."

Hands on her hips, her mom tried to give Everly an "I raised you better" glare. "People will want to see you open your gifts."

Everly had an argument ready. She opened her mouth and

started to speak because she was thirty years old and didn't have to open presents on her fake birthday if she didn't want to.

But her father came out to the porch banging a pot with a wooden spoon.

"Lots of food, so make sure you all eat," he boomed when people quieted. He was no stranger to speaking in front of people. "I'd like to say a few words."

He looked over to where Everly, her mother, and her aunt stood, and though she loved her father, her stomach twisted with the idea of him turning the spotlight their way. Stacey, Chris, and Tara watched from the other side of the yard.

"I have had the pleasure of having some wonderful women in my life. But no two make me happier or prouder than my beautiful wife and lovely daughter. I love you both with all my heart."

Everly's eyes watered. Her mom put a hand to her chest and made a humming sound. Her dad put the pot and spoon on the food table and picked up a bottle of beer. "To my girls. On their birthdays and every day."

Everyone raised their glasses or bottles, and Everly drank deeply, cooling the fire in her throat. *Survived. Done.*

She should have known better. Her dad set the beer down while everyone was still toasting, then bent to pick something up. When he lifted a bat in the air, Everly's airway closed. Her mom clapped her hands together.

"What's a birthday without piñata smashing?"

Everyone laughed and cheered, and Everly's gaze locked on Stacey's. Her friend shrugged, her look emanating empathy even from a distance.

"Get up here, Evie. You get first swing."

She shook her head, dug in her heels when her mom started nudging her forward. She was seven all over again. Humiliated and being forced to stand center stage with everyone watching, waiting.

"I couldn't believe when I cleaned out your closet and found this old thing," her mom said under her breath.

Wait. What?

She dug in her heels, looked at her mom.

"All those years, I wondered what had happened to it. Of course, we won't be able to eat the candy out of it. Come on, sweetie, get up there."

Nooooo. No. No. No.

Her throat was closing. *Breathe. Your throat isn't closing. You're panicking. Hell yes, I'm panicking. If that's the piñata from my closet, it's not full of candy!* Her nails dug into her palms, stinging, but she only pressed them harder.

"Aw. My girl is still shy. That's okay. Who wants to swing?" her dad said, looking around, holding the bat out.

She loosened the pressure on her palm, torn between rushing forward and running away. She had to stop this. What was wrong with her? Why couldn't she move? Speak? Shout?

"I'll take a swing," Chris said, walking over to her dad.

Everly's gaze flew to him, and her heart stopped trying to kick its way out of her chest. She pressed her hand there, certain it had just given up and stopped.

"Me, too," Stacey said, followed by Tara saying the same and a chorus of others.

Her mother laughed. "You're missing out on the fun. I want a turn," she called, heading to the crowd.

Everly stood frozen, stuck in the moment like she wasn't actually there. Chris lined up the bat and took a swing. The thwack of contact echoed and made people cheer. Aunt Jules slipped her hand into Everly's, squeezed it.

"They mean well," she said quietly.

Maybe she was wrong. *Oh, please, be wrong.* Everly squeezed her hand back, words impossible.

Being twenty years old, it happened quickly.

The worn, gray, bedraggled pieces of paper fluttered to the ground as the donkey burst with a loud pop. Cardboard, paper, confetti, a couple of candies, and years' worth of condoms she'd slipped away erupted into the air.

"No," Everly whispered.

Laughter erupted, and Everly felt like she might dissolve into the grass. Or burst into flames.

People scrambled to pick up the "prizes," scooping it up from the ground. Hoots of laughter pierced Everly's ears.

"They're flavored!" someone yelled.

"Mine is ribbed," someone else called.

"What the heck?" Her mother's voice could be heard through the din.

"Jessie! Did you put these in here?" her father yelled through laughter.

Everly pulled her hand out of her aunt's hold, shook her head when her aunt tried to speak. Her parents' laughter felt like shoving large granules of salt into a bleeding wound.

Stacey appeared at her side. "Come on."

She took Everly's hand and pulled her toward the side gate. They slipped through it, unnoticed, the boisterous commentary fading with every step. When they got to Everly's car, Stacey swung around and faced her, irritation shining in her typically easygoing gaze.

"I'm sorry. I should have texted you to give you a heads-up. From now on, we have a special code word. It'll mean your parents are comin' in hot."

Everly could only laugh. It came out half-strangled like maybe she was choking on her mortification instead. "That's all I'm saying. That's not even their fault, though. Not entirely."

"What?"

Everly leaned against her car. "Remember I told you how she was always slipping condoms in my purse growing up? I shoved them all into the donkey in my closet. She found it and thought it was full of twenty-year-old candy."

Stacey groaned and leaned her head on Everly's shoulder. "I'm so sorry. You can definitely add *no surprises* to your rules list."

Everly shook her head. "It's full. You need to start your own."

Stacey lifted her head and leaned beside her on the vehicle. "My parents would have been scandalized. I always thought you exaggerated a little with your stories about your parents. I can't believe how hard they laughed."

Everly looked up at an airplane flying overhead.

They stood in the silence for a moment before Stacey spoke again. "It could have been worse."

"How?"

Stacey giggled. "We could have been live on TV."

Rolling her eyes, Everly pushed at Stacey's head.

Her friend's smile slipped. "I'm sorry I didn't warn you."

"It's okay."

"I got you a present," Stacey said, lowering her lashes.

Everly groaned.

Stacey pulled something from her pants pocket and held it up between two fingers. It was a glow-in-the-dark condom. She waved it back and forth.

Laughter jostled her shoulders. "I hate you a little."

"Come on! I couldn't help it. Tell me this wouldn't be fun. It's like a whole different kind of lightsaber. Aren't you a little curious?"

Everly shoved her shoulder while Stacey bobbed her eyebrows up and down, slashing the condom through the air, making a whooshing noise that Everly suspected was meant to sound like an actual lightsaber.

"I'm good with never knowing," she said, glancing back at the house.

"I find your lack of curiosity disturbing," Stacey said.

With a resigned sigh, Everly turned back toward her childhood home. She couldn't hide forever. Stacey tucked the condom in Everly's pocket, but Everly removed it and tossed it back at her. "I already tried my new thing for this month. It's your turn."

"Challenge accepted."

[19]

Chris tuned in to the station's channel on his laptop while dialing his mother's number. Stacey and Everly were doing a half hour of music that would be finished soon, then the entire staff would gather for their weekly meeting.

"I wondered if you'd forgotten my number," his mother said instead of hello.

He smiled. "You know the phone works both ways, right?"

She laughed, and he smiled wider. "I've heard it does. How are you, sweetie?"

He sat down at the conference table, scrolling through the station's website. "I'm good. Busy. The station is doing a unique promotion featuring one of our producers—"

"You're saying that like I don't follow what you're doing," she interrupted.

Chris stopped scrolling. "You follow the station?" Pride burst in his chest.

"I follow *you*. I feel like you've found your niche. The Facebook posts are fun. I'm looking forward to seeing who Everly chooses."

His heart constricted. "She's still got a few dates." *Including one tonight.* "She's amazing. Even though the idea of this blindsided her, she's handled it with charm and grace. She's become some sort of media darling, and if you knew her, you'd know she hates it. We were already turning things around here, ratings-wise, but this cinched it. There's no way we don't end the year on a positive note."

"I like the sound of your voice," his mom said through the phone.

He wasn't entirely sure what she meant by that. He could picture her lying by a pool after a morning of coordinating charity events. She kept herself busy giving back to others. Sometimes he wondered how his parents had fallen in love; they were complete opposites. *Which is why it didn't last.*

"My voice hasn't changed since I was twelve, Mom."

Her laughter floated through the line. "I mean when you talk about the station and Everly. You sound . . . home."

Chris leaned too far back in the chair, nearly toppling himself. "I don't know about that. I'm heading *home* in less than six months. I've got plans to unite all Dad's HR departments and communication systems. I've got surveys ready to go for each of the companies to find out where they think we're lacking. I've been waiting for this chance. It's what Dad has promised me."

"I know that, sweetie. But is it still what you want?"

Mostly. "Of course."

His mom was quiet, but he didn't get a chance to ask her what she was thinking because some of his staff started to trickle in. "I have to go. I'll talk to you soon?"

"Anytime. Just remember, honey, if you're happy, maybe it's okay to stand still."

A smile tugged at his lips. Was she drinking before noon or purposely speaking in riddles? "Sure, Mom. Love you."

"Love you back."

Mason sat down across from Chris and grinned. "Chatting with Mom on your break?"

Chris laughed. "Unlike you, I don't get a break."

Jane, the receptionist, joined them. She had a pile of files in her arms, and Mari trailed behind her, the two of them finishing a conversation. Mari and Mason exchanged an odd glance, making Chris curious.

Chris turned up the segment as Stacey's voice cut in. "Well, lovely listeners, that's our show for today. Remember, our girl Everly has date four tonight. Tonight's candidate is Andy, a twenty-nine-year-old model. Evs, if you don't feel well, I'm happy to fill in for you. Hmm. She's giving me a look, you guys. I think she wants this one for herself."

Jane and Mason laughed.

Stacey continued, "Log on to our Facebook page tomorrow for the details. In the meantime, I'll be giving away a gift card for Mocktails to one lucky follower on our Twitter account tomorrow. Just make sure you answer my question of the week and use the hashtag."

Advertisements started up. They had about forty-five minutes of ads and music before the next deejay would chime in.

A few minutes later, Chris and all his staff, minus the remote deejay, gathered around the conference room table.

They went through the agenda, adding to it. Chris's eyes drifted more than once toward Everly. Her hair was down again. It looked really good, soft around her delicate features. She'd worn it up so often that seeing her like this still surprised him. Not nearly as much as the events of her birthday party had.

Kitty, their sales manager, spoke up first. "We're selling more ad time than we ever have, and our reach is growing. We have a couple of national companies that just signed up to work with us."

All good news. Chris needed to take a closer look at the figures for the subsidiary companies under the radio's umbrella and see if a steady cash flow through one arm would be enough to keep the others functioning.

"Which means we should be trying new things now while we can pull in more listeners and advertisers," Mari said, again looking at Mason.

He shrugged, and Chris had no idea what was going on between the deejay and his producer.

"Everly has an idea," Stacey said.

Chris was in the middle of looking her way when he caught the flicker of irritation on Mari's face. He turned to Everly and smiled. It felt like days since he'd seen her, and that was stupid since it had only been a day. But he hadn't chatted with her alone, away from a crowd, on the phone, or via text in a couple of days. *The last thing you need to do is start making her a part of your daily routine. She's an employee. Like Mari or Stacey or Mason.* Only looking at them across the table didn't make him want to move closer and see if he'd catch a hint of vanilla.

"Go ahead," Chris said.

Everly glanced around the room, and he wondered if she picked up the tension from Mari. "I think we can grow the station and our audience in a new way. I'd like us to consider doing a podcast. Stacey's segment on her opinions and whether people share them is one of our most popular. I think people enjoy the interaction—the human piece that is often lacking from online engagement."

"I love podcasts, and my favorites are always the ones where listeners are invited to take part. Interviews and guest spots can be fun and pull listeners in," Mari said, turning her body toward Everly.

Chris smiled, folding his fingers together under his chin as he listened to them go back and forth.

"Exactly," Everly said, her face lighting up. God, she was stunning when she really dug into something she enjoyed or felt passionate about. He wondered . . . no. He wouldn't let himself wonder about her passion in any area other than work. The sooner he left California and returned to his real life, the better. He was getting muddled, being pulled from his goals.

The conversations continued as they talked about segments, weekly promotions, schedules, and the live event coming up. By the time the next deejays were needed in the booth, they'd almost wrapped up. Everly stayed seated while Chris chatted with Jane about the upcoming staff party. When she left, he took a seat near next to her.

"You okay?" He liked the flush of happiness on her face. She was good at her job, and when she forgot to be nervous, well, she was magnificent.

"I am. I just wanted to apologize again for my party. I'm sorry you got dragged into it." A deeper blush rose up her neck.

He tore his eyes from the view and met her gaze. "Don't be. The take-home gifts were awesome."

Everly's eyes widened, and he was just about to tell her that he was totally joking when a laugh burst from her lips. She covered her face with her hands, her shoulders shaking.

He chuckled. It had been more than a little shocking to see condoms shooting out of the cardboard donkey. Her parents were unlike any parents he'd ever met.

Pulling gently at one of her wrists, he smiled at her reassuringly. "I was really honored to be part of it. No need for apologies."

She nodded. "If you say so. Just don't, uh, rely too much on those *goodies*. Most of them are about fifteen years old."

Now his eyes widened, and as she told him about her mother stuffing condoms in her purse at every opportunity, he had a moment of longing. He loved his parents, but he couldn't imagine them being that relaxed with him. His mother was gentle but firm and had always invited them to speak freely, but none of them had wanted to discuss their sex lives, and she'd seemed happy to pretend they never had one.

Their father . . . well, he was too busy building an empire after his own father died, and when he did have time, he was usually dating or marrying a woman who had no interest in his kids.

"You're lucky," Chris said as she stood up.

"Because my parents believe in safe sex even if it's glow in the dark?"

Laughing, he stood beside her. "That and because they care. You matter to them."

"I do. They're a lot to take sometimes, but you saw them on one of the good swings. When they're happy together, their love is amazing to witness."

"Not so much when they aren't?"

She shook her head. "I realized I don't know much about you when my dad was grilling you the other night."

They walked out of the room together toward his office.

"What do you want to know?" he asked.

She shrugged. "Do you like working here?"

His gaze narrowed. "Sure. It's great. You guys are great." Did she sense something? He hadn't told them he was leaving because that was a sharp dart to an overfilled balloon. Staffers didn't feel like giving their all to management that wasn't sticking around. Plus, he didn't want to worry them. He'd leave them in better shape than he'd found them, and his successor would carry forward with their triumphs.

"You have siblings?"

"Three. All older. One sister, two brothers."

They went into his office. Was she curious or wanting to know something in particular? He liked the idea that she might want to know more about him.

"Is this what you imagined yourself doing?" She leaned against his desk, much the way he had a few weeks ago when he'd run the promo idea by her and Stacey.

"No. Not really. I mean, not broadcast media in general. Communications, yes, but I never thought about the radio aspect of it." *Tell her. My dad owns the station, so I was given the opportunity to turn the place around as my final level of the jumping-through-hoops game.*

"Now I just need some deep dark secrets," she said, straightening.

His breath caught in his throat, but when she followed the statement with a laugh, he relaxed.

"I feel like everyone knows so much about me now, and I hardly know anyone," she said, her tone quiet, almost reflective.

"Do you feel exposed?" He didn't like the idea.

She shook her head. "Not as much as I thought I would. I've started to realize that being so introverted and nervous hasn't just stopped people from getting to know me but *me* from getting to know *them*."

Something like pride and affection mingled in his chest and filled his body with energy. This *was* good for Everly in ways he couldn't have predicted.

"You're a very special woman, Everly."

Her breath hitched, and her gaze fastened on his like a magnet finding its mate. The words hung between them. He was afraid to speak because he didn't want to take back what he believed so strongly, but he also didn't want her to feel uncomfortable.

His phone buzzed, and Jane's voice filled his office. "Line two for you, Mr. Jansen."

"I'll let you get back to work," Everly said, leaving the office.

Chris's heart rate doubled, and he took a few deep breaths before picking up the phone.

"Jansen," he said.

"It's me," his father said curtly.

Chris sighed. "What's up, Dad?"

"I axed the publishing company. Legal has started the paperwork," his dad said without preamble.

Shit. What? There were five companies under the Harco Media Entertainment umbrella—the radio station, an ad agency, a publishing house, a digital software company, and a cybersecurity firm. Chris was doing his best to unite all of them because of their commonalities and hoped to amalgamate them in some way rather than getting rid of any of them.

"Why would you do that?" He gripped the phone so tightly, the skin around his knuckles went white.

"Let me think. What was that reason again? Oh, right. I own the places; I wanted it gone. It was a conflict of interest with another company I'm looking at."

Chris breathed in and out slowly, through his nose. "These five are under my control right now. You had no right."

"I didn't call to argue this," his father interrupted. "Just sharing the information before the emails came through. Didn't want you to be surprised. I know how you like your communications." His dad laughed like Chris's background, education, and interest in that field were a joke.

Less than six months. He was almost there. *As long as Dad follows through and doesn't screw you over.* He hated the thought. His mother's words from earlier ran through his brain. Was he happy? Professionally, if his dad weren't involved, he would be. Which brought up the question of whether or not he could ever really find his place when his father kept changing the playing field.

[20]

Everly yawned on her way into the station. She couldn't keep up with her social life, which was a problem she'd never encountered. Both dates this week had been lacking in the entertainment, enjoyment, and interest categories. Her fourth candidate, Andy, had met her at the restaurant with an entourage. She hadn't noticed at first, but when he kept looking around, she realized that he'd brought a group of friends. When he asked to introduce her to them, she'd faked a headache and cut the evening short.

Last night, curled up on her couch, alternating between reading, watching cooking shows, and searching animal shelters, had been her favorite night this week. She'd texted back and forth with Stacey and Chris. Chris had wondered if she was going to kickboxing, but she'd been too tired to go. She smiled now, remembering that she'd promised to kick his ass the next time they sparred. Maybe it was all talk, but she was looking forward to the next class and had asked Stacey to join them.

***

Everly stopped short when she got to the door of the conference room. Stacey was standing in front of the whiteboard where they sometimes jotted down ideas, an actual pointer in her hand.

She'd created a Final Four bracket of Everly's dating life, going as far as calling it *the Road to the Final Two*.

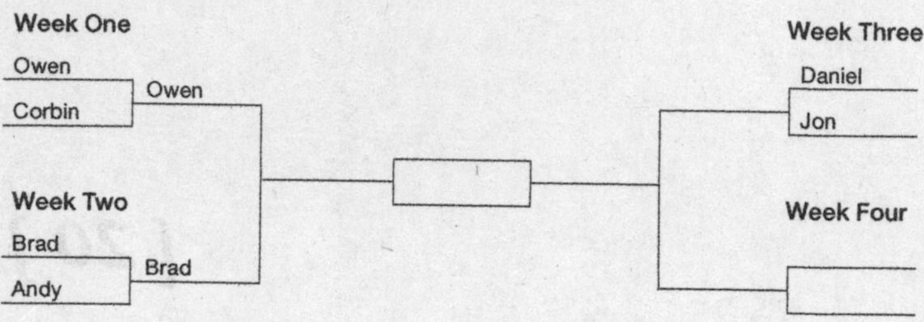

No one had noticed her standing in the doorway, eyes wide, fingers clenched around her purse. Their conversation buzzed through the room and her head as their voices pitched with excitement. Two of the station's deejays argued that Andy should be this week's choice. Kitty leaned back in her chair, tapping a pen against the table while she stared at the board.

"My money is on Owen. It doesn't sound like these two latest ones were worth her time."

Stacey used her finger to wipe a smudge outside one of the empty rectangles. "Brad sounded okay. They might not be Everly's type, but I have a very good feeling about next week's candidates. Did you see Daniel's profile picture? Though I guess looks aren't everything since Andy the model thought he could bring all his buddies for free food."

Everly stepped into the room, unstuck her tongue from the roof of her mouth. "You're betting on my dating life?"

Everyone swiveled in an almost comical synchronization. Elijah, who produced for Christine, who sat beside him, took a sudden interest in his notepad. Kitty bit her lip, her deer-in-the-headlights gaze moving to Stacey.

"No. Of course not. We're just organizing the . . . choices," Stacey said, lowering the pointer.

Everly pointed a finger at Kitty. "She just said her money was on Owen."

Christine looked up. "He was a cutie." She rested her chin on the heel of her hand.

She started to deny it, but at this point, if she had to choose, Owen was the front-runner.

Kitty stood up, straightened her gorgeous, white linen blazer. "We signed our biggest ad yet. Ridgeview Motors just signed a six-week contract for your segment."

She forced her lips into a smile. This was benefiting everyone. "Excellent," Everly said. She moved farther into the room, trying to ignore the fact that her love life, such as it was, was written out on the board.

"We really weren't betting, Ev. But if we're having conversations around the table, you can bet other workplace employees are, too. All of this is doing exactly what we wanted—generating interest and money for the station. I heard it from a friend of a friend that 102.9 is trying to come up with a kick-ass end-of-summer promotion."

"It can't suck all that bad to know so many guys want to go out with you," Christine said.

Elijah looked up from his doodling. "You're such a quiet person. Doesn't this make it easier for you? It's like central casting doing all the screen tests and just sending you the best possible actors." As a wannabe movie star who'd opted to produce over full-time auditioning, it made sense that he would see it this way.

If this were a movie and not her real life, maybe it would be a relief.

"That's a great way to look at it," Stacey said, walking over to the coffee and pouring a cup. She brought it to Everly.

Accepting the mug, she brought it to her lips and reminded herself that these people were as close to friends as it got. Other than Stacey and Tara, Everly didn't have many constants in her life. It was time to start letting people in a little further, regardless of where she ended up on her road to the final two. *Now you're doing it.*

Give them something. This is what people do. They sit around and talk about their dating lives, complain about their spouses and pets. This is how people get to know each other. You were just saying to Chris that you needed to let others in more. Get to know them as well. Take a chance. She smiled. *Be bold.*

"We can put Brad as moving on," she said, the words thick in her mouth as she gestured to the bracket for week two. Then she gave them a bit more. "Owen really was nice." She pressed her lips to the rim of the cup like she could hide behind it.

The conversation veered to first kisses and dating disasters the others had experienced. Surprised by how good it felt to hear their stories, she got caught up in listening to everyone else. For a few minutes, anyway.

"Since we're all here, we could start our air-check meeting a few minutes early?"

Stacey gave her an affectionate smile that did nothing to soothe the unrest she felt. "Always the taskmaster."

"That's what he said," Kitty said with a laugh.

Everly rolled her eyes, but the others laughed. The meeting was fine, but the nerves that took up residence under her skin didn't fade throughout the workday.

The nerves hovered over her day in and day out, more constant than they usually were. By the time date five rolled around, she was positive it would be easier to endure than the days leading up to it. As she got ready for her dinner with Daniel at the restaurant she'd selected, she told herself this would be just like the last four. She could absolutely do this. Again. Dressed in jeans, a patterned tank top, with a blue cardigan, she sat in her car outside Chows.

He's probably already in there. She looked at the time on her dashboard: 6:58. *Go in. You're here on time, and you're going to be late.* She forced herself to get out of the car, walk across the parking lot, ignore the tightness in her throat. It wasn't closing. A couple ahead of her laughed loudly, their heads close together, his hand on her back. They went into the restaurant, and the man held the door open for Everly.

Pulse pumping abnormally loud in her ears, she shook her

head and kept walking past the door. She skirted around to the side of the building, which was basically an alley. When she leaned against the wall, every jagged groove of the brick pressed into her through her sweater. Everly counted in her head, hugging her purse to her chest.

Just breathe. You're overwhelmed, but you're okay. Or her throat was literally closing. *It's not. You know it's not. One, two, three, four, you're definitely late now.* Which only made it worse. *This is your job.* But it wasn't. Her job was sitting in a booth, planning programming, working in a partnership with a person she knew. Someone who knew *her* in return. This wasn't her job and it wasn't her and she couldn't go in. Everly's breathing turned choppy like violent seas.

Goddamn it, just breathe. It's dinner at a restaurant with a good-looking firefighter. Hardly something to freak out over. That didn't fix her breathing or cool her heated skin.

Just go in. One step at a time. You know how to do this. She pushed off the wall. *It's just dinner.* She took a step out of the alley. *You've eaten here before, and you like it.* Everly walked toward the entrance, but at the last second, she veered to the left and practically sprinted to her car. When she slid inside, the interior filled with her sawing breaths. She tossed her purse on the passenger seat and tugged at the sleeves of her cardigan. It was too hot. Yanking it off one arm, she adjusted her body in the seat, pulling while the soft cotton seemed to stick to her heated skin. When it was off, next to her purse in the passenger seat, she felt marginally better.

Wrapping her hands around the wheel, she pictured a box unfolding. All—the—way—open—and—closed. And again. Slowly inhaling, faster exhale. Tears burned her eyes.

You've come so far. You've already done this four times and survived. What's one more? The words were low, nearly whispered, but they echoed in her brain. She knew from reading anxiety sites online and the few workshops she'd taken that beating herself down for this would only make it worse. She'd gotten so much better in that area, too. One tear slipped, but she swiped it away, scratching her cheek with her nail. The sting of it made her gasp. She'd also learned that sometimes she just couldn't push past the fear.

She couldn't do this, and if she thought about the fact that this was somehow equivalent to not showing up for work, she'd be back to hyperventilating. So she started the car and headed for home. By the time she got there, she was able to breathe.

Everly locked the door behind her and hooked her keys by the door. Grateful to be home, she thought it'd be easier to settle, but she knew it wouldn't work while she was letting others down. Using the app Chris's brother had made, she texted Daniel to tell him she'd become unexpectedly ill, which didn't feel like a lie, and asked if they could reschedule. She said sorry a record number of times and set her phone down before even checking his response.

Having an anxiety attack was a little like having a bad hangover and an asthma attack at the same time—at least, in Everly's experience. Head fuzzy, body heavy, she moved slowly as she stripped out of her date clothes and stepped into the shower. The warm water pulsated over her skin, and the scent of her soap—raspberry and honey—filled her nostrils, bringing calm the way a pleasant memory could. Pressing three fingers between her breasts to the place where her sternum ached, she went through the breathing routines she'd known since she was old enough to google *anxiety* on the internet.

It took almost as much energy to *not* berate herself as it did to slog through the shower, let the repetitive motion of washing and rinsing her hair settle everything inside of her body. She didn't know why it was called fight *or* flight when it should in fact be fight *and* flight. That was the actual human response when stuck in a harrowing situation. For Everly, every time something like this happened, she fought herself as she fled. Fight *and* flight. Until she had no energy left.

Turning off the water, she dried off and got into her coziest clothes, made a cup of tea, turned down the lights, and turned on the television. Later, if she thought about it, she'd blame the exhaustion. People didn't understand the fatigue that came with having a brain that never stopped. So she didn't stop herself when her fingers dialed his number, didn't ask herself why it was him she wanted to reach out to.

He answered on the first ring. "Everly. Are you okay?"

Tears fell, and she nodded even though he couldn't see her. Pulling in a measured breath, she dug deep for the strength she needed to say the words stuck in her throat.

"I could use a friend," she whispered, ignoring the truth. She needed a friend. But she wanted Chris.

"I'm on my way."

[21]

Whatever words she'd rehearsed in her head slipped away the minute Chris walked toward her, worry furrowing his brow. Dressed in a pair of jeans and a hoodie, his hair mussed, she wondered where he was coming from. A casual date at his house? A woman's home? *Why do you care?*

At the moment, she didn't. She'd called, he'd come, and the relief of that pushed everything else away. Including her typical reserve as she stepped into him and wrapped her arms around his waist, letting her head rest on his chest so she could hear his steady heartbeat. His arms closed around her automatically. He shut the door with his foot and just stood there, holding her, not saying anything. It was her definition of perfect.

He didn't rush her, but when she felt like she could talk about it, she stepped back. He bent his knees and looked into her eyes. "Are you okay?" His voice was hushed, but he wasn't looking at her like she was weak, and for some reason, it made her feel stronger. She *wasn't* weak. Just tired.

She nodded, about to speak, but then his eyes widened, his hand coming to her face. His thumb swept, feather-light, across her cheek, reminding her of the scratch. His skin on hers made her cheek feel like a hot spot.

With a frown, his other hand went to her upper arm to hold on. "What happened?"

"Oh. I . . ." Where'd her words go? Why did it feel like her cheek had its own pulse beneath his thumb?

"Everly? Did you hurt yourself?" His tone was so tender and concerned. It threatened to unravel her again.

"I scratched myself by accident." She walked into the living room with him on her heels.

Belatedly, she realized she hadn't followed through with contractual obligations. The thought hadn't run through her head in her panic or the aftermath. Now, she couldn't help but wonder if she'd get in trouble. Whirling around with this new concern, her breath caught in her chest, snagging like cloth in a zipper. He wasn't looking at her like she was an employee or worried about whether she'd fulfilled her end of the bargain.

He's looking at you like a friend. Someone he cares about. Don't make it more. You do that. You see things that aren't there.

"I didn't go," she blurted. Pressing her fingernails to her palms, she gave him the rest before she could chicken out. "I couldn't do it. I'm sorry. I just . . . It was too much tonight. With the road to the final two and the jokes and my parents' party last weekend . . . it just . . . I'm sorry."

Chris tilted his head, opened his mouth to speak, and then stopped. He ran both hands through his hair and shook his head. "Okay." The word bounced off the walls.

Everly's heart hammered. Did he not understand? Loosening her fingers, forcing steady breaths, she tried again. "I got to the restaurant, and I couldn't go through with it. I came home and texted him, apologized. It's the only time it's happened, and I think I've done a pretty good job of going through with all of this. I—"

Her words died when he took two giant steps forward, looking at her in a way she *didn't* recognize. Not from him. He reached out but paused like he was waiting for approval. She gave it by putting her hand on his chest. Why was she touching him so much? *You always want to be held when you feel like this. Usually, there isn't a strong, sexy man available at such times. Boss. Boss. Boss.* Maybe if she said it enough, she'd remember.

He pulled her close, both her hands flattening on his chest between their bodies. Chris sighed into her hair, resting his chin there, but more than that, his body sighed into hers. Dual sensations, comfort and electricity, tangled together, all their wires crossing. She didn't know what to do, so she gripped the fabric of his shirt between her fingers. It was soft. Soothing.

"I don't care about the show right now. We can push everything back a week, reschedule. Whatever. None of it matters. Just you. All that matters is you're okay."

Everly's lungs forgot their purpose, opting to take a break altogether. Her heart joined in. Traitor. Both of them useless inside her body.

"You're trembling," he whispered, leaning back to look down at her face.

Their gazes met. Like runners from a starting block, both of her organs jumped back in the game, working overtime. Everly's gaze wandered to Chris's mouth. If she just went up on tiptoes or he lowered a fraction. Her brain went fuzzy again, but this time, it felt delicious, like the chocolate pie he'd brought weeks ago. Sweet and indulgent. She licked her lips.

The moment stretched, becoming nearly dreamlike. Hazy. Heated. She desperately wanted to stay trapped in it.

"Everly," he whispered. Flecks of gold shone like stars in his eyes. She wanted to wish on them.

Giving her a tight squeeze, he stepped back, putting distance between them and pulling Everly harshly out of the moment.

Embarrassment set her body on fire from the tips of her toes to the ends of her hair. What was she doing? *You weren't thinking.* She turned away, seeking space . . . clarity . . . fresh, un-Chris-scented air.

She hurried to the kitchen, grabbed a water without another word. With shaky hands, she twisted the top off the bottle. The ridges on the cap ate into her already sore palms, making her wince. His footsteps sounded loud in the quiet of her home.

Chris took the bottle from her hands, opened it, but set it down. Everly almost whimpered but bit her lip to keep from making a sound. Chris turned her palms over, and she looked down to see what he was staring at.

Marring her skin were angry red crescent shapes, the grooves still easily visible. She'd broken the skin in a few spots. Tears burned her eyes. Through lowered lashes, he met her gaze. His thumbs moved softly over her palms, caressing tenderly, like his touch could erase the hurt.

"You had a panic attack."

Sucking in a sharp breath, Everly whipped her hands away, stepped back, and smacked her hip into the fridge. *Damn it. You're going to be covered in battle wounds.* She picked up the bottle and gulped it down while he stared. *Nothing like being judged for how my brain freaks out without my permission.* He'd think she was weak or incapable. *No. You think that. It doesn't make it true.*

As if he could read her, he stepped back, giving her space to drink her water. How did he do that? Read her so well? The fact that he could tempted her to open up, to let go. When she set it down, half-empty, her breath was uneven.

Tomorrow, or later tonight, she'd replay every minute of this, from the moment he walked into her house, and cringe at her words, her actions, her neediness.

He watched her, almost curiously. Intensely. It made the moment more intimate.

"Why does it upset you for me to recognize that you had a panic attack?"

She ground her teeth together. *Because I hate the words. Panic should be reserved for bears chasing you or skydiving.*

"It makes me feel weak," she said softly, surprising herself.

Chris moved closer. "You're one of the strongest people I've ever met."

She snort-laughed and didn't have any energy left to feel embarrassed.

Smiling, his eyes locked on hers, he closed the distance so they stood side by side. "Strength isn't always something a person can see, Everly. I don't know the extent of your . . . anxiety, but I do know that even when something scares you, you push through. That makes you strong *and* brave."

Her heart fluttered. She wanted to believe his words. She wanted to write them down on a Post-it to reread later.

Standing shoulder to shoulder, she enjoyed the silence nearly as much as she liked talking to him.

"In college, I'd been crazy about this girl for months. We went to a lot of the same mixers and parties and spent a fair amount of time making eyes at each other across the room. I couldn't get the nerve to ask her out," Chris said, not looking at her.

She turned her head, studied his profile. "I can't imagine you being nervous to ask someone out."

His face turned, and his eyes cut to hers. "You'd be surprised. I'd just gotten out of a fairly significant relationship." Folding his arms over his chest, he looked straight ahead again, as if telling her cupboards would make it easier. "She approached me one night at a party, asked me to dance, seemed pretty into me. My beer-drenched brain thought so, anyway. We made plans to meet at a coffee shop the next day."

He paused like he was back there, reliving it. "I was so nervous. I bought this stupidly large bouquet of flowers. I show up, see her right away at the counter. I hurried over because I wanted to buy her drink. She hugged me hello, beamed over the flowers. I pull out my wallet, wondering what the hell she ordered that cost twenty bucks, not that I minded spending the money."

Everly didn't realize she was leaning into him until he looked down to where their arms grazed. She didn't move away. There was a buzz of awareness humming over her skin. Saying they were friends didn't lessen the impact, so she ignored it.

"What happened?"

Half his mouth tipped up in a smile. "We grabbed the food and drinks. I thought it was weird she'd ordered more than one coffee before I got there. We're heading to the back, where she says she already grabbed a table, and there's this big, burly jock I recognize from the football team. She sets everything down, goes to his side of the table, and kisses him. Then she introduces us and says, 'This is Chris, baby. He's the guy I was telling you about. He aces every one of Bayerman's quizzes.' Then she looks back at me and asks if I can tutor her boyfriend so he doesn't lose his scholarship."

Everly's mouth opened, but no sound came out. Nervous laughter tickled her throat right along with mortification on his behalf. She could vividly imagine him standing there, flowers in hand, trying to make sense of it all.

"That's horrible," she said.

Chris shrugged. "It sucked. I tutored him, though. He was a good guy. I didn't ask a girl out for a long time after that. I just wanted you to know that even though I don't totally get what it's like for you, we all have moments. Ones where we want to disappear into the ground, praying for a do-over."

Struck with the overwhelming urge to hug him again, she pushed off the counter. "It means a lot to me that you'd share that. Thank you."

She'd stepped away, but with a hand on her arm, he brought her back, turned her to face him again. "It means a lot to *me* that I'm who you phoned tonight."

Nodding, her throat thick, she gestured toward the table. Setting her water down, she swallowed the lump blocking her words.

"I don't get . . . attacks like that often, but tonight, I got overwhelmed. I can't pinpoint why." That wasn't exactly true, but how did she tell him that it was a dozen little things that would be normal to anyone else that had set her off? Not only was she unable to stop it, the inability to do so made her feel . . . less.

Chris grabbed one of the chairs while Everly slid into the bench seat. He straddled it backward, making Everly's mind shut down for one quick second. He looked so confident and sexy; so very *male*. Her breath fluttered.

Chris crossed his arms over the back of the chair. "You could have called me. Told me you were feeling overwhelmed. I would have made an excuse for you."

"You shouldn't have to. I should have handled things differently. I apologize."

His jaw hardened, drawing her attention. A few days' growth covered his skin. If she stroked her hand along his cheek, would there be a subtle, sexy rasp under her touch?

"I don't want your apologies. You know that. Not as your boss and not as your friend."

She smiled. Apparently, he was into labels. *Panic attack. Jock. Friends.*

"We are friends, aren't we?"

The look he gave her would have made her laugh at another time. It was the absolute male equivalent of *Duh*.

"We do seem to check all the boxes. We've hung out, we talk on the phone, text. We've brought each other dessert. I went to your birthday party."

"We do *not* need to talk about that," she said, hoping her tone was a warning.

The subtle smirk made it clear, warning or not, he was going there. "You just don't think about donkeys practicing safe sex all that often in life."

She closed her eyes. Yup. He was talking about it.

Make me disappear. Poof. One little splash of magic. Pretty please? Universe? Let me open my eyes and have him be gone.

She opened one eye and saw his wide grin. Everly slapped a hand over her eyes.

Chris reached over to pull her hand away.

Laughter gurgled at the back of her throat. She fought it. He stood, came around the table to slide into the bench seat beside her.

She turned her head, her cheeks *hot*. "It's not funny."

His lips twitched, his head tipping to the side. "I think it is. Though not entirely. It's also a little sad."

Her brows crashed together. "Huh?"

"Just think, no matter what a donkey does, his girl is always going to think he's an ass." Without warning, a laugh escaped. One short bark of it and she pressed her hand back over her mouth.

Chris chuckled. "See?"

They both tumbled into the kind of laughter she hadn't experienced in longer than she could remember. Her sides hurt, her eyes watered, and she forgot all the things she had to worry about. When she regained enough composure to speak, she looked at him, laughter wanting to escape again.

"It's my own fault. Why didn't I just throw them away? My mom's still texting apologies asking if I'm mad." Removed from the situation—as in, not standing in the spray of cardboard and condoms—it *did* seem pretty hilarious.

"You came back to the party and acted fine. You've moved through every level of this contest with grace and dignity. Obviously, you're fighting down the nerves. It's not a wonder they fought back."

Why did he get it? More important, why didn't he *judge* her for it? Whatever the reason, it made her want to be up-front with him. He deserved it.

"I'm pretty good at managing them. I guess everything came to a head tonight. I offered to reschedule with Daniel."

Chris nodded, his smile slipping entirely. "There you go,

then. Everything will be fine." He looked at his watch and glanced around. Her heart rate accelerated.

She didn't want him to go.

"Do you want to stay for a bit? We could watch a show or something?" That was friendly. She did that with Stacey and Tara all the time. The way his lips tipped up, just marginally at the corners, made her feel like they were sharing a secret. The quiet smile unfurled something inside of her; like the sun rising on a chilly morning, it warmed her chest, her body.

"Sure. I need to run out to my car for a minute."

He stood up and started for the door. Everly wondered if he needed to call someone—maybe the date he'd left? Did he need to make excuses? Did he have plans?

"If you have other things to do . . . ," she said, not finishing the sentence. He turned around at the door.

"I don't. At all. What's that show you and Stacey always talk about?"

"*Veronica Mars*?"

"Let's watch that."

Everly licked her lips, still staring. Trying to loosen the sudden restriction in her chest, she joked, "You trying to be one of the girls?"

"Not quite. I wouldn't mind seeing it, that's all. Then maybe I can be in on the inside jokes you two are always making."

"Oh, I'm afraid not. You'd need years of training and mind melding for that to happen."

He chuckled, and she realized the sound made her happy.

Setting up the show so that she didn't spiral into what-ifs, Everly debated making popcorn as she waited for him to return. It didn't even register that she wasn't nervous about the fact that he would. She couldn't remember the last time she'd hung out with anyone other than Stacey where she didn't feel the need to review possible conversation topics in her head beforehand. There was no pressure with Chris. If he hadn't made it clear more than once that he wasn't interested in her—she didn't think it was just the work thing—she might feel differently. She *knew* she would. She'd probably need itch cream. But she didn't, which meant they really were friends. She didn't know why she had to tell herself repeatedly, as she waited for him to return, that that would be enough.

[22]

Chris gripped the small gift bag, a range of emotions battering him from the inside out. He stood outside of her apartment for a minute, trying to get a grip on everything whirling through him. He'd almost closed his mouth over hers and given in to the desire that had been building for months now. She'd glanced up at him with so much trust, he'd stepped back. He truly *wanted* to be her friend. Yes he wanted more, but he wouldn't jeopardize what they were headed toward for something he couldn't follow through on.

"This is enough. More than you thought you'd have with her," he said before taking a calming breath and turning the knob.

The scent of popcorn hit hard, making him smile. She was incredible. He'd seen her struggle with her nerves, smooth them over, and bounce back like a punching bag. That kind of inner strength was sexier than anything he'd seen. The pleasure of her calling him, reaching out to *him*, and now, inviting him to stay would keep him awake tonight.

"I'm just making a snack," she called from around the wall.

"You didn't have to do that." They'd agreed to friendship, but could he be friends with a woman when the way her eyes switched color in the right light haunted his dreams? *You're about to find out.*

"If I hadn't, I'd be hungry," she replied, peeking around the wall.

Chris's laugh came out rough. "True."

When he'd gone out with Rob, they'd ended up having a couple of beers, playing some pool, and chatting about work stuff. There wasn't a woman in the place that pulled his interest the way Everly Dean did.

When her gaze went to the gift, she scowled and damn if he didn't find that cute, too. He wasn't sure he could handle getting too close only to leave, but he could take this. Tonight. Because she'd *asked*. That didn't come easy for Everly Dean. *At least you'll know she's found someone to make her happy. To treat her like she deserves.* He hoped.

She came out of the kitchen a moment later, her arm wrapped around a large blue bowl. In her other hand, she held two bottles of water.

"You change your mind?" she asked.

"Huh? No." He shook his head, slipped off his shoes, and walked over to the couch.

She set the waters down and sat as well, the bowl of popcorn leaving a nice amount of personal space between them. Not enough to diminish the scent of her shampoo or soap. He'd be craving berries long after he moved away.

Everly picked up the remote as he held out his hand, offering her the gift.

She eyed it, her lids lowering. He couldn't help but laugh. She looked like he was passing her a bomb.

"Why did you get me a gift?"

Putting on a serious expression, he straightened his shoulders as though about to give a lecture. "It's a typical New York custom, when one celebrates a birthday, to offer that person a present. Do they not do that here in Los Angeles?"

He *loved* the way her lips quivered with amusement.

"Come on, you let Stacey give you one," he teased.

Her cheeks went red like he'd swiped paint over them. What the—? He thought back to what Stacey had said and felt his own face heat up. He shoved the bag forward. "Just open it. I guarantee it's *not* anything like Stacey would give you."

Everly removed the tissue paper and took out the small wrapped present. When her fingers pressed in, her brows scrunched and curiosity shone in her eyes. "What is it?"

Shifting toward her, he again pulled out his lecture voice. "You West Coasters need a lot of training. So, what happens is, you *unwrap* the gift by taking the paper off. Then inside, you'll find the present."

Everly reached out and shoved him, surprising him, making him laugh. "You're quite the comedian."

"Just helping you out."

She found a spot of tape and scratched at it. Chris hid his smile by rubbing his hand over his mouth. He should have known she wasn't a ripper.

When she removed all the paper and saw what lay beneath, her breath caught and her bottom lip slipped between her teeth. He'd had a hard time keeping his eyes off her mouth, and now he was drawn to it again.

She moved the paper and held up the small, soft cat squishy that fit easily in her palm, her eyes blinking rapidly.

"It's a—"

She looked at him, and the shine in her eyes caught him off guard. "I know what it is. It's a stress toy."

He hoped she wasn't offended. Shit. What if he'd offended her?

"This is the most thoughtful thing ever." Her hand flexed and released around the cat.

Rubbing at the back of his neck, which felt overheated, he shook his head. "That can't be true."

He really hoped that giving her a stress ball wasn't the most thoughtful thing someone had done for her. It couldn't be. Because she deserved so much more.

"It is true. It's discreet and soft, and I really love it."

Going on instinct, he took the hand that wasn't holding

the cat, turned it over, and ran a fingertip along the dulling red crescents that still showed. His heart and stomach twisted in opposite directions from the sight of them. "Maybe it'll help with this."

She nodded and pulled in a shuddery breath. Their eyes met, and the effect was more potent when he was touching her.

"Thank you," she whispered.

"You're welcome," he whispered back. He swallowed around the tightness in his throat as he pulled his hand back. "So, *Veronica Mars*. Female PI, right?"

Blinking away the moisture, Everly smiled. Chris's heart flipped over like a pup eager for attention.

"A teenage PI, and she's completely badass. You'll owe me for introducing you to the show."

Getting comfortable, he shifted on the couch, keeping the distance between them so he'd be able to concentrate. "We'll see. Have you watched *Justified*?"

She shook her head and grabbed some popcorn. He felt ridiculously pleased that she didn't put the squish toy down.

"No. Is it good?"

"If you want badass, you need to watch Raylan Givens."

"Hmm. Okay. I'll watch a few episodes, and we can compare their badassery."

Chris laughed. He did that a lot around Everly. "Speaking of, you going to try kickboxing again?" He wasn't about to admit he'd been back to the gym twice in hopes of running into her.

She looked almost bashful. "I went to a morning class. It was good but I liked ours better so I'll probably go back to that one."

"Good. I could use a sparring partner," he said, smiling at her, lifting his brows. He kickboxed with Rob. Definitely a friend-zone thing.

Her face scrunched. "I don't know, Chris. That might not be a good idea."

Disappointment lodged in his gut—he started to nod, to

agree, then her face lit with a brilliant smile that socked him right in the chest.

"I don't want my kicking your ass to put a strain on our budding friendship."

Another chuckle escaped, and he tried to think of another woman—*person*—who made him feel so at ease. The more time they spent together, the more her guard seemed to come down. She was *funny*. He hadn't expected that.

They settled into the show, and Chris had to admit it was pretty good. He honestly wasn't sure if it was what he watched on-screen or just the experience of sitting with Everly in her home, with her relaxed and comfortable in his presence, while they shared popcorn and laughter. He'd have to watch a couple of episodes at home and see if he still felt the same. What worried him, and he wasn't a worrier by nature, was the idea that when he wasn't around her, when he left, wherever he ended up, nothing would feel the same. That he'd have an Everly-size hole when he finally said good-bye.

[23]

Everly stood outside of the gym, unsure of which part of the day was knotting up her stomach. Of all the . . . *God. Just label it.* Of all the *anxiety*-related issues she cataloged as just part of who she was, the one that bugged her most was not knowing what caused the restless uncertainty inside of her. It was as though she could feel the extra energy vibrating through her, around her, under her skin, making her hyperaware, extra jumpy, and sometimes more emotional.

It was one thing to be put into a situation—a party, a date, dinner with her parents—and have it push her buttons. She could *deal* in the moment. When she approached the unknown, her thoughts barrel-rolled over her sanity. But she'd been to the gym twice now, so it shouldn't *still* make her pulse frantic.

"You didn't have to wait out here for me," Stacey said.

Everly swallowed down a yelp and spun around to see her friend. Dressed in workout clothes that were both sexy and functional, which Everly envied, Stacey grinned.

"No worries," Everly said. *Or irony. Definitely no irony in you using that phrase.*

Stacey put her fists up in front of her chin. "We could go a couple of rounds out here."

Laughter soothed some of the vibrations, making them more manageable.

She pulled the door open and waved Stacey through first. "I'm good, Rocky."

Stacey strutted past her. Whoever she'd gone out with the night before had left her extra feisty. She'd made nonstop jokes on the air this morning. A couple were about Everly's dating life, which earned her friend an equal amount of succinct whiteboard messages, but most were pretty funny.

"I'm thinking more Wonder Woman," Stacey said.

The door swung shut behind them as they walked to the counter. "No. You're more Black Widow." *You could ask for lessons.*

Stacey's eyes widened. "Yes. I think you're right."

Everly stopped before they got to the counter, looking at Stacey expectantly.

"What?"

Everly rolled her hands. "Who am I?"

"Oh." Stacey gave her a once-over and put her hand to her chin. "Pepper Potts."

"What? She doesn't kick anyone's ass," Everly said, louder than she'd meant to. There was absolutely no reason to be upset by a joke she'd started, but *Pepper Potts*?

"She's totally badass," the woman at the counter said.

Everly and Stacey looked her way, and heat suffused Everly's skin. She didn't mean to draw anyone else's attention. Especially not for a ridiculous conversation.

Stacey pulled her wallet out of her duffel bag and walked up to the counter. "Right? Pepper is the behind-the-scenes muscle. She's got the freaky kind of power that makes people—well, Tony—do things and think they're his own idea."

The young brunette, who looked like she lived at the gym, pointed at Stacey. "Yes. Exactly. She's a quiet badass on top of being a physical one. She kicked some ass in the final movie."

That was true. When it dawned on her that they were really discussing this with a stranger, she was a little embarrassed, but oddly pleased with the comparison. She pulled out her own wallet.

"Kickboxing, please," she said after Stacey paid.

"We've got a special starting. Ten classes for 25 percent off."

"That's a good deal," Stacey said, glancing at Everly.

She rubbed her fingers along her bank card, the numbers softly scraping against her thumb.

"No?" Stacey asked, stepping closer.

Everly shrugged, the nerves from earlier returning. *Take a leap. It's time.* Looking from Stacey to the brunette, she nodded. "Yes. Okay, yes. I'll pay for ten, please."

Stacey raised her fist for Everly to bump it, but instead, Everly rolled her eyes at her friend.

The class didn't start for another ten minutes, and Chris's friend wasn't in the room when they got there, so Everly followed Stacey's stretches, trying not to think about whether her *boss* would show. Since he'd given her that squishy cat two days ago, she hadn't been able to get him out of her head. He'd already been in it, sort of. The back of her thoughts. Now, he was front and center. Which was why she'd started referring to him as *boss* in her head instead of *Chris*. Best to keep those lines firmly drawn. Work was her constant, and once this radio promotion was over, maybe it would go back to being her security blanket as well.

A few more people filed in, bringing the group to nine, including Everly and Stacey. At least she'd come with someone so she wouldn't be the ninth wheel in this case. The teacher's partner. Rob hurried in with only a minute to go until the class started. He was already out of breath, and Everly wondered if he'd been teaching another class.

"Hellooooo, cutie," Stacey whispered.

Everly frowned, looked from side to side to make sure no one heard. From the looks on the other women's faces, and it was *all* women tonight, they agreed with her friend.

"He's totally out of breath. Maybe he shouldn't be teaching," Everly whispered back.

"Sorry, ladies. A treadmill challenge was issued, and I had to prove who was the best before coming."

Some of the women laughed. One near the front, wearing *very* bright yellow spandex workout clothes, put a hand on her hip. "That'll just make it easier for us to take you down."

Everly's brows furrowed deeper when Rob winked at the woman. "You could try."

The rest of the room laughed, but Everly was too caught up in wondering how people could just throw themselves out there like that. She'd been embarrassed for having a silly conversation with her friend in front of someone. Every now and again, there were situations that knocked Everly upside the head with a reminder of how different she was from the general population. When it happened, she wanted to curl up inside of herself. Or burst free.

Stacey nudged her hip with her own. "Hey, space cadet. Put your dukes up."

Her attention refocused in time to see Rob look their way, giving her a chin nod in recognition before his gaze locked on Stacey. His words trailed off, and his eyes widened marginally before he went back to what he was saying.

Interesting. She glanced at Stacey, who seemed oblivious to the heated stare the instructor sent her way.

"Okay. We'll go through the basics, work on combining some of the moves, and then we'll partner up. If everyone is okay with it, I'd like to do some work with the punching bags for the last twenty minutes. Sound good?"

The other women agreed with a chorus of yeses, including Stacey. Everly sighed. Maybe she should just get a punching bag for home. That way, if it hit her back, there'd be no witnesses.

As she went through the blocks and punches Rob modeled, coming around the room, critiquing their stances and follow-through, Everly fell into the motions. When she was trying to understand something, it was easier to turn down the white noise in her head. Having Stacey beside her helped, though she couldn't settle entirely with the combined scents of perfume and sweat reminding her she was in a roomful of strangers. Really fit ones. Including Stacey, who moved through the motions like she'd been doing it since she could walk.

"Have you done this before?" Rob asked, hands on his hips. He wore a black tank top, soaked through with sweat, and stood too close for Everly to concentrate. She lost her balance and put her other foot down as Stacey nodded, swiping the back of her arm across her forehead.

"I've been to a few classes. Here, actually, but with another teacher," Stacey said.

Rob's eyes traveled along her body, and again, Stacey seemed unaware of the heat in them. *So, you're an expert at picking up on pheromones now? Because you've been on . . . what? Four and a half dates?* Oh yeah, she was counting Daniel because they'd rescheduled and, technically, she'd shown up. Thank goodness for technicalities.

Rob reached out to reposition Stacey's arm, pausing to get permission before he actually touched her. Her respect for him increased immediately. He smiled at Everly.

"You're back and doing well. You need to widen your stance a bit," he said, showing her. She was relieved he didn't reach out to reposition any part of her, while at the same time, curious about what Stacey thought of him. Her friend talked about her dates with an easy humor, but Everly had yet to meet any of the guys she went out with.

"Thank you," she said.

"Everly, right?"

She almost laughed. As perhaps the most awkward dater ever, even *she* could pick up on Rob's attraction to her friend. Either Stacey was really not paying attention or she was playing it really freaking cool.

She nodded. "This is my friend Stacey. Rob is a friend of Chris's."

Rob held out a hand. "Deejay for the Sun. You've got a very recognizable voice," he said, holding her hand a beat longer than needed.

Stacey didn't seem to mind. "Thank you. Have you worked here long?"

He nodded. "Since inception. I own it."

Anything else he planned to say was cut short by a woman asking for guidance on how to follow through.

Everly waited for Stacey to make some of the usual comments she made around cute guys, but her friend was suspiciously silent.

She sidled up to Stacey and leaned toward her. "No running commentary about his butt or what his abs might look like?"

Stacey feigned a punch at her and laughed, also leaning forward. "No, why? Do you want to see his butt and his abs?"

Everly's face flamed. "No!"

Others looked at them, so she glared at Stacey but bit her tongue. It could have been Everly's overactive imagination, but it felt like Rob spent considerably more time hovering around them than the rest of the women. He shot several looks their way, but Stacey maintained an unusual focus on her movements.

By the time they went to the punching bags, Everly felt like she'd swallowed a pound of sand.

"I need to refill my water," she told Stacey, trying *not* to breathe like an obscene caller.

"'Kay," Stacey said, pulling her phone out.

Waiting in the line at the fountain, Everly kept her gaze on her feet. Easier to avoid eye contact that way. *Nice. Friendly as usual.* She lifted her chin. *You're out. That matters. Focus on the good.* The rules were actually helping her navigate her focus. *Uh-huh, that's why you spent last night tossing and turning, thinking about how Chris's laugh made you enjoy* Veronica Mars *even more.*

"Your turn," someone said behind her.

Everly jolted and sent an apologetic look, moving forward in the line. *Yeah. Really focused.* Weaving her way through the gym, pleased that she felt a little more settled than the last two times she'd visited, she found her class already starting on the punching bags. They were in the far back corner of the gym in a matted area, not far from where people lifted weights. There were six bags, and five of the women had taken a position in front while Rob taught them how to steady the bag, how to hit it, and how to move around.

"I'm not so sure about this part," Everly whispered.

Stacey grinned. "Why? This is the good part. You can take out all your aggressions on it."

Everly side-eyed her friend, lifting her brows. "Is that what you'll be doing?"

Rob called Stacey to the bag and used her as an example of how to step into a punch.

"Everly?"

She turned, her insides already cringing at the familiar voice. Simon stood staring at her with his mouth slightly open. Speaking of rules—there was a law in her universe that said she could only run into people she didn't want to when she looked her worst. He, of course, wasn't even sweating. Maybe he'd just arrived.

"Simon." Her voice came out smoother than she expected. She waited for her pulse to kick into high gear, but it remained the same as it was a few seconds ago.

Stacey appeared at her side. "What are you doing here?"

"Working out," Simon said with a dismissive glance toward Stacey.

"Weird. I thought you liked your workouts more horizontal with women who weren't your girlfriend," Stacey said, tilting her head like she was thinking it over.

Everly's gaze went cartoon-character wide, and she slapped a hand over her mouth, a giggle tickling her throat.

Rob approached her other side. "Everything okay?"

Simon scowled, saying to Rob. "Fine." He turned to Everly, the sneer still present. "Can I talk to you for a second?"

Hard pass. "No."

Stacey slid closer until her shoulders were brushing Everly's. "You can get lost, though."

"I'm not talking to you," Simon said, teeth gritted.

"And it doesn't sound like Everly wants to talk to you, so why don't you go finish your workout and leave her alone?" Rob's voice was calm and smooth, but it was clear the question was not a suggestion.

"Five minutes," Simon said.

"Is that your personal best?" Stacey asked. She leaned into him, not even pretending to whisper.

Everly lowered her chin to her chest and bit her cheek to keep from laughing. She should *not* be laughing. There was nothing funny about running into her ex after he'd recently bashed her on another station. The memory infused her with irritation.

Simon started to speak, something unpleasant if the sneer on his face was any indication. Everly squared her shoulders, holding a hand up.

"Stop. Honestly, he's not worth the time." He wasn't. He wasn't even worth the energy it would take to insult him.

His gaze whipped to her, showing surprise. "Everly."

"Go away, Simon. Before one of us says something we shouldn't."

"Or kicks you right in the—" Stacey started.

Simon cut her off. "Screw you, Stacey. I know that contest was your idea. It has your stupidity all over it."

Rob's chest puffed up, but he glanced at Everly, making her want to weep with appreciation that even though it was clear what he wanted to do, he paused long enough to let it be her choice.

Giving him a surprisingly genuine-smile, she whispered, "Yes, please."

Rob's next motions were like a choreographed dance. He stepped into Simon, raised one hand, snapped his fingers once, his other hand going to Simon's shoulder as two huge, muscled men came out of seemingly nowhere and flanked him.

"These gentlemen will escort you out of my gym. You're no longer welcome here," Rob said, his voice tightly controlled.

Everly closed her eyes, realizing belatedly that they were making a spectacle and that others were staring. Her pulse picked up, and the sweat beading at the back of her neck was no longer from overexerting herself. *You will not panic. You will not flee. Breathe.* She tapped her fingertips against her thumb. Index, middle, ring, pinkie, repeat. Repeat. Repeat. Flickering in the base of her brain, though, was pride. She'd done it. She'd stood up to someone who didn't deserve her time. She hadn't been a bitch, which, in her opinion, was the easy road. She'd held her own and felt good about herself. *If only people weren't watching you.*

"Breathe," Stacey whispered, pressing her hand to Everly's back.

"You know what? I'm going to go," she said quietly. It was a good decision. *Her* decision so it didn't make her a coward.

"Don't. Don't let that ass chase you out of here," Stacey said, her voice atypically harsh.

"If you need a minute, you can go to my office," Rob said in a much softer tone.

"I don't. I don't need a minute," she said. She needed a whole bunch of them, all to herself.

The other women hovered around them, and a few of Rob's staff checked in, glancing at her but speaking only to Rob.

"Don't go home," Stacey said when Rob walked back to the class.

"I don't feel well," Everly said, trying to rein in her fluttery breaths.

"You're fine."

God. Wouldn't that be something if you actually felt that way? Fine? Instead, she felt overheated and nauseated.

"It's not like I won't be back. I have nine more visits paid for." She'd force herself to use them, but she'd had enough for tonight. "I'll see you tomorrow." The need to go clawed at her. Baby steps. She'd handled herself, she deserved some space. *No one is looking at you.* She walked toward the exit, refusing to keep her head down. Stacey stayed at her side, and when they exited the building, Everly gulped in the fresh air.

"Why do you do this? Why do you let someone who doesn't matter have so much control over you? Don't you know how much better you are than he is?"

Simon wasn't controlling her—it'd be easier to fight if he were. Everly bent at the waist and put her hands to her knees. "This isn't about him. I needed some air. Some space. Even Pepper Potts needed a damn minute after kicking ass. I kicked ass in there. Be proud of me, or at least don't question me. I didn't question you when you got all weird around Rob. So how about you let this go?"

"What?" The one word rang out sharply, disrupting the quiet evening.

Everly stood up, feelings tripping over each other. "You." She pointed to the building. "In there. You're the queen of flirting and sexual innuendos, but when he talked to you, you clammed up like I do at a staff party."

"You don't attend staff parties," Stacey said.

Everly rolled her eyes. "Nice deflection."

"I was there to work out, not hit on one of Chris's friends. I was there for *you.* Why is it the people who love you don't get to have an impact on your actions or how you feel about yourself? You'll let some creep you dated for five minutes chase you out of a building but won't take any of us at our word that you deserve better."

Everly's jaw dropped, and blood rushed to her head. "I *know*

I deserve better. I walked away from *him.* I know you don't get how hard it was for me to do that just now, but it was. A public confrontation? I don't *do* that. So excuse me if I need five fucking minutes after to decompress without people staring at me."

Tears burned her eyes as guilt kicked her in the lungs. Stacey always had her back even when she didn't understand the whats and whys of Everly's quirks.

"I'm sorry. I'm sorry. That was uncalled for. Thank you for coming tonight. Finish the class. Please? So I don't feel worse than I already do?"

"Everly," Stacey said, surprise and hurt etched into her features, woven into her tone.

She felt the sigh Stacey held back.

More than all the other things she hated feeling, Everly despised being a burden or a weight on her friend.

"I'll text you later." But sometimes, there was nothing she could do about it. She couldn't stand here and pretend she could let everything roll off her shoulders. When Stacey stepped back, her face a mask of disappointment, Everly's heart muscles clenched. Maybe she didn't deserve friendship. She dismissed the thought, angry at herself for wallowing. *Go home. Get over it. Focus on the good.* Why the hell was that so hard when there was so much of it?

[24]

Everly forced herself not to think of Simon or feeling awkward at the gym or to give in to the nagging urge to text Stacey that she was sorry. She'd tell her again in person, but there was no reason to interrupt any more of her evening. Instead, she kept herself busy by working on her Facebook posts and her own journal notes.

It surprised her how much she enjoyed this piece of it. The idea of sharing without having to engage in back and forth conversation was freeing. She kept the posts short when she was reminding listeners which candidates were coming up and a little longer when describing the date. Tonight's post was about rescheduling the last date and how it could be tricky, even for someone with a limited social calendar, to fit dating in. The other surprise was the comments on the posts.

There were several instances of *Way to go, Everly* and lots of *You go, girl,* which was an expression she just couldn't pull off. Sometimes she answered, others she didn't. The interaction was part of bringing the audience into the fold, but she hadn't expected to enjoy it.

Her eyes stopped at a comment made after she'd posted about canceling on Daniel.

> **Ally Meyer** You're so inspiring, Everly. I'd never get the nerve to reschedule. I can't even find the nerve to say *yes*.

Everly's fingers hovered over the keyboard. She was no one's guru, but she could give her own perspective.

> **Everly Dean** Thank you, Ally, but trust me when I say I take it one step at a time. Saying yes that first time and making yourself follow through really does make the next time easier.

It sent a strange thrill through her that her experience was impacting others. What if she could help others be brave by being brave herself? Not in a public forum or anything. She wasn't signing up to give TED Talks, but interacting on Facebook in small degrees was okay.

She smiled when she saw dots pop up under her comment. Was Ally commenting back? It could just as easily be someone chiming in to be negative. There were a lot of *Take Simon back* comments peppered in between the good ones.

> **Ally Meyer** I'm going to try. The next time my crush asks me out, I'm going to say yes. Any suggestions for how to make myself believe he'll actually *want* to ask again?

Everly laughed. She was treading in unchartered waters. No one asked her for dating advice. It was surreal and a little unsettling. *Don't screw it up. Just be honest. What would you do?*

> **Everly Dean** If you want the truth, I made a list of rules for myself. Things I wanted to follow through with. I needed it if I wanted to reach my goals. Could you do something similar? Make a list of what makes you awesome, just to remind yourself when you're feeling unsure? Obviously, there's a reason he's asked more than once.

She almost added, *You go, girl,* but fortunately stopped herself.

An instant message from Ally popped up. Everly opened it,

pulse pumping. She didn't want a stalker or anything. *She's not a stalker. Just a girl who feels like you do.*

Ally Meyer Thank you for taking the time to respond. I'm going to do that. It'll be good to have something to remind myself. Good luck on your next date. I'm still rooting for Owen.

Everly thanked her before shutting down the computer. Unable to wipe the smile from her face, she thought about the interaction, about the podcast she still wanted to push. Mari had seemed on edge about Everly getting another spotlight. It wasn't what she was after, though. She just wanted to create something that would resonate with people. Ideas started to simmer. She didn't have to be sole producer of the podcast. Everly had never wanted *or* needed the spotlight. She just wanted to be good at her job.

A small smile played on her lips as she thought of ideas to bounce off Mari and Stacey. The five words on her screen pulled her heart back into her stomach.

MOM: Come visit at my office?

Everly sighed and closed her laptop, getting up from the table. She took her phone with her as she walked toward her bedroom to grab a light sweater. As she went, she typed the response her mother was no doubt expecting because this was so far from the first time, she couldn't even remember.

EVERLY: On my way.

***

Her mom's office was actually a converted home. They owned the entire home, but she ran her massage practice out of the bottom. The top unit was shared by a chiropractor and a physical therapist. The entrance and living area had been transformed into a waiting area, the former kitchen was now a staff break room, and two of the three bedrooms were massage rooms. The third bedroom was an office for her mom, complete with pull-out couch and television. It was a pretty sweet setup.

Everly knocked, ignoring the knots growing in her stomach. Her mother opened on the second knock.

"Hi, sweet girl." She pulled her into a tight hug.

"Hi, Mom," Everly said, her voice muffled by her mother's embrace.

"You didn't have to come," she said, stepping back and waving Everly in.

Uh-huh. And if she hadn't, she'd never hear the end of it. The sound of a game show came from down the hall, along with the scent of lavender. What had been the catalyst this time?

"Did you have dinner?"

Everly slipped off her shoes and walked toward the office. "No. I went to the gym and was going to eat after," she said. She hadn't been hungry after the gym. Simon tended to ruin her appetite.

"The gym? Good for you. I'll order Chinese."

"I'm not hungry, Mom. What are you guys fighting about?" Why did they have to do this dance? Why couldn't they remember she was their kid, not their friend, not their counselor? *Uh, because you never say anything?*

When she walked into the office, she stopped abruptly. "What is that?"

"Do you like it?" Her mom came up behind her, poked her head over Everly's shoulder. "It's my new hobby. Life portraits of the male form. And if you must know, *that's* what we fought about."

Everly tried to look somewhere else—at the television, the couch, the floor—but it was impossible not to stare at the life-size canvas she'd set up against the wall. Where had she even gotten a canvas that big?

Her mom moved around her and walked over, gesturing to the painting—if it could actually be called that—with wild, fluttery hands and a smile.

"I've been taking a course here and there at the college. Your father was all offended when he found my drawings around the house. But look at this, Evs. This is the human body in all its glory."

Everly choked and nodded at the same time. It looked more like stretched beige cloth with a tennis ball shoved into the top of it and strange limb-like things—*Please let that one be a leg and not something else*—sprouting out from different areas.

"Is it . . . um, abstract?"

Her mother's smile flatlined. "No. Oh, honey, you don't have an artist's eye. Plus, it's not finished. This is just the beginning."

Everly absolutely did not want to know what it was the beginning of. And she hoped never to see the end. *Oh God, what if she gives it to me as a gift?* There was no hiding that thing at the back of a closet. It was bigger than her closet.

She sank down on the couch, oddly unsettled as if there were a third, faceless, well-endowed presence in the room.

"Dad didn't like the drawings?"

Her mother sank down beside her. "No. Men can appreciate—a.k.a. drool—all over women's bodies and talk about their great butts and boobs and everything else, but I can't comment when I see a well-shaped man? I mean, excuse me for noticing a really tight, firm—"

"Mom." The word snapped out of her mouth like a shot. She held up a hand. "Got it. Appreciation is one thing, but would you like it if Dad were drawing the female form?"

Her mother's eyes widened and filled with tears. "I asked him to take the course with me. I'm sure they'll get some female models soon."

Everly's jaw dropped. "You looked at a real person for this?"

She nodded. Proudly. Everly did her best to avoid looking at the painting again.

"Wow." She'd gotten her mother's jaw structure and nose. How come she hadn't gotten any of her guts?

Her mother jumped up. "Let me grab some snacks." She rolled her eyes, but they landed on the painting and all she wanted was a blindfold.

Everly checked off the list in her head: she'd come back with two glasses of wine, snacks she'd prepared, even though Everly didn't have to show up, and then she'd say how she didn't feel seen or understood. Sometime tomorrow, her father would give his side of the events. Everly was expected to show an openly divided loyalty. It was exhausting.

Pulling her phone out of her purse, she glanced at it and saw a text from Chris.

CHRIS: Rob said you ran into Simon. You okay?

She typed back a quick response.

EVERLY: I'm fine. It was just a moment.

CHRIS: . . .

Everly waited.

CHRIS: Want company?

A gentle shiver traveled over her skin.

EVERLY: I'm at my mom's work.

CHRIS: Getting a massage?

She smiled even as her cheeks heated.

EVERLY: No. When she and my dad fight, she comes here to "cool down." It's complicated.

CHRIS: Most things are. Text me if you change your mind. I'll just be watching VM.

"You should latch on to whoever is making you smile like that," her mother said, carrying two way-too-full wineglasses. She set them down and went back to the kitchen, returning a minute later with a platter of cheeses, crackers, and veggies with some hummus dip.

Everly slipped her phone back inside her purse and picked up her wine. It was too sweet for her taste, but she wouldn't drink it all, anyway.

"So?" Everly braced for whatever her mom would say. She'd always thought by thirty, she wouldn't care. That she'd be immune to their back-and-forth game in the way she was to reality shows—they piqued her interest, but she could easily turn off the TV. With her parents, though, it was one of those ones that sucked her in even when she knew she shouldn't watch. She couldn't look away or pretend it didn't matter.

Her mother leaned back with a sigh. "Tell me about the smile first."

It was nowhere to be found. "It's nothing."

Her mom leaned over and poked her in the shoulder, a playful grin tilting her lips. "One of the lucky bachelors?"

Nope. Just the . . . purveyor of said bachelors.

"How's that going?"

Two dates left and it's over. "Fine. It's . . . okay, I guess. I have another date tomorrow." She knew how this worked—give a little to get the intel. "I had to reschedule last time, so it's a makeup date."

Her mom's smile shifted into something else. Something Everly didn't want to see. "Oh? How will you *make* it up to him?"

Huffing out a breath, she tapped the fingers of one hand on her thigh. "I don't like when you do this."

"What?" Her mom blinked innocently.

She knew exactly what. They'd had the conversation enough times.

"You wanted me to come, so just tell me. What's going on with you and Dad?"

Pasting on a phony grin that—to her credit—she didn't use often, her mom leaned in. "I have an idea. Why don't the two of us hit whatever hot spot is all the rage these days?"

Blinking rapidly, Everly tried to wrap her head around the sentence. *Take it slow. No temper. She's hurting.* Hidden well or not, Everly knew her mom didn't enjoy their blowups. Who would?

"I have no idea what would be considered a hot spot right now. Like, zero. And as to anything being 'the rage'? I don't think that's a thing anymore."

Her mom poked her in the shoulder again and then grabbed a piece of cheese from the platter. "We should switch spots. You act like you're thirty years older than I am. Youth is wasted, sweet girl. Tell me about the date tomorrow."

She wore yoga pants and a fitted tank top. Her dark hair was pulled up in a messy bun, and her face was makeup-free. Since she'd inherited her mother's lack of cleavage, Everly hoped to age in a similarly graceful fashion.

Everly continued to stare until, finally, her mom's shoulders dropped and she knew it was time.

"Marriage is hard, Evie."

There's a news flash. "Yeah, Mom. That's why people go to counseling or talk things out, make changes." *The hard part is what you work at, persevere through.* That was the whole point of the commitment.

"He doesn't see my talent. My need for a creative outlet. He insulted my work," she said, holding her wine in both hands.

Hobby, Mom. It can't be work unless you actually commit to it. Maybe that's a more common theme than I'd thought. She never returned to one of her blowout hobbies, so she never actually got better at any of them. Not balloon animals, crocheting, cross-stitching, fishing. The chances she'd become the next Picasso were slim.

Everly pushed back at the irritation roiling through her, but she hated this, everything about it from being in the middle to wondering if they'd ever actually pull the plug. How could anyone live with that kind of uncertainty? She couldn't. Some people called it a piece of paper, but in her mind, you sign it, you mean it. You don't run off when things take a sharp turn.

"Why do you do this to each other?" *To me.* The words came out harsher than she'd intended.

Her mother's eyes widened. "Do what? I'm trying to navigate growing older with a man who says he's changing and I'm not changing with him. He thinks our life is boring and we need more excitement. I asked him to try one of my hobbies. He wants to travel or to maybe try something new in the—"

Everly cleared her throat, interrupting her mom. "I'm begging you not to finish that sentence or even the thought." There were so many things a kid never needed to know about their parents.

Her mom rolled her eyes and sighed. "How are you such a prude? People have sex, Everly. It's normal and natural, and sometimes, when a dry spell happens, you need to spice things up. I'm not opposed to that."

Everly's brows pushed together, and she picked up a piece of celery. "It's like I didn't actually say, 'Don't tell me,' out loud."

"This is how he gets his way," her mom said, bottom lip quivering. She pointed to her artwork. "Belittling the way I express myself."

Despite Everly's impatience with the situation and both of her parents—because no doubt both of them had a hand in whatever had caused this round—guilt and pity swamped her.

She wanted them to be happy but had no idea how to help that along.

"It's not healthy for you guys to go back and forth like this. Did you try telling him he hurt your feelings? Did you try to understand how he felt when he said he didn't like seeing his wife draw nude men?" Everly grabbed another piece of celery, suddenly hungry.

Her mom lowered the sound on the TV. "It's easy to judge when you've never been in a serious relationship, never mind married, sweetheart."

Crunching into the tasteless vegetable, she figured it was a good thing her mouth was full. Maybe she'd never been married, but she knew when she did, it would be for good. Choosing to spend your lives together shouldn't resemble a freaking yo-yo every time one person didn't get their own way.

She swallowed, hoping the extra seconds smoothed her tone. "Relationships, marriage or otherwise, are supposed to be a mostly positive thing. I don't need to get married or have been married to know that this back-and-forth you guys do isn't healthy. If you love each other, you make it work. If you really want a hobby, get one and stick to it. Don't do it as a way to get back at him for something. Stop coming here when you're mad. Talk to your husband. If you can't do it on your own, ask for help. There are professionals for this. You love each other. Leaving can't be just one of the option boxes you check when you're mad."

Where had all that come from? She blinked, nerves swirling at the look of shock on her mother's face. Everly picked up her wineglass again and gripped the stem tightly, taking a long swallow.

"I didn't invite you over for this. I just wanted company," her mother said quietly. She hadn't invited her at all—she'd sent the "I need you" code, and Everly had gone.

Lowering her glass and her gaze, Everly nodded. "I'm sorry," she said softly.

"You don't understand. Maybe one day, you will."

That had always been her hope. To one day understand them. *Not today, obviously.*

By the time she left, Everly felt wired. Unsettled energy coursed through her, looking for an outlet. *Maybe you should go back to kickboxing now,* she thought. She did have nine classes left. She was actually looking forward to going, but tonight, she was too tired.

On the drive back to her place, she thought about how she'd managed to piss off two of her favorite people today: her mom and her best friend. Thinking about it only made her antsier, so instead of heading for her home, she detoured to the grocery store.

The parking lot of Save N' Shop was quiet when Everly pulled in. Adulting at night was far less crowded. Maybe this could be her new thing. She smirked. Stacey would so veto that as trying a new thing. A little thorn lodged in her ribs. She didn't like when things weren't okay with Stacey. Or not knowing whether there was more she should apologize for. She grabbed a basket. *Things will be fine. You'll text her later, Stacey will blow off your apologies, the slate will be clean.*

Maybe my something new should be to cook something. If those little kids on TV can do it, I can. Maybe. She was a decent cook—as in, she didn't starve even without takeout. *How about a dessert?* She passed the baking aisle, stopped, and decided to check it out. *Something chocolate? Chocolate is always good. Chocolate caramel pie, in particular, is very good.* That same shiver she'd felt with Chris's text grazed her skin, making her heart feel like a live wire. She started to talk herself out of making a dessert that would cause her to think *more* about the man she shouldn't be fixating on. *Do you have to pick apart every little thing you do? Make it into something more? It's a dessert. Get over yourself, Everly. You're not proposing marriage.* Pulling her phone out, she looked up the ingredients.

"This isn't so hard. I can do this," she muttered, scrolling down the list.

"I have no doubt you can," a deep, male voice said.

Everly's head snapped up, her skin prickling with the embarrassment that came along with talking to oneself. She locked eyes with Owen Baston. Bachelor number one. The smile that took over her face was shockingly genuine. It stretched her cheeks.

Her heart flipped out like a hamster on speed, stuck on one of those wheels. "Ha. Thanks for the vote of confidence."

Owen's eyes twinkled with amusement. "My pleasure. What is it you can most definitely do?"

Warmth flooded her chest. He was cute, sweet. Funny. "Make a salted chocolate caramel cake."

Owen hummed low, the sound nearly as sexy as the scent of his cologne when he leaned in. *Hmm.* Definitely sexy. *Not shiver-inducing sexy but nice.* Nice was good. Nice was safe. Safe was *awesome.*

"Sounds delicious. Even if it goes wrong, you have to try."

Why did that feel like good life advice in this minute?

Owen smiled. "How are you?"

"I'm good. You?"

"Not bad. Work is good, life is good. I can't complain. How's the dating game?"

She laughed and knew she'd curse herself later for how loud it sounded in the empty aisle. "Exciting as always. Just two more to go."

"Before you choose the lucky guy?" He said it in such a genuine way, her flutters softened.

"Before I narrow it down, anyway."

His phone buzzed, and he got extra points for not bothering to pull it out and check it. "It's probably against the rules, but do you want to go grab a coffee?"

"Oh, I shouldn't have coffee this late at night. No caffeine, really. I'll never sleep. When you get older, caffeine can actually affect you more easily." *You take dork to a whole new level, Everly Dean. Way to go.*

To her surprise and relief, Owen laughed. The sound was deep and rough and sent what she was willing to call a mini-shiver over her skin. "I forgot your age, clearly. How about some warm milk?"

Everly bit her lip, trying not to giggle awkwardly or smile like a loon. It was getting late, she hadn't bought the few groceries she needed, and it hadn't been the best of evenings all the way around. *Be bold. Even if it's scary.*

Owen watched her through dark blue eyes with caution and consideration. She got the sense he wouldn't push if she said no. It wasn't actually against the rules. *Technically.*

"Sure. That sounds good," she said, going with her gut but needing to add, "I can't be out for long." It was reflex to add the escape hatch. Just in case.

He smiled warmly. Sweetly. "Do you turn into a garden vegetable?"

She fell into step beside him, dessert forgotten. "Pumpkins are actually a fruit." *That's it. Reel him in, dork-a-saurus.* She stopped, looked up at him. "Let's pretend I didn't say that."

He bit back his chuckle, but it was there. She could see it in the creases around his eyes. "I'll wave my magic wand and it'll be like it never happened."

Everly liked how easy it was to laugh with him. This was what she needed: a sweet, funny, good-looking man who made her feel *something* but not too much. One who wasn't off-limits. One she could open up to but not lose herself in. Owen was absolutely right. Even if it didn't work out, she had to try.

[25]

For only the second time in her life, Everly stood outside someone's front door, way too early in the morning, unsure if she should let herself in. She had a key. It was a you're-welcome-any-time-don't-even-knock key. She'd never used it before because there'd been no reason. Now felt like a valid reason.

Stacey hadn't returned her text the night before, so maybe she needed some space. Stacey never needed space. Without being overbearing, she was as "in your face" as a friend could get. They'd been spending more time out of work together than *at* work for the better part of three years. If they were fighting, they'd smooth things over and things would be fine. Shifting from one foot to the other without letting either foot actually leave the ground, she chewed the inside of her lip.

Unless you've finally maxed out her patience. Unlike chocolate, caffeine, or batteries, there was such a thing as too much where Everly was concerned.

It's going to be time for you to go to work if you don't knock one day soon. Just go in. She knocked with her free hand, keeping her fingers curled into her palm when she lowered her arm. Seconds that felt like minutes passed without response. She knocked again, curled her fingers deeper, and wished she'd remembered to put Pepper Potts in her pocket. Yes, she'd named her squishy cat from Chris. No one had to know.

The door swung open, and Stacey appeared, looking less than impressed. Her hair was knotted into a messy bun more on the side of her head than the top. She wore an oversize hoodie and loose flannel pants and a scowl.

Everly didn't cover her shock with any amount of grace. "I don't think I've ever seen you without makeup."

Stacey yawned, not bothering to cover her mouth. "Well, if that was your goal, showing up at the crack of dawn is the way to do it." Her squinty gaze focused on the bag in Everly's hand. "What's that?"

Everly gave her best "I'm sorry I'm high maintenance" smile. "Double chocolate fudge doughnuts. From Baked."

Stacey stepped back. "Permission to enter, granted." Once she'd shut the door to the tiny bungalow home, she grabbed the bag. "Gimme."

Laughing, Everly followed her into the kitchen. The bungalow used to belong to Stacey's grandmother, but she'd inherited it after her grandmother's passing several years earlier. It was part of her decision to settle in San Verde despite opportunities to work at bigger stations.

While Stacey started coffee, Everly glanced around the kitchen. Dishes from the night before, and probably the night before that, were stacked on the counter. Old newspapers sat on the small round table. In the window over the table, a once-leafy plant drooped.

Everly went to the sink, grabbed a glass from the cupboard, and turned on the water. She poured a small amount on the plant, waiting for it to drain into the tray below, listening to the sounds of Stacey grinding beans and shuffling around.

Her skin felt too tight. She hated fighting. Hated conflict. Especially when she was the source.

"Thanks. If I ever have kids, they're going to be in trouble if you don't visit more often," Stacey said, jutting her chin in the plant's direction when Everly set the glass on the counter.

Taking a deep breath, trying to fill her lungs with courage, she faced her friend. "Tell me what to do to make us okay. I'm sorry I acted weird at the gym last night. I'm sorry I left, that I overreacted. I'm sorry I'm high maintenance, fussy, and all the other adjectives you could probably label me with. But along with the negative ones, like *finicky* or *anal*, I want you to know you can also add *loyal, loving, trustworthy*, and *reliable*."

Stacey blinked several times, leaning against the edge of her aged countertop. "That was a *lot* before coffee. What are you even talking about?"

The air whooshed out of Everly's lungs. "I can't stand you being mad at me."

"Good thing I'm not, then. Have you been up for hours worrying about this?" Stacey's eyes narrowed.

Of course. Unnecessarily so, apparently. Everly scoffed, averted her eyes. "No. Hardly. Whatever."

"You forgot *convincing* on your list of adjectives."

Stacey turned and grabbed two cups from the glass-fronted cupboard.

"Maybe it's time to see someone," Stacey said quietly.

Everly purposely sidestepped this. "I'm seeing too many people. This is part of why we can't be fighting. I need you. I'm multi-dating."

Stacey spun. "What?"

"You heard me. You can't be mad at me. I need you."

"I'm not mad at you. We're circling back to the 'you should *talk* to someone who can help you work through your anxiety' conversation because I'm sure you've created new indents in your skin worrying about something that wasn't a problem. Now, if you value your life and want me to share the doughnuts, tell me what you mean by *multi-dating*."

Everly opened her mouth.

Stacey held up a hand. "Wait. Let me grab the coffee; you get the doughnuts and meet me in the living room."

All breathing functions returned to normal, and adrenaline pumped through Everly's veins. They were okay. *No reason to worry. Ah, but then what would you do with your time?* It'd be interesting to find out.

The living room was completely retro, but by current decorating standards, it was hard to tell if it was on purpose or because Stacey had never updated after her grandmother died. After removing the box from Baked from the bag and setting it on the coffee table, Everly curled up in the yellow wingback chair, tugging the soft crocheted throw over her legs. Stacey joined her only a minute later, setting both coffees on the table. She tugged two napkins out of the pocket of her hoodie.

"Explain yourself, Dean."

Everly smiled. "First, are you sure we're okay? I felt like we didn't leave things okay last night."

"We're fine, Evs. Even if we weren't, we'll always be fine. There's nothing we can't get through. You're my girl. You know that. You're quirky as hell, and I love you. All those little idiosyncrasies you, for some reason, dislike about yourself are just a small part of why I love you. You're for real, Evs, and so is our friendship. Don't ever doubt that. Ever. Or I'll kick your ass."

Everly laughed, tears filling her eyes. *No tears.*

Stacey's expression softened along with her voice. "I wish I could help you loosen up, stop your brain from spinning. Not because it bugs me but because I see how hard it is on *you*. You're exhausted, babe. But I'll always be here for you. Just as you are. You accept me, I accept you. That's how this works. Now, do you want to lose out on a doughnut? Because you've been warned. No more mushy stuff. Spill it. Did you get naked with someone?"

Everly was leaning forward for the doughnuts and nearly fell at Stacey's words. She sputtered unintelligibly before saying, "No. Of course not."

Stacey grabbed one of the chocolatey pieces of goodness and brought it to her mouth, saying just before her bite, "This may be part of your problem and why you have so many quirks."

Picking up her own doughnut, Everly licked chocolate off her index finger. "I disagree, but regardless. Guess who I ran into last night? Never mind. Guessing takes too much time. Owen. Bachelor number one. He was in the grocery store, which I stopped at after I visited Mom at her office, and he asked me to go for a drink."

Watching her friend's jaw drop open was mildly satisfying. "But no naked?"

Huffing out a breath, she took a bite. "Of any sort."

Pointing with her doughnut, Stacey asked, "Your mom was at the office ? I'm scared to ask. What was it this time?"

Everly cringed. "Nude paintings."

Stacey slapped a hand over her mouth, then moved it. "Of herself?"

"No!" Everly shuddered. "Actually, that might have been better. She's taking a course on how to draw people in their birthday suits. Only the one she drew looked more like he was wearing a wrinkled bodysuit."

Stacey burst out laughing. "I'm oddly intrigued and kind of want to see it."

Everly waved a hand, not wanting to get into that conversation. "You don't. Trust me. Save yourself."

"Okay. Was Owen still dreamy at second glance?"

It was easy to smile when she thought about him. *That's a good sign.* "He was. Also, he was still sweet, funny, and charming."

Stacey sat straighter. "I think you're smitten."

"I could be." She had a strong suspicion he was going to be the one she chose.

"Did you at least want to get naked?"

Everly sank into the chair, breaking off a chunk of doughnut. "Are you secretly a sex addict?"

Polishing off her own treat in record time, Stacey made loud, sucking motions while cleaning off her fingers. "I can neither confirm nor deny."

"That's exactly what someone who was secretly addicted to sex would say."

Stacey shook her head. "You can't know that. Anyway, this isn't about me."

"No. It's about me, who never goes out and somehow ended up on a date last night and has another date tonight." *And has a secret crush on our boss.* In her mind, she slapped a hand over her mouth. Where had that thought jumped in from? *Uh, reality?* God, she hated her brain. *You do not like Chris. You do not like Chris. He's your buddy. Like Stacey. Your kickboxing partner. Who looks delicious both before and after a workout. Shut up.* Why did her brain never listen? *Owen. You want Owen. Owen would look good after a workout, too.*

"It's about time. You deserve to play the field and see what's out there for you. One of these guys is going to give you tummy flutters. I can feel it."

Ha. The wrong one. "I don't know, Stace. I had a panic attack the other night. That's why I had to reschedule."

All humor fled from Stacey's gaze. "Dude. You're supposed to call me when these things happen. Why didn't you?"

Everly shrugged. *Because it never stops being embarrassing? I called Chris, and he came over. I . . . lost track of everything else.*

"What did you do?" Stacey grabbed a napkin, wiped her hands, and then crumpled it up, tossing it back on the table.

"Chris actually came over. We watched *Veronica Mars.*"

"What? You watched our show with someone else?" Stacey unfolded her legs from the couch and got up. "I need a moment."

Everly laughed, heard the water running and was still smiling when Stacey returned, hands clean. She picked up her coffee.

"Question," Stacey said, leaning on the arm of the couch.

"I'll allow it," Everly said, picking up her own cup.

"Have you considered the possibility of getting naked with Chris?"

Her heart went a kind of haywire she hadn't experienced before. Like she'd taken an adrenaline shot straight to it. In slow, calculated movements that required a lot of effort, Everly brought her mug to her lips, sipped, tasted nothing, and set it down. "I'm not sure why you're so fascinated with the idea of me naked. Maybe it's more than a sex addiction going on for you. I'm not running around looking for men to strip naked."

Stacey sank back into her spot on the couch with a sigh. "Trust me, friend, you'd be far more relaxed if you were. But for real. Was I imagining a little spark of lust between you two?"

"He's my boss. He's *our* boss. We're becoming friends." She folded her hands together.

"So, no, I wasn't imagining it."

"He's in charge of our job security." Her fingers linked together.

Stacey sat forward. "You like him."

"He's a perfectly nice human being."

Setting her coffee down, Stacey pressed both palms flat on the table. "You *really* like him. 'Perfectly nice human being'? You don't like human beings. They talk too much. This is serious."

Despite feeling like the room got a hundred degrees hotter, Everly let out a deep belly laugh. "You're such a dork."

"You're a dork in love with her boss."

Picking up the napkin Stacey had crumpled, Everly tossed it in her face. "You take that back. I'm not."

Laughing, Stacey tossed the napkin on the ground, and Everly did her best to ignore the urge to pick it up. Or flee from the conversation. "Be honest. Do you think Chris Jansen is dreamy?"

Her annoying insides trembled, waking up at the sound of his name. The thought of him. "He's attractive."

"Uh-huh. On a scale of one to I'd-sleep-with-him, where is he?"

Everly's cheeks felt like fireballs. Stacey pointed, making it clear that her expression gave her away.

"Oh my God. I was teasing at first, but do you seriously like him, Ev?"

Picking up her coffee, Everly took another drink, but it had cooled too much to be enjoyable. "It doesn't matter. Stop. I need your advice."

"On what? Whether or not to bang our boss?"

She nearly choked on her own spit. "Jesus, Stacey. I'm not banging anyone, and if you say that's part of my problem, we *will* be fighting, because that's not what any of this is about. I don't want to be alone for the rest of my life. I'm not happy dating a string of men and figuring out how to act around each one. I thought by thirty, I'd already have kids. That I'd have a loving husband who made me laugh and swoon in equal measure. Instead, I'm dating like a college coed and breaking out in hives every second day."

Stacey got up and came over to sit on the arm of the chair, putting her feet on the other arm, creating a bridge over Everly's lap. "Okay. Okay. Breathe. Slow down. I'm sorry."

She rubbed Everly's back, making her feel both comforted and needy at the same time. Damn it. Why couldn't she have a normal freaking conversation? No wonder she hadn't settled down or found the one.

"Do you want to stop the contest?"

"No," she whispered. Clearing her throat, she said it again, louder. She realized that was actually the *truth*. "I don't. Stace, last night, a woman contacted me and thanked me for being brave. She talked to me a bit about her own anxiety. I felt like I actually helped someone. I have two dates left, one later today. I think Owen is going to be the front-runner. It's more than that, though."

Stacey waited. Like Chris had. No rushing. Just patience. Her heart muscles spasmed as she leaned into her friend.

"I feel good. I'm learning things about myself. I stood up to Simon even though I had to leave after. I hung out with Owen last night. I invited Chris over to hang out. I made someone else want to be brave."

She was surprised to see tears fill Stacey's eyes. "You're awesome. I keep telling you that."

"Even with all that, I'm tired. I'm ready for things to go back to normal. Whatever that means."

"It will. In the meantime, you're doing this incredible thing. This is so far out of your comfort zone, you probably can't even see the fence *around* your zone. I'm proud of you. Not everyone could do this."

Everly tilted her head back and arched a brow. "You could. You could do this in your sleep."

Stacey pursed her lips, pressing them tightly together. She leaned down and whispered, "Because I'm afraid to fall in love at all."

Everly wasn't sure she'd heard her right. "What?" She put a hand on Stacey's shin.

"What you said about Rob? You weren't wrong. I got all weird because it was a different kind of internal butterfly thing going on. Usually, it's just the lusty ones that wake up when a cute guy is around, but these ones, they felt heavier."

Everly frowned. "I'm trying really hard to follow, but is *butterflies* a synonym for *feelings*? Because you could just say *feelings*."

Her friend's gaze shifted, became more playful. "I'm a serial dater because I'm terrified of finding the one. I mean, I'd have to stop dating," Stacey said dramatically.

Everly laughed. "I can't tell if you're being serious."

Clearly done with the conversation, Stacey swung off the chair. "Me neither. That's the thing, Ev. We all have our quirks. Even Chris, I'm guessing. So, finish up the contest, and then maybe it's time to ask yourself a very important question."

When her friend said nothing else after a moment, Everly asked, "What?"

Stacey's lips tipped up in a cross between a grimace and a smile. "Whether or not you've already met Mr. Right. If he's been right under your nose the entire time."

A lump lodged in Everly's throat, and goose bumps dotted her skin. No, she didn't want to ask herself those questions. They'd found a new normal between them; she knew he cared for her, but he didn't like her that way. He'd had ample opportunity to put it out there—she winced, thankful she hadn't said *that* out loud—if he wanted more.

She'd be able to tell if he *liked her* liked her. *He gave you a birthday present that was thoughtful and sweet.* He'd called her *Ms. Dean* for the last ten months. *He worried about your hand like you'd stuck it in a fire.* He'd only recently started to make eye contact. *His voice goes soft when he says* Everly. He'd hardly spoken to her since he'd started there. *He came up with a plan to save your job.* He was actively helping her find other men to date. *He came the moment you called, no questions asked.*

Everly slumped back in the chair. Life after thirty was supposed to be easier. Clearer. She was supposed to feel better in her own skin or some *Cosmo*-esque phrase like that. She was supposed to know exactly what she wanted and have a surefire plan for how to achieve it.

Stacey watched her closely, amusement simmering in her gaze.

Everly sighed. "Go ahead and laugh. This is thirty. I'm screwing it up, but you're next, my friend. You're next."

[26]

Chris pushed away from his desk and went to his mini-fridge for a soda. He didn't mind hanging around the office late. It was quieter, easier to focus. *Easier not to think about Everly out on a date.* Supposedly. He stopped by the window, opened his soda, and took a sip before staring out at the parking lot. It was mostly empty. Other than the janitor, no one else was in the building. On Saturday nights, they had their remote deejay take over.

Walking over to his desk, he loosened his tie and pulled it over his head, tossing it on the couch. He sat down, putting his soda away from the files, and looked at the information in front of him. The station was doing well. They'd tripled their ad revenue with this promotion alone. He was pissed his dad had cut the publishing company out before Chris had a chance to see what he could do, but that left more money for the other subsidiaries. Harco Media Entertainment, which still housed the station, the digital software firm, an ad agency, and a cyber-security company, could be one of his father's key players.

He'd recently compiled a list of all his father's companies so he could start thinking about what came next for him—bringing it all together.

His father had always held a varied portfolio, wanting a little piece of all the pies the world had to offer. Chris had several ideas of how an increase in communication between those companies would improve profit. He wanted to stop letting go of underperforming corporations. If his father would just take a damn breath between buying and selling, Chris had a strong feeling they could launch his father's name into the Fortune 500 sphere.

Before he returned to New York, his immediate goal was to shore up the three remaining subsidiaries connected to the station. He'd just finished drafting an email to each of their management teams requesting a meeting. They needed to work together, combine their efforts, and utilize the current success of the station. Chris wanted to touch base with Wesley, his tech-obsessed brother, about the idea of merging the cyber-security firm with the digital software. If he could successfully amalgamate these, he hoped he could do something similar with his father's other holdings.

Chris was just about to open up his laptop when a familiar voice spoke from the doorway.

"Is your job always this boring?"

Chris's head snapped up. His brother Noah leaned against the doorjamb, a goofy grin—one that probably matched Chris's—on his face. Chris shoved back from the desk, and they met in the middle of the room and embraced, patting each other on the back, laughing through their *Hey, mans* and *hellos.*

When he pulled back, Chris looked Noah over. God, he'd missed his brother. They talked and texted constantly, but it wasn't the same. Unlike Chris, Noah enjoyed the whole millionaire playboy gig. Wearing designer jeans and a button-up, his hair was expertly styled—something he'd perfected by hogging the bathroom starting at age fifteen—and though there were creases around his dark eyes, he was aging well. Noah was the carefree one. Wesley was the introverted genius. Chris wasn't sure what he was in the group. Maybe he'd figure it out when he was finally where he was supposed to be.

Noah clapped him on the back. "You look like shit. Like you've been here way too many hours staring at a bunch of boring papers. You ever leave this place?" Noah wandered over to the desk to finger through said papers.

Chris rolled his shoulders, loosening the knots in his neck. Between the kickboxing class and being hunched over the desk, he was stiffer than he'd been in a long time. *Maybe it's time to get out of the office, then. Stop avoiding life so you don't have to think about Everly with other men.* He grabbed another soda and tossed it to Noah, who stood there grinning.

"I missed you," Noah said, popping the tab on the drink and tipping it back.

"Missed you, too. What happened to phoning when you were coming?"

Noah shrugged. "Thought I'd surprise you, see if I could catch you up to no good."

Chris laughed, and it felt good. He'd made friends in California, but it wasn't the same. Noah was his best friend. He was closer to him than to Wes, though all three of them got along and had a hell of a time when they were together. He sat down on his sofa while Noah kicked back in the chair behind Chris's desk.

"So, this is where the magic happens, huh?"

"I don't know if it's magic, but the contest has brought in a shit ton of revenue, and Dad's happy. I'm in the middle of putting together some recommendations for moving forward."

Noah tipped his head to one side. "You going to promote from within to take your job?"

He hadn't thought of that yet. The idea of leaving had started coming with a painful stitch in his side that he couldn't explain. The intention was always to leave. "Why are we talking business? What the hell are you doing here, dude?"

Noah laughed, opened the top drawer of Chris's desk, and rooted through. He found Chris's stash of Starburst and unwrapped one. "Same old, same old. I'm here to see my brother." He popped a strawberry square into his mouth, crumpling the wrapper, shooting it toward the garbage can and missing.

Chris got up and grabbed the wrapper from the floor, shooting his brother a sideways glance. "Uh-huh. Sure. What else?" Noah had a restless streak. It'd gotten him into trouble more than once.

"Thought I'd check out some properties. See that one mansion for myself even though they took it off the market. Sucks, but I figure there's got to be more. Ever feel like you were looking for something to settle everything down inside of you?" He leaned forward, unwrapped another strawberry.

Yup. Found it, too. She's about five foot six, with brown hair and a kick-in-the-solar-plexus smile. Chris grabbed a Starburst from the stack that spilled once he'd ripped the wrapper. Noah would eat every last pink one if Chris didn't grab one now. He unwrapped it and popped it in his mouth, evading the answer.

Noah didn't notice. "I just needed a change of scenery."

"So, you're staying with me indefinitely?" Chris didn't mind, but he wouldn't purposely miss out on a chance to razz his brother.

"If that's okay. First, I worried about cramping your style, but I remembered you have none and probably haven't been laid since you got here. If anything, having me around can only improve your life." Noah stood up and walked over to Chris.

Chris punched him in the shoulder, and Noah twisted, grabbed Chris, and tried to pull him into a headlock. It didn't matter that they were thirty-one and thirty-two, they went at it the same way they had since they could crawl.

Noah had Chris bent at the waist and was reaching for his boxers when he taunted, "Say, 'I missed my big brother,' or you get a wedgie."

"What the hell, dude? No wedgies. Not cool." Chris grabbed one of Noah's legs. "Don't make me."

"None of that sounds like what I told you to say," Noah said, adjusting his grip.

That one slip gave Chris the wiggle room he needed. He grabbed a handful of Noah's thigh and pinched.

Noah shoved him back, hopping on one foot. "Motherfu—"

"You left yourself open for that one," Benny, the night janitor, said from the doorway as he lifted the garbage can and dumped it into the bigger one on his cart.

Chris's face went hot as he straightened his clothes and glared at his brother and held back his laughter.

"Sorry, Benny. This is my brother Noah. He decided to come for a visit. He doesn't get out much, so he forgets how to act around humans."

Benny and Noah both laughed. Benny replaced the garbage bag and looked at Noah. "You coming to work here, too? You need to tone down your polish, boy."

The staff estimated Benny was somewhere between ninety and one hundred and twenty. No one knew for sure. He'd been there long before any of them, including the radio station. The running joke was he'd come with the building.

Noah looked down at himself. "What's wrong with what I'm wearing?" He pointed at Chris. "He's wearing suit pants. Isn't he too polished?"

Benny looked over at Chris, one side of his mouth tipping up in a crooked, toothy grin. "Nope. Not with his underwear sticking out like that."

Noah gave another bark of laughter and shook Benny's hand as Chris righted the waistband of his boxers *and* his pants. Jesus. Five minutes with his brother and they were teenagers again. *It feels great.*

Still smiling after Benny moved down the hall, Noah rubbed his stomach. "That guy is awesome. All your staff like that?"

Chris let out a breath. "Yeah, actually. They are, in their own ways." He pulled out his phone and sent a reminder to himself to book a place he'd been looking at for their first annual staff appreciation celebration. Damn, they all deserved it.

Noah pushed Chris's shoulder. "I'm starving. Anything to eat around California that isn't made of kale or raw fish?"

Chris grabbed his keys, wallet, and pocketed his phone. "Yeah. There's a burger shack you'll love."

Noah rubbed his hands together. "Now you're talking. You wanna show me around this place on the way out?"

The tour wouldn't take long. Chris walked Noah down to the two meeting rooms past his office before they turned in the other direction. They stopped in the meeting room, where the whiteboard still held Everly's dating bracket. The sight of it turned Chris's stomach. But they were all keeping track, and the visual made it easy.

Noah jutted his chin toward the board. "*This* is where the magic happens, then?"

"You're not at Hogwarts, dude. There's no magic. Just hard work."

Noah bumped his shoulder. "How many people you have here?"

Chris gave him a rundown and explained a bit about their meetings. "You want to try out broadcasting?"

Noah laughed. "I don't think I could do it. Who's on the air now?"

Chris led the way out of the room and down the hall. "Remote deejay. It's pretty cool, actually. She has a four-hour Saturday-night segment. Keeps costs down because she produces for herself from home, and it gives listeners something different. She's from Australia, so the accent really pulls people in. I'm actually thinking of upping her hours."

"No producer? Then is that a deejay?"

Chris turned around to see his brother looking through the side window of the office they'd just passed. He hadn't even noticed the light on. Walking over, he peered in and saw Everly.

His heart did a strange jump. Like it was trying to get up the next step but couldn't quite reach.

He frowned. "Give me a second?" Pushing his brother aside and back, he knocked as he opened the door.

Everly looked up from the binders she was poring through. Her hair was pulled back at the front, highlighting the makeup she'd put around her eyes, making them look smoky and sexy. She blinked in surprise, and he noticed her lashes were thick and long. A tremor rumbled through him. She wore a pale pink blouse, and the color was soft and striking at the same time. She tended to go for shades of black and gray, and seeing her in another color did something to the wires in his brain, making him stare a little too long.

"Hey," he said in a sandpapery voice.

Everly rested one hand on top of the other and smiled at him. She looked tired. Beautiful. Always so freaking beautiful it stole the air from his lungs and made him feel winded. But tired.

"Hi. What are you doing here?"

He leaned on the doorjamb, nudging Noah, hoping he'd take a hint. "Same as you, from the look of things. I was finishing up some work. What do you have there? Why aren't you on your date?"

He hoped the last question came out evenly. Nonchalantly like, *Oh, what'd you have for dinner? How was it? Did you want to marry him?*

Her brows furrowed, and a little line appeared on her forehead. "I made Stacey ICE me."

Noah snorted with laughter behind him. Chris leaned back and glared.

Everly leaned forward. "Is someone with you?" She tried to peer around him.

"Just my idiot brother. Noah, this is Everly Dean. Ev, this is one of my older brothers, Noah."

Noah leaned in and shook Everly's hand. When he stepped back, he looked at Chris and arched his brows in a way Chris chose to ignore.

Chris focused on Everly. "What do you mean she iced you?" Jesus, if that didn't conjure up images . . .

Note to self: Do not think of Everly and icing in the same sentence. His mouth watered.

"In case of emergency. I made her call and say she needed me about fifteen minutes into the date. In that fifteen minutes, he joked a total of seven times about the fact that I'd have to do something pretty nice to make up for bailing last time. The restaurant was loud, he didn't seem to mind. He just yelled over the music and the talking. I'm pretty sure that he would have used the same decibel in a library or hospital."

Chris cringed, hating that her evening had gone like that.

Noah leaned against the table like they were old friends shooting the breeze. "Not cool. Only two dates left, though, right?"

Chris's surprise must have shown.

Noah laughed. "What? You didn't think I was Team Everly? I'm keeping up with the action. I love your Facebook posts."

Everly smiled, her real smile. Not the one that didn't reach her eyes. "Thank you. It was two until tonight. Now it's one. I've dated more in the last few weeks than my entire life."

Chris chuckled despite the surprise he felt at Everly opening up to his brother. Though, why wouldn't she? Every other woman did.

"What are you working on?" Chris asked, glancing at the promotions binder she was looking through. He stepped closer, leaned over her shoulder to see.

Her breath hitched, so low he hoped he was the only one who'd noticed. One hand rubbed over the other. Did he make her nervous? A good nervous? Was there such a thing? Did she have any idea how much he enjoyed being with her? What would it be like if she felt the same?

"I had an idea for the podcast thing. I wanted to look back over some of the things we've tried in the past. I need to talk to Mari. I feel like she's feeling on the outskirts of things. There's no reason. I want to put together a proposal that'll mean us joining forces with a real talk segment. We'd invite successful professionals to share their truths. I'm not making sense." She turned, enthusiasm making her more animated. Their knees brushed. "Someone thanked me the other night for sharing my story. We see so much of the polish online. 'I ran a marathon.' 'I baked eight dozen cookies and iced them like Martha Stewart.' But what if we showed the tears halfway through the run or the eight dozen cookies that ended up in the garbage before the perfect ones were ready?"

The idea pulled him in immediately, and when he caught her gaze, he felt the flicker that shimmered there all the way through him. Everly Dean was beautiful, but when she was excited about something . . . she was indescribable.

Noah whistled, putting his hands in his pockets. "I love that idea. We were just going to grab some food. You should come with us. Tell me about this little town my brother's been stuck in for so many months now."

Everly's face blanched for just a second at Noah's wording, and Chris was back to wanting to punch him. She licked her lips, making Chris's stomach tighten. She locked her hands together and nodded before she spoke. To his utter surprise and delight, she turned her shy smile and sparkling eyes Chris's way and said, "Sure. I could eat."

Chris wasn't sure if he could eat with her there looking like she'd walked out of one of his dreams, but who needed food when he could fill up on the sight of her?

[27]

Everly squeezed the steering wheel until her fingers touched the base of her hands around it. The Saturday-night traffic was worse than normal—maybe. She actually had no idea, because she rarely went out at night. And now she was heading from one date to another.

"So not a date." The Burger Shack was about twenty-five minutes from the station, and though Chris had suggested they drive together, Everly had quickly made an excuse, saying she needed her car, which she now desperately wanted to turn in the direction of home. At this point, she was basically a walking nerve ending in a pretty shirt. But driving her crazy, more than the nerves, was the desire to *be* with Chris. To see another side of him. To watch more of the fascinating interaction between him and his brother that revealed a completely new side to him. *You're going. Rule seven: Find your happy. This counts. Seeing a new side to someone you now consider a friend makes you happy.* She was so good at glossing over the rest of her feelings.

"Hey, Siri," she called. The beep sounded and waited. "Text Stacey."

"What do you want to say to Stacey?"

"I'm heading to the Burger Shack with Chris and his brother Noah. I need you to meet me there. I don't know why I said yes, but whatever you're doing, come there. Please don't be on a date."

Everly pulled into the right lane, stopping at the light.

Siri's cute male-accented voice responded, "Your message to Stacey says: I'm heading to the booby shake with Chris and his lover Noah. I need you to meet me there. I don't know why I said yes, but whatever you're doing, come there. Please, I'll be your date."

"Do you want to send?"

"Yes." The light changed. "Wait, what?"

"Message sent."

"Son of a bitch."

"I don't know how to respond to that."

Forming an *o* with her lips, Everly breathed out a long breath and pressed the gas. "Me neither, Siri. Me neither."

When the phone rang, she pressed Connect on the steering wheel and braced for Stacey's response. Nothing like autocorrect to make a girl's life worse. *At least it wasn't to Chris.*

"Are you okay?" Stacey asked as Everly drove. Palm trees lined the streets in between one-level, mostly concrete homes.

"What? Yes, why?"

"Multiple reasons, but the first is because you need to be told that when you do the booby shake with a boy, you shouldn't ask people to tag along. I mean, unless that's your thing, but it's not mine, so I'm going to pass on that one."

"Shut up," Everly growled.

"Reason two is because—and I hate to break it to you—Chris is definitely not your type if his lover's name is Noah and if he is, in fact, his brother? Sweetie, turn the car around no matter what kind of heaven he promised you."

"I hate you. Tell me you're coming."

"Already in the car. I never miss out on the booby shake."

"Please stop," Everly said, taking a right at the next light.

"Oh no. That's just not going to happen. Is the brother hot? I thought, for sure, you'd be home by now."

She gave a quick recap of her evening and then described

Noah without using the word *hot*—though, clearly, her friend was a master decoder.

"Sexy and hot. I think I'm going to like Chris's lover."

"You have to stop." The Burger Shack parking lot was crowded, and suddenly Everly's chest felt that way, too.

"Nope. Rules of friendship state that I must mock you when you give me such straightforward reasons to do so."

"There is no rule that says that," Everly said, breathing through her nose.

"You haven't seen my book."

"You'll be here soon?"

"Yup. Order me a chocolate-vanilla shake with Oreos and whipped cream. You're buying."

"Obviously."

Chris and his brother were waiting by the door when Everly approached, feeling very overdressed for the beach-themed restaurant.

Her radar wasn't the best, but she was pretty sure Chris's gaze traveled up and down her body with appreciation. Either way, the thought that they might have warmed her skin more than the evening humidity. She'd chosen a pair of pale blue capris, wedge sandals, and a pale pink top that looked sheer but had a darker pink camisole underneath. She'd watched a tutorial on how to do her eyes, and after almost blinding herself with an eyeshadow brush, she was pretty pleased with the result.

"Chris was worried you were going to head home," Noah said.

Chris shoved him, making Noah laugh. Everly's face felt warmer than the rest of her body. "Of course not. I said I'd come."

She held the strap of her purse with one hand and her keys in the other. They dug into her palm, but she ignored the sting. Noah opened the door and held it for them. Chris moved closer and put a hand to her back, leaning down so his breath tickled her ear.

"You don't have to stay," he said as they walked forward.

She turned her face when they stopped by the hostess station. "Do you want me to go?" she whispered, very aware of Noah directly behind them. Her skin felt alive and tingly. Why was she so aware of her skin when Chris was near?

"Not even a little bit, but I'm worried you're going to snap your keys in half."

Everly bit her bottom lip, loosened her fingers, not sure if it was sweet or just embarrassing that he noticed those little things.

"Where's your cat?" His eyes danced with humor, and her ribs loosened by half.

"Pepper is in my purse," she whispered back.

"Pepper?" His voice was low.

She closed her eyes, breathed through the accidental slip. When she opened them again, Chris's gaze had heated. "I named her Pepper Potts."

His grin blinded her. "She's kick-ass."

Everly smiled. "Yes, she is."

She might not be great at the dating game, but she could feel as well as see the happiness and warmth in the way he looked at her now.

Noah leaned his head toward them, right between the two of their faces. "Just to be sure, I'm not supposed to interject here and make a comment about a *cat* being in your purse?"

Chris's eyes closed and opened slowly. He stepped away from Everly and glared at his brother. "I'm going to smother you in your sleep."

Noah chuckled and winked at Everly. "He can't stay up later than I can, so I'm not worried. When we were younger, Wes—that's our other brother—Ari, our sister, and I used to dip his hand in warm water when he passed out at 9:00 p.m. on the weekends."

Everly didn't even try to suppress the giggle. She locked eyes with Chris, attempting a pitying look. He shook his head and sighed.

"How many?" a hostess asked in an uber-cheery voice.

"Three," Chris said loudly, making Everly choke back a laugh.

"Oh, wait. Four. I invited Stacey. I hope that's okay," she said. Her pulse scrambled. She shouldn't even be here. She should have said no, and she definitely shouldn't have invited a fourth. What if Chris thought she expected him to pay? Was this awkward for him with his brother visiting? Had she totally crashed their reunion? *They invited you.*

He reached out and squeezed her shoulder, his hand there and gone in the space of a breath. Normally, she tensed when people touched her without warning, but his touch had the opposite effect.

"It's fine. Always." Chris turned back to the hostess. "Four, please."

She gave him a megawatt smile back, glancing at him and Noah with more than a little interest. "You've got it. Right this way."

Should she wait for Stacey? Everly looked back over her shoulder, but all she saw was Noah. He must have read her mind, or maybe she had a flashing sign over her head.

"I'm sure your friend will find us," he said, nudging her forward.

They settled at the back of the restaurant at a table in the corner by the patio doors. Laughter and music filled the room. Servers dressed in palm tree–covered shirts passed each other with full and empty trays, grinning and singing along to the songs. Up two steps and across the room, a small group of servers sang a very fast and complicated version of "Happy Birthday." Everly shuddered. If there were *more* than nine circles of hell, being sung to, *loudly*, by strangers, in a public place would have a spot on her list.

"Your server will be right with you," the hostess said, setting four menus down.

Everly worked to keep her fingers still, her eyes darting around the restaurant. Noah picked up a menu and opened it.

She felt Chris's stare and knew she should pick up her menu, but she just needed a minute. Or five. *Just breathe. You've been here several times, Stacey is on her way, you like being with Chris. It'll be fun to hear some more stories about him. Right, because you need to get attached to a guy who isn't in your final two bracket? Though Daniel is definitely not getting through to the next round, unless the final date is unbearable. Next week is the last week. It's almost done. Owen looks better and better every minute. Safer.*

When Chris's fingers nudged hers, she jolted.

Noah glanced at them. "Be back in a minute." He got up and left the table, heading in the direction of the restrooms.

Chris leaned closer, in her space but not so far in she couldn't breathe. "Hey. Are you okay?"

She opened her eyes wider because that totally added believability. "Yup."

"You know you're the worst liar ever, right?"

She added a smile. "Uh-huh."

The look in his eyes softened, smoothing out the rough seas raging inside of her. He nudged his hand a little closer and just his pinkie finger touched her own. Sparks shot along her arm—apparently that was a real thing and not just in books—like static electricity but sharper, distracting her from breathing too fast. His pinkie covered hers like it was offering her much tinier one a hug. *A two-pinkie dog pile. God, you're a dork.* Her insides went all warm and squishy, and for some ridiculous reason she could not think about, she felt like crying.

A flurry of blond hurried toward them. "Hey. Fancy meeting you two here," Stacey said, pulling her purse off from across her chest.

Chris moved his hand and stood up, pulling the chair out for Stacey. "Glad you could join us," he said evenly.

Clearly, his heart wasn't blocking his throat like Everly's. Noah came back to the table and looked down at Stacey. Her technicolor blouse looked gorgeous on her, and Everly was positive she'd interrupted a date in progress. Guilt tugged at her, but the relief of having her friend there was too palpable to pay it much attention.

Noah's lips quirked up on one side, reminding Everly of Chris when he didn't have his guard up. Like the other night when they'd watched television together.

"If you're our waitress, you're not very good at your job. But since you're lovely and appear so happy, I'll let it go this time," Noah said.

Stacey tilted her head back, and the sexy smile Everly had seen more times than she could count took over her friend's face. "Are you the brother?"

Noah put his hands in his pockets and nodded, a grave look on his face. "That's the word on the street. If it helps, I'm the better-looking and more charming of the three."

Chris shook his head, letting out an exasperated huff. "Jesus. Sit down, you idiot. Stacey, this is my brother Noah. Noah, Stacey." He waved a hand between them. "Don't hit on each other. Seriously."

They both opened their mouths, their mutual shock comical. A laugh burst from Everly's chest, and she slapped a hand across her mouth.

"Something funny? Maybe a text or something?" Stacey gave her a sickly sweet smile, and Everly bit her lip, trying to contain further giggles.

Noah sat beside Stacey and shook her hand. "I'll do my best not to hit on you, but I'm fairly hungry, so I might not be responsible for my actions if we can't order soon."

Stacey nodded and picked up a menu. "Noted and completely understandable. I make no promises whether I'm hungry or not."

Chris caught Everly's eye, and they shared a smile before picking up their menus. Maybe she could handle part two of an evening she'd wanted to put behind her hours ago. With

Stacey there, she could breathe easier and know that she could be on the listening end of the conversations. She could do that.

Listening and observing were her sports. She was a gold medal champion in both, which was the only excuse she had for looking at the menu without actually seeing the words. Observations: the scent of Chris's cologne and the proximity of his hand when he set his menu down, the way his laugh was a little gruff, sort of like he'd slept on it, his affectionate smiles toward his brother even as he rolled his eyes. By the time their waitress joined them, with water and apologies, Everly still wasn't sure what she wanted. From the menu.

[28]

The service at the restaurant was beyond slow. Normally, this put Everly on edge. She didn't like feeling stuck, but it felt different with Chris and Stacey—one of whom she was very comfortable with and one who gave her this dual, confusing sensation of ease mixed with nerves. Noah was hilarious, and listening to Chris try to defend his actions as a younger sibling gave Everly a completely new view of him.

Noah hooked one arm around the back of his chair, casually elegant and completely at ease with himself. He finished his pint and set it down. "Our dad isn't the most affectionate. Our mom is. She used to tell us that if you want to be really good at something, you have to practice and work hard."

They'd finished their dinners and were waiting for their bills. The restaurant was quieter, but music still played in the background. The smell of french fries and burgers permeated the air, and Everly was sure she wouldn't be able to eat again for days. The milkshake had been unnecessary but delicious.

"I'll pay you to stop talking," Chris said, leaning back in his chair, clasping his hands over his stomach, drawing Everly's attention.

A quick, hard flash of curiosity danced through her mind with the force of a tornado, making her wonder what he'd look like *under* his shirt. She choked on the last of her milkshake.

"You okay?" Stacey asked, her eyes playful.

Everly nodded, eyes watering. "Fine."

Noah grinned at his brother. "When Chris was about six, he took his favorite stuffed bear—he slept with that thing until he was fourteen."

Chris crumpled a napkin and tossed it at Noah. "Screw you." He looked at Stacey, then Everly. "I absolutely did *not*."

"I could be a bit off on the age. Might have been sixteen. Anyway, he takes this bear to our dad in his home office, just offers it to him. I was reading, and Wes was playing on the computer. We just liked to be around our dad, and as long as we weren't bugging him, he didn't mind us hanging out in there, absorbing his business sense. He looks down at Chris and says, 'I can't play with you right now.'"

"This is completely against the bro code." Chris groaned, draining his soda glass. He glared at his brother, but there was no heat in it. This is what they did. It made her wonder what it would have been like to have a sibling.

"No way. This is good stuff. Keep going," Stacey said. She was digging into the last of her milkshake, pulling out chunks of Oreo with a spoon.

"Chris tells Dad he doesn't want to play. He tells him that he can borrow the bear to hug. My dad stops doing what he's doing. He hates being interrupted, but he stops and says, 'Why would I want to hug your bear?'" Noah's grin was contagious. "Chris says, 'Because you don't know how to give hugs. You can practice on Bear, and I'll tell you if you're doing it right.' Our dad went three shades of red. Wes and I couldn't stop laughing."

"Oh my goodness, that's absolutely adorable," Stacey said through her laughter.

Everly glanced at Chris. Despite his smile, she didn't think he enjoyed the story. She hated the image of him craving attention he didn't get from his dad. Maybe because she'd been on the receiving end of having tales told about her to provide comedic relief, mostly by her parents, she could read that in his body language.

"I think it's sweet," she said quietly. "Did he practice?" Her dad would have. He had faults, but giving affection wasn't one of them.

Chris ran a hand through his hair and scoffed. "No. He took the bear away and told me to go play with my brothers—who are both jackasses, so I probably went off by myself."

A pang of sadness struck her heart. No, her dad definitely wouldn't have taken the bear away. She wondered what other little secrets went into making Chris the man he was. Noah was more outgoing and had a different presence than his brother. Though she could see some similarities in the eyes and the nose, she found Chris more attractive in a less obvious way. Noah was all sharp cheekbones and magazine smiles. Chris was . . . real.

"Aw. We weren't all bad," Noah said, folding his arms and letting out a weary sigh.

If he'd come from New York, the flight was probably catching up with him. The day was certainly catching up with Everly.

"I'm not sure whether to be happy or sad I don't have siblings," Everly commented.

"You have me," Stacey said, holding out a bite of Oreo for Everly in challenge. Everly shook her head, so Stacey shrugged. "Your sister from another mister." She ate the Oreo and dropped her spoon, making it rattle against the glass.

Everly laughed. "True. The best part of that is when you're too outrageous, I can make it clear we're not actually related."

Both of the men laughed, and Everly saw Noah exchange a glance with Chris.

"You have awesome employees."

Stacey sat straighter, adding some sass to her expression. "Hell, yeah, he does."

Chris sat up straighter. "The station has excellent employees all the way around, from the janitors to the producers. It's part of what's kept it going."

"Can I quote you on that, Mr. Diplomacy?" Noah grinned at

Stacey. "Come on, he won't tell me any good stuff. Any drama? Good gossip? Any of you hooking up in the break room?"

Chris coughed, and Everly felt her own face redden. "Shut up, Noah. There's a no-fraternizing policy. My employees are all trustworthy, dependable, and great at what they do."

Noah pretended to pout. "But surely a little policy could be waived if two people were mad about each other."

"Sometimes I think Mari and Mason are secretly in love," Stacey said.

Chris did a double take. "Really? I can't see that." He must have realized what he said. "I don't think that's the case, and I'd feel a lot more comfortable if we talked about something else."

"Chris is the serious one," Noah said with a sigh.

Stacey grinned. "No shit. What are you?"

Noah arched an eyebrow. " The exceptional one."

"And Wes?" Stacey asked, her smile widening.

"The geek. It's a lot of weight to carry on my shoulders, but I've gotten used to it."

"I think you like for people to think you're a lot more confident than you are," Everly said quietly, not even realizing the words came out of her mouth.

All three of them looked at her, and her pulse hiccupped. Uh-oh. Insulting the boss's brother was probably not a good idea.

To her surprise, Chris chuckled, and Noah leaned in. "Really. Tell me more."

Everly bit her lip and shook her head. "Sorry. No. You just . . . I mean, clearly, you're all those things you said. I generally find that people who have to draw attention to those things about themselves have underlying feelings that they're lacking those things." Oh God. Why did she keep talking? "But you aren't, so you shouldn't worry." *Someone stop me. Stacey, stop me!*

Instead, her friend looked amused. "If only you could psychoanalyze yourself as well as you do others."

Swallowing the butterflies trying to force their way up her

throat—very uncomfortably—she tugged at her napkin, tearing bits off. "Don't get me started on you, Miss Commitmentphobe."

Noah laughed, deep and loud. "Damn. I like these two. When do I get to meet the rest of the staff?"

A bus girl came to take the rest of their dishes away, silently reaching between them.

"Yeah, what about that? We were supposed to have some staff shindig. Bonding and beer and all that," Stacey said.

Chris was eyeing Everly with a hint of a smile, like the other night when she'd felt as if they were sharing a secret.

"Very soon, actually. I'm putting it at the top of my to-do list."

Everly nibbled on her bottom lip. That was interesting. Usually, the top of his list had ratings, followed by policy, ratings, and ratings.

"I want in. I can help you plan," Noah said.

Brows furrowed, Chris shook his head. "You're not staff. I'm not planning a kegger."

"I'm like staff," Noah said.

Everly realized she was watching Chris quite closely when she saw his jaw tense, his gaze fly to his brother's, with an imperceptible shake of the head. What the—?

"Fine. You can come," Chris said as the waitress approached with the bill.

She started to put it on the table, but Chris swept it up.

"You don't have to do that," Everly said quickly. Her jaw clenched tightly. Almost painfully. "That wasn't the expectation. I'll pay for mine and Stacey's."

Chris turned his head and locked his gaze on Everly. She worked to keep her breathing even. "No expectations, Everly. It's my pleasure. Honestly, it's fine."

"Don't worry about it," Noah said, standing and stretching. "Chris would never let you pay. He's weird like that. Mr. Responsibility."

"I hope you're still in good shape, because it's about an hour walk to my place from here," Chris said, giving the woman his credit card.

"Well, thank you. This was an unexpectedly fun evening," Stacey said, also rising.

"Yes, thank you. It was really fun to meet you, Noah." Everly stood and went around the other side of the table to stand near Stacey.

"Same goes. Come here," he said, pulling her into a hug. Surprised, Everly kept her hands by her side, but he didn't seem to notice. He released her and did the same with Stacey, who returned the gesture easily. Noah grinned at Chris, then back at them. "I practiced on Bear, so I'm really good at it."

As he signed the credit card slip, Chris muttered something under his breath that Everly didn't catch, but she laughed along with the others, anyway.

The guys walked them outside and said good night, leaving Everly and Stacey standing by their cars, which were parked close to each other.

"Interesting night. You look fantastic, by the way," Stacey said, leaning on Everly's car, seeming not to care about her black leather skirt.

"Thank you. So do you. Thank you for showing up. Did I wreck a date?"

"Nope. You saved me, so we're all good. Are you okay?" Stacey eyed her in the way her mom used to when she tried to sidestep love interest inquisitions. At fifteen, Everly hadn't wanted to share gossip about boys with her mom any more than she did now. Speaking of which, she needed to return her father's phone calls. He and her mom had been tag teaming her voicemail for days.

"I'm fine. It was nice to meet Chris's brother." Spending more time with Chris didn't suck.

"Sure was. Gave us a little insight to our mostly stuffed-suit boss, who has a wicked crush on you," Stacey said, pulling her keys out of her purse.

Everly's jaw dropped. A couple of guys walked by, smiling at them, but Everly turned toward Stacey, who, of course, gave them a finger wave. Everly grabbed her hand and pulled it down.

"He does not. Did you hear what he said about no in-house dating?"

"Yup. Didn't stop him from making I-want-you eyes at you all night. Maybe that's why your past relationships haven't worked out. You clearly ignore the signals."

Everly sputtered. Actually sputtered, making a strange, unintelligible sound while she waved her arm again.

Stacey laughed. Hard. "Well said. Great comeback."

"How can I love you and want to throttle you so often?"

Her friend shrugged, not one trace of remorse on her beautiful face. "Don't know. It's a mystery. Definitely part of my charm. Which I'm telling you because of the aforementioned missing of signals and not because I secretly don't think I'm charming."

"I need to go home," Everly said, suddenly overcome with a bone-deep exhaustion.

"Me, too." She leaned in for a hug, squeezed her harder than usual. "Good to see you laugh tonight. Really laugh. And relax. Happy looks good on you, my friend."

Stacey kissed her cheek and turned, giving Everly the same finger wave she'd given the group of guys. Everly watched her walk a couple of cars over before sliding behind the steering wheel. She sat for a moment, letting the quiet interior settle around her like the comfort of a weighted blanket.

She rested her head against the seat and tried to think of what was pressing down on her most. The dates. The weird feelings for Chris. Her parents' back-and-forth. Or just the massive milkshake she'd consumed.

Opening her eyes, she started the car and then slid her hand in the side pocket of her purse. She pulled out Pepper, which was oddly soothing, holding it in her hand as she drove home, doing her best to think about nothing at all.

[29]

The staff was wrapping up their air check meeting—a playback of the shows from the week before—on Monday morning when Chris switched gears. The fact that Everly recognized he was about to slip out of work mode only worried her slightly. As people got closer, they picked up on tells. That's all this was. *I bet once you spend some quality time with Owen, you'll pick up on his nuances, too.* That was her latest diversion. Whenever she thought of Chris, she made herself think of Owen. Sweet, cute, available Owen.

"I've been putting this off for too long, but with all the extra hours you guys have been putting in, I wanted to do something to show how much I appreciate you," Chris said, looking around the table.

"You flying us to Hawaii?" Mason kicked back in his chair, giving Chris a toothy grin.

"Not quite. But there is a beach involved."

"I like the sound of that," Stacey said. She was doodling on a piece of paper while they chatted.

"I rented a house on the beach for next Saturday. All you guys have to do is show up. I'll have food, drinks, and entertainment covered."

It shocked Everly to realize that she felt excited. *At the idea of socializing? Who are you? Where's the real Everly Dean?* What was happening to her?

Chris grew more enthusiastic. "We'll have a lot to celebrate by the end of the week."

Everly's happiness deflated like a balloon. Right. She'd have made her final decisions on her love life.

"That's awesome. That sounds fun. Where is it?" Stacey asked.

"I'll have Jane send out all the information. There's plenty of room for everyone to stay the night. I've arranged for pre-taped segments and the remote deejay to cover Sunday's spots."

The staff started talking over one another, but Everly's nerves crept in like a stealthy fun-sabotaging ninja.

"Hopefully no one minds, but my brother will be joining us. He's out visiting from New York. Please feel free to bring your significant others," Chris said.

"Oh, maybe Everly can bring her final choice. We don't have to advertise it before the big reveal, but you'll know by then, right, Everly?" Mason sat forward.

She nodded. "I guess, but I don't want to bring anyone to a staff function."

"But you'll come, right?" Chris asked.

She turned her head. They were seated beside each other, and the minute their eyes locked, Everly felt like the others faded into the background.

"Of course."

"Can we get back to work now? Is the meeting over?" Mari slapped a hand on the table, jolting Everly out of the moment.

"Sure. Sorry," Chris said, appearing flustered like she felt. Which couldn't be true. *He has a wicked crush on you,* Stacey had said. She was definitely more adept at picking up cues than Everly, but she couldn't be right about that.

When Mari stood, Everly remembered what she'd wanted to do today. "Wait, I wanted to talk to everyone about something."

All eyes turned her way, filling her stomach with lead. She took a deep breath. Stacey smiled at her, giving her a thumbs-up.

Chris moved his chair slightly closer. "What you were

working on on Saturday?" He asked it so quietly, she almost didn't hear him over the thunder of her heartbeat.

"Is that okay?"

"More than." His ready encouragement boosted her confidence.

She pressed her hands flat to the tabletop so she wouldn't fidget, then looked at her colleagues. Mari looked slightly pissed. Everly might not be great at social cues, but she hoped what she was about to say would eliminate the undercurrent of competition between them. Everly had no desire to compete with these people. They were . . . *Holy shit. They're your friends. Your work friends, but still.*

She sat straighter, telling herself to pretend she was cool. *Stay cool, Ponyboy.* She grinned at the image of Veronica Mars saying that.

"I'd like to piggyback on the success of the dating promo by doing a real talk series. We can look into podcasts because I think it's great to branch out, but after doing some research, I don't know if we need to." They didn't look irritated, so she continued, "In the age of social media where everyone posts their best self, I feel like a lot of people would benefit from the truth. The other night, I chatted with a woman who talked about how hard it was to put herself out there. She said it was uplifting to know she wasn't the only one. People want to know they're quote-unquote normal. Whatever that even means. The point is, no one wants to feel like they're alone. When we look at everyone else's achievements, we feel less than. My proposal is that we do a series of interviews and chat spots with successful people who are willing to give us the gritty details."

Mari shifted in her seat. "Gritty how? Like who's cheating on their husbands and nanny cams?"

Everly pushed down on her instinct to sink farther into her chair. *Explain it better.* She glanced at Chris and Stacey. Neither of them looked ready to rescue her. She smiled. She didn't need rescuing.

"Not at all, Mari. More of a 'this is what I've gone through in my marriage while building a successful company, having children, and *not* cheating on my spouse' discussion. I'm talking CEOs who share their slips down the ladder rungs before they reached the top. Supermoms who don't mind sharing that the secret to their success is buying a dozen cupcakes instead of staying up all night icing ones she didn't have time to bake in the first place."

"People are getting back into radio because of the human connection," Mason said.

Everly pointed her finger at him and said, "Yes," loudly. She bit her lip, her cheeks heating up. "Sorry."

"Never apologize for your passion," Chris said.

"Human interest stories where we get to see the flip side but still with a happy ending," Mason said.

Everly's heart thundered in a new way. With pure excitement.

"The grit beneath the gloss. Not just ugly stories but more the mud they trudged through to get to the top. So people don't think it's as easy to do as it seems when they post the picture on the top of some mountain."

They were getting it. They were excited, and they were actually getting it.

Ideas bounced around the table, everyone having a story about a struggle they'd faced to get to where they were. Everly realized as she listened to them that they were *all* different. They all had their *thing;* Stacey feared commitment, Mari didn't know if she was good enough at her job—hell yes she was—Chris said he struggled with getting his father's approval. Every one of them faced battles the others weren't privy to. She spent so much time wishing she were different, calmer, chiller. If she'd been anything other than who she was, if she'd taken a different path, she wouldn't be sitting here right now feeling like she finally belonged.

[30]

The house was awesome. Noah showing up, along with this inexplicable *need* to show his staff how much he appreciated them, gave Chris the idea to rent something beachside. They could have done a restaurant or someone's house with a caterer, but he really wanted them to let their guards down. *You want to get to know them better. All of them.* He wasn't getting attached; he was just doing what any good boss would.

"Dude. This place rocks. Maybe I should buy this," Noah said, looking around. The two-story, almost-beachfront property was available for staff parties, weddings, vacations, or whatever else people could come up with.

"Maybe you should figure out what you want to do before you purchase anything," Chris countered.

Noah opened the double doors off the galley-style kitchen. Crisp ocean air wafted through, easing leftover tension out of Chris's shoulders. He'd intended for Jane to take care of the details, but once he'd started, he wanted to finalize everything himself. He wasn't sure why it mattered so much to him, but once an idea struck, Chris couldn't let it go until he saw it through.

"Not all of us have had our lives mapped out since we were kids," Noah said, bringing Chris back into the conversation.

Grabbing a couple of beers from the party-size fridge, Chris brought them out to the deck and stood at the rail beside his brother.

"Nothing wrong with a plan. It'd stop you from wondering where to go next," Chris said, clinking his bottle to Noah's.

"Yeah. That's one way to look at it," Noah said, taking a drink.

Chris glanced at his watch. He had a caterer showing up shortly, and then the staff would be here soon. They had time to sit around, shoot the breeze. It felt like forever since he'd done just that. The fact that some of his favorite people would spend the evening with him was a huge bonus.

"What's another?" Chris glanced at Noah.

"It's good to have a plan and all, but not if you never look up."

"What's that supposed to mean?"

"Why do you want to be like him so much?"

Chris reared back slightly. How they went from talking about the house to their father was beyond him. "What the hell, Noah? I bring you a beer and you insult me?"

Noah half smiled. Chris was only partially joking, though.

Turning so he could rest against the banister, Noah looked Chris straight in the eyes. "You sure the plan you laid out for yourself is still what you want?"

Irritation prickled along the back of his neck. "Of course it is. You think I worked this hard, bounced around fixing company after company, just so I could keep doing it?"

Noah tipped his beer back, fine with making Chris wait for his answer. "I don't think you should have had to jump through any of those hoops in the first place. None of us should have. You seem happy here, man. Do you even know that?"

Chris shook off his unease, taking a long drink of the beer that no longer tasted good. "I'm a happy guy. Why wouldn't I be?"

"No. You seem happy *here*."

"I'm not meant to stay *here*, Noah. This was always temporary." Even if saying it put a clutch in his chest.

Noah rolled his eyes. "Because that was the plan."

Chris set his bottle down hard on the rail. "Yes, it's the fucking plan. What's wrong with that? What are you getting at? There's nothing wrong with the path I'm on. It's *you* who is aimlessly wondering what to do next because Dad said no to some warehouses. Speaking of being like him, you're one to talk. You jump from one goddamn thing to the next wondering why you're not satisfied. Stand still and maybe you will be."

Chris's lungs squeezed. Why did he feel so mad right now? What the hell was Noah's problem?

"Back at you, bro. Stand still. Reassess. You can be pissed all you want, but I'm worried you're going to get back to New York only to realize that everything you wanted . . . *everyone* you wanted . . . was right here in California. You can't plan for everything, Chris. Sometimes you have to let life just happen."

Chris leaned in. "My life is finally *starting* to happen." Everything he wanted was within his grasp.

Noah shrugged. "Keep telling yourself that. Just answer one thing."

Chris waited. Noah stared at him, giving nothing away.

"If I tell you to think of something that makes you truly happy, what's the first thing that pops into your brain?"

Everly. Shit. Her image snuck in without any effort at all. He'd seen his father throw away wives the way he did businesses, and he wasn't about to do that with Everly. She deserved more. He had a plan that involved New York. Once he was waist deep in it, he could think about the next step.

Noah set his beer down. Chris glared at him, grateful when the doorbell rang.

"I'll get it." Chris started to walk away, but when Noah chuckled behind him, he raised his hand and shot his brother the finger. Noah only laughed harder.

***

The sun had lowered itself in the sky as if it were settling in for the best part of the evening. Streaks of red and orange blazed out from each side of the orb, creating a painting-like view. There was a path leading from the house down to the water. A few of the staff had headed that way when they'd heard about a bonfire at the beach. Mari and Mason were playing Frisbee with Kitty and Luke, both of whom brought significant others.

Jane was chatting with Benny and his wife, enjoying the wide variety of finger foods the caterer had set out. Noah was showing Stacey how to play boccie ball and stopping every five seconds to laugh gregariously at something she'd said.

Chris glanced around, trying not to seem like he was looking for someone specific. Everly showed up on her own, right after Stacey. He hadn't talked to her about her final date, but he didn't want tonight to be about work. *Or the men she's dating.* He'd thought the two friends would come together, but Stacey claimed Everly had a list of things that she had to do. Apparently, she was serious about her lists. The thought of it made Chris smile.

He walked out into the backyard, watched the Frisbee game for a few minutes, and then decided to take the path down to the beach.

He expected—okay, hoped—to find Everly by the beach. He was surprised to see her sitting off to the side of the entrance to the main area. She sat, knees drawn up to her chest, on a bench, staring out at the ocean with a quiet focus he didn't want to break. It was no hardship to stare. She wore a soft gray shirt and a pair of cargo shorts. Her legs were paler than her arms and face. Now that he was looking at her, he realized, she rarely wore shorts. Capris, the odd dress here and there, but rarely shorts. She'd looked beautiful in pink last weekend, but tonight, she looked soft and sweet. Approachable. It struck him that, over the last several weeks, she'd started to share more sides of herself even if it was just through subtle changes in her wardrobe.

"You don't have to stay over there," she said quietly.

Chris laughed, walking over. He settled beside her. "Clearly, my application to ninja school should be denied."

She turned her head to smile at him. "Stealth you are not."

"It's beautiful here," he said, meaning the ocean but unable to look away from Everly.

"It is. I love the water. I never make time to come enjoy it." She looked back toward the seagulls diving in the shallow waves.

He took a long swallow of his beer, and when she looked at him again, he offered it to her. She took a sip and then scrunched her nose in an adorable way.

"I hate beer. I try it every now and again because so many people love it. My dad is in a craft beer craze. That's how he's handling the latest break with my mom. But I can't get used to it. It tastes like . . . wet bread."

Chris laughed, taking his beer back. "Wow. I guess our taste buds are different, because I was thinking more nectar of the gods."

She grinned. "That would be the Oreo milkshake at the Burger Shack."

"Also delicious. So, your mom and dad aren't together right now?" Was it weird that he wished he could erase the sadness in her tone?

She rested her head on her knees, and Chris had to fight down the urge to put his arm around her and pull her closer.

"It shouldn't matter. I'm thirty years old. I don't need my parents to stay together to make me happy. But it would make me happier if they didn't both think they needed to get me on their side. It's like this covert competition to see who can hang out with me more right now. They don't understand that I don't want to hang out with *anyone*." She scrunched her nose again. "Present company excluded."

Another chuckle rumbled from his chest. The ocean breeze had tendrils of hair dancing across her cheeks.

"Obviously," he said. "Your dance card has been rather full lately. Come to any great conclusions?" He hoped she understood that he was asking as her friend, not the person who'd orchestrated her busy social life. How did she see him? He wondered if maybe she'd found something more with one of the men. Owen? Everything else aside, he'd be happy if she was. Regardless of whether she chose one of them or not, she deserved contentment. Whatever that looked like for *her.* He'd never really thought about that aspect of caring for someone—the idea of wanting them to have what they wanted or needed. Her happiness increasing his own.

"Definitely," she said, lifting her head again.

Chris's heart thundered in his chest. He lifted his beer but didn't drink. His throat was dry, but he knew it wouldn't taste good while he wondered about her declaration. Her final date post hadn't revealed anything significant except that of the two this week, Daniel was out. But maybe she'd known from the start. The final two were being announced tomorrow. His breath froze in his lungs.

"I conclude that I'm not a very good dancer. Or in this case, dater."

The muscles in his chest loosened so he could breathe again. "I don't believe that." If he was leaving, which might happen sooner rather than later, he needed her to understand how *he* saw *her.* "You're an . . . amazing dancer. You're bright, funny, and beautiful. This isn't about any of those guys, Everly. It's about you. You realizing it's your choice. All of it. Wherever you want to go, personally or professionally, you'll get there. You deserve great things because you're a great person."

He didn't mean to stare at her lips but found himself fascinated with the way they formed a small *o* as if he'd surprised her. His gaze moved up, reaching Everly's.

"That was a really nice thing to say," she whispered.

"Maybe, but it's also true. You amaze me," he replied. The moon was casting a glow, stars were dotting the sky, and the moment, all of that combined with sitting next to her, felt a little like magic. The kind that brought out the truth.

"You don't get out much." She sat straighter, put her hands flat on either side of her.

Chris covered her hand. "Don't do that. You kick ass, Everly. In so many ways."

She blinked several times, then smiled at him, lighting up his chest the way the moon lit the sky.

He didn't want to ask, but he needed to know. "Did you choose?" His pulse caught in his throat.

Everly turned her hand over under his, essentially linking their fingers, though neither of them curled in to tighten the grasp. He didn't think he'd ever been so aware of his hand.

"Yes," she whispered. She turned her head, looked down at their hands before looking up at him. "At least, I think so."

He nodded, removed his hand but not his gaze. This was good. Excellent. His other hand gripped the bottle so tightly he forced himself to loosen his hold.

They stared at each other longer than either of them should have, and the more he looked, the more he wanted to move closer, pull her near and tip her face up to his, feel her lips move under his own, and find out once and for all if she tasted as good as she always smelled. *She chose.*

"You do that sometimes," she whispered, her face a fraction closer.

His own breathing hitched now. "What's that?"

"Look at me like you're thinking things I can't imagine you thinking," she said, her voice still so quiet it was hard to hear her. Except that he could hear her because he was hanging on every word she said. His heart was having a seizure behind his rib cage.

"I think all sorts of things," he said, his own voice husky. Things he shouldn't, *couldn't* entertain. Happiness came from setting a goal, achieving it. He was so close. *So is she. So close you could kiss her, just brush your mouth over her lips.*

"About me?"

All. The. Time. They were close enough to share the same tiny molecules of air. They were breathing each other in and out. Chris's heart took up residence in his ears, the steady thump drowning out the waves rolling in.

Everly blinked, her eyes moving to his mouth, lingering there long enough to have Chris biting back a groan. Their fingers linked. Not by accident. Chris wanted to kiss Everly more than he wanted anything. More than going home, gaining his father's approval, or taking his rightful seat at the helm. When he'd arrived in California, those three things had been his sole focus. His mission. They were nothing compared to the desire thrumming through his entire being in this second. Business, his father, they didn't exist. His home? It was wherever he could see her face. Touch her. Breathe her in. In that moment, Chris would have turned himself inside out and upside down if it meant having even the smallest chance at being in Everly's heart. Of finding a way inside of it.

"Hey! We're going to play Never Have I Ever. Come on, oh boring ones. Let's go. I saw ingredients for margaritas," Stacey said, bouncing over out of nowhere. Noah was trailing behind her chatting with Jane, who must have joined them without Everly or Chris noticing.

"Whoa, what's going down, Charlie Brown? Why do you look so serious, boo?" Stacey settled herself more *on* Everly than beside her. "Mmm. You smell good. Doesn't she smell good, Chris? You make me want cookies."

Everly laughed and pushed Stacey away from her. "You're drunk and do not need margaritas."

"Whatever, Mom. I'm having one, and you can't stop me."

Everly shook her head, her smile tight. "I *will* stop you, because one of us needs to make you act responsibly. You're going to feel sick tomorrow, and we have the event for Rob." She stroked a hand down Stacey's hair, gentling the words.

"Hmm. Rob. Right. Make you a deal. You play Never Have

I Ever, and I won't have a mar . . . mar-har . . . when did that get hard to say?"

Chris laughed with the others, but something very much like disappointment settled in his gut. He didn't feel like playing a game right now, but he definitely had something that fit. That would always be true for him. *Never have I ever had the pleasure of kissing Everly Dean.*

[31]

Everly joined the others around the propane fire pit on the wide, wooden-planked deck. She couldn't even process how gorgeous this home was. It was like something out of a magazine. She loved her apartment. It was her happy place, but one day, she could imagine buying a home, making it her own. *Not one like this, though. A little out of your price range.* People settled on or around two L-shaped outdoor couches. The furniture was set up for conversation with a gas fireplace in the middle. *Are you hoping that by thinking about furniture and houses, you won't think about how close Chris's mouth was to yours? Or how you wanted to close the space between you more than you wanted to breathe?*

"You look pretty serious. You okay?" Chris sat beside her looking like he wasn't at all shaken over what almost happened.

Her lungs paused. Everly was almost 100 percent positive that if Stacey hadn't interrupted, she and Chris would have kissed. Even now, just thinking about the "almost" had her stomach swooping like a trapeze artist, thrill and terror mingling together. She couldn't think about what "actually" would do to her body and mind if it happened.

If he's fine, acting like nothing almost happened, you can do that, too. "Porches are nice," she said, swallowing loudly. *Really? "Porches are nice"?* "I mean, I was thinking about how beautiful this house is and that if I ever buy a house, I think I'd like a nice big veranda like this."

There. Coherent sentences, even breaths, lungs functioning normally. *Just don't look at him. Or think about the fact that your thighs are touching. That's just so others fit. Others you work with. Your coworkers and friends.*

"I agree," Chris said, no censure or judgment in his voice. "I'd sit out here every morning for coffee and watch the sun come up."

Now she looked at him as the others talked, laughed, grabbed drinks, and sat down. "Same."

She couldn't help the grin that blossomed. Maybe they weren't so different. Maybe there were ways around . . . his eyes traveled to her mouth, and her stomach tightened with want. Pure, unadulterated, to-the-core *want.* She'd been on six dates in the last month. And the man she wanted was sitting right beside her, looking like he'd like to pick up where they'd left off, several inches closer to each other.

"Everly," he whispered.

One of his hands held a beer, and the other rested on his thigh. With the subtlest of movements, that no one would see even with the moon glowing behind pockets of clouds and the strings of small outdoor lights along the patio roof, his hand touched her own. Tiny vibrations of sensation, like miniature pulse points, beat up her arm, burrowed into her chest, and she sighed, locked her gaze with his.

His eyes were questioning, and all she could do was widen her smile.

"Okay," Stacey said, half falling, half sitting in the chair across from them. She looked around at the group. "Everyone have a drink? Excellent. This is how this works for those of you newbies. Someone starts by saying, 'Never have I ever,' and they complete the sentence with something they've never done." She stopped, looked around to make sure everyone was with her so far.

Everly laughed, but it felt like an out-of-body experience, because even though she was listening to Stacey, 99 percent of her focus and attention was on the two inches of skin touching Chris.

"We got it, Stace. None of us are as drunk as you," Mason said, laughing and raising his beer.

"Cool. That's not all. Whoever *has* done whatever the person says they haven't done . . . Wait . . . Is that . . . Yeah, that's right. If you *have* done what they say, you have to drink. Got it?"

"Maybe you should switch to water," Everly said, that 1 percent of herself beginning to worry Stacey should just be tucked into bed.

"Meh. Noah watered down my drink, anyway. Buzzkill."

Noah gave a hearty laugh. It was similar to Chris's but did nothing to the butterflies in Everly's stomach. Nope. Those were apparently trained to respond to men she shouldn't want. *Man. One man.*

"Why don't you start, Stacey?" Noah said, throwing his legs up over one side of the chair he was draped on.

So much more casual than Chris, but she noticed when he'd stopped by their meeting last week, he had the same air of authority that Chris did when speaking to a group.

Stacey tapped her lip with one finger. "Okay, never have I ever . . . oh! Never have I ever skinny-dipped." She grinned like she'd just won a prize and glanced around the room.

When Jane tipped her drink up first, several people hooted and hollered.

Stacey's jaw dropped. "Sweet, button-up-collar Jane? Really? I need to up my game."

Her girlfriend, a long-haired brunette with a distinctly bohemian style, put a hand on her shoulder and joined her in taking a drink, but neither added to the story.

"My turn now?" Jane looked up at her girlfriend. She seemed very into her, and Everly felt bad she didn't know more about some of the people she'd worked with for years. She needed to stop being so closed off. *You're working on it.*

"Never have I ever . . . played a musical instrument."

Several people took a drink, while Stacey claimed that one was boring. When Chris drank, Everly arched a brow.

His pinkie rubbed along hers. How many freaking nerve endings could one little pinkie have? And since when were they all hardwired to other important parts of her?

"Flute," he whispered. "In junior high."

She bit her lip to keep from grinning about this new information. "Nice."

Mason took a long drink. "Picked up a guitar at sixteen because I figured chicks dig it. I was not wrong. I also was not good."

Laughter prolonged the game while others shared stories.

"Mason's turn," Stacey said, cozying into her seat a little more, her head drooping.

"Never have I ever gotten drunk playing one of these games," Mason said.

Several people drank, including Everly. Chris looked at her, and even though they were surrounded by people and music and waves crashing in the distance, she felt like they were in their own bubble.

"That surprises me," he said.

"I was a teenager once, you know," she said after taking her drink.

"Everly's turn," Kitty said.

"Why's it my turn?"

"You haven't gone yet." Kitty shrugged, like the reason was obvious. Others looked her way. When she was younger, there were times she had to pull on an invisible shield that let her get through things, like speaking in front of her class, with minimal panic. Faux confidence brought on by necessity.

Counting to ten in her head helped to loosen the pressure in her chest. Chris's finger sliding over hers, covering it like he had last weekend at the restaurant, pushed everything else out of her head.

"Never have I ever dated someone who I knew was going to be my forever," she said. Even knowing Owen was her choice of the bachelors, who was to say where it would go? There was a slight pause, and she cursed herself for turning things so seriously, but what was she supposed to say? *I've never had sex outside? I've never done anything terrifying? I've never done anything exciting?* She didn't need people to know these things even if there was a strong chance they wouldn't remember tomorrow.

When Jane and her girlfriend drank at the same moment, eyes locked on each other, a chorus of *awws* sounded along with some colorful commentary from Mason, Luke, and Noah. Luke and his wife were leaning against one of the railings, drinks in hand. He leaned down and whispered something in her ear that made her laugh. Everly's heart clutched with want.

Everly noted Chris hadn't drank when she'd said hers. Had he ever been in love? Thought he was?

"You go, Jane's girlfriend," Stacey called.

"Petra. I've introduced you three times tonight, Stacey," Jane said, laughter underlying her tone.

"Petra. Right. Hey, Petra. I love your skirt."

"Hi, Stacey. Again. Thank you, and all right, let me think. Never have I ever . . . I don't know. Uh? Never have I ever been married."

Everly glanced around, grinning when Mari, Kitty, Benny, Luke and their respective spouses drank. She turned her head slightly to look at Chris. He was already looking her way.

She would have kept on staring if his brother hadn't spoken up. Or yelled, more accurately.

Noah leaned across others to nudge his brother in the arm. "No cheating. Even quickie marriages count, little brother."

Everly's heart slammed full force into her rib cage. What?

She watched his fingers tighten around his glass. When her gaze moved back up, he was glaring at Noah.

"Whoa! You were married?" Stacey asked, sitting up so she could lean forward to point at him.

Everly felt him stiffen at her side but couldn't take her eyes off his profile. His jaw tightened, his shoulders went back just a touch. He wouldn't meet her gaze.

Noah cleared his throat, giving a forced laugh. "He was married for about five minutes." He picked up a handful of chips from a bowl on the table beside him, popping a couple in his mouth like they were discussing the latest sports highlights. "Our dad was *pissed*." He saluted his brother with his bottle of beer. "One benefit, right?"

Chris huffed out a sound between a growl and a laugh. His eyes caught Everly's. Her throat went dry, and her pulse beat too fast. It probably wasn't healthy for it to beat that fast. Now everyone was probably staring at her, staring at Chris.

"You're not still married, are you?" Stacey asked.

Even drunk, her friend could read Everly's thoughts.

Chris's jaw dropped, and he shook his head. "No. I'm not." He looked into Everly's eyes like he was trying to hold her in one place with his gaze. "I'm not. And it wasn't only to piss my dad off. That was a definite side benefit, but we . . . I think we confused love with something else entirely. We were young."

Everly didn't like the feeling in her chest or the way it was winding through her body, freezing up her insides. He was married, but he'd never been in love? Why else would anyone get married? She couldn't fathom a reason to tie herself to someone through the bonds of marriage if there wasn't love involved. Was she the only one who thought marriage deserved some honor? Some respect? It wasn't something a person bounced in and out of as if it were a trampoline.

"Your turn, bro," Noah said.

"You guys suck. I'm not getting to drink at all," Stacey said, flopping back into the cushions.

"Let me fix that," Chris said, his tone light and fun while Everly's heart was bouncing around. "Never have I ever embarrassed anyone on-air while ten thousand people listened in."

Stacey sat up with a ginormous smile. Her drink sloshed over the rim of the cup. "I've definitely done that."

More laughter, but it sounded far away to Everly. She felt like she was at the other end of a tunnel, watching from far away. Her leg bounced up and down, slowly at first. She tapped her fingers against her cup and inched her other hand away from Chris. *His history is none of your business. He's not married now. What difference does it make? None. It makes no difference. You didn't actually kiss. He's not yours. You choose Owen. You're choosing Owen. You like Owen. Even if brushing up against his entire body couldn't do what Chris's pinkie finger manages. That's a good thing. Who wants to live with this much adrenaline pumping through them all the time? It'd probably give you a heart attack. That's right. Being with Chris would be too much on your system. So stop.* She pictured a stop sign. Then she pictured banging her head into it.

"Who hasn't gone?" Stacey asked. "Kitty, you go."

"Let's do something else. Mason, there's a guitar in the living room. Go grab it and sing some bad songs," Noah said.

"Hey, it's my turn," Kitty said. The guests looked her way. "Never have I ever gone on a blind date." She beamed at them.

"There we go," Stacey said, taking a long gulp of her margarita. A couple of the others drank, too, but Stacey was so happy about being able to, no one paid attention.

Everly couldn't pay attention to anything but the pinball game happening inside of her head. It didn't matter if he'd been married. And divorced. But it made her wonder what he would do in a situation like her parents. Would he go all in and make it work, or would he wash his hands and convince himself he'd done his best? How could anyone really know? *Why does it matter?* She hadn't imagined the heat between them earlier. The "almost" between them was stronger than any actually she'd ever known. If she traveled that road only to find that he wasn't someone who would stick . . . she didn't know if she could handle it.

"You cold?" Chris asked, leaning in so his breath tickled her cheek.

"No. Why?" She couldn't look at him. She tapped her fingers on her legs. They actually did feel cold to touch.

"Your knee hasn't stopped moving," he said.

"Sorry," she said quickly, not hearing what Mari said for her turn. Everly got up, not meaning to do it so suddenly but not entirely in control of her movements.

"Hey, where are you going?" Stacey asked, holding up her glass. "Can you get me something else? I don't like my drink."

Pushing her own feelings down deep, Everly took Stacey's wrist instead of her drink. "Come with me."

They wove their way through the group and into the kitchen. Everly gulped in air. She started to shiver. Maybe she was cold.

"What are we doing, Evs?" Stacey leaned against the counter. She picked a few grapes off one of the platters.

"I need to go, but I need to make sure you're okay first."

Stacey squeezed the grape between two fingers and scrunched her nose up, her eyebrows down. "Why do you have to go?"

"I'm tired. My head hurts a bit. You need to stop drinking."

Stacey straightened up and grabbed a napkin, wiped her hands. "What's wrong?" Moving to Everly, she put her hands on her shoulders, bent her knees, and met her gaze. "What's wrong?"

I'm confused and possibly have feelings for someone I shouldn't. Someone I don't know all that well. I'm dating strangers and forgetting what I want for myself. I'm not sure I actually know. Rules or no rules, I feel like I'm messing things up. Tears pushed, so she pressed the fingernails of one hand into her palm. "Nothing. I'm just really tired. Overwhelmed. Please don't make a big deal of it."

Though she was nowhere near sober, Stacey nodded, and Everly saw that she was taking her seriously. "Okay. I'll stop drinking. I'm going to sleep in one of the guest rooms. I won't be late tomorrow. Promise. You still love me even if I'm drunk?"

The french doors leading off the kitchen opened, and Everly's heart rate quickened. "Always. I'll see you tomorrow."

Without glancing over her shoulder, she grabbed her purse from the table, hating how rude she was about to be—leaving without saying good-bye—but she couldn't breathe. Couldn't pull air all the way into her lungs, and worse, she couldn't explain why, so she needed to go. She needed space. She made it to the front door, breathing like a marathon sprinter.

On the front steps, she released her nails from her palms, and her lungs flexed a little. She'd parked near the end of the drive, having shown up later than others and knowing she'd want easy access when it came time to leave.

She was almost there. *Just get in your car. Go home. Everything is fine. It's all just hitting you. Eight dates in a month? That's more than the last five years of her life.*

"Everly, wait," Chris said behind her.

Clarity hit her like a wave rocking her backward. It was *Chris* she was running from. She needed to escape from him. All at once, sitting next to him, she'd realized she *did* like him. That she wished he were one of her dates. All her dates. Immediately after that had sunken into her brain, he'd admitted to being married and divorced. It struck her then that she didn't know him. Not knowing someone was the reason she'd spent her birthday morning cleaning coffee stains off her pants.

He'd followed her, and now she had to face him. Along with her own feelings.

She stopped at her car but didn't turn around. She felt him behind her as his footsteps crunching over the gravel came nearer. His hands came to her shoulders, and they stood like that a moment. She could still hear the waves in the distance and laughter from the other side of the house. She could hear her heartbeat in her ears and both of their breaths sawing in and out.

Instead of turning her, Chris dropped one hand and walked around her, coming to stand in front of her, his fingers trailing down the arm he was still touching.

Everly clenched her jaw and stared at his chest. *Don't look up. Don't look up.* Softly, and exquisitely, painfully slowly, Chris brought his other hand up and pulled her close, pulled her *into* him, wrapping her up in his arms. The lump in her throat doubled in size when her cheek rested against the hard surface of his chest.

"Is this because I said I was married? It was years ago, Everly. I was twenty-one."

Everly blinked back the tears she didn't want to shed, forcing herself to lean back to see his face. Rule six: Be bold, even if it gives you hives. It wasn't *just* that. It was so many things that she didn't know how to voice in this moment. She *felt* too much. It made her brain hurt. *Him holding you makes everything else hurt less.* His arms tightened, hers rested on his waist. "I just need to go."

"There's something here. For both of us," he whispered.

His admission sent a shiver through her body. Everly reached for logic and reason. "You're my boss."

"I'm also your friend," he whispered, his head lowering.

Her breathing hitched, her heart doing some jumping jacks in her chest. "Yes. I don't want to lose that." He mattered to her more than she'd let herself admit. "I work for you. You're my boss." She was repeating herself, but it was all she had. Hadn't that been his reasoning?

"What if I weren't?"

She swallowed. She couldn't think about that right this second. "How long?"

His thumb grazed the skin of her lower back. "Was I married?"

She nodded emphatically, her head feeling disconnected from her neck. *Great. A human Everly bobblehead.* She didn't know why she needed to know.

"Three months. It was a mistake. We thought we felt more than we did, but when it came time to actually be *married*, we knew we were too young. We were friends. We didn't love each other."

Being married is hard, Ev. So why was she fighting so hard to find someone to spend her life with?

Chris's right hand moved and cupped Everly's cheek, his thumb caressing her skin. Warming it. Fighting the chill and her reserve.

"I didn't mean to feel this way about you," he whispered, his face coming closer.

"What way?" She couldn't assume. She couldn't pretend she knew what she was doing.

"Like if I don't kiss you, something inside of me might break."

The next breath she took shuddered in and out raggedly. Their eyes were tethered, fixed on each other with an intensity Everly felt through her entire body.

Time had a way of slowing down, nearly pausing during intense moments. Every second felt like two, moving past in a hazy blur. Chris's face filled more of her vision until his forehead pressed against her own. He closed his eyes, took measured breaths while hers felt suspended. Everly wondered if he could hear her heartbeat as her fingers dug into his waist.

When he opened his eyes, she saw uncertainty clouding them, and it shut down her lungs. What the hell were they doing? They couldn't uncross this line.

"Everly," he whispered.

She shook her head. She couldn't process any of this right

now. She needed to go. It was too hard to unclutter her brain when they were sharing air.

"I have to go. Let me go," she said.

Chris stepped back. Everly got in her car, fought with her seat belt and the desire to dive back into his arms. When his hand pressed to her window, she looked up at him, at the sadness in his gaze. Everly wasn't built for back-and-forth, highs followed by lows. Her parents were champions in that way, but it was never what she wanted. She'd rather have steady, predictable feelings than be unsure in any way. Chris made her feel like she was standing in the middle of a teeter-totter, unable to maintain her balance. *You've got two second dates. The second of which will be Owen, then this is done. The audience was choosing the other but neither Brad nor Jon appealed to her more than Owen. Whether you go out with Owen again after the contest or not, you can go back to your quiet life.* Nothing inside of her felt quiet right now. The longing she'd felt in Chris's arms was like a brass marching band in her chest. So not quiet. How did she get past that?

Easy. You pretend it doesn't exist.

[32]

After working the on-location event Sunday, Monday came too quickly in Everly's opinion. Stacey, who'd been quiet yesterday, nursing a hangover, was back in full form and ready to go. Everly pulled up the website on her laptop, glanced at Stacey as the music was winding down. She gave a nod, just to make sure they were on the same page.

"That was One Republic closing our thirty-minute, no-repeat set. I like their lead singer. He's got so much energy. We should go see them the next time they're in town, Evs," Stacey said into the mic.

Everly shook her head, giving her a bland look. When Stacey started talking again, Everly's eyes wandered to the glass. She hadn't seen Chris yet today. He hadn't shown up at the event, which wasn't out of the norm, but a small piece of her had been disappointed. Which was silly, because she needed to straighten herself out before she saw him again. He scrambled her thoughts.

"Now, the moment you've all been waiting for, particularly you bachelors. As our wonderful listeners know, Everly has been narrowing her playing field as the weeks have passed. Just a recap for those of you joining us, who can still get in on the fun: Evs went on six dates. Three men advanced to the second date round. If you've been following along, you know those three are Owen, Brad, and Jon. With only two second dates available, listeners chose their favorite and Everly picked the other. Thank you to everyone who shared their opinion. The choices have been selected. Evs, drumroll please."

Everly pressed a button, indulging her friend. It was almost easy to pretend they were discussing someone else's life.

"Our top two, going head-to-head for my girl's affections are . . . Owen Baston and Jon Remeyer." Stacey paused, letting Everly press a switch for a crowd clapping.

"The next stage of the competition works like this. Listeners get to read the bios online and pick their favorite of the two. Ultimately, it's Everly who makes the choice, but those people who guessed correctly will be entered to win a very special prize. Your votes need to be in by midnight tonight. Everly's last two dates will be this week with a final reveal next Monday. Have I mentioned how much I love you listeners? Who knew you were all a bunch of romantics? How about a love song to set the mood? Get to our website and cast your vote."

Stacey pressed a couple of buttons and removed her headset, smiling at Everly. The music would play for another half hour. Normally, they'd head into a meeting, but Everly wanted nothing more than to go home, curl up on the couch, and forget about dating anyone.

Stacey came through the door they shared. "Hey. Wanna grab some lunch?"

Everly grabbed her bag, closed her laptop, shoved it in, and stood. "I'm pretty tired, actually." She didn't meet her friend's gaze.

"Any idea what's going on with Chris?"

Everly's head snapped up. "What do you mean?"

Stacey watched her carefully, leaning against the doorjamb. She shrugged. "He and Noah came in before you got here this morning. Chris was on the phone, arguing with someone. They've been holed up in his office since. Something is going down. Jane wouldn't give me any details."

Everly laughed. "Because Jane isn't a gossip."

Stacey sighed. "Yeah. I know. But I like her, anyway."

Walking toward the door, she waited for Stacey to move out

of the way. She swallowed around her nerves—if Stacey sensed anything, she'd pounce. Everly didn't know how to talk about the feelings ricocheting around her chest, so it was best to leave them untouched.

"We leaving?" Stacey waited a beat. "Everly?"

"Hmm?"

"Look at me."

She lifted her chin, nibbling the inside of her cheek.

"I'm bringing lunch to your house. I'll see you in twenty minutes."

"Stace, I just want—"

"To pretend there aren't a dozen things on your mind. To hide from everything until you have no choice but to face it. We're going to talk. You're going to open up to me, Dean."

She wanted to feel indignant at Stacey's bossiness, but this was her best friend. They didn't keep things from each other until Everly had spiraled so far into her confusing feelings, she didn't know how to voice them.

"If you say no, I won't confide in you."

Everly stiffened. "About what?"

Stacey leaned in. "I'm not telling. But it's important. It's real. You're the only person I want to talk to about it, but if we don't do that anymore . . ."

Everly's lips quirked. "Stop. Point made. Grab sushi. We've had too much junk food lately."

"Yes, Mom."

Everly left work laughing, doing her best not to think about all the things she needed to say. Words, like feelings, couldn't be stuffed back into the boxes they belonged in once a person let them out. Which was why it was good she and Chris hadn't kissed the other night. Who needed that kind of complication? A relationship with him—not that he'd said he wanted one, just that he'd wanted to kiss her—would be something like her parents'. Exciting one moment, uncertain the next. Even as friends, that was how it'd been so far. Everly didn't like roller coasters—figuratively or literally.

She'd open up to Stacey, sort through her feelings, get things down on paper, then they'd focus on her friend. It was time to make someone else's dating life the priority. Two more dates, neither of them firsts, but Everly was ready to wave the white flag, pick Owen, and start living her life again.

***

Stacey wiped her mouth, finishing off the last California roll. "Rob asked me out."

"Chris's friend," Everly said. A smile tugged at her lips, but she didn't give in. Her friend deserved happily ever after as much as anyone. If she got all the feels with Rob, maybe he was the one. Everly wanted that almost more for her friend than she did for herself.

Stacey nodded. She was the most confident, outgoing, straightforward person Everly had ever met, yet she didn't look at Everly's face. She fidgeted—*fidgeted*—with the take-out container. The grin started in Everly's chest, warming it and taking over her face, making her cheeks stretch. She bit her lip to keep from laughing with glee. When she had herself under control, she cleared her throat. Stacey still didn't look up.

"My little girl is growing up," Everly said with mock seriousness.

Stacey's gaze jumped to hers and quickly turned to a scowl. "Not funny."

"You like him. You always go out with men you like."

Stacey nodded, stacking her empty container on top of Everly's.

"Why are you so scared of getting into a relationship that might go somewhere?"

Donning a look Everly had seen only a few times—a false bravado—Stacey swung her hair over her shoulder. "Seems unfair to take myself off the market just for the possibility of something lasting."

Leaning back in her chair across from Stacey, who cuddled into the couch, Everly crossed her arms over her chest. "All this time, we thought I was the one with relationship issues."

Stacey arched her brows. "Dude. You so are."

Laughter bubbled up. She nodded. "Truth. But so are you. Maybe everyone has their own demons around this sort of stuff." She thought of her parents.

"Of course everyone does. But we're not talking about them."

Everly got up and went over to the couch, curling her knees under her as she sat next to Stacey. "You're the bravest person I know. Rob seems like a good guy."

"I agree. A good guy. Not a *good-time* guy."

This clearly troubled her friend. "Have you ever been in a serious relationship?"

"A long time ago. It didn't end well. I promised myself I would worry only about me. That I wouldn't sew myself into something long term, because nothing lasts."

"Now you sound like me."

"I don't want to hurt someone," Stacey said, playing with an invisible thread on her pants.

"It's the risk anyone who wants to find someone takes."

Stacey looked at her through lowered lashes. "This contest has made you wise."

Everly rolled her eyes. "It's hard to take the risk. It makes me feel . . . almost normal that it's hard, even for someone like you."

Laying her head on Everly's shoulder, Stacey sighed. "It's all fun and games until someone falls in love, Evs. I like my fun."

"Maybe it's possible to have both. The fun and the love."

"You think I should go out with him."

Resting her cheek on Stacey's head, she nodded against it. "I will. If you tell me what's up with you."

"I think I'm falling for Chris."

"Duh."

Everly pinched Stacey's arm.

Stacey jumped, laughing. "Ouch. Come on. You think I don't see that? Or the way he's crazy about you?"

"I don't want complications." Now, Everly focused on her own invisible thread. She didn't want to feel vulnerable, capable of being hurt again. She had a feeling that she hadn't known real hurt yet because she'd never felt anything like this before. If it was this . . . *big* before they started, it might kill her if they did get together and things ended.

"Life is full of them, Everly." Stacey sat up.

"Sure. But sometimes you can choose which ones you let in."

"You just told me to go for it."

"I'm not you. Chris isn't the one."

"You sure?"

Everly nodded.

Stacey tipped her head to one side and held out a hand. "Let me see it."

Resistance was pointless, so even though her cheeks went hot, Everly got up and grabbed her journal off the cabinet by the door. She flipped it open to the page she'd finished before Stacey arrived.

"Oh my." Stacey stared at the list Everly had already memorized in an effort to stay strong and choose Owen. *Hmm. I should make that into a shirt.*

Reasons It Can't Be Chris:

He's my boss.

He's becoming my friend—don't want to lose that for something that might not last.

Sometimes I'm not even sure he's into me.

He gives me butterflies. Even when we're doing something mundane. That can't be good for me even if it's a happy kind of nervous.

He's too observant.

I can't come out of my shell with someone who won't push me to do so.

He says he likes me, but he's helping me find a guy.

He knows too much. Hello, condom piñata.

He's been married. This shouldn't matter, but it does. I want someone who will take this step only once. Forever.

I can't shake the feeling there's something he's not saying.

Stacey looked up. "Ev."

She shrugged. "They're all good reasons."

"Are they? You say I'm the brave one, the risk taker, but Ev, you're amazing. You've done this whole contest thing with grace and dignity. People are turning to you for understanding. For hope."

She scoffed. "That was one person."

Stacey scooted closer. "That you *responded* to. There are way more DMs than that, and I know you were reading through them. The fact that you found the courage to respond, to recognize that you could help someone else, is huge." Stacey took a deep breath, probably to keep from getting too fired up. It made Everly smile to know her friend was so willing to see the good.

Stacey nudged Everly's shoulder. "We're going to do the new segment. It's going to help others. You did that. You didn't just come out of your shell, you broke it down. Smashed it to pieces."

Everly wanted to disregard the praise, but those were things she felt proud of. "I don't want the highs and lows. I just want a middle-of-the-road, make-me-content, no-surprises, steady kind of love."

Stacey gripped her hand. "Then you're selling yourself short."

Again, she shrugged, tired of the conversation, of thinking so much. Of *feeling* so much. "Maybe. But it's safer."

[33]

Everly pictured putting her phone down, walking away, coming back in, say, twenty minutes.

"I'm telling you, Evie, that woman staring at another man's junk is more than I can handle," her dad ranted, pausing only to take a breath. At least he had survival skills. She wouldn't want him to pass out from talking too much.

"Sort of like my hard limit is *you* saying the word *junk*, Dad. I have to go." She didn't really, but she was so tired, she couldn't even feel guilt. Setting the phone to speaker, she set her dad on the counter, grabbed a bagel, popping it in the toaster.

"How did you get to be such an uptight prude, sweetie?" Laughter tinted his tone.

"Steady diet of parents who overshare, provide condoms, paint nudes, and discuss said nudes."

Her dad's chuckle made her smile. "You're a good girl. How's the dating going?"

"Almost done. Actually, the listener voting results should be in." She grabbed her phone, pulling up the station's website.

Yup. The votes were in. Owen won by a landslide. Everly smiled. He was her choice, too. The fact that thousands of Californians agreed with her boosted her confidence. She *could* pick a good guy with long-term potential.

"It's Owen," she said out loud, forgetting about her dad for a minute.

"Owen. He was the first one, right?"

Everly nodded, remembering he couldn't see her. "Yes."

"Who's your choice?"

Chris. "Owen," she said somewhat forcefully.

"That's my girl. Sounds like you're smitten."

Her bagel popped just as her doorbell buzzed. "I have to go."

"Love you, Evie."

"Love you, too, Dad. Forgive Mom. Move on."

"Give me marital advice when you make it six months in a relationship, baby girl."

"Touché."

Everly disconnected and left her bagel, going to the door. She pressed the button for the intercom. "Hello?"

"It's Chris."

Her heart grew wings and freaking fluttered. Everly looked down at her chest. *Stupid heart. What is wrong with you?*

"Jansen," he added. She heard the smile in his voice. If she were making a list of reasons why it *should* be him, his smile would go at the top.

She pressed the release button and unlocked her door so he could let himself in. Going back to her bagel, she spread cream cheese like it was the most important and engaging task on earth, her breath hitching when he knocked once and let himself in.

"Everly?" The door closed.

"In the kitchen. Want a bagel?" *Smooth line. Dating queen, indeed.*

"I'm good, thanks."

When she turned from putting away the cream cheese, he was standing there in the small opening between her kitchen and dining area. Dressed casually in jeans and a waffle-knit T-shirt, he looked . . . well, he looked really damn good.

She picked up her plate and stared at him. He could fill the silence.

"Don't let me keep you from your nutritious dinner," he said, nodding to the plate.

She wasn't hungry anymore. "Why are you here?"

"Why did it bother you so much that I was married?"

Shock struck her like a pedal against a drum. "It didn't." She walked past him, brushing his arm as she went to the couch. He followed after her.

"You froze up. You left."

"I don't like to socialize. I've done more than enough of it lately. I wanted to go home." She curled into the corner and stared down at her bagel.

"I know I'm your boss, Everly. We can come back to that later, but I can't stop thinking about how you pulled away when you found out."

She looked up, her chest constricting from the seriousness of his gaze. "What difference does it make? Why are you doing this? The listeners just voted. Owen is their pick. He's mine, too, so maybe it's good you're here. I want to forget about the second date. Just name Owen the winner . . . bachelor . . . whatever."

He stared at her hard enough to make her focus on her bagel. "Why did it bug you so much?"

She sighed, met his gaze again, unable to hide her frustration. Why the hell was he pushing her on *this*? "I apologize for overreacting. I'm just in a funny place with all the dates, my parents arguing, and this . . . whatever it is that happened between us. I thought we were getting closer. Becoming friends. Finding out that way was a shock. It threw me off, but it shouldn't. Your past is none of my business. We're just friends."

What she felt for him was bigger than anything she could imagine feeling for Owen, and that scared the hell out of her. Overblown, uncontrollable feelings led to terrifying hobbies. Everly just wanted quiet. *Right. Quiet, safe, comfortable.*

He tunneled both hands into his hair and sighed, pacing in

front of her coffee table. "I know that. I told myself that. Along with a hell of a lot of other things."

Chris sat down on the other end of the couch. At least he was able to read her need for space. "We were twenty-one. There was a group of us, all good friends. We took a road trip. I was mad at my father, who is . . . Let's just say he's somewhat controlling. Her dad worked for my dad, and that pissed my dad off. It just happened. We thought it would make us truly feel like adults, but we were wrong. A few months later, we decided to call it quits and stay friends. She's remarried and has three kids."

They'd acted on impulse—on feelings. Her parents' marriage was built on the same shaky foundation. Everly wanted a base of titanium and concrete. She closed her eyes, gathered her strength, and looked up at him. Why was he telling her this? She didn't want to know about his ex-*wife*. God, why did that gut her to think about it? She put her plate on the table. "This is none of my business."

He shuffled over and took her hand. "I disagree. We *were* getting to know each other. I'm not hiding from you. I want to know more about you because there's something here, Everly. This isn't typical for me. I don't get tingles just holding a woman's hand. Except for with you. Work complicates it, and I know you're finishing up the dating, but be honest with me, with yourself: Tell me you *don't* feel something back."

She felt more intimacy with just the touch of his hand than she ever had with any other man. But she couldn't just jump. It didn't work like that. She had a list. She had reasons. Good ones. He was a roller coaster, and she wanted the teacups—a ride that threw her off balance but was easy to recover from. Acting on chemistry had led her down the wrong path many times. Attraction fizzled. Sure, this ache she felt in her chest for him and these feelings were different from anything she'd known. That just made her trust herself less.

"What if it didn't work?" The whispered question surprised her. She hadn't meant to ask.

Chris stroked a finger over her palm, making it hard to focus. He stopped, looked up. "What?"

She pulled her hand back, clasped both together, and put them in her lap. "What if we try, and it messes everything up? I mean, sure, you stayed friends with your ex-wife." She took a deep breath, hating how much she disliked the whole friends-with-the-ex thing. "We work together. I don't have that many friends. If it doesn't work, I could be out of a job. Down a friend."

"Jesus. These two situations are nothing like each other. I'm a thirty-one-year-old man who is a hell of a lot surer of my feelings than I was as a kid. My marriage has nothing to do with how I feel about you. It was a mistake. On both our parts. Why do we have to go into anything thinking about it *not* working out?"

"Because things don't. Things happen. Life is hard. Marriage is hard. How do you know that if you got married now, you'd do anything differently? What if you got married and it wasn't working out?"

His face contorted with exasperation. "I . . . I don't know. Are you asking me if I believe in divorce? Yes. I do. There's a reason my mother didn't stay with my father. She's happier without him. Should she have lived in misery her whole life just because she made some promises?"

Some promises. "Those promises mean something," she whispered. Why did people make them if they couldn't *keep* them?

"They *did.* But people change. God, look at your own parents. They can't decide one way or the other. Tell me you don't wish they'd get a divorce—just be done with all the back-and-forth?"

Her heart muscles tightened. Everly breathed through her nose. "Actually, I wish they'd stop looking at being apart as an option. I wish they'd stick by the promises they made. There shouldn't be an out."

He sprang up from the couch, startling her. "So, you think if two people are wrong for each other, they should stay together?"

She stared, hard, at her plate. The cream cheese was melted now, and the bagel looked soggy. "No. I just think they shouldn't get married if they aren't in it for good."

"Sometimes people don't know where life will lead them, Everly. You can't be that naïve. There's no way. Why does this even matter? If I were still married, we wouldn't be having this conversation."

The muscles wouldn't loosen, and it felt like her heartstrings were looping themselves around her ribs, pulling corset-tight. "We shouldn't be, anyway."

"Fine. You want to pretend you feel nothing, fine. That's great. Let's do that."

Tears pressed. "Okay."

"Seriously?"

She stood up, irritation and sadness pulling her in opposite directions. She stalked closer. "Yes. Seriously. Why mess things up? I care about you. We're friends. Looking for more is a risk I don't want to take. Especially with someone who has no staying power."

"Excuse me?"

She stepped closer, her vision tunneling a little. "You heard me. What do you want? You want to date me? Sleep together? Hook up? You clearly don't believe in putting your all into a relationship, working it out no matter what." She knew she was being unfair, possibly even taking a bit of her anger at her parents out on him. Even knowing, she couldn't stop herself. *Self-sabotage. So much easier in the long run.*

His face lowered so they were almost nose to nose. The scent of his cologne along with the heat of his body, the heat in his eyes, messed with her head.

"No matter what? What about your ex? He cheated on you. You think you should have stayed with him despite that? Huh? Pressed through the tough times and forgiven him?"

Everly lifted her hands, unsure what to do with them, and then crossed them tightly across her chest. "That's different. We weren't married."

"Fuck, Everly. Neither are we. I just said I had feelings for you, and somehow that's led to you not only judging me for mistakes I made when I was twenty-one goddamned years old but also deciding I'm not fit for long-term boyfriend material. People get married. They get divorced. The world isn't black and white. Bad things happen. Hard decisions get made. You don't get to make decisions about who I *am* based on one thing from my past. Any more than I should do that to you. Look at who I am now. That's all I'm asking you to do. Look at *me*. Right now."

His voice was rough. Tears filled Everly's eyes. She blinked them away, swiping at the few that escaped.

"I want to get married one day. I'm tired of playing around, wasting time. I want someone who won't give up. Who won't give in. I'm not exactly low maintenance," she said, her voice breaking. He reached for her, but she stepped back. "I can't fall for someone who will run when things get hard."

Chris's eyes widened as they filled with hurt. She immediately regretted her words, not just because of how they clearly impacted him but also because he'd never given her a reason to doubt him. She, of all people, should know better than to judge a person based on one thing. Would she want to be seen only for her anxiety? There was so much more to her than that one thing. This man, standing in front of her like she'd wrecked him, had believed in, trusted, lifted her. He made her laugh, think, and want to try harder. He made her wonder what it would be like to fall in love without a safety net. He made her want that. He saw her as she really was—anxiety and all. She was throwing that away because she couldn't stand the uncertainty. Tears clogged her throat.

Chris cleared his throat. Stepping toward her with more compassion shining in his gaze than she deserved. "I just want to point out that all this time, I've been fighting what I feel for you. Every bump that's come along with getting closer to you, getting to know you and be your friend? It hasn't been me running, Everly. Not once. It's been you, every time."

Something—desperation or panic—clawed at her, making her lungs fail. She gasped for breath and let out a sob.

Chris reached for her but dropped his hand when she shook her head rapidly. "There are no guarantees in life, Everly. That doesn't mean you can't trust what I feel is real. That it could, that it *would*, last."

He left. Everly went to the door and locked it, smacked her hand against the hard wood, then lowered her forehead to it, not fighting the tears that fell. Angry at herself, at him, at her parents, at how much she wanted to go after Chris and how much she wanted to disappear and pretend they hadn't met, she let herself cry, muffling her sobs in her hands as she sank down to the floor.

[34]

Everly did something she'd never done before. Ever. She called in sick two days in a row when she wasn't sick. Her date with Owen was tonight. Though she still felt some lingering guilt, she'd had a quick lunch date with Jon, more to tell him that she'd made her choice than because she was torn between the two bachelors. Nope. That's not what she was torn about. If she barreled forward, didn't give herself time to think—or *overthink*, as was her norm—she felt good. Buoyed. One foot in front of the other, she was taking charge of getting what she wanted out of life.

After Chris left the other night, after she'd pulled herself up from the floor, dusted herself off, and put her overwrought feelings on a shelf, things had been clearer. She'd known what she needed to do.

The past few days, before she'd straightened herself out, were mired in a Chris-haze. Sure, his words woke her up at night once she'd managed to fall asleep. That gave her the perfect motivation to paint her bedroom pale blue, staying awake until she'd all but crashed into the tray of paint. Wednesday morning, she put on a brave face before heading into work, surprised at the relief she felt when it turned out that Chris wasn't there. She'd slipped out of work, telling Stacey what she was up to as she ran out the door. By the end of the evening, her life was going to be in perfect order, and she'd finally be able to breathe.

Everly drove to one of her favorite restaurants, keeping her brain busy by singing along, badly, to a song she liked. When she arrived, the parking lot was nearly empty. The lunch rush crowd would have finished up earlier. She spotted her mother's car and went into the restaurant, squeezing her hands into fists.

Her mom waited in the lobby. They embraced and then turned to reply to the hostess who'd greeted them.

"Two?" the woman asked.

The door opened behind them, and Everly glanced over her shoulder, her stomach and heart colliding into each other. She looked back at the hostess. "Three."

"What?" Her mother turned and saw her father and stiffened at her side. "Everly."

"What's going on?" her dad asked, staring at his wife. Everly noticed the spark of longing in his gaze, giving her hope that her plan wouldn't push both of them away from her. It was a chance she needed to take. *Ha. See? I can totally take risks without knowing the outcome.*

"We're having lunch," Everly said, her voice rigid as she gestured to the hostess, who was waiting to lead them to a table.

They settled around the table, all of them flashing fake smiles until the hostess left, promising the waitress would be right with them.

"What are you doing, Everly?" Her mother leaned in, over her opened menu.

"You have some nerve, sweetheart," her father said, crossing his arms over his chest, stretching the shoulders of his dark suit.

"It might seem like that but really, I'm just doing something either of you would do, and *have done,* without a second thought. I'll explain everything after we order. I need to speak to both of you and didn't want to do it separately."

Her mother's expression morphed into worry. She reached out to hold Everly's hand. "Are you okay? Is it something bad?"

Everly swallowed. "No. Just something I need to tell you guys."

The tension was thicker than the ten-page menu as they smiled through the waitress's greeting. The second she brought their drinks and left, both her parents turned and focused on Everly.

"What's going on? Are you all right?" Her father folded his hands on the table. They might be divided on many things, but they'd never wavered in their love for her. She loved them back just as fiercely, but if she didn't take this step, she'd resent them.

Everly took a deep breath and let it out. She put her hands on her lap, tapping her fingers on her thighs, focused on the movement and light touch as her heart rate settled.

"I'm okay. I didn't mean to scare either of you, but I have something I need to tell you, and I need you to listen to me and respect what I'm about to say."

Her mom's lip wobbled, and she reached out to take her husband's hand. He took it without hesitation, saying, "We're here, and we're listening, sweet girl."

They were so *weird*. Maybe Everly hadn't been married or even truly in love, but she hoped that if she ever found the one, she wouldn't do what her parents did to each other. To her. She'd admitted the full force of their damage to herself the other night, realizing this was the starting point of her having what she wanted.

No more delays. "Your marriage is your business just like my life is my own. We might not agree with each other on everything, but how you choose to love is entirely up to you. My whole life, I've accepted the dichotomy of your marriage as normal. I've let myself believe it didn't impact me in any way other than that I wanted to avoid something similar." She inhaled, forcing herself to continue. "I told myself I wasn't impacted by what you do to each other, but I was wrong. Who you are with each other—in good times and bad—has shaped who *I* am. It's clouded my ideas of what I want, or don't want, for myself. I've been so mad at you both so many times over the years. Now that I'm older, I realize I only have control over me. My life. How you guys choose to be married is up to you, but how I let it affect *me* isn't. I asked you both to come here today to tell you that I won't do this anymore." Her lungs all but collapsed, and air whooshed out. Her shoulders sagged. There. She'd said her piece. Just like she'd practiced.

"What on earth are you talking about?" Her father's voice carried through the empty restaurant.

"What won't you do anymore?" her mother asked, pulling her hand out of her husband's.

Everly waved a hand in their direction. "This back-and-forth you two do? I won't be part of it anymore. I'd love to be able to tell you to decide one way or the other—be all in or all out, whatever makes you truly happy, but it's not my place. As your daughter, the person whose emotions have been yanked back and forth like a yo-yo since I was seven years old, I'm saying no more. You don't get to drag me into it." She held up a hand when they started to speak. "Let me finish. Watching you act like newlyweds one day and then enemies the next has taken more of a toll on me than I wanted to admit. Unknowingly, I've let your relationship influence my own beliefs. If you two get divorced, I hope you both find love again. You are both amazing people. You both *deserve* happiness. I was positive that I just wanted you guys to stay together. You made vows, promised to get through anything. But I'm not seven anymore. I'm not naïve. I know now that it doesn't always work out like you want. Sometimes, how you *want* to feel just isn't the way you do. There's no right or wrong. What works for you won't ever work for me in a relationship. Of that much, I'm sure. Whether you stay apart this time or not, there's no more texting me and calling me to fill in the gaps of loneliness you feel because you're missing each other. When you're together, you get so wrapped up in the renewed newness that you forget I exist sometimes. This pendulum you swing wrecks me."

She paused and took a long drink of her water. Her mother's eyes were brimming with tears, and her father slipped his arm around his wife's shoulder.

Everly swallowed down her tears with the drink. "I'm asking you not to put me in the middle. Call me on a regular basis and check in regardless of your relationship status. I promise to do better in that regard, too. When I say I promise, I mean it. I've cut you guys out of a lot of things because I can't handle the stress of not knowing from one day to the next whether you'll be together or apart."

The waitress came, seemed to sense the mood, and didn't make small talk while she set down sandwiches and fries. She asked if they wanted top-ups of their drinks, then scurried off.

"I had no idea these things weighed so heavily on you," her mother said, unwrapping her fork and knife from the napkin roll.

"Because I haven't told you. I make jokes or blow it off or go with whatever the status quo is. I don't think I even knew how much it's been hurting me. I plan on being more open. Or trying to be, at least. While we're on the topic of what needs to change, I don't like birthday celebrations. I don't like big get-togethers, especially surprise ones. I *hate* surprises. They make me uncomfortable. I don't want to pretend anymore. You're both so social. I envy that sometimes, but it's not who I am. I need you to respect that and never again, for as long as you both shall live, ever give me a piñata or condoms."

Laughter burst from her father. "I told you she was still mad."

Her mom tipped her head back to look at him. "You did. I don't always listen." She looked back at Everly. "It's not as cut-and-dried as *do we or don't we*. We love each other, and no matter what happens, we always will. One thing that never changes, though—we love you more than anything."

Her father nodded, took a bite of his sandwich.

"I know," Everly said, cutting her sandwich into smaller

triangles. "I love you back. I'll always be here when you guys *need* me. It just can't be to fill the void. I can't be your best friend when you need to gossip about what Dad did this time. Dad, I can't be your go-to dinner date at a moment's notice when you're apart."

He nodded, his eyes suspiciously bright. He looked at his wife, making Everly wonder what he was thinking. When he looked back at his daughter, he smiled. "For your next birthday, maybe we could just have one of those cakes you like from your friend's bakery."

She smiled back. "That sounds good."

Her mom huffed out a breath, straightening her shoulders. "Maybe I should take up baking."

After a second of silence, all three of them laughed. The tension lifted. Everly told them about Owen, pushing all her other worries aside. She didn't need them to sort everything out right now. She just needed to say her piece and have them *hear* her so she could move on to the next item on her list.

***

Lunch with her parents, even though it ended well, relieving her of a years' old burden, took a lot out of Everly emotionally. To give herself a bit of extra time, she'd texted Owen to let him know she'd be a little late, telling herself it was fine. *It's okay to say what you need. If someone wants to be with you, they'll accept it.*

Though nerves covered her like an extra sweater as she walked into the restaurant, she didn't second-guess herself. In the past several weeks, she'd stepped up in her own life. This was just one more step. Not a leap, but those left a person with broken ankles. Her feet were firmly planted. Steady.

She wasn't running. Owen was a good man. Good-looking, successful, sweet, and funny. *We have a good foundation.*

"Hey," he said from behind her.

Everly whirled to face him, her breath catching when she

saw the single pink rose in his hand. Her eyes locked on it, then wandered up to meet his gaze.

He shrugged, a charming half smile curving his mouth. "It seemed fitting. You know, like that *Bachelor* show?"

She laughed, nodding. "It's beautiful."

"So are you," he said. When he handed her the rose, he leaned down, brushing his lips across her cheek. Just a whisper of a touch.

Everly's lips trembled.

"Your table is ready," the host said.

Owen put a hand to her back as they wove their way behind the host. They slid into the booth on opposite sides of each other. Everly reminded herself to breathe. *Open mind. Look at him. He's so cute. Easy to read. Easy to be with.* He wore a dark gray golf shirt and a pair of Levi's. Who didn't love a man in Levi's? *No one. That's who.*

She set the rose down on the table. "I thought I'd be more nervous. I don't want to be at all, but I am. Just a bit." *Here comes the babble.*

Owen laughed, the sound light and fun yet still masculine. Little lines gathered at the corners of his eyes when his smile was at full blast. It was a good smile. "It's okay to be nervous. We can't control everything." He reached across the table and took her hand. She didn't pull back. Her hand fit inside of his. It was . . . comforting. Comfortable.

"No kidding. I'm not a big fan of what I can't control," she admitted.

A waiter came to their table and told them the specials.

"I'll take the Santa Fe chicken salad," Everly said, passing over her menu.

"That's my favorite," the waiter said. He turned to Owen. "For you?"

Everly saw Owen's lips move as he ordered his own meal and tried to imagine sitting across from him every night for a very long time. The waiter took the menus and walked away, but Everly was lost in trying to figure out how she'd feel if he was the one. Would she know already? *You can't know. You choose someone, they become the one through hard work, commitment, and promises you keep.*

"You okay?"

She blinked. "Hmm? Yeah. I was just thinking."

Owen folded his hands on the table. "About?"

"Whether we're a good long-term match," she said before realizing she hadn't meant to actually say it out loud.

Owen laughed. "Wow. Okay. No pressure. How's it looking so far?"

Her cheeks went hot, and she picked up her water, took a sip. "You have a sense of humor and aren't put out by my habit of blurting out random things."

"I asked what you were thinking. It's okay to tell me and be honest."

Was it? She folded her hands so she wouldn't move her fingers and leaned in. Okay. Fine. "You're with someone for a long time, but things aren't what you'd hoped. The excitement is gone, you fight all the time. You want different things. Do you do whatever it takes to get back to where you started, or do you cut your losses, decide not to waste your time trying to find what you lost?"

Owen blinked, took a deep breath. His lips formed an *o* as he let it out. "Life is rarely that cut-and-dried. It depends on so many different things. Should two people give up without trying? No. But what if they do try, what if they fight like hell to get back to where they were, but that road is closed? I think if you love someone, hell, even if you just care deeply for them, their happiness comes first. So does your own. Life is long enough to make the effort but too short not to let go if it's just not there. You can't force something you don't feel. That's not fair to anyone."

She wasn't sure why his words made her chest heavy with emotion.

He shrugged. "This is heavier than I'd expected. Really, I think two people have to build a foundation. You pick a person who checks all the boxes for you in the beginning. Then, if you can, you keep choosing them time after time."

Her heart fluttered. "Yes. You do. You keep choosing them. That's exactly right." If she'd scripted his words, he couldn't have given her a better answer.

"I'm glad you wanted to go out again. I'm glad you chose me."

"Bookends." First and last. She smiled. "A perfect fit."

"This has been a little unconventional. The waiting was hard. I'm excited to see what's next. I know there are no guarantees or anything, but I've always thought if you go with your gut, just follow your heart, it'll lead you where you're meant to be. No guarantees. But no regrets that way either."

The waiter appeared with a basket of bread. "To start," he said, smiling at them.

When he left, Everly's breathing evened out. This steady, sweet, charming man could be her one. He was real. They liked each other. They had something they could truly build on. Life came down to choices. Making one and sticking with it. No regrets.

[35]

Chris pressed End on his phone and tossed it on his bed. His father wasn't taking his calls. There was so much anger and frustration vibrating off his skin, Chris wouldn't be surprised if his father could feel it all the way across the country.

Linking his fingers behind his head, he paced the length of his bedroom. When he'd arrived in California, his life had been a perfectly organized entity. Like a Jenga tower before someone took it apart. Over the course of the last year, the more time he spent with Everly, the more the pieces disappeared. Now, he felt like he was one breath away from the entire thing crumbling.

It wasn't just Everly either. His father had gone behind his back, emailing the advertising company to inform them their doors were being shut. He had no goddamn right. But he had the power and wielded it how he saw fit.

Chris had made a decision before telling Everly how he felt. He wanted to stay. Talking with Noah had confirmed it. He'd planned to tell his father he needed more time here until he could figure out the best approach.

Now, there was no point in having that conversation. Everly was out on her date with her bachelor of choice, she'd shot him down because of something he'd done when he was barely an adult, and his father was dangling his career in front of him like everything was a big, stupid game.

One where he lost everything.

He lowered his hands. "Stop." If Noah were here, instead of out on a date—how did that guy find a social life so fast?—he'd be telling Chris to knock off the pity party and figure shit out.

"Nothing to figure out. Everly's too scared to take a chance. Dad will rake you over the coals until he feels you've earned your place back, then it'll be business as usual." At least, once that happened, he'd be in New York rather than here, watching Everly build her perfectly structured life on her divorce-free foundation.

Damn, he was mad. Which beat the hurt he'd been feeling since he left her house. He left his room and went to the kitchen to grab a beer.

Dressed in pajama bottoms and a T-shirt, he leaned against the counter, his entire body weary, popped the top, and took a long swallow. He set it down and sighed. He and Everly had been avoiding each other for days. There was no way he believed she was sick the last two days, so today he'd made sure to show up after her spot was finished. He could do that for a couple of more months while he trained Mari to take over as station manager. He had a meeting with her and Mason tomorrow to offer her the promotion. She'd earned it and would do a good job. If his father would return his damn calls, he'd be able to tell him he was heading home sooner than expected.

The idea of being face-to-face with his father turned his stomach. The ad company had been dissolved behind Chris's back. Would his life always be like this? What other option did he have? In the back of his Everly-addled brain, he'd thought she'd want him. He'd stay, run the station, prove to his father that it was worth the time, money, and effort.

When he heard the buzzer for his apartment, he felt relief. Maybe Noah's date hadn't gone well. Sure, he should wish his brother well, but right now, he'd rather hang out with him. If for no other reason, to get out of his own damn head. Chris pulled the door open, leaned on the jamb, waiting for the elevator to arrive.

The elevator door slid open, and whatever smart-ass comment Chris was going to make to his brother died in his throat. Everly walked toward him, dressed in a pale blue dress that cinched at her waist and flared out after that. Her hair was up, off her face but in a way he'd never seen. It was like one of those updos women did where it looked easy but probably took several engineers to orchestrate. Her makeup was soft and striking. Her shoulders were stiff, her gaze laser focused on him. She looked like she was on a mission. *She's breathtaking.*

She stopped in front of him, and even in her black slingback heels—damn, those were sexy—she only came up to his shoulders.

Her gaze nearly scorched him. She poked him in the shoulder. "I don't want it to be you. I have a list of reasons why it shouldn't be."

She unzipped her purse, reaching in to pull out a folded piece of paper. Even as he scrambled to form words, his throat impossibly dry, she slapped what he guessed was the list, against his chest.

She returned her eyes to his. He could freaking drown in them. Why the hell did he feel so much for this woman?

Around the dryness, he mumbled, "I don't need your list, Everly. You were more than clear the other night. I'm not likely to forget all your reasons anytime soon."

Still, he reached for the paper and scrunched it in his fist. She smelled like vanilla. He wanted to lower his head, bury his nose in her neck to breathe her in endlessly. *She made her choice.*

"I went out with Owen tonight."

His heart skidded to a stop. There it was. Her choice. Why did she feel the need to ram it down his throat? Hadn't he taken it well? He'd wanted to grab her and kiss her until she couldn't breathe. Instead, he'd left. Let her make her damn decisions even if he knew it was wrong for both of them.

"I know that. I hope it was perfect." Regardless of how mad

he was at her for not taking a chance on them, he wanted her to have what she wanted. If she was happy, it was enough.

Everly looked down. Chris curled the fingers of his other hand into his palm so he didn't reach out to touch her. To lift her chin.

She looked up again, her eyes bright. Wet. "It was." She tilted her head to the side. Chris felt like she'd ripped his skin off his body. His heart slammed up against the wall of his chest.

Awesome. "That's great. I'm happy for you." His words came out like gravel sliding over a metal grate. It wasn't a lie. Not completely. He was happy at least one of them could pretend this was the best thing.

You're leaving. You won't have to stick around to watch her fall in love.

Surprising him, she stepped into his space. He inhaled the scent of her shampoo, all that was Everly. The list crinkled in his hand. Her eyes darted down to it, then back up.

"That list has good reasons on it," she whispered.

His heart felt like a blinker on the fritz. "I'm sure it does. Why are you here?"

Chris didn't know how much longer he could stand there, looking at her, inhaling her, without saying to hell with it and kissing her like he'd wanted to for twelve long months.

Everly pressed her hand to the same spot she'd slapped the list. Her brows drew together as her palm flattened over his out-of-control heart. The look she gave him sparked something so deep inside of him, it felt like his entire being was on fire.

"I'm here because there's nothing I can write down on any list that will get *you* out of my mind. As much as I've tried to force it, my heart refuses to be logical. I have no idea how this will end, but I know if I don't try, I'll regret it. I'm so scared of absolutely everything. You understand that, right? You do. I know you do. So, it should tell you something that more than anything right now, I'm scared of not taking this chance. Of not taking the leap. With you. Regardless of how I land."

It was a good thing his jaw had already opened during her speech, because it would have dropped to the floor when she flattened her body against his. Fisting her hand in his shirt, she went up on her tiptoes, locking her other arm around his neck.

Something inside of him broke. Or maybe it mended. Righted itself. His hands moved without permission, tunneling into her hair, knocking pins to the ground as he captured her face between them. His mouth moved, touched hers, and that first taste unleashed everything he'd held back and tried to ignore. Her lips were intoxicating, the little sound she made in the back of her throat electrifying.

She was right there with him, pressing her gorgeous body in that beautiful dress as close as she could, kissing him like he was air and she'd gone without it too long. One of his hands streaked down her back while the other stayed tangled in her hair. She let out a sexy little gasp when he changed the angle, took the kiss deeper, touched his tongue to hers, and did his best not to swallow her whole.

The depth of his desire threatened to overwhelm him. He couldn't touch enough of her at once. Hands sliding over her subtle curves, Chris picked her up, letting her feet dangle above the floor. It was easy to reach her this way but still not enough. Without breaking the kiss, he walked into his apartment, kicked the door shut with his foot. Her arms locked around his neck.

Turning them, he pressed her back to the door and brought both hands to her ass, boosted her up so he could get closer. Immediately, she wrapped her legs around his waist. It still wasn't enough. There was no such thing as close enough to Everly Dean.

He'd dreamed about kissing her more times than he could count. It was beyond anything he could have imagined. That quiet, introspective nature was nowhere to be found as she took what she wanted from the kiss, let her hands run up his back, into his hair. The sexy contrast of softness and strength turned him on to an alarming degree.

He told himself to slow down, even as her lips traced a path down his cheek, along his neck, making him whisper her name. Their heartbeats were erratic. He didn't know whose was beating harder, but he felt like they were nearly in tandem. When her mouth found his again, he gentled this kiss. He pressed his lips to her nose, her cheeks, her forehead, then leaned back only enough to breathe. With one hand, he smoothed back the tendrils of hair he'd knocked loose. His head spun, his pulse was a live wire setting off every nerve in his body.

Everly shuddered in his arms. He couldn't stop touching her, staring at her, scared this moment might not be real. She smiled up at him, her cheeks flush, her eyes burning into his, the soft contours of her body nestled against the hard planes of his. She was real. Chris pressed his forehead to hers, wanting to imprint this on his soul. God, she was precious.

"Why did you wait so long to tell me how you felt?" Her hands moved over his face, his jaw, caressing his cheeks as if she were memorizing the feel of him under her fingers. He caught one hand, kissed each of her fingertips.

"For all the reasons you already said. I'm your boss. We work together." *I'm leaving. Fuck. I'm leaving.* He breathed in and out, refusing to worry about that right now. He'd figure something out. *They'd* figure something out. After. After they sorted through this part.

"I didn't even think you liked me until six weeks ago." Her fingers played in his hair, and her nose brushed against his in the sweetest of touches.

He groaned. "Self-preservation. Easier to keep you at a distance."

She rolled her hips and tightened her arms around his neck. "I don't like the distance."

A rough laugh escaped him, and he kissed her again, loving the taste of her lips, the scent of her skin, the feel of her against him. "Me either."

He carried her over to his couch and sat with her still in his arms. And then he did what he'd wanted to do practically since the moment he'd met her—he kissed her like there was nowhere else he needed to be and nothing else he'd ever wanted. He explored her with his hands and his lips as she did the same. Until time spun out and all he could think or breathe or feel was Everly Dean. Until nothing else existed other than this one woman who tied him in knots and set him free in the same moment. This was a woman worth fighting for. Worth making changes for. He couldn't think about all the things he needed to tell her, what he'd need to do to make sure they could be together. It was too much and not enough all at once.

She pulled back. He'd lost track of time. Staring at him, her breath ragged, she touched his chest, met his gaze.

Covering her hand over his heart, he smiled up at her. "What happened? You said you made your choice. Why the change of heart?"

She laughed, low and sweetly. "It was less a change of heart than a decision to *listen* to my heart."

His own heart flipped over in his chest. "I'm so glad."

"I'll choose you again and again and again," she whispered.

His heart tumbled. Right into her hands. "I'll choose you back."

Tomorrow, he'd do whatever he damn well had to do to make that true. Because now that he'd kissed her, held her, touched her? He'd choose her over anything else.

[36]

Everly adjusted her pillows, then rolled to her side. She couldn't sleep. Her body was vibrating with an energy she'd never felt. Owen had been so gracious when she'd explained that her heart belonged to someone else. Just saying it to him made her heart feel like it might implode. She'd had no idea what to expect with Chris, but she'd done it.

She could still feel the imprint of his lips, the feel of his hands memorizing every nuance of her body. Those casual touches and pinkie grazes had been nothing compared to the fireworks of actually kissing him.

"Thinking about it isn't helping you sleep." She rolled over to her back again.

Since she couldn't *stop* thinking about him, she gave up, threw her blankets back to crawl out of bed. Padding out to the kitchen, she turned on the kettle to make some Sleepytime tea. While it steeped, she picked up her journal, then took it and her tea back to her bedroom.

She couldn't believe she'd left the list of reasons it couldn't be him at his house. She'd texted him as soon as she got home.

EVERLY: I forgot the list. Don't look at it.

CHRIS: Are you joking? I'm going over it now.

Her cheeks had burned.

EVERLY: Rip it up.

CHRIS: Not a chance. We'll go through it point by point so I can change your mind on every issue.

EVERLY: You already did.

CHRIS: Won't stop me from proving you made the right choice over and over again.

She'd bit her lip, staring at the screen, a new kind of warmth rushing to the surface of her skin.

EVERLY: That sounds . . . intriguing.

CHRIS: You're everything, Everly. Don't ever doubt that.

She hadn't known what to say in response to that. Instead, she'd texted good night, to which he replied, "Sweet dreams."

"They would be, if I could sleep," she said to herself as she crawled back into the bed. The tea at her side, she pulled the covers up over her bent knees, opening the journal to her list of rules.

She smiled, putting a check mark by number one. Definitely focusing on the good. She put a star next to number two. She was thinking, seriously, about getting a cat. Just one. Maybe two. Definitely not a hoard. She'd worry about her birthday when the time came, but maybe it was time to stop dreading them. Now that she'd told her parents what she didn't want, maybe they'd listen.

Number four, try something new each month, had been a big surprise. Kickboxing was perhaps one of the most surprising ones. It filled her with an inner strength, making her feel more powerful just by attending the classes.

"Number five, definitely achieved." She put a check next to it. The entire team was buzzing with ideas for their new show. Between that and the get-together Chris orchestrated, she felt closer than ever to her staff.

A shiver ran through her when she read number six. *Be bold, even if it gives you hives.* Tonight was the first time she'd understood why people did crazy things for the rush of it. She'd made the first move and been bolder than she'd ever been in her life. Something had clicked into place when she'd admitted her feelings. *The safety harness on the roller coaster.* She grinned. Getting on the ride might be terrifying, but it was also exhilarating. Freeing. There'd been not one hive in sight.

She put a smiley face next to number seven. *Find what makes you truly happy. And hang on to it.* She'd done that in so many surprising ways. Opening up to her parents had removed the cement block weighing on her chest. Even the dates, which she'd worried so much about, had played a role in her current state of happiness. Going on them had taught her things about herself. They'd taught her about what she didn't want as much as what she did. Being honest with herself about her feelings for Chris was a whole new plane of finding her happy.

Everly chewed on her pen a moment, staring at number eight. "Ironic," she said. She'd told herself to choose men who made her feel something, yet she'd all but run from the man who made her feel more than she ever had. She crossed out the rule. She didn't need that one anymore.

If she *felt* any more for him than she did right now, her heart might explode. Maybe part of her worry had been how he saw through her nervous habits, saw deeper than her social anxiety. He didn't sidestep it; he knew it was part of her, but he accepted it the way he did any other aspect of who she was. He made her feel *seen*. More, he made her feel like he *liked* what he saw. She felt stronger when he looked at her like she was all he could see. Number nine—*believe in herself*—was going to take some time, but she was on the right road now. For so long, her anxiety had been this hovering cloud she couldn't shake. In the last six weeks, she'd realized, she couldn't, and didn't need to, get rid of it. She needed to stop holding it against herself. Facing it, learning how to accommodate it, had given her a new kind of freedom. One that hopefully would let her be kinder to herself.

She laughed at number ten.

"Make the first move." She put a huge check mark next to it. "Done."

She closed the book, shut off the lamp, and snuggled farther into the blankets. Her tea had gone cold, but she didn't need it now. Despite the giddy, restless feeling stirring her blood, her eyes grew heavy, and she fell asleep thinking about how tomorrow would be the start of something new and amazing. They had things to discuss and work through, but she'd been wrong about one thing—she did *know*. The first touch of his mouth to hers had sent flashes of what could be through her mind. She'd known. He was a man she'd choose over and over and over again.

***

Butterflies danced in her stomach as she took the stairs up to the radio station the next day. She'd dressed with more care than usual, choosing a pair of dark jeans and a pale yellow T-shirt. Maybe she'd try something vibrant one day, but for now, the softer sides of the color wheel were growing on her. They had a staff meeting at ten thirty, which would give Stacey enough time to do a live segment before they transferred over to the computer until after the meeting. They needed to do a wrap-up segment for the show. Each of the men had signed nondisclosure agreements, but it was time for all of them to get on with their lives, which meant clueing the listening audience in to the final results.

She hesitated before pushing open the door to the lobby. *Stop it. You're going to work. You've done this every day for years. Nothing is different. Not about your job.*

"Hey," Stacey said from behind her.

Everly jumped, letting out a little yelp.

Stacey laughed. "You were so far in your own head you didn't hear me behind you. You okay?"

Pressing her palm flat to her chest, she glared at Stacey, who continued to laugh.

"I didn't make you pee, did I? I hear that happens after thirty," she said, poking her in the shoulder.

"Pretty sure that's after babies, not thirty."

"Hmm. Can't be too careful. Where were you last night? I texted."

Right. She needed to tell her friend everything. "Can we talk about it later? I have a lot to catch you up on."

Stacey's brows drew together. "Did you sleep with Owen?"

"Why do you always think I slept with someone when I say we should talk?"

She shrugged. "Wishful thinking."

Everly's heart rate calmed, and she opened the door, let Stacey go ahead of her. "Speaking of such things, what'd you decide about Rob?"

They stopped in the lobby, and her friend blew out a breath. "I'm going to go for it. We're going out tonight."

Everly grinned. "That's awesome. I'm proud of you."

Stacey rolled her eyes. "Aw, shucks. Thanks, Mom."

They were still laughing when they walked down the hall toward the booth. They put their lunches away in the break room, waving to Jane, who was chatting into a headset. It was so weird to know a different side of these people. In all the years she'd worked here, Everly had kept a small piece of herself closed off.

She let Stacey in and felt like she was amicable to her coworkers, but seeing everyone together outside of work was different. It made her realize she didn't really *know* the people she worked with. Jane was much less reserved with her girlfriend around, Luke was far more affectionate with his wife than she would have expected of the gruff and tough janitor, and Mari was far less serious.

"Morning, ladies," Mason said, coming into the room. "Any clue about the big announcement Chris is making?"

Everly's butterflies returned, and they were sporting weighted wings, all but punching her rib cage in rapid succession. "At the staff meeting?" He wouldn't announce . . . *them,* would he?

Mason filled his coffee, glanced over at Everly. "Mari thinks something is up. Said he was making some changes and wanted to talk about where the station is headed."

Everly's breath whooshed out quietly. Okay. Not them.

Stacey filled a mug after Mason and took a sip. "We'll find out soon enough. Maybe his brother is moving here and joining the ranks."

Jane walked over and joined them. Everly thought about how strange it was that they'd never huddled in the break room to converse before. At least, she hadn't. Maybe all of them had and she'd just kept her walls up.

"Noah is in real estate. I don't think he wants to be in broadcasting. I need to go buzz someone in. He's here to see Chris, so that might delay your meeting."

They chatted a bit more about a few on-location event requests that had been emailed in.

"I'm going to go set up," Everly said. She should definitely make more of an effort to engage, but for now, baby steps would have to do.

Walking out of the room, she was too aware of her pulse. It was beating harder than normal. Faster. *You've worked with him every day for a year. You can handle one more day of normal until you figure out what to do from here.*

She was worried that when she saw him, little hearts would pop up over her head as if she were a cartoon character.

"You can't just walk back here," Jane said to a man who came barreling down the hallway.

"He won't answer my calls, then I'll speak to him face-to-face. He's probably too much of a damn coward for that, but I'm not. Where is he?" The man was probably in his fifties, average height, his gray hair a little long on the top. Everly clocked the details like they'd be important later. Mason came up behind her with Stacey.

"What's going on?" Mason pulled Everly back as the man kept stomping forward.

"Which way is *Mr. Jansen's* office?" Blotchy red spots covered the man's face.

"Sir, I'm calling security," Jane said.

Chris came out of his office, worry etched into the lines of his face. "What's going on?"

The man pointed at him. "Are you him? Are you Mr. N. Jansen of Quality Corporations Incorporated?"

Chris stopped, his expression one of surprise before he masked it with professionalism. His eyes met Everly's for the briefest of seconds before he focused on the irate man.

"I've called security," Jane said.

"I'm saying my piece, and then I'll go. As much as I want to punch you, I won't. You cost me my company, put my employees out of work. I won't lose anything else to you. You're not worth it."

Everly felt Stacey step closer and take her hand. She hadn't realized she was pressing her fingers into her palm, but now it stung.

"You must be Mr. Lee. Why don't we speak in my office?" Chris said, gesturing to the door behind him. His tone was almost resigned. Defeated. What was that about? Who was this man?

"So, you *do* know who I am. Guess I should be flattered, huh? That if you were going to dissolve my company, through email, you at least knew my name. How magnanimous of you.

Do you want to sit me down in your office and tell me doing that was just business?"

Chris's jaw tightened, and Everly held her breath. She watched his chest rise and fall, realizing he was trying to maintain composure.

"What I'd like is to let my employees get back to work. This doesn't concern them at the moment. I'd very much like to sit down with you to discuss what happened."

The man reared back, threw his hands in the air. "What *happened? You* happened!"

Chris stepped closer. "That might be what it looks like, but if you'd just allow us some privacy, we can talk."

Security came down the hall, assessed the situation. Chris put a hand up to hold them off.

Mr. Lee laced his hands in his graying hair. "We were struggling, but that doesn't mean we wouldn't have made it. I sank everything I had into this ad company. We *were* turning things around. You didn't even have the decency to seek out other solutions. You can't just make decisions that impact dozens of people with the swipe of a freaking signature."

Chris winced. "You're missing valuable pieces of the puzzle. It's not as black and white as you're making it seem." His eyes darted to his staff. To Everly. His mouth tightened.

Mr. Lee growled, taking a step forward. "My life savings were in this company. Now, it's gone. No warning. Just gone. I looked up your company. You don't care about anything other than profit and proving you can take someone's legs out from under them."

Chris's eyes blazed fire. His back stiffened. "You know nothing about *me,* Mr. Lee. If you won't take me up on my offer of a private discussion, I'm going to need you to leave."

Mr. Lee pointed at Chris, the fight sagging out of his stance. "You'll never know what it's like to build something from the ground up. You'll never know what it's like to lose everything."

The security guard sidled up to the man. Mr. Lee's breathing had gone ragged, and Everly was close enough to see sweat forming at his temples.

"Sir, I'm going to escort you out," the security guard said. Everly didn't know his name. He worked the whole building and a couple of others in the same area.

She blinked, trying to pull her breath in. Mr. Lee shook his head, pulled a piece of paper out of the inside pocket of his suit jacket. He held it up, ripped it in half. "Gone. Just like that."

"I'm sorry," Chris said quietly, holding the man's angry stare.

Everly could see in his face, his eyes, the way his body tightened that he was. He was truly sorry, but nothing made any sense. Mr. Lee shook off the security guard's touch and turned around, stomped down the hall toward the exit.

The rest of them—Jane, Everly, Stacey, Mason, and Mari, who'd come out of the meeting room—stared at Chris. His gaze found Everly's, and everything inside of her tumbled like rocks off a cliff.

"Staff meeting, now." Chris pointed to the meeting room.

"I'm so sorry. He said he had an appointment," Jane muttered.

Chris was still looking at Everly when he replied, "It's not your fault, Jane."

Stacey went ahead of Everly, releasing her hand. She couldn't look away from Chris, her heart pounding, a feeling of dread making her stomach queasy. Even though he was standing right in front of her, she felt like he was disappearing.

They filed into the meeting room, sat around the table, the tension thicker than fog. Everly felt like she could choke on it. The muscles around her ribs tightened. She rubbed the pad of her thumb over her other fingers, counting to herself.

Chris ran a hand through his hair and paced at the front of the room. When he stopped, facing them, she got the distinct feeling that whatever happened next would change everything.

"I'm sorry about that scene. I should have maybe foreseen something like that," Chris started.

Stacey leaned closer. "Breathe, sweetie."

Everly nodded, gripping one hand with the other, pressing her thumb into her palm.

Chris rubbed a hand over his chin. She'd felt the slight stubble that grew there all over her neck and cheeks last night. She could *still* feel it. He leaned forward, putting his hands on the table, his shoulders dropping slightly.

"There are things I should have said before now. My father owns the radio station and its sister companies. There were five in total, but this one is the most profitable. My father off-loaded one recently without warning. Mr. Lee ran the ad agency. I'd been looking into ways to keep it alive when my father dissolved it without warning. Mr. Lee has every right to be mad, but that particular decision wasn't mine."

Everly's brain went foggy.

"Wait, you *own* the station?" Mason sat forward.

Chris took a deep breath. "My father owns it. Nathaniel Jansen."

"Just to be clear, you purposely kept *who* you were a secret from us?" Stacey's words slashed through the tension. They weren't harsh or judgmental, more curious. Like she was just clearing something up.

Everly bit her lip, focused on the pressure of her teeth against the delicate skin of her mouth.

"You have a right to be angry. It seems weak now, but when I first arrived, you were all on edge with having changed management and ownership several times." He sighed, straightening, then shrugged. "My first day here, a few of you were taking bets on how soon the new owner would cast you guys aside. I'm nothing like my father. I work for him. I came to do a job here, and I didn't want my role clouded by the connection. I'm sorry." His gaze locked on Everly.

Everly sucked in a sharp breath. "You said he wanted to fire Stacey and me. It was your *dad* who wanted to get rid of us?"

Chris nodded slowly.

"He did, yes. But I fought to save your jobs. And this station because it matters."

"So, is the station still in trouble? Do we need to find jobs?" Mari got up and walked to the whiteboard, erasing the doodles Mason had created at another time. Her movements were jerky, like her words. "From what Mr. Lee said, it sounds like your dad snapped his fingers and made the company disappear. Are we next?"

Chris shook his head. "No. You don't need to find another job. The numbers are fantastic. You guys all did that. My father knows this station is worth the time, money, and effort. I'll speak to Mr. Lee, but I don't want you guys worrying that you're going to be replaced or shoved to the side." His words should have soothed, but Everly couldn't help thinking about the few times he'd mentioned his father—the resentment in his tone. He'd married a woman, in part, to spite the man. He sounded, through Chris's own descriptions, like a ruthless individual.

Mason leaned back in his chair, studying Chris. "Did you fight for the ad company?"

Chris turned his head, met his employee's assessing gaze. "I was blindsided before I had a chance."

Mason pursed his lips. "You can't really guarantee what your father will do, can you?"

Taking a deep breath, Chris's eyes darted away. "I can't. I might not deserve it, but I'm going to need you guys to trust me."

Stacey let out a sardonic laugh, then winced. "Sorry." She glanced at Everly, who didn't know where to look or what to think.

"Why do you work at a radio station as a manager if your father owns"—Jane asked, glancing up from her computer, then gesturing to the screen—"what looks like an empire?"

The others peered over. Not Everly. She didn't move. She was scared that if she did, she'd come apart.

"Holy shit," Stacey said, getting up to look over Jane's shoulder. "You're mega loaded."

Everly's eyes widened. She looked at Chris, seeing the irritation flash in his expression before he shook his head. "My father is rich. Can we please get back to the issues at hand rather than my father's wealth?"

Mason crossed his arms over his chest. "The issues being you're actually like those undercover boss guys, but nothing really changes, right? We go on as we have been. Our jobs are safe."

Everyone focused on Chris. "I wasn't doing anything undercover. For now, it's business as usual."

No one seemed to know what to say. Questions bombarded Everly. Was his life in New York? Why *did* he work here? Was this why he'd kept them at arm's length until recently? How much sway did he have over his father if the man decided to cut his losses? Had Chris really stood up to his father on their behalf?

"There's really nothing more to be said right now. I need you guys to get back to your day. Everly, could you stay a minute?"

They waited a beat and then started leaving the room. Stacey squeezed her arm, giving her a "You will tell me everything" look on her way by. Chris walked over, shut the door, then turned to her with a crestfallen expression.

Her lips quivered. "You lied," she whispered.

"Everly," he said.

She inhaled deeply, breathed out through her mouth. Standing because she couldn't sit any longer, she paced the room as he had earlier.

"You can say you didn't, but omitting the truth about who you really are, your purpose here, that's the same as lying."

He stepped in front of her, stopping her in her tracks. She

looked at him, her body trembling. "I lied. You're right. It was by omission, but that doesn't make it okay. You, of all people, though, should understand."

Her brows furrowed as she tried to figure that out. "Why?"

Moving a touch closer, his look begged for understanding. "You don't want to be judged by your parents, Everly. I didn't want to be judged by my father. He's not a man I want to emulate."

She could understand that. Resisting the urge to touch him, *hug* him, she asked, "Then why do you work for him? Why would you come work for a station that you've had to fight every step of the way for? Why do you want to please him badly enough to have hidden that from all of us?"

He swallowed audibly. Everly's heart stuttered. There was more. He said nothing for a moment, like he was gathering his words carefully.

She clasped her hands together as she waited.

"The deal has always been that if I wanted to run a company on my own, without interference, I had to jump through his hoops. It's the same for both of my brothers. If anything, he's harder on us than he is on anyone else in his employ. I'm not whining or playing the poor little rich boy card. I'm just telling you, I came here to prove myself. I didn't want to have to defend myself at the same time, so I didn't say I was related to the owner."

She nodded, her fingers loosening until a thought occurred to her. "You haven't been running this company without interference, though. He tried to get rid of Stacey and me. He *did* get rid of the publishing company and now the ad company. Did he break his word?"

Even mad at him for the dishonesty, she felt bad for him because he shouldn't have to *prove* himself to his own father.

"No," Chris said, the one word coming out harsh.

Everly stepped back. "Then what . . ."

Chris closed the distance between them, his hands cupping

her shoulders. "I needed to prove I could turn the station around before getting my choice of companies to run. I'm supposed to take over as executive director of communications for his company."

"Supposed to?"

"I'm not taking it."

She shook her head. "Why?"

He dipped his head. "Everly."

She pushed her hands up between them, hating the shiver of need that came with touching him. "What? You're staying at the station for me? You don't have to do that. You can go, be the communications director or whatever. We don't have to work together."

"That job is in New York, Everly."

She sucked in a breath. Chris dropped his hands.

"You've always intended to go back?"

"Not anymore. Things have changed."

That was an understatement.

She let out a sharp, painful laugh. "From the beginning, this job has been a stepping-stone for you to get to where you really want to be. Now, what? You're going to give that up because we kissed? Somehow I'm supposed to believe you won't one day regret or resent giving up everything you've worked toward because we have some chemistry?" He started to answer, but she cut him off. "Did you even want to manage the station? Do you have any interest in this arena at all?"

He sighed. "No. I didn't. But there are challenges here that I never expected that made me like it. What we have is far more than just a little chemistry. You know it. I can be happy here because I'm not staying for business. I'm staying for you."

For some reason, that only made it worse. It was too much pressure. She'd just reached the point of *believing* they could work. What if they didn't? He'd already made it clear there were no guarantees in life. She couldn't be his reason. It would make her feel like a dead end. A detour on the path to what he'd really wanted.

She bit the inside of her cheek and willed her words to form coherent sentences. "Why? Why would you do that? Until six weeks ago, you barely saw me. Barely acknowledged me."

His face fell. "Everly. You know why." His hurt tone cut through her, but she couldn't stop herself from finishing.

"You couldn't even tell me who you really are. Your father owns an empire. You're meant for more than a small town. You jumped through all these hoops because your career matters to you more than anything else. You *told* me how important it is to you. We just . . . You can't throw it all away for something that hasn't even begun. For something that could end."

He touched her arm, and she pulled away. "Don't say that. I want *you*. We can make this work."

Everly crossed her arms over her chest, wanting to move but afraid her feet wouldn't carry her. "Can we? What if it ends up not being what you want? We know what your thoughts are on things that don't seem to have an easy solution. Cut and run, right?"

"Damn it, Everly. Do not throw my divorce back in my face. You want to talk, I'll tell you everything you want to know. But don't use that against me."

"Okay. Let's talk." She gripped the chair. "How long have you liked me?"

His brow furrowed, like he sensed a trap. "Since the moment I looked at you."

"Then tell me why you suggested I date a bunch of strangers. Tell me why, if you liked me so much, you came up with that solution to save the station."

His jaw tightened, and Everly's heart spasmed.

She nodded. "Because business comes first. Always."

"I thought I was leaving. I never planned on telling you how I felt. I thought I could help you find happiness before I had to go."

She scoffed, her jaw dropping. "Oh." Now she stalked away, nervous laughter bubbling from her throat. "Isn't that nice. You turn the station around, make Dad proud, and do a little pity project on the side. How lovely."

He huffed out an impatient breath. "Jesus. Stop turning my words around."

She whirled, pointed at him. "The bottom line—that's a term you understand, right? The bottom line is you were willing to let me be with someone else to prove something to your father. You held back because you never intended to stay. I get that there are no guarantees in life, but I need to be all in with someone who doesn't hold back. Someone who will give me *everything*—their heart, their trust, their honesty. That's what I have to give. That's what I deserve in return. I can't be with you if in the back of my mind, I'm always wondering if you'll be sorry you stayed." Her voice cracked. "If you'll be sorry you stayed for *me*."

She stepped around him, desperate to escape before her tears did. The hurt and frustration etched into the lines around his mouth, his eyes, clawed at her heart.

"I'm willing to stay," he whispered. "Once again, you're the one running."

She shook her head. "Self-preservation," she said, throwing his words back at him.

Stacey hurried after her when she grabbed her purse and fled for the exit. She didn't think about work or shirking her responsibilities. All she could focus on was getting out of the building, getting away from Chris, being alone.

Stacey had other plans. "Hey. Hey! Stop it. What's going on?"

Everly hurried to her car, her hands shaking as she pulled her keys from her purse. She unlocked the door and yanked it open.

"Just go." She slid in and started the car.

Stacey opened the passenger side and jumped in.

"What are you doing? Get out. I need to be alone."

"Do what you need to do, but I'm not going anywhere. You're in no shape to drive, so I'm okay if you want to just sit here and not get us into an accident. But I'm not leaving you alone. Cry, scream, do whatever you need, but you are not alone, Evs."

She swallowed down the tears, put the car in Drive. "I'm fine." She held the tears back and thought that she and Chris had something in common—they were both liars.

[37]

Chris grabbed one of the rolling chairs and rammed it into the wall. Yanking at his tie, he pulled it over his head and threw it on the boardroom table. The staff had scattered, and he had no idea what was being played on the radio right now, but none of it mattered.

Noah walked through the door and looked at Chris. "What the hell is going on, man? I saw Everly run out of the building with Stacey. Your receptionist looks like she saw someone get run over. Mason and Mari are running Stacey's spot."

"Go away, Noah. Now isn't a good time." He picked up his tie and wrapped it tightly around his fist.

"Clearly. What happened?"

"Just go somewhere else, okay? I don't have time to screw around with you. You wouldn't understand, anyway. You jump from one thing to the next without a plan, never stopping for a damn minute to see where you're going. Everything is messed up. I don't want to get into it with you."

Noah pursed his lips, nodding and slamming the meeting room door. He pulled a chair out from the table and sat down, put his hands behind his head, and leaned back.

"First of all, fuck you. Maybe I jump from one thing to the next, but I'm happy with my life. I don't need it color-coded, mapped out to the minute. Besides, this isn't about me. Second, calm the hell down so we can fix what you broke."

"Jesus. You're so much like him sometimes, it drives me nuts. This can't be fixed. I can't throw money at it and make a deal. I can't sweet-talk my way through this, okay?"

"You want to do this now? Okay, then. Back at you, bro. You're more like him than you want to be, too. You don't think outside the box. You're too black and white. You keep things in separate boxes, and when there's spillage, shit blows up, and instead of dealing with it, you wanna shove everything back into the right place."

Chris stopped pacing and stared at his brother. "I have no clue what you just said."

"There's always a solution, Chris. I'm not talking about money. Punch something if you need to. Preferably not me, because I will punch you back. Whatever you gotta do. But pull yourself together. Let's do what we do and figure this out."

"You have no idea what's even going on."

"Nope. But I'm pretty smart, little brother. You're all tied up in knots, your girl ran out of here crying, and your staff looks like a bomb exploded. Seems like they all might have found out about Dad and the business being a stepping-stone."

Chris deflated, his anger morphing into hurt, his heart twisting at his brother's words. "She was crying?"

Noah's face softened. "Not quite, but she looked close. What the hell happened, man?"

Chris sank into his chair and pressed his head back against the cushion, rubbing the heels of his hands against his eyes. "I screwed everything up."

He filled his brother in on Mr. Lee, the staff finding out, and his conversation with Everly.

"It's time to tell Dad to go screw himself. Sometimes I think his real full-time job is messing with us like puppets."

Chris laughed at the analogy. "Little hard to do that when he's holding the strings."

"Cut them, then. We have our own money. You're an excellent businessman. We don't have to live by his decree. I'm not going back, man."

Chris startled. "What?"

"I'm staying. I like it here. I don't want to be in New York anymore. Under his thumb."

Chris leaned forward, dropped his hands between his knees. "You're moving to California. Just like that?"

Noah grinned and put his feet up on the table. "Well, I do like to jump around from one thing to another, but I can actually picture myself standing still here. Figuratively. I'm looking into more houses. I can make my own real estate investments here on the West Coast. It's sunny here more often than not, I like the people, the vibe, and my little brother is going to live here if he gets his head out of his ass and figures out what he wants."

Chris swallowed the lump in his throat. Noah made it seem so cut-and-dried, but he hadn't seen Everly's face. He hadn't felt her shut down, step back physically and emotionally.

"Well? What do you want?"

The answer was simple. "Everly."

***

When Chris arrived home that night, the fatigue went straight through to his bones. He'd spent the day putting a plan into action, which involved lawyers, conference calls, and talking with both of his brothers.

He let himself into his apartment, realizing the emptiness of it mirrored how he felt inside. He had to believe there was a way to fix things with Everly, but not tonight. If he let himself think about her, he wouldn't be able to pull himself out. He'd be on the phone or at her door, begging for another chance. He had to settle things first. That was the only way to give her some of the guarantees she needed. One thing at a time. If he knew his father the way he was sure he did, he didn't have much time to get settled.

Sure enough, as he sat down on his couch, his phone lit up, showing his father was trying to FaceTime him. Nerves resurfaced. He breathed in through his nose and out through his mouth.

"You've got this. If you don't, well, you have nothing else to lose at this particular moment."

With that, he swiped Accept.

"Dad. It's nearly midnight in New York. Late night." *Keep calm. Don't let him rile you.* Those were Noah's words. *The numbers are in your favor.* That, of course, was Wes's wisdom.

"What the hell did you do?" New wrinkles had formed around his father's eyes and mouth. Definitely not laugh lines. His graying eyebrows furrowed; he held the phone too close to his face.

"I did a lot today. Are you referring to something specific?" Chris sure as hell hoped he sounded more nonchalant than he felt. If his heart beat any harder, his father would hear it through the phone.

"Don't give me that. You know what I'm talking about. I got an email from that ad agency saying I was in violation of the contract. He actually gave me a goddamn ultimatum. You want to explain how he knew about the primary contract regarding the dissolution process?"

Here we go. "I got blindsided, Dad. I had no idea you were pulling the rug out there. When Mr. Lee came at me today, irate, I got our lawyers on it, figuring we'd better lock this down before it got out of hand. I had them comb through all the individual contracts we have with each of the subsidiaries as well as the primary documents. I thought I was being thorough, making sure he didn't have any room to take action against us." Chris took a breath, his hands shaky. "I had no idea it wouldn't turn out in our favor."

That part actually was a shock. It had been Wes's idea to look through whatever documents they had available. Chris had suspected his father of bending rules, to get his own way in the past, but what he'd done with the station nearly crossed ethical lines. The contracts with the subsidiary companies were standard. The one for the radio station, however, implemented several clauses that overrode many of the terms the smaller companies agreed to.

His father's face contorted with anger with every word. Chris worked to keep his expression passive.

"You told him!" His father spat the words, actual spittle flying from his lips.

Keep calm. "I absolutely did not." Nope. Noah had. He'd gone to Mr. Lee, encouraging him to take a look at the fine print. Most of the companies wouldn't bother reading any extra paperwork, but they had access to it. Once Mr. Lee found it, realized what Noah *wasn't* saying, he'd taken the necessary action to make sure his father knew getting rid of the smaller company wouldn't be quite as easy as he'd hoped.

"Then who did?"

Chris shrugged. "I'm sure you can get it dismissed, Dad." He needed to wrap this up before he gave in to the renewed anger that was surfacing.

"That's not the point. I won't have you sabotaging me like a child out for revenge."

Chris gripped the phone tighter, keeping it a reasonable distance from his face as he began to pace the room. "Again, I don't know what you're talking about, but while I have you on the phone, I'd like to mention that being caught off guard by Mr. Lee wasn't pleasant. You had no right to step in. More than that, you had no reason."

His dad started to speak, but Chris was done playing. "You gave me the reins in theory, but you've questioned me every step of the way. When I don't do what you want, you break promises, go back on your word, or change the rules of the game."

"This is how business works. If you haven't figured that out yet, maybe I was wrong about your ability to succeed at all." His father's tone deepened. Hardened.

They stared at each other through the small screen. He *wished*, even willed himself to feel more for the man staring back at him.

His dad waved a hand dismissively in front of the screen. "This is a waste of time. My lawyers will make this go away. Even if they don't, it doesn't matter anymore. Get your ass home. Part of this is my fault. Thought you were ready for the next step, but clearly, you're not. As for the station, none of that matters. I'm selling the entire thing piece by piece. Even if this Lee guy thinks he has a leg to stand on, there'll be nothing to fight for."

Chris nearly shot out of his seat. "What?"

His dad shrugged. "We don't need this in our portfolio."

Chris lost whatever calm and cool he'd fooled himself into believing he had. "You haven't got a goddamn clue what any of us need. The only person you care about is yourself. You had no right to undermine me, go behind my back. It wasn't that this was too much for me; it was that you couldn't keep your hands out of it."

"Watch how you talk to me. It's my company. My hands *built* every bit of it, so of course they're in it." His father's eyes went hard, like his aging jaw.

"Bullshit. Grandpa built this company. He'd be sick if he knew what you've done to it and this family. You've torn both apart bit by bit so there are only fragments floating around resembling what he put his heart and soul into."

His father's fist came down hard. Chris heard the thump through the computer. "My father was stuck in the past. This is the way forward. You and your brothers are spoiled. Indulged. You've had everything given to you."

Chris wished he could pace. "Given to us at a price I'm no longer willing to pay."

He didn't have to play by his father's rules. He and his brothers had joined forces years ago, creating a contingency plan that Noah reminded Chris of today.

His father's face went a deep shade of red. Chris worried, for a split second, that he was having a heart attack.

"What the hell are you talking about?"

"I can't keep jumping through your hoops," he said. "I won't. I want to be happy more than I want to please you."

"You're a damn fool. What the hell is wrong with you?" His dad was practically snarling through the monitor.

Chris smiled. "Nothing. I finally figured out what's worth chasing in life, and it isn't your approval."

"You're going to walk away from your dream, from what you've worked for all these years, because I made some decisions without your approval? You're acting like a child. You're going to lose everything."

Chris shook his head. "I hope not. I've had my head down, working toward this goal for so long, I never stopped to make sure I still wanted it. I came here to prove something to *you*, but instead, I found out who I am. Having it all means something entirely different to me than it does to you. I don't want to fill your shoes. I want to walk in my own. Good luck with your wedding."

Chris pressed End before his father could say anything more. He was too tired for any more circles. That chapter was closed. The rest would play out however it would, but he knew now, professionally, he'd be okay. He always thought he needed his father's backing, his approval. He didn't discount how lucky he was to have the opportunities given to him, but in each of those roles, he'd been the one doing the heavy lifting. He'd done the work, risen in the ranks, and still never received an ounce of appreciation from his father. So he'd go it alone, or he'd work for someone else. Either way, he'd survive professionally. The most important thing he'd learned was that what he did for a living was not how he wanted to be defined.

When he thought of what kind of man he wanted to be, the answer was simple: the kind that deserved Everly's trust, heart, and love.

[38]

More than all the things she wished at this moment, Everly wished Stacey hadn't followed her all the way into her apartment. She felt like that game from when she was a kid—Operation. One slip, one wrong touch, and everything would go off inside of her. She wanted to be alone when it did.

She slipped her shoes off, tossed her keys somewhere near the hook, and went to the couch. She snagged the stupid squishy cat she freaking loved off the coffee table and sank into the corner.

"You want some tea?"

"No, thanks. You can go. I'm fine. I'll text you later." The fact that she got that many words out in a row made her proud. She could hang on a few more minutes. She flexed her hand. *In, out, in, out.*

"Ev, talk to me."

She clenched her hand so the cat's head sort of squeezed out of her fist. *Nope. No more talking.* She wouldn't get through it. Her mind was spinning with facts. *Dad owns the station, not who he said he was, never intended to stay, divorced.*

"What the hell is that thing? It's creeping me out!" Stacey walked across the room and leaned over Everly, looking down at her hand.

"Stress cat." Everything was building inside of her. She could actually feel it piling up. Her emotions were a tower of cards; the slightest breeze would send her crashing down, but all she could do was watch. Wait for it to happen.

"That's weird."

She let out a strangled laugh. "Yup."

"Evs."

She shook her head, closed her eyes and her fist as tightly as possible. The couch shifted, and Stacey's side was plastered to hers. She breathed through her nose.

"I'm not going anywhere," Stacey whispered.

The card tower tumbled. Slowly at first, a few tears trickling from beneath closed lids. Her friend's sharp inhale released the rest, and then she couldn't see even with her eyes open. Everything was blurry and wet, and she couldn't squeeze the cat hard enough to stop the sob that escaped.

When Stacey's arm came around her, she caved and leaned into the hug. To her credit, Stacey didn't try to talk her through it. She just held on, and that's what Everly did, too. She held on and let all the cards scatter.

The litany of awkward moments that lived in her head on repeat—her parents, Simon with a woman on top of him, announcing her failure on the air, the goddamn piñata full of condoms, the first piñata full of distraction and devastation, her parents' back-and-forth, back-and-forth, their faces when she said she'd had enough. Chris.

Her chest ached and her face was soaked, and still Stacey didn't let go. Everly would die of mortification later, but for these few moments, she couldn't bring herself to care.

She had no idea how long it was before her tears ran dry. By the time they did, her entire body ached and she'd all but molded her body to Stacey's. The feel of her friend's hand stroking her hair was so soothing, she closed her eyes. Just a few more minutes and she'd pull herself together. Just a few more minutes.

***

Everly's eyes felt like they'd been glued shut and sprinkled with salt. She blinked and got stuck in that hazy moment of knowing something was wrong but not being sure what.

She turned her head and realized she was lying on her couch, facing the back of it. Instead of sitting up, she shifted and turned over, saw Stacey sitting in the chair across from the couch, a book in her hand, a cup of tea on the table in front of her, and Everly's notebook beside it.

Her mouth felt like she'd eaten sandpaper, but she licked her lips and managed a gravelly, "Hey."

Stacey smiled and put the book down. Everly realized she was covered by the blanket she kept on the back of the couch. She worked herself into a sitting position, still too groggy for the embarrassment to swallow her whole. That would come next. Once she was all the way awake to appreciate it.

"How're you doing?" Stacey's voice was soft. It made Everly smile because it was so different from her gregarious tone that infused people with happiness.

"I feel like I swallowed and bathed in sand. What are you still doing here?" Everything rushed back. *Kissing Chris. Work. Angry man. Lies. New York. Stacey following her. Sobbing. Stacey's date!* "Your date with Rob. What time is it?" More awake now, she sat up straighter and pulled the blanket in front of her to fold it.

"I've rescheduled," Stacey said, eyeing her in a very strange way.

Everly groaned. She probably looked like she'd been hit by a truck. Crying was never pretty, but falling asleep before cleaning herself up was something she didn't want to imagine. Unfortunately for her friend, she was staring right at her. "I'm a mess. I'm sorry. Please don't reschedule for me."

"Jesus, Everly. Would you leave me if the tables were turned?"

Everly sat back down, surprised at the bite in Stacey's tone.

"Well, no. But I didn't mean to ruin your night. I know tonight mattered."

Stacey sat forward, and it took a minute—hazy post-tears brain—but Everly realized she was mad.

"You know it mattered, because I let you in. You're supposed to do the same. You're my *best* friend. You're my person."

Everly's pulse hiccupped. "You're mine. I'm so sorry I messed up your night."

"This isn't about tonight or a date." Stacey got up, her movements jerky and tense. She walked over to the window and leaned on the wall next to it, staring outside.

"Why are you mad?"

Her friend glanced over, and the sadness she saw in her gaze made Everly's heart clutch. "The whole social anxiety thing? I didn't get it at first, because why would I? I love crowds, people—the more noise the better. I'm cool with all that, but the closer we got, which wasn't an easy road in the first place, the more I understood that this was part of who you were. So you don't like to double-date, go to clubs, or sit at a crowded lunch table. Who cares? Once you loosen up a bit and start to trust someone, you're pretty damn cool. Funnier than I'd originally thought, probably the sweetest person I know. Likely, that comes from how much overthinking you do. God, your brain must be fucking tired. I can*not* imagine being in there."

Everly's mouth hung open. She had no idea where this was coming from or where it was going. The words were raw, genuine, and surprisingly on point. She *was* tired.

Stacey wandered back over and flopped into the chair with her legs stretched out. "The thing is, I've made it clear in a million ways—at least I thought I had—that I accept you. I *get* you even if I don't get what goes through your brain."

"I know that. I love you. You *know* that." Her heart got all panicky. Why did this feel like a breakup?

"I love you, Evs, but you can't keep people at arm's length. Well, you can, but not *me.* The other shoe is not going to drop on our friendship. I'm not leaving. Not when you're being so shy you seem like a snob to others, not when you babble like an idiot because your nerves get the best of you, not when you cry like your heart is breaking. How could you think I'd leave you alone through that? Why would you want me to? Why the hell would you put yourself out there to go on all those dates when you're in love with Chris? Most of all, why would you keep all of this from me?"

The hurt in her tone slashed across Everly's skin like claws. "I—" She shook her head, her throat closing up. "I'm not. I'm not in love with him. I wasn't trying to keep things from you."

Stacey leaned forward and opened the notebook, pointed at Reasons It Can't Be Chris. Everly cringed. She knew she should have ripped up the original. "It's not love. It's just . . . feelings. None of this matters anymore."

Stacey tossed the book down. "How can it not matter? How can you say that? You didn't cry when you were seven years old and your parents wrecked your birthday party. You didn't cry when you walked in on Simon fucking someone else. I've *never* seen you cry like this, Everly. You bounce back time after time after time. But not today. Not after Chris."

Everly's lips trembled. She pressed her fingers to them, worked to gather her thoughts. Letting out a slow, careful breath, she lowered her hand. "That was just a buildup of everything. I'm sorry for that."

Stacey's jaw dropped, and she stood up again. "I don't want you to be sorry. I want you to know that I'm not going anywhere no matter what. Cry all over me, snap at me when I do something stupid, say no every single time I ask you to go to a new pub or restaurant. I don't care. But don't shut me out. Open up to me. How long have you been crazy about Chris? How the hell can you say he's never been in love? Have you not seen the way that man looks at you?"

Everly shook her head, unable to process that. She stood up, set the blanket on the back of the couch. "That's not true. It was just attraction built up over time. It doesn't matter." She turned and faced Stacey. "I can't think about him right now. It hurts. I never learn. I believe my parents every time they say this is the last time, and I'm still surprised the next time. I go out with guys that I know aren't right for me because then I can say I always knew. The few times I've taken a chance, let myself think it might work out differently, it always blows up in my face. I told him I'd choose him. He said the same, but he was never really in a position to make that true." *Not if he'd always planned to leave.*

She walked closer, wrapped her arms around Stacey, and rested her head on her shoulder, breathing in the familiar scent of best friend and strawberry shampoo. "I *was* going to tell you everything, I swear. You're my person, too. It just all seemed to happen so fast." She pulled back, gave Stacey a watery don't-stay-mad-at-me smile that worked because Stacey rolled her eyes and shoved Everly's shoulder.

"I just want things to go back to the way they were. I have you. My job. I don't need more than that." Although that made her sound quite needy, didn't it?

"One of those things is a guarantee. The other—" Stacey bit her lip.

Everly's heart hammered. "What?"

"We have a few emails to read."

"Okay." She said the word slowly, watching Stacey's face.

"Mr. N. Jansen emailed all employees. Effective immediately, the station is in the process of being sold. There's no guarantee we'll get to keep our jobs or that the station will even stay open."

Everly looked around as if there were a hidden camera, not understanding what Stacey was saying. She'd only left work this morning. How on earth?

She stared at Stacey. "How long did I sleep?"

Though there was absolutely nothing funny about this

moment, Stacey burst out laughing. She slung her arm around Everly's shoulder and leaned her head against hers.

"Quite a while. We're going to be okay, Evs. No matter what."

Everly had absolutely no idea how her friend could say that and believe it.

[39]

Everly woke up the next morning feeling like she'd drunk too much. Grabbing her phone from the nightstand, she sat up and, bleary-eyed, checked her email again, hoping last night had been a nightmare.

She didn't pull up the email from Chris's dad, though. The newest one caught her eye.

To: sunbroadcaststationemployees@allmail.com
From: chrisjansen@allmail.com
Subject: Moving forward

Hi, everyone. I wanted to take a moment to apologize again for a few things. The first being not telling you my father owned the station. There's a wall that goes up immediately when new management is introduced, and when I joined the station last year, I wanted to avoid that as much as possible. I didn't want to be judged one way or the other based on *who* I was. I didn't expect that you'd all become more than employees. The family atmosphere you've created, despite the numerous changes you've all endured over the past few years, is remarkable and commendable. I'm honored to have been part of that. I regret any hurt I've caused by not being entirely honest.

Going forward, that will change. I know that you've all received the email from my father. He wasted no time there. It's true. The station is being sold, but I want all of you to know that your jobs *are* safe. I know I don't deserve your trust, but if you can find a way to do that, trust me, for just a bit, I will explain everything. I need to return to New York, but I will be back. In my absence, Mari will take over as station manager, and Mason will produce his own show.

When I get back, I'd like to have a meeting with all of you. By then, I'll have more answers to the many questions I'm sure you'll have. For now, please know that in all the years I've been jumping into my father's newest acquisitions, I've never felt more at home than I did with all of you.

Sincerely,
Chris

Blinking away the tears that formed, Everly wiped her cheeks with one hand, staring at the email with the other. He was returning to New York. The station was sold. *Your job is fine.* Why didn't that feel like more of a relief?

Everly pulled up another email. It was the post she'd never made public. She'd emailed it to herself and posted an entirely different one for the station website. *That* one had explained that her heart wasn't ready to make a choice despite some great options. It had, in her opinion, been funny and poignant—closure to an experience that had taught her more than she'd ever expected.

A text popped up on her screen.

STACEY: You okay?

EVERLY: Yeah. Just got up. Reading the email.

STACEY: I figured. You okay?

EVERLY: You just asked that.

STACEY: I know, but you lied the first time.

Everly laughed out loud as she typed.

EVERLY: I guess I don't need to avoid work today.

STACEY: Is that what you'd have done? Weird. I thought you were shy, not a coward.

Surprise widened her gaze.

EVERLY: Ouch.

STACEY: We all have our quirks. Mine is being bluntly honest.

EVERLY: Noted.

STACEY: Will you call him? Text him? Have his babies?

Renewed sadness swamped her, but she didn't cry. No more tears.

EVERLY: It was over before it began.

STACEY: Coward.

EVERLY: I'm going to let that go because I cried all over you last night.

STACEY: And stopped me from getting some.

EVERLY: Your birthday is coming up. I'll get you what you got me.

STACEY: Say it. Or type it. Come on.

Everly's cheeks heated.

EVERLY: I need to get ready for work.

STACEY: You can't type it, you're not going to buy one. Besides, I have plenty.

Everly shook her head, laughing, the sadness mingling in with the humor creating a strange juxtaposition in her chest.

EVERLY: Ever hear of online shopping?

STACEY: Well played. I look forward to my birthday, then. See you soon?

EVERLY: Always. Stace?

STACEY: Evs.

EVERLY: Thanks. ❤

STACEY: Always.

She set her phone back on the nightstand. As she got ready for her day, she did her best not to think about Chris and how the station would feel different without him. How everything would feel different without him.

"Good thing it wasn't love," she told her reflection when she stepped out of the shower. She dried her hair and did her best to keep her brain busy, but it kept flitting back to Chris.

Good thing it had been over before it began, because she couldn't imagine what it would feel like if she'd gone all in. If she'd told him that he consumed her thoughts and made her want things she was scared to want. Good thing she hadn't had a chance to give him more of herself. To give him everything. She just didn't understand why, if her brain *knew* it was a good thing, her heart couldn't get on board.

***

Over the next week, Everly did her best to focus on her job. She went each day, did all the things she'd always done, and went home to enjoy her nice, quiet life. The new promotion Mari had suggested for Mason's show, which included a cruise with the deejay, had listeners spinning with excitement. Despite that, she was surprised to see daily comments popping up on her final post. She hadn't given their listeners much: a few well-edited paragraphs of appreciation, how it'd take more time to find the one, but they'd always share music. It was a cop-out, but a succinct one. Why was everyone still invested? Her heart ached when she thought of how things *had* worked out—even if just for a moment.

***

The week after everything happened, she stood outside a nondescript building, hesitating to pull open the door and walk through. This could lead to all sorts of issues. She could regret it immediately or, worse, after a few weeks. She heard a car door shut behind her, the footsteps across the concrete.

"Are you waiting for me or just scared to go in?" Her mom approached her, pressed a kiss to her cheek.

"A little of both."

"Oh, baby girl," her mom sighed. "I'm sorry we messed you up."

Everly laughed, shocked at the statement. She turned to face her mom. "I didn't say you did. I just said I couldn't get caught up in your relationship back-and-forth. Aside from that, you and Dad are great parents. I love you. So much. You know that, right?" Did no one know how she actually felt about them? *Kind of hard when you keep that locked down to avoid rejection*. Totally Stacey's voice in her head. She pushed the thought away.

Her mom put an arm around her. "We do. But we also

know we've always treated you as more of an equal than a child, and maybe we've thrown things at you that you weren't ready to absorb. It was unfair."

"Just to say, Mom? I'm absolutely never going to be ready for you to throw condoms at me."

Her mom chuckled, stared at the glass doors with Everly. "We learned our lesson. Speaking of which, your dad and I start counseling tonight."

Everly turned her head, searched her mother's expression. "You do?"

Her mom nodded, a tiny smile curving her lips. "You were right. We can't keep doing this. I'll admit, without giving you any unnecessary details, that there's a certain . . . rush to the getting back together. And maybe even the splitting up. But it's not healthy. We want to be married. We love each other, but that doesn't mean things are easy."

She could easily imagine how love was anything but easy. It was messy and complicated, and there was no list in the world that could simplify it because how could you simplify something that was based on emotion? On feeling?

"I'm glad, Mom. I'm rooting for you guys."

"Me, too, honey. You really can't ever be sure, you know? But not being willing to take the risk because you're scared of the outcome isn't really living."

Everly thought about that, squeezing the cat toy in her right hand.

"Can I just say one more thing?" Her mom turned to her, brushed a hand down Everly's hair.

"Sure."

"Even if it doesn't end up perfectly, there will be so many moments of happiness and joy that it'll offset the imperfections. Just because it's hard doesn't mean it's not worth it."

Everly nodded, unzipped her purse, and put the squishy cat inside. She squared her shoulders and smiled. "I'm ready."

"Good. I was thinking you should get two."

Everly stopped in her tracks. "I just wrapped my head around one."

Her mother nodded like she understood completely. "But one is so lonely. They need a partner. Someone to play with. Fight with. Someone to love."

It amazed her that at thirty years old, her mother could still teach her something.

"You're absolutely right." Everly looked up at the shelter sign and nodded. "Two kittens it is."

[40]

What people failed to mention when they got kittens was the kittens were nocturnal monsters who took pleasure in bouncing around like furry pogo sticks. What was she thinking getting kittens when she had a full-time job? Mac and Wallace kept her up most of the night. *Which is fine because you weren't sleeping, anyway.* In between pulling the kittens off her curtains and each other, she'd thought about Chris and her parents and her lists and her life. She didn't know when he was coming back or if he was staying, but she knew she wasn't over him. She thought of texting him but couldn't make herself do it. Because what if . . . She hated what-ifs.

A nervous restlessness kept her from entering the building. She knew he was back. Stacey texted a He's Back! gif. Pressing her back to the concrete building, she focused on watching Stacey walk toward the station instead of on the mounting tension spiraling inside of her brain.

"You good?" Stacey asked.

"I'm a coward."

Stacey's eyes narrowed. "I ain't friends with no coward."

Everly laughed. "Stop. I'm serious."

Stacey leaned beside her, looked down at Everly's phone, where she'd brought up the post she'd never posted. "What's that?"

Everly turned her head. "The truth. I didn't post it because

I was scared. If I see him and he doesn't feel the way I do, I'll never share it."

"Okay. If you share it, regardless of how he feels, are you going to second-guess yourself eight million times?"

Everly nodded.

Stacey laughed. "At least you're honest."

"Is it a now-or-never thing?" Stacey's voice was gentle.

All of the things she'd pushed herself to do should make her proud. She *was* proud. It wasn't everything, though. She could post it after she saw him, after she knew how he felt. After she knew if he'd still choose her. That was the safe thing to do. She had the tiniest inkling of what her parents must feel every time they thought of starting or stopping. Love wasn't safe. It was a jump off a high-dive platform into unknown waters. For them, they trusted each other to eventually be wading around, ready to rescue them if they sank. She now understood the safety factor in that. For them.

Everly couldn't guarantee Chris's feelings, but the least she could do was acknowledge her own. It wasn't brave if she wasn't scared. It wasn't a risk if she knew all the answers.

She pressed Post on the words that had been sitting there, unseen by the world, unsaid by her. Stacey sucked in a breath when the post went live on the station's Facebook page.

Everly's heart hammered out of control.

Stacey gave a loud whoop, shoving her friend in her enthusiasm. "I take it back. You're totally Black Widow."

Laughter bubbled up over all the doubt. When Stacey yanked her into a hug, Everly forced herself to put it aside. She had no idea what they were in for, but she'd been brave. She'd taken a chance. He didn't know it yet. But he would.

The energy in the building was immediately tangible when they walked into the station. Walking to the break room, Everly focused on breathing. Breathing was good. She could do this.

Stacey grabbed a coffee. "Did you read the email this morning?"

Everly gripped the countertop. What had she done? It was out there for all the world to see. Her heart wasn't on her sleeve—it was on the internet! *Breathe.* "No. What email?"

"We've been bought out by some company called SCI. They're sending someone in to meet the staff, but Mari is the new station manager, and they're hiring another remote deejay. Mason is taking our spot because it's easier to manage on his own. He's not getting another producer. Evs. You and I are getting the morning spot."

Everly's eyes widened, and her heart rate galloped. Had Stacey known all of this and let her post, anyway? She gaped at her friend, her knuckles going white. *Breathe. You did the right thing. You didn't do it for him. You did it for you. Focus on the good. Goddamn it, Everly. Focus on the good.* "That's . . . fantastic." It was. It was fantastic. Wonderful. Why couldn't she breathe? Her chest was too tight. Women were more likely to have heart attacks, and they didn't always present like people thought. Was her back sore, or was she imagining it? That could be a sign.

"Hey," Stacey said, pulling her hand off the counter and gripping it. "It's okay."

"He's really not staying," she whispered.

"Oh." Stacey put her arm around Everly's shoulder. "Oh, Ev."

She clenched her jaw and breathed deeply through her nose. Stacey looked at her. "Talk to him."

Everly nodded. "After." She'd waited this long.

Stacey grabbed her hand and pulled her toward the door. Everly took one more deep breath, but it got caught in her throat when they walked into the hallway and Chris was standing right there.

"I'll make sure everyone is in the room," Stacey said way too loudly. She squeezed Everly's hand on her way by.

Chris stood in front of her, quite close, actually, staring at her like she might not be real. His gaze swept her body, head to toe and back again, and Everly shivered.

"Hi," he said. One syllable had her heart racing but her breathing evened out.

"Hi."

He smiled, just one side of his lips hitching up. "It's good to see you."

She wanted to launch herself at him, but he gestured for her to go first, to go ahead of him. She felt him at her back and had to physically stop herself from turning and crashing into him. From wrapping her arms around him and telling him she didn't care about any of the other stuff. That she wanted him. That she chose him. And would every time.

Chris stood at the front of the room looking at his entire staff, a soft smile playing on his lips.

"Hell of a week. Thank you for meeting with me again. First things first, Mari, congratulations on your appointment to station manager."

Everyone clapped, and Mari looked nervously excited. "Thank you." She looked at Chris, a subtle shade of pink coloring her cheeks. "Sorry about . . . you know, you *not* being station manager anymore."

Chris laughed. Instead of his typical suit and tie, he wore a pair of jeans and a light sweater. He looked delicious. His gaze caught Everly's, and he winked at her, sending a tremor through her veins. Stacey arched and then waggled her eyebrows.

"I'm good with how things are. Trust me. Managing this station was never what I wanted," he said, looking at Everly. She held his gaze even though she could feel the sweat beading at the back of her neck.

"I came here because it was one more step toward where I wanted to end up—or where I'd *thought* I wanted to end up. Broadcasting isn't my thing. I let my dad bounce me around because I didn't really know what I was looking for." He rubbed a hand over his face, then walked closer, putting his hands on the back of the leather chair in front of him. His gaze never wavered. Everly knew people noticed. How could they *not*? But she never broke eye contact.

"Turns out, what I wanted couldn't be reached through any of my dad's demands. As you know, the station has been sold. The paperwork is finalized. It was a quick sale. My father was eager to unload as one final way to show me he was in charge."

Why was he still smiling? His father sounded like a jerk.

"We're sorry to lose you, Chris. We really are a family here, and you're part of that, man." Mason leaned his forearms on the table.

"That makes me happy. Thank you."

"Do you know who bought us? How can you be sure they'll keep the station and not just . . . ?" Jane asked, her voice tense. Her eyes darted to the table and then back up. "How do you know they won't just dissolve the company?"

Chris sat down in the chair, looked around the table. "Like he did to the other company? I know how to hedge my bets. I'm confident the station will do nothing but thrive going forward."

"Do you know who SCI is?"

Chris folded his hands in front of him and looked at Jane. "Those letters I asked you to bring in? Can you pass them out now, please?"

Jane stood up and went to the side table, grabbed a box, and began handing out orange manila envelopes to each of them. Their names were written across the front.

"If you could just wait a moment before opening those, I'll explain." Chris smiled at Jane. "Thank you. SCI stands for *Squishy Cat Industries*," he said, his gaze zeroing in on Everly. She sucked in a sharp breath, held it. "My brothers and I have formed our own company. Under that umbrella will be the station, the cyber security and digital software companies that are still connected to us, and a very small-scale advertising firm that, under our guidance, will be run by our friend Mr. Lee, who I'm sure you all remember. While my oldest brother, Wes, is staying in New York, Noah is moving here, and I'll help him run his real estate development company. See, what I realized when I came here is that I don't have an interest in a specific business but business in general. I like figuring out how to take small companies and make them stronger so they have the ability to last."

He paused, and Everly felt like they were the only two people in the room. "I like seeing what makes them work and what doesn't and figuring out a way to bring them back to life. That's what I'll do. For lack of a better term, I'm a consultant who owns one-third of SCI. I'm not your station manager, but I am still your boss. As such, you each have a new contract in front of you. Review it and let me know if you have questions or issues with what's there."

Everly looked around the table. They all shared expressions of awe and surprise and . . . relief. She looked back at Chris.

"There are some policy changes, some updates, salary increases. We've been able to save some money in a variety of areas, and the station is currently doing better than ever financially."

"What sort of policy changes?" Stacey asked, playing with the opening of the envelope. "I'm not wearing a uniform."

Chris laughed. "There are a few outdated policies—like no fraternizing with employees. Odd word, *fraternizing*. It can mean a lot of things. Since it was so vague, we took it out. Because if you care about someone, nothing should stop you from sharing it. Which means . . ."

Everly's breath hitched, and Chris's lips hitched up.

"Despite all measures being firmly in place to prevent any workplace harassment, say you accidentally fall for someone you work with, we won't stop you from pursuing your happiness. Mari and Mason, you can quit hiding your relationship," Chris said, smirking in their direction. "Wes is a master hacker. He found several emails. No one is losing their job over falling in love as long as you show up for work and do your job."

Everly's breath whooshed out of her lungs. Mari and Mason

looked at each other, and the smiles on both of their faces added to the energy of the room.

Stacey pointed. "I knew it!"

Mason laughed, moving closer to Mari. "Hard to hide it when you care so much for someone."

He's right about that.

"Now. I know I've dropped a lot on you guys, but if you could give me the room for a few minutes, you can take some time to look over your contracts, hopefully sign them, and return them to Mari when you're done."

Everyone stood up, so Everly didn't know what to do. Mason and Mari shook Chris's hand. The other deejays and producers did the same, but Stacey and Jane both hugged Chris. Everly stood, watching everyone file out the door.

"Ms. Dean? If you could stay behind?"

He walked over as Stacey closed the door behind her, leaving them alone. Everly clutched the envelope in her hand, doing her best not to scrunch it up in her fists.

"Your envelope is a little different. I'd hoped you could open it up in front of me."

"Now?" Her voice came out as a squeak.

"I thought of a grand gesture, maybe throwing up my list on the big screen so there were no doubts, but I didn't think you'd want that."

Her heart fluttered so hard she lost her breath. Grand gestures were good things, right? He stepped closer, reaching out to tuck a strand of hair behind her ear. "I changed my mind, though. I wanted you alone for this. Just you and me."

She had so much she wanted to say. She leaned into his touch and closed her eyes, and her chest expanded. She could breathe.

"Open it," he whispered.

She carefully pulled the glued flap open, too aware of how close he stood, how much she had to tell him, how much she wanted him, how good he smelled. Her fingers shook. She pulled a single piece of paper from the envelope.

She read the title, tears immediately filling her eyes. *Ten Reasons It Will Only Ever Be You.* Her eyes scanned the list, and her heart moved into her throat. She looked up at him through lowered lashes.

He rubbed one thumb over her cheek, causing the tear to fall but catching it. The paper shook in her hands. He brought his other hand to her cheek and did the same thing with his thumb, then leaned in and kissed the spots where the tears had been. He pressed his forehead to hers and closed his eyes as if he were breathing her in, absorbing her into himself.

When he opened his eyes, they locked on Everly's. This close, with their noses touching, he was a little blurry, but he was here and he was real, and she wanted this enough to ignore the fear.

"I love you," he whispered.

The paper crumpled in her hand. She jumped back and smoothed it. She hadn't even had a chance to read it thoroughly, but already knew she'd want to save it forever.

Her breath shook as happiness swamped her. "I said it first!"

He laughed. "I'm pretty sure I'd remember if you did."

She shook her head, tears blurring her vision. Setting the paper down carefully, she pulled up Facebook on her phone, shoved the screen in his face, her fingers gripping the edges.

She watched his eyes scan over the words she'd gone to sleep with every night in her head since she wrote them.

> I lied to you guys. I told you that I didn't find love, that I was okay with that and appreciated you, anyway. The truth is, I did find love in the least expected place but still because of all of you. I've never printed these words down before, but I have severe social anxiety. So much so that I will likely never publish these sentences, but if I do, I'll struggle with the fact that I did. The day

I announced my misfortune on the air was a turning point for me. It showed me so many things about our listeners, the world, and mostly, myself. I'm brave when I need to be. I don't need to change who I am to feel good about myself, but I do need to push myself to be better. To be more. Because otherwise, I'm just standing still. I didn't fall in love with the bachelors you chose not because they weren't great guys. No, the reason it didn't work is because my heart recognized the one even before I was ready to see it. I wouldn't have been able to see it without all of you having my back, showing me it's okay to get knocked down as long as you get back up. It's okay to fall in love while being scared to death. I am. I'm scared that he won't choose me. That I'll be too high maintenance or I'll mess it up. Those things might happen, but it won't change the fact that I love him. That he's who I choose. Chris, I choose you. I always will.

His eyes blazed bright when he took the phone from her hand, set it on the paper. Taking her hand, he yanked her close. "You are the most amazing woman I've ever met in my life. You humble me. From the minute I met you, something inside me shifted. I didn't know what it was at first, but now I know it was my path. What I wanted out of life. I like business. I have enough money not to work, but I always will because it's a challenge and a puzzle and I enjoy that. But when I met you, I realized there was more to life. I fought it because . . . well, because I had a plan. My own list, if you will." He smirked, and she laughed, locking her arms around his waist. "I'm sorry I withheld so much. The only way I can explain it is I didn't want to be judged by who my father is. I've spent my life trying to be nothing and everything like him all at once."

She reached up, stroked his cheek, loving the feel of his skin under her fingers. "I understand."

His brows drew together. "You do?"

She nodded. "I always worry that if I open up too much, all people will see is the anxiety. It consumes me sometimes, worrying about that. But I've recently learned that even when people see it clearly, it doesn't always push them away. Not the ones who matter, anyway."

"You matter, Everly. More than anything. I said I'd never been in love, but I was wrong. I wanted to call you or text so many times this week. That expression about feeling like you're missing a limb or a piece of yourself? It's true. I did all the things I had to do to get back here to you, but the entire time, I felt like I was operating without my heart."

She gripped his wrists, hanging on. "I'm sorry about . . . everything. The things I said. Not giving you a chance to explain." Her eyes darted to his chest. She took a deep breath and met his gaze again. "How I reacted to you being divorced. That's kind of a personal issue for me, but I'm working on it."

He turned them so he was leaning against the table and pulled her between his legs, his hands going to her hips. "I didn't fight for my marriage at twenty-one because I was a kid. I wasn't in love. You asked me if I believe in divorce. I do. Because I don't think people should spend their lives in a bad situation if they truly aren't happy. But that doesn't mean I see it as an option. As a way out. It might be for some people, but if you give me . . . if you give us a chance, I wouldn't want the option. There's nothing I wouldn't do for you, Everly. That includes fighting for you no matter what. That includes making promises and never breaking them. Never giving up. If you let me, I'll choose you over and over and over again. Forever."

Tears spilled over, and she gave in to the desperate need to hug him. She wrapped her arms around his neck and squeezed him until he made a strangled noise. She pulled back, laughing through her tears.

"I'll choose you back. I promise. Every time," she said.

He cupped her jaw, stared at her lips before meeting her eyes. "You might have said it first, but I said it *out loud* first."

She bit her lip. Was there such a thing as *too* much happiness? Her chest was going to burst. "I love you."

Chris grinned, kissing her nose. "Despite all the reasons it shouldn't be me?"

She laughed, pressed her body tightly to his, loving the fact that she could. "I was lying to myself. It'll always be you."

He kissed her forehead, moved along her temple, his breath fluttering over her skin softly, heating it, healing her heart and making her pulse race wildly. By the time his mouth found hers, her breathing was ragged. She locked her fingers in his hair and kissed him back, reveling in the feel of him against her, the taste of him. She could spend a lifetime kissing him if there wasn't so much more she wanted to do. His hands roamed, pulling her tighter into his space until not even air fit between them.

He came to his senses first, right about the time she was wondering how sturdy the tables actually were. God. He made her forget everything. He made her want everything. With him.

When he pulled back, he left only a fraction of space between them. "I, uh, arranged a few days off for you. I was hoping I could maybe have a few dates with you."

Everly's groan morphed into a laugh. "I want nothing more than to spend time with you. To be with you. But I cannot take another dinner out or crowded restaurant for a while."

His fingers tightened on her waist, sliding up and down. He pressed kisses along her collarbone, up her neck, stopped at her earlobe, and whispered, "Good thing none of our dates involve leaving my house. That's why they invented takeout and Netflix."

"God, you're perfect," she said as his lips touched hers again. His words belatedly pulled her back. "But it has to be my place."

His brows moved down, and his forehead creased. "I don't care where we are as long as we're together. But do you not feel comfortable at my place?"

She smiled, her cheeks stretching with happiness. "I'm comfortable with *you*. It's not your place, it's just . . . I recently adopted a couple of needy roommates."

His frown was instant, and his right eyebrow arched up adorably. "Roommates?"

She nodded. "Yes. Wallace and Mac. I hope you like them."

She couldn't read his expression exactly, but she could make a guess at where his thoughts were headed. She bit back the giggle that wanted to escape.

"Where exactly are Wallace and Mac sleeping? Are they a couple? Why do you need roommates?"

She smoothed her fingers along his forehead crease and then pressed her mouth there. Her heart danced in her chest as she grinned at him.

"They sleep on my bed. With me. I hope you don't mind a crowded bed," she said.

He started to speak, but she cut him off. "They're not a couple. They're actually brother and sister. I needed them because I've wanted kittens for a while now but was afraid to make the leap. I mean, what if it didn't work out? What if they tear my furniture up? What if they wreck my stuff or hate me? What if they hate each other and fight all the time?"

Chris's grin sent spirals of pleasure through her body. "That's a lot of what-ifs."

She nodded. "That's how my brain works. It can be exhausting." She said it with a smile but meant it as a warning.

He pulled her close. "Good thing I've never needed much sleep. You can't get rid of me now, Everly."

Her fingers curled into his shoulders. Happiness was almost as terrifying as fear. "I don't want to get rid of you. I love you, remember?"

He laughed. "Trust me, I won't forget. You won't forget I feel the same. Because I'll tell you over and over and over again."

She could definitely live with that.

[41]

Everly carefully inched up in the bed until her back was against the headboard. She used the flashlight on her phone to locate the folded piece of paper she'd set on her nightstand. Glancing over at Chris to make sure she hadn't woken him, she unfolded the paper she'd read a dozen times. The words were etched on her heart, but she liked seeing them in print. Chris slept with Mac curled up in the crook of his arm and Wallace on his stomach. His very drool-worthy, sculpted stomach that she'd spent considerable time admiring up close.

The sound of his breathing and the kittens' dual purrs were the best soundtrack she'd ever heard.

She read over the words one more time, imprinting them on her brain before turning out the light and snuggling into Chris and the kitties. But she didn't sleep. She just lay there, smiling into the dark, thinking about his list. And how incredibly happy she was that she'd stepped outside her comfort zone so she could be sure that where she landed was exactly where she was meant to be.

Ten Reasons It Will Only Ever Be You

1. *The thought of you fills me with this inexplicable happiness.*

2. *Your face is the first thing I want to see every day. What I want to fall asleep to every night.*
3. *I've become addicted to making you laugh, just to hear the sound.*
4. *I love the way you analyze a situation from every possible angle. Including ones I didn't know existed.*
5. *You don't just make me want to be a better man, you make me feel like one.*
6. *Nothing is impossible beside you.*
7. *You're sexy, adorable, pretty, brave, and amazing. (That's technically more than one, but it's all sort of wrapped up in an incredible package.)*
8. *Your heart. You give so much without asking anything in return. It makes me want to give you everything. Forever.*
9. *You don't want to go out every night. (Don't tell Noah, but I'm actually happier in small groups, too. Like groups of two. You and me.)*
10. *Your brain. It fascinates me the way you have a thousand thoughts to every one of mine. I could spend eternity listening to you.*

    I love you. I'm in love with you. I'll choose you every single day forever if you give me the chance. I won't give up or give in. It'll always only be you.

Acknowledgments

People probably don't believe this part is harder to write than the book. Not because there's no one to thank but because this is the point where the author becomes terrified of missing anyone who made their journey easier, happier, bearable, or possible.

The good news is it's not an Academy Award speech so it can go on endlessly. The bad news is if I forget someone, I'll forever be reminded, in print, that I forgot. If this happens, let me know and I'll mail you a handwritten thank-you note for the role you played in helping me see this dream through.

For now, let me do my best to make it clear how much I appreciate so very many people. Alex. There are not enough words. Ironic, right? You believed in me and this story at a time when I was done believing in myself. Working with you has made me fall in love with writing all over again. Thank you. I hope we have many, many books together.

To Mara and the many other people at St. Martin's who are behind the scenes helping this book come to light, thank you. I probably owe more than a thank-you to anyone who had to correct my comma and semicolon usage.

To Fran. We did it. We're going to keep doing it. You told me we would. Thanks for truly believing it and helping make it happen.

To Christy for helping me to be funny, for making me laugh, and for lifting me up.

To Renee and Kim, thank you for your ears and shoulders and kind hearts.

To Tara for believing from the first story you ever read for me that I was headed here. Even when I didn't.

To Rob Michaels for not only being a great deejay and a funny guy but for being gracious, helpful, and doing open chair which gave me this idea.

It's starting to feel like they're cuing the music and there's still so many people! Stacey, Cole, Sarah, Sara, Charlene. To Shannyn and Robin who read it first when it wasn't ready for human eyes. To Nicole, for so many things it's hard to list. But mostly, for believing in me so hard.

To Kira Archer, Lauren Layne, and Lyssa Kay Adams. I feel so cool that you read my book. It's impossible to state how important it is to find your tribes. They hang on to you even when you feel like you don't belong or deserve to be there.

To my kids for their patience and constant cheerleading. I'm better because of you two. To Matt. How is it that twenty years later, you make me laugh more than ever? I'm so grateful for you.

To Brenda. Thirty years. That's a hell of a lot of staying power. You deserve an award. What you get is me. To everyone who gets up every day, powers through the worry, pushes past the doubt, you are not alone. None of us are.

Thank you to anyone who reads this book. You have no idea how privileged I feel to be sharing it.

Look out for Sophie Sullivan's next escapist rom-com!

Coming soon from